AMBER EYES

Also by S.D. Grimm

CHILDREN OF THE BLOOD MOON:

Scarlet Moon | BOOK ONE

AMBER EYES

CHILDREN OF THE BLOOD MOON

BOOK TWO

S.D. GRIMM

an imprint of
GILEAD PUBLISHING

Published by Enclave Publishing, an imprint of Gilead Publishing,
Grand Rapids, Michigan
www.enclavepublishing.com

an imprint of
GILEAD PUBLISHING

ISBN: 978-1-68370-074-6 (print)
ISBN: 978-1-68370-075-3 (eBook)

Amber Eyes
Copyright © 2018 by S.D. Grimm

Edited by Ramona Richards
Cover design by Kirk DouPonce
Interior design/typesetting by Beth Shagene

Printed in the United States of America

To the man who made it possible
for me to pursue my dreams,
my husband, my friend,
my Captain America, thank you.
I love you.

ACKNOWLEDGMENTS

If I'm being honest, this section of the book is a place where I feel humbled and thankful and truly blessed, because I realize how many people believe in me and my writing. I recall the times people made sacrifices for me, rallied around me, encouraged me, prayed for me, rejoiced with me, and believed in me. And I'm grateful beyond what words can express. I love writing. I love it in my soul and down to my bones. But it involves blood, sweat, and tears—sometimes literally—and it's because of all that support I get from others that I can pluck away at my keyboard every day, doing what I love.

And so I say thank you.

Thank you to the amazing people at Gilead, who have been helpful and wonderful throughout this publishing process. Thank you especially to Steve Laube, who loved my story enough to bring me on as a writer.

To my amazing editor, Ramona Richards, who saw what I saw in my story and also knew what I needed to change to get that picture to come through at its clearest.

To Julie Gwinn, agent extraordinaire, who does so much more behind-the-scenes work for me than I ever expected.

And to the people who have encouraged me and believed in me and helped me to learn and grow as a writer. You all are part of my team, and I'm grateful for each of you: my amazing Speculati friends (Charis, you are included here!) and my fabulous Paladin crew—whom

I got to know after I'd written this book. You all help me through our friendships and writer fellowship more than you know.

And to my family and (non-writer) friends. Mom and Dad, I wouldn't be the writer I am today without your willingness to foster creativity in me. Molly, you are the best friend and encourager I need. Philip, I cannot thank you enough for your never-ending support. My "cisters," Eve and Cecilia! I love how you encourage and pray for me all the time. And my beautiful children. I cannot thank my God enough for all of you.

I thank God for giving me the desire, the talent, and the willpower, and the amazing team of people to help me to make my dreams a reality. I couldn't do it without him, nor would I want to.

Never least, thank you to my amazing readers. Every tweet, picture, post, and email makes my day. You all are the best.

I am truly blessed.

BEAST IN THE WATER

She doesn't look powerful." The woman with wild red hair glared as she spoke, and the fire in her eyes made Quinn tremble.

Fire.

It burned. Bit her skin. Nothing soothed her blistered arms. Quinn huddled at the base of the tall tree they'd tied her to. Dull, diseased wood scratched her exposed and burning skin. This forest was so different from the warm, sunny place they'd taken her from. Everything here was gray and overgrown with brambles. Prickly ropes bound her hands. Her wrists itched. Thinking about the itching took away from the pain.

A smug smile lit the red-haired woman's face. "Ready to be compliant now, are you?"

Quinn trembled. Why did they hurt her? What had she done? She wasn't powerful, whatever they thought. But when she denied it, they burned her. Bound her hands. Picked her up with wind they controlled and slammed her back against the trees.

The trees mourned with her. They didn't want to hurt her, but they were powerless.

She glanced at Enya, her only friend. The huge colorful bird wasn't okay. The netting they'd thrown around her had bent her wings. Sunset-red, deep-purple, and fiery-orange broken feathers poked out between the tight ropes of the netting. They floated like wisps on the wind. Once vibrant and shimmering, they fell like shattered hopes. Soon they'd turn gray—everything here dulled to gray. Enya looked like a crooked mess, lying in a heap on the cracked earth. Her thoughts didn't reach Quinn anymore.

Tears slid down Quinn's cheeks.

"Sabine," The red-haired woman spoke to the woman with yellow hair. "It's time to tell the Mistress we have the girl."

Sabine dipped her fingers into her jerkin and pulled out a cloth. She crouched in front of Quinn and unfolded it. A stone rested in the center, small and shiny.

Sabine held it out between her two fingers. "Do you know what this is, girl?"

Quinn shook her head, and her tangled brown hair caught Sabine's hand. The stone flew from her grip.

"Stupid child." Sabine smacked Quinn's already stinging face.

Quinn crawled backward as best she could in her cumbersome bindings.

Sabine laughed. "I can still reach you."

A gust of wind cradled Quinn. It held her in the air for a moment then forced her hard against a tree. Bark scraped her back and her head bashed against the trunk. The wind released her and she fell to the ground, huddled low with her head hidden. If this was what people were like, she hated them.

Sabine yanked Quinn's hair and forced her head up. "Get me the stone."

On her knees, Quinn crawled toward the stone and picked it up with her bound hands. It warmed to her touch. The shiny black exterior changed, turning red along the edges, and a picture flooded the center. Quinn stared, captivated.

The woman who looked back at her from the stone was beautiful, with silver-blue eyes and long hair so dark it resembled a moonless night. *So you're the girl. You're only a child.* Her voice was like a sharp hiss.

What girl? Before Quinn could ask, the picture changed. Nothing but blackness and two amber eyes. Frightening eyes. Not quite human. Whoever was behind the eyes spoke to her. *Don't worry. I'll get you safe.*

Quinn gasped. His voice seemed kind, but who had eyes like that? *What* had eyes like that?

The eyes softened.

Strange eyes. Strange but kind.

She wanted to call out to whoever was behind them. *Please. Help me.*

Sabine snatched the stone from her. "The Mistress spoke to you, didn't she?"

Quinn nodded slowly.

"What did she say?"

Quinn sat numb.

"Janice." Sabine motioned to the red-haired woman.

Janice snapped her fingers, and a flame grew in the center of her left palm. Quinn shook. Not the fire again. Tears raced down her cheeks as Janice stepped closer. The flame in her hand shot up higher.

"She asked if I was the girl."

The fire in Janice's hand died.

Quinn huddled closer to the tree as Sabine's narrowed eyes searched her face. She walked over to Janice and leaned close. "The Mistress says someone infiltrated the stone."

"Who?" Janice asked. The fire sparked up again.

Quinn's body shook. "Please, don't. I didn't see anyone else!"

Sabine's eyes narrowed. "We'll find out. First, we are to shackle this girl to the black island of Castlerock."

The woman with red hair straightened her back, and her eyes grew wide. "Surely the Mistress doesn't mean to send her there."

"Don't worry. She'll protect us from the beast."

"How?"

"Do you doubt her powers?"

"She has been trapped for a long time."

"I'll go alone. Then I'll collect your share of the power when she is released."

"No one takes my fire. I'll come." She pointed to Enya. "What about her bird?"

"Kill it." Sabine's lips curled into a devilish smile, and Quinn's stomach squeezed.

Enya's half-closed eyes looked at Quinn, and her small, quiet voice leaked into Quinn's thoughts once again. *"Be brave, little chick. Remember: a burned heart can rise from the ashes."*

"What does that mean?" Quinn asked.

A ball of flame lit Janice's palm and pulsed. It grew. She looked at the red bird in the net and threw the ball of fire. It exploded and consumed Enya.

The bird's thoughts winked out from Quinn's mind, leaving a hole, hollow and empty. A sob clawed out of her throat. Gone. Nothing but a pile of ash. Enya was wrong. Quinn didn't want to be with other humans. Not if they were this cruel.

Janice untied the rope from the tree and jerked Quinn's bindings. She fell forward. Rocks scraped her bare arms and bit through her clothes. She scurried to stand before they dragged her.

Janice laughed. "We're going to take you to your new home."

They took a rowboat across the inky waters up to the island where lush vegetation covered hundreds of boulders at the base of a mountain. The breeze smelled sick here. Not clean. Not alive with the freshness that comes from living, beating trees.

Then they shackled Quinn to the base of the mountain with cold, metal chains, and they tossed her the rest of their rations. Birds had always fed her before. Would they come in the presence of these women? With Enya gone, would anyone come?

Sabine knelt next to her. "The Mistress thinks you're special. You're nothing but a scared child."

Thunder rumbled below the surface of the black water. The ground quaked. A long, serpentine neck shot straight up into the air and towered over them like an ancient oak. Liquid slid over its green and yellow scales like tiny black rivers. Dark, moving veins. It snaked its head closer. Horns encircled the creature's crown, curved and spiky. A single black eye sat in the center of its head and jagged, white teeth outlined its massive jaw. Smoke poured out of its nostrils.

Quinn wanted to scream.

"The beast," Janice whispered. "Tell the Mistress to call it off." She held a ball of flame in her hand and shot it at the beast.

It opened its mouth and a stream of fire ate her tiny flame. Its head dove down fast, and huge jaws snapped around the woman with red hair. Swallowed her whole.

Quinn screamed.

Shaking, Sabine took out the stone from her pocket. "Call off the monster!" she said into the rock. "Call off—"

The beast closed its jaws around her, and the stone clattered against the rocks and landed near Quinn, but too far away for her to reach.

Then the beast snaked its head closer. Quinn sat still and silent as a newborn fawn, but her heart thrummed. Its black eye blinked. She saw her face in the depths of its pupil. Frightened. Dirty. Alone. A shiver pulsed through her, but she dare not so much as blink. Slowly the monster retreated and sank beneath the quiet, black water.

Quinn shuddered, staring into the stone. *Please, someone help me.*

CHAPTER 1

THE ENEMY'S SHADOW

Logan stood on the top of a wooded hill facing the direction of the palace, the wolves with him. He'd come here again because of the pull in his chest, like a string attached to something but always out of reach, or a dream he was supposed to remember hours after waking. It had to be telling him where to find the remaining three Deliverers. Specifically his son.

The unreachable tug urged him to stay near the palace. For two days he had. But it made him jumpy. Danger still lurked there. He felt it in the air. Smelled it in the wind. Sword oil and chainmail filtered through the scent of spruce and moss. And the smell of horse grew stronger tonight.

Jayden may have killed Idla, but a bigger threat seemed to pulse below the surface.

Westwind nosed the air as a breeze filtered through the pines.

"What do you smell, friend?" Logan asked.

"Horse and rider mixes with deer and rabbit. And the scent of fear stains the soil here. Something isn't right."

"Perhaps they're looking for my son." Logan's heart jolted at the thought of it.

Westwind didn't say anything in return, but Aurora's voice entered his thoughts. *"If your son is still in these woods, he's nowhere near here."* She sounded sad and comforting. So similar to Rebekah. The wolf retained Rebekah's normal speech inflections even though the two of them were no longer bonded. It was both a comfort and a curse—hearing his wife's voice daily, having a piece of what used to be her heart now bonded to him.

The memories stung more since he'd seen Rebekah at the palace. She hadn't sounded like the Rebekah he'd known and loved. Her eyes held none of the warmth they used to.

She'd become a cold and heartless killer. A pawn of the palace.

And he still loved her.

He closed his eyes and breathed in, banishing thoughts of her—feelings toward her—to the deepest corner of his heart. He would find a way to get his son from her grasp. But how much would being raised by Rebekah have poisoned his son's heart toward the Feravolk?

Westwind turned to him, his eyes gleaming as traces of the approaching dawn reflected off of them. *"I understand your desire to stay, but I think it's time we fled. Unless you want to risk meeting this danger head on."*

"It's my duty to protect the Deliverers. That includes my son."

"Yes." Westwind cocked his head. *"It also includes Jayden. Keeping her close to the palace is like planting her in a black lion's lair. Come back for your son when you are ready with an army. Don't risk the Deliverer you have."*

"You think I should abandon him and find the other two?"

A hint of sorrow filtered across the bond along with Westwind's quiet pause. *"I don't think abandon is the right word. But you typically make decisions with your instinct. I think your heart has been taking over."*

Sunlight pierced the darkness, making it easier for anyone who could be tracking them to see, despite the camouflaged cloaks they wore. Logan bowed his head. The wolves were right. He should leave.

"Aurora and I are going to check the perimeter again, then we'll look in on Jayden. Perhaps you'll let Gavin talk some sense into you." Westwind's eyes gleamed greenish gold in the moonlight as he turned to leave.

Logan glanced right as someone approached him with soft footfalls. It was only his friend Gavin.

His boots padded against the soil as he drew closer to Logan. "Melanie says Callie found the scent of one set of tracks on top of our trail. Someone is following us."

Melanie's mountain lion would know. As much as he wanted it to be his son, Logan couldn't rule out the possibility that they had been found. "A scout? This area carries the faint scent of horses and chainmail."

Gavin didn't speak right away, but when he did, his voice remained quiet. "This evening, Glider saw a group of horses and riders to the east. I had him follow them, and they've bedded down for the night. If they're working with a scout, it's not the same one on our trail."

"Thankfully, Gavin's eagle would tell them if those riders found their trail. So we're still in the clear for now."

"For now." Gavin leaned his shoulder against a tree and glanced at Logan.

Logan bowed his head under the weight of that look. "I've kept us here too long."

Gavin grasped Logan's shoulder. "We'll find your kid. We'll find all the Deliverers and help them save Soleden. Our people. Your burden is mine, friend."

Save Soleden. Hadn't they done that when Jayden defeated Idla? Deep in his heart, Logan knew of the danger Gavin referred to. "Do you think the Mistress is escaping?"

Gavin took his time breathing in. "All the signs point to it. Evil creatures, like those black lions you met, are her creations, banished into the prison with her. If they've found a way out, she won't be far behind. In the end, Queen Idla was just a pawn of the Mistress of Shadows." He tipped his chin up to the full moon. "Besides, isn't it starting to look red to you?"

A slight hint of red, like blood, spread over the moon's glowing surface. "I was hoping it was my imagination."

"But you knew it wasn't. Otherwise you wouldn't be out here trying to herd the Deliverers."

Logan closed his eyes. Gavin was right. It was time to leave before it was too late.

"*Logan.*" Westwind's thoughts punctured his mind. "*Someone has spotted you. The intruder is fleeing. Aurora and I are on her tail, but Jayden and Ryan are following us.*"

Logan's stomach tightened and so did his fists. "*Which direction is the intruder headed?*"

"*East.*"

The direction of the palace.

CHAPTER 2

WHITE LION

Everything was black as pitch except the white lion. It paced in front of Ryan. Yellow-moon eyes bored into him. Blood seemed to splash across the creature's coat as it moved, as if it carried the liquid inside like a goblet of red wine.

The lion lunged. Paws smacked into Ryan's shoulders and pushed. His back slammed into the ground. Claws dug into the scars above his birthmark. Scars the black lion had made with pearl-white claws when it attacked him in the palace. All he could think about was the fire in his veins that the black lion venom had pulsed into him. And he shook.

The white lion stopped. Licked a blood-red paw and stained its tongue crimson.

Ryan stared into the creature's uncaring eyes. "Get out of my head."

"You're the one keeping me here."

"I'm pretty sure I'm asking you to move out."

The claws pressed harder, and this time it crouched on top of him. Pressing. Purring. Tail thrashing. He needed air.

"As long as your heart is dark, as long as my taint lives within you, I'll remain."

"Taint. Again with that word." He couldn't help but recall what Anna, the Whisperer, had told him about her friend who had been tainted with black lion venom. A friend Anna was told to kill.

Ryan swallowed.

The claws kneaded. Pricked.

He swung a fist at its face and scraped at its eyes.

The lion growled. *"That was a mistake."*

Fire shot through his blood. Scorched his insides. He screamed.

"Ryan."

This voice wasn't the lion's. It was hazy. Distant.

"Ryan?"

He sucked in a breath and opened his eyes. Hands pressed against his chest, but this time the weight was light enough for him to breathe. He slammed his arm into the body and knocked his attacker off of him. Quick to his knees, he crouched over the attacker, hands ready to strike.

"Ryan, it's me!" Jayden stared at him, eyes wild and round.

He moved away. "Jayden? I'm—I'm sorry." All the emotions pricked into his skin like his blood was suddenly trying to cool, trying to bring him back to reality. The dark of night still shrouded their camp. Empty trees towered above, lean in the moonlight. His sisters lay sleeping beside a snuffed fire.

No lion. No blood. No claws. Only Jayden, and she shrank away from him.

She rubbed her wrists.

"Did I hurt you?" He reached for her and she pulled back. "I'm sorry." He winced at his words. Couldn't he say anything else?

"It's okay." She stared at him like a spooked horse.

"It's not okay."

"Are you going to tell me what's bothering you?"

"I didn't mean to hurt you."

She sighed and touched his arm, soft and tender. "Do you want to tell me about it?"

Not really. He bit the inside of his lip and tried to think of anything that wouldn't make him sound crazy. Nothing came to mind.

She squeezed his hand. "It might help you to talk about what happened in the palace."

"A black lion attacked me." His words sounded flat.

"I know."

And he'd killed it. With fire from his hands.

After that, the fever dreams from his first encounter with black lion venom had grown stronger. Voices *and* hallucinations. He hoped it had nothing to do with the fact that a taint pulsed in his heart—taint left there by black lion venom. It all made for pretty poor conversation and even lousier joke fodder. If he could at least crack a joke—make her smile—perhaps she'd think things were heading back toward normalcy.

Oh no. She stared at him with the pity eyes. Not the pity eyes. "Blood was pouring out of your chest, Ryan. I didn't know they could do that."

He flashed a smirk. "Cats with hidden talents."

"Ryan, please. I think this is serious." Her eyes pleaded with him. She wanted to know what happened. She wanted to know how he was doing because of . . . Ethan. His throat tightened and his heart ached. He'd left his brother to die. Alone. And now she was here with him— the brother she hadn't fallen for.

What was he supposed to say? That he hated himself for being a coward? That he would cry himself to sleep if his father hadn't told him crying made him look weak? Admitting all of that out loud wasn't an option. He'd already told her it was his fault for dragging Ethan into this mess, and she looked so appalled that he—well, he should have taken Ethan's place.

He sighed and shook his head.

"All right." She stood to leave. "If you don't want my help, fine, but talk to someone. Please?"

He opened his mouth. The words "I want to tell you" were so close to coming out, but he stopped them. Because he *didn't* want to tell her that evil had fused to a part of his heart. He had to figure out how to solve this on his own. Before he went crazy. Well, crazier.

Before Logan decided to kill him.

○

Jayden stared at Ryan and opened her talent. His feelings typically flooded into her, but since they'd escaped the palace, his emotions seemed distant. Had she lost his trust?

She held his gaze and probed with her talent. Eye contact was a door-way into someone's emotions. Some were harder to open, but Ryan's usually tumbled into her as if they were her own. Blood thundered in her ears as her heartbeat sped to match his. Sorrow caused her chest to ache. Uncertainty squeezed her stomach. Yet he sat there with a lopsided smile.

Why wouldn't he tell her what was troubling him?

His eyes narrowed and his feelings siphoned out. The imaginary door slammed shut. He averted his gaze and lay back against his bedroll, staring up at the canopy of trees, hands behind his head as if he were carefree.

When did he learn to close me off like that?

She sighed and headed the few steps to her own bedroll, which lay on the other side of a cluster of blankets occupied by a tangle of three red-headed girls and a dog. How Ryan's sisters had slept through his screaming amazed her. Then again, Jayden hadn't been sleeping well either.

She smiled at Scout's furry body curled up among the girls, his fur almost the same shade as their hair. Wren, the youngest, held the dog close as she slept, and Scout twitched his paws in what Jayden hoped was a happy dream. He hadn't been his usual tail-wagging self since Ethan was gone. The dog's movement seemed to cause the middle sister, Kinsey, to wake. She sat up as soon as she saw Jayden, carefully removed herself from between Chloe and Wren, and scooted to the edge of the blankets. "How's my brother?"

Jayden bit her lip. "He seems fine."

Kinsey patted a vacant part of the blanket beside her and smiled. Something in her eyes resembled a look her mother might've used. Then again, Kinsey had a lot of wisdom for a fourteen-year-old girl. "Lying to me? Not a good idea."

Jayden joined her. "He won't talk to me."

"My brother is stubborn, but you can get through to him."

Only if he let her in.

Kinsey hugged her knees and dusted a dry leaf off the edge of her blanket. "I know you loved Ethan, but you love Ryan too, don't you?"

Jayden's breath caught. Did Ryan's sisters still think of Jayden as his betrothed? Did he? An ache settled in her chest. She'd always love Ryan. He brought a piece of home back to her. He was family. But after she'd met Ethan, she realized there was a different kind of love to be had.

Ryan was like a fire—wild and warm, comfortable in a forge, perfect in a hearth, but never quite tame. Ethan was the wind before a storm. He moved her. Made her feel his power and strength. Pushed her to see things she never would have looked for.

Fire was easy to be near, but difficult to get truly close to, whereas wind . . . consumed her. Tangled her hair. She could feel its touch on her face for hours after it dissipated.

Now Ethan was gone.

Kinsey sniffed, bringing Jayden's attention back to the conversation. "Our father told Ryan to go and protect you that night the Feravolk razed the town. I kept wondering why. You had four brothers. Why would my father send our only brother to protect you when the whole town was under attack?" She looked into Jayden's eyes. "Father knew you were a Deliverer. Didn't he?"

Jayden stared with her mouth open. "I don't know."

"I wondered if maybe our family moved to Tareal because he was supposed to protect you. He was always so jumpy about things. It makes sense. You and the other Deliverers were born to save the Feravolk from extinction. Ryan knows this. He'll protect you whether you love him or not."

"But I do love him. I—"

"I know." Her smile was rueful. "And it's okay."

A soft sound caught Jayden's attention, and she turned to see two wolves approaching. Westwind, the taller of the two, led his mate—Aurora—over to where Jayden sat with Kinsey. He eyed her and cocked his head.

She smiled at his greeting and extended her hand. He brushed against it, turned in a circle, and pressed his warm body against her leg. She fondled his ear. "Must be my watch. Tell Logan I'm already awake."

His golden eyes seemed to soften in the moonlight, and he opened his mouth in what looked like a smile.

"I see you're a step ahead of me."

"How do you know what he's saying?" Kinsey seemed to want to lean closer to and yet back away from the wolves at the same time.

Jayden shrugged. Westwind was quite capable of making his

thoughts known to anyone willing to listen. She glanced at him. "It's a full moon tonight."

He tilted his head, and his eyes seemed to squint as he stared at her. Jayden chuckled. "Should we howl or something?"

His body shook against her leg as he laughed.

Kinsey seemed to like this, and she leaned closer.

As soundlessly as he'd laughed, Westwind rose. His ears swiveled. His body stiffened. Aurora stood, too. Both wolves dipped their heads low and growls rumbled in their throats.

Jayden grabbed her daggers and stood. "Intruder?"

Westwind's eyes flickered in the moonlight as he nodded. Their combined growls brought Scout to his feet.

Ryan also jumped up. "Does Logan need help?"

Westwind and Aurora tore off into the woods, Scout chasing after them. Ryan glanced at Jayden before he followed.

Kinsey touched Jayden's arm. "You're not—"

"I'm not letting Ryan go alone."

CHAPTER 3

AN URGENT MESSAGE

Jayden pressed her back against the tree's mossy bark and quieted her breathing. Dawn's first sliver of light peered over the horizon, making it easier to track the intruder and follow the wolves. This intruder's stealth made her difficult to get close to. The wolves had been able to track her, and Jayden and Ryan had been able to follow Logan and Gavin. Finally, they were close enough to surround and catch her.

Jayden risked a glance around the tree. Had the woman seen her? A Feravolk cloak hid the woman's face, but the wolves seemed to think she was a threat, and that was enough for Jayden.

She pulled out her dagger. Felt its weight in her hand. Let its power to calm her emotions fill her. At this distance she'd have to back up a pace to get the shot she wanted or wait until the woman moved to the right spot. Just a step or two farther.

One step.

Her heart thundered. Not yet.

Calm.

She breathed deep. Back straight, weapon ready.

Two steps.

She whipped her arm back then forward. Her dagger sailed out of her hand and shot toward the tree. It pinned the woman's Feravolk cloak to the trunk.

The woman pulled at the camouflaged fabric, but three deep, resounding growls stopped her. Westwind, Aurora, and Scout encircled her.

Jayden moved in, and the wolves and dog moved to let her pass. She stood in front of the prisoner. "For one who wears Feravolk garb, it seems strange that you'd run from wolves." Jayden clutched the hilt of one of her longer daggers. "They seem to think you're a threat." Blade against the woman's neck, Jayden reached forward and pulled back the woman's hood.

The woman lifted her blonde head and looked into Jayden's eyes.

Jayden gasped as a fire lit in her chest. Thea.

The assassin who'd broken her promise and sealed Ethan's death.

Jayden pressed her weapon harder. "I should kill you now."

"I have news. Call off your wolves and put your weapon away."

"What news?" Logan's voice boomed behind Jayden. His blue eyes pierced deep into Thea.

Westwind bared his teeth.

Gavin and Ryan stepped out from behind trees and brushed back their hoods. Melanie's mountain lion, Callie, dropped out of the tree Thea stood closest to.

"Don't you trust me?" A smirk flickered across Thea's face.

A growl rumbled in Scout's throat.

"Relax." Thea raised her hands. "I surrender. I'm on your side, remember?"

"Our side?" The flame in Jayden's chest could no longer be controlled. She pushed her dagger into skin. Blood dripped out.

"Whoa. Relax, Jayden. She surrendered." Ryan gripped her arms and tugged her to his chest.

She looked down at her dagger. At the thin line of blood on the blade.

"Well, Softheart." Thea's sultry voice scalded Jayden's insides. "I didn't expect a warm welcome, but where is this fire coming from? Did killing Queen Idla awaken your thirst for vengeance?"

Jayden lunged for Thea, but Ryan pulled her back. His breath heated her hair. "Whoa, what's she doing to you?" he whispered.

"Doing?"

"You're acting strange."

"She promised to protect us but got us captured anyway. She's responsible for Ethan's death." Every word burned her from the inside out.

"I'm responsible?" Thea's eyebrows shot up. Her blue-eyed stare cut deep. "You're the one who trusted me. The one who made an alliance with an *assassin*. You entrusted Ethan's life to my sister and me. *We* got you out. His death isn't on *my* hands."

"How dare you?" Jayden broke free and lunged, her dagger pointed at Thea.

Her arms jolted as her weapon hit steel. Logan's sword. He stood between her and Thea. When she saw his face, his calm filled her. The hate melted.

Hate?

Thea's emotion. Jayden's hands shook. What had she done? "What am I—"

"Jayden." She registered Ryan's faint touch on her shoulder. "Look at me."

She faced him and his worry leaked into her. If other people's feelings were flooding her unbidden, her talent was out of control. She breathed deep and focused on the dagger's power to help her tame the emotions. "I don't know what came over me."

Ryan touched her cheek to keep her from looking back at Thea. "She's playing with you. Don't listen."

She touched his hand. "I—I didn't—"

"It's okay."

"Oh, Charmer." Thea chuckled. "Regardless of what Jayden thinks, I kept my end of the bargain. I can't help it that your little soldier thought he should sacrifice himself for you."

Ryan dropped his hold on Jayden and fisted his hands. "Don't you dare."

Logan pressed a hand on Ryan's chest. "Gavin, find some rope and get Thea out of here before I kill her myself. She might have information, but she's stalling."

Jayden watched as Gavin led Thea away.

Was it true? Did Thea have some power over her? Maybe it was all the guilt eating her from inside, pumping through her heart with every painful pass.

The sun rose fully over the hillside now, such a dark orange that it resembled blood. So much blood.

She had to keep her emotions in check. Losing it like that again was not an option. Thea might be right, but all she was trying to do was rattle Jayden. It wouldn't work. She tightened her grip on her weapons and marched after Gavin and Thea.

"Whoa. Where are you going?" Ryan held his hands up in front of her, but it didn't stop her.

"Thea can't be trusted. She's nothing but a liar." She said it loud enough that Gavin stopped, pulling Thea to a halt with them.

Jayden kept barreling after them. Logan tailed her now. Apparently her little tirade had caused some mistrust.

Thea looked over her shoulder. One corner of her lips curved, and her gaze pierced Jayden's. "Your soldier's alive. At least he was when I left. I imagine Kara's helping him get out of the palace as we speak."

Logan drew his sword. In three strides he had reached Thea and grabbed her wrist. He whipped her around until her back smacked against his chest. His sword blade pressed against her neck. "I don't tolerate lies."

Her hand gripped his arm, unable to remove the blade from her neck. "It's not a lie."

"I saw him myself. General Balton stabbed him." There was a catch in Logan's voice.

"He's alive, but that's not what I came here to tell you."

Jayden stormed forward and raised her dagger. "Then tell me, or die."

CHAPTER 4

HIDDEN INTENTION

Serena clutched the hood of her cloak closed at her throat and peered out of the edge of the forest—the edge of safety. The trees seemed to brush up to an invisible wall outside the city gate. Green, rolling hills led up to the high wooden fence, and a small, red-dirt road wound through the hills like a path of sunset on the hillside. The open, Healers called it. The world where people lived—people who could not know her secret.

Serena breathed deep. That thought always scared her when she reached the edge of the wood. And it was hard to deceive others when by very nature she couldn't lie. Neither could Dash. She stroked Dash's opalescent mane. "You still want to come with me?"

The unicorn snorted and dipped his head. *I'm not letting you do this alone. Besides, I don't think anyone in this city would notice a unicorn even if I didn't cloak my horn. Unless, of course, I healed someone.*

"Dash, don't even talk like that." Healing someone out in the open could lure the wrong eyes. Dangerous eyes. She shuddered. *I don't think these people are going to be as oblivious as you've made them out to be. I'm sure things must have changed in the last hundred years since you visited.*

He snorted again. *Try five hundred.*

"How old are you, friend?"

His sides lifted as he heaved a sigh. *Serena, you know we don't think of age the way you do.*

"Right. Your impetuousness keeps you feeling young."

"I am young."

"For a unicorn." She patted his neck.

"You're sure you want to do this?"

"There isn't enough information in Salea or our library. I have to know, Dash. I—I can't describe this longing. This pull. It's like when I was drawn to you."

"Yes, but this Ethan fellow left without you. Twice. He likely doesn't share the bond."

True. The first time she'd met Ethan was outside the Blind Pig Tavern in Salea. He was losing a fight to six men, and she'd bailed him out of it. He'd pushed her away then, but the second time he'd asked her to go with him. That meant he might have felt the bond—or whatever it was. That's what she had to find out.

"Ready, then?" Dash's voice pulled her out of the memory.

Ready to leave the cover of the trees and venture into a city? Never. The thought always made her stomach clench. The Circle would have her hide if they knew what she was up to on these supply runs. A rush of uncertainty flooded through her blood, and that only emboldened her. She released her grip on her cloak and straightened her back. *"Yes."*

Dash's horn dimmed—a hazy ripple outlined it. If she wasn't touching him, she wouldn't even be able to see it. His fur also seemed to lose its shimmer. He would now seem nothing more than a white horse. Serena pulled her black mask from her satchel. She wouldn't put it on yet.

When she wore it, she was Swallow. A bolder version of herself. Some cities may know her as a mysterious masked swordswoman, but not Erinecath. She'd never been here. Serena was as much a stranger here as Swallow. But she would be Swallow. Serena wasn't safe outside of The Valley of the Hidden Ones.

Her bones buzzed. A shiver skittered over her skin. Erinecath awaited.

As Dash stepped out of the woods and headed toward the old dirt path, she breathed in. The air felt different out in the open. The wind stronger but warmer. The sun uninhibited. The sky unobstructed.

Free.

Dash chuckled.

"What?"

"You're like a child in a field of wildflowers."

"How do you mean?"

"You want to run. To smell each flower and see how it's different from the last."

Serena tipped her head to the side. "That seems right."

He chuckled again. "Hold on."

She gripped her friend around the neck and Dash ran. He raced through the meadow, sending butterflies into flight. The wind rippled through her hair. Right here, right now, this place—the place in between where she headed and where she she'd come from—seemed suspended in time. A place she could just pretend to be a child again. Carefree.

As soon as she stepped into Erinecath, she would be bound again by who she was. But right here, right now, with the wind against her mask-free face, kicking up butterflies with her only family, she could breathe.

Too soon she put on her mask, and Dash trotted right up to the city gates.

The men who stood guard outside the city gates looked up from their books. "What business?"

"I wish to visit the library."

Both men smiled and motioned for her to enter. She smiled in return. Dash stepped inside, and Serena slid off his back. The cobblestones beneath her feet were worn and smooth. Some were red. Others were dark gray, still others were blue or white. Each seemed to have its own pathway to a different direction of the city. The white path led through the center of the city and right up to a huge, blue-domed building.

Serena lowered her hood and gasped. "It's magnificent."

A man with circular spectacles and a short white beard—following a spiral pattern of the blue stone that eventually straightened and headed north—stepped around her, nose in a book. "Good day to you." He didn't even look up.

She giggled. "Good day, sir."

Another man, younger and severely bowlegged, stepped around her, taking the red path. "Good day to you," he said.

Serena watched him sidestep Dash and continue south. She covered her mouth with her hand to hide a smile.

Dash chuckled. *"Sometimes little changes in a thousand years."*

"A thousand, truly?"

Dash nuzzled her with his white nose. *"Get inside before all the books are gone."*

She walked up the marbled steps, passing three men who all said, "Good day to you" to her and one another as they took to their colored paths and headed away from the library.

She stepped inside and immediately breathed in. Spinning in a slow circle, she looked up into the domed ceiling. Her gaze drifted over the walls and rows of books. Reliefs carved onto the outside walls mirrored the colored frescoes inside. Beautiful. She touched the drawing of a dragon on the south-entrance wall. Its green wings were splayed open, and it seemed to overlook a city below. The Circle taught her to believe this creature meant to swoop in and kill, but this dragon stood with a man touching his shoulder. He didn't look like a murderer. His red eye seemed to look fondly on the human.

How perfectly strange.

Frescoes soared up into the dome as well. Pictures of winged horses and dragons and willow trees and birds on fire. "It's beautiful."

"Shh!" struck up in a chorus around her, and she bit down on her lip. Apparently they didn't like much in the way of noise here.

Serena wandered between the shelves, taking in the mixed scents of paper and ink and glue. Finally she found a dusty shelf near the back of the library filled with books on bonds.

By the time Dash mentally nudged her, Serena sat on the floor surrounded by at least seven books and three melted candles. Hopefully her sack would be large enough to borrow what she wanted. She closed each book, running her hand over the covers and noting the titles again. *The Bonds of Kin, The Tie of a Bond,* and *When Evil Binds* made it into her bag. The rest she placed on the shelf. Then she headed to check the books out.

The librarian looked up from his book long enough to notice her. He motioned to her mask. "Is it a feast day?"

"No."

"Are you a woman?"

She crossed her arms. "I thought it was obvious."

"Well, er, yes, but women don't usually come here."

"Is my being here a problem?"

"I—um—well, no."

Lie. And she didn't need Healer abilities to detect the untruth, either. She tapped her fingers against her bicep. Perhaps the Circle was more right than she'd given them credit for.

The man got out his ledger. "Who is requesting to borrow this book?"

"You can call me Swallow."

He breathed in a tight breath, and Serena silently dared him to refuse her.

A book slammed next to her on the desk, and someone slid it close to her pile. "She'll take this one, too."

Serena glanced at the person next to her. An old, wrinkled, and hunched woman with milky-white eyes. Serena held her hand up in front of the woman and opened her talent. No sight. The woman wasn't suffering though, so Serena didn't feel a pull to heal her. She looked at the book, and her stomach squeezed. There was no title on the front cover, so she opened to see the first page. *A Journal of the Whisperer of the Second Age.*

A Whisperer? What would she need with this book?

The sightless woman seemed to look right into Serena's mind. She didn't say anything, just nodded. "You'll need it."

Truth.

Serena moved the book closer to the reluctant librarian.

"Here you are, Miss Swallow. Enjoy the reads. And a good day to you." His voice seemed tight as he handed the stack back to her.

She smiled and turned to thank the old woman, but she'd disappeared. Serena placed the books in her sack and headed out.

Outside, Dash approached her, slapping his tail against his rear leg. *"You seem flustered."*

"It's just so strange here."

"Ready to leave then?"

"Yes."

Dash chuckled. "So didn't you have a good day?"

Serena rolled her eyes. Then she froze. A growing pain nagged at her insides. It exploded, revealing the cause, then reduced to a small ache. She touched Dash's flank and removed her mask. This problem didn't need Swallow's help. It begged for Serena's. "I'll be right back."

"Serena, no. You can't heal here."

"Tell me you don't feel that pain?"

Dash paused. "I do."

"Someone is dying, Dash. How can I not help?"

"If you do and the Circle finds out, or worse, someone here tries to imprison you—they will hunt you down."

"I don't care what the Circle says, and I don't value my safety over someone's life. I'm healing someone today." She raced around the library to the north side, where the cries of a woman grew louder.

"Please! I have come all this way. You have to help him!" She held the limp form of a small boy in her arms.

Serena placed her hand over her heart.

The woman stood on the steps of a small house behind the library. A sign on the door read, "Physician."

A man stood in the doorway, staring at the child. "I'm sorry. There's nothing I can do."

Truth.

Tears streamed down the woman's face, and her knees seemed to weaken as she stumbled closer to the man. "You're the best physician in Soleden. What do you need? More money? This is all—"

"Madam, we cannot help your boy. Modern medicine—"

"I can help him." Serena reached the bottom of the stairs.

Dash followed.

"I am tired of living in the shadows, Dash. Are you with me?" She looked into Dash's huge, brown eyes. It would put him in danger, too.

"Always."

The woman ran up to Serena, her boy in her arms. "Whatever you can do."

"She can do nothing. Erinecath has no female surgeons. This woman is nothing but an inferior—"

"I can save your boy's life." Serena lowered her hood, revealing her unmasked face. "Set him here." She knelt on the ground.

The woman laid her son on the grass.

Serena pressed her hands on the boy's side. Something inside of him had ruptured. Infection was killing him. She'd have to funnel it into herself. This would take a lot of energy.

Strength drained from Serena's body as she leaned over the boy. Pulled his pain into her own body. Everything else muted. Shouts resounded around her. A tremor rocked the earth. Dash must be defending her. She had to hurry, had to save the boy.

Finally, the pain stopped pulsing into her. It was done. She leaned back and the world around her returned in full color. She felt weak. Drained.

Dash reared, his hooves flailing, as he kept the mob of men away. They shouted words like "monster," but one voice rose above the rest. "We could study her."

A tremor shot through her heart and she stood. *"Dash?"*

"I'm coming."

The boy sat up and blinked. "Mommy?"

Everyone stilled. "She did it." Whispers spread through the mob.

The woman stared at Serena. Her eyes widened. "You're—"

Serena cupped the woman's hands. "Your boy was healed here, at the home of the physicians in Erinecath. You understand?"

"Yes. Thank you," she whispered. "And bless you."

"It's my duty. My purpose." Serena mounted Dash, and the unicorn bolted at a speed no horse could match. Serena clung tight to him.

"You did the right thing, Serena."

Serena looked over her shoulder and kept her hand on her hood to keep it in place. *"I know. It's hard, though."*

"To do the right thing?"

"Sometimes. But I meant that it's hard to know when to disobey the Circle."

"Just keep following that small voice in your heart."

She smiled. *"You?"*

He snorted. *"You know what I mean."*

"I do. And thank you for letting me heal him."

"I don't think we'll be coming back here any time soon."

"Me either."

"Serena?" Dash's voice held a tremor, and she looked forward. The breath rushed from her lungs. The gate was closing.

"Hold on." Dash leapt over the gate. Serena grabbed his neck and held tight. Even as the shouts behind them dissipated, he kept running.

CHAPTER 5

CRUMBLING PRISON

Ethan opened his eyes to darkness. Shadows and light pulsed and flickered above him, a reflection of torchlight. By the looks of the jagged, rocky ceiling, he was still in the tunnel beneath the palace grounds. The last thing he remembered was General Balton stabbing him in the chest with a sword.

His heart beat faster. No sounds of battle. Only the quiet drip of condensation leaking off cave walls. How long had he been out?

Where was Jayden?

He opened one of his talents but didn't sense any threats for Jayden, but it was too much to hope that she wasn't in danger. That meant she was either too far away from him or . . . no, she was alive. He had to believe Ryan had gotten her to safety.

Dim light made it too difficult to see much of anything. He reached for his sword and cringed. Moving was a bad idea. Everything hurt. Gingerly, he touched his right arm where the enemy's sword had bitten deep. A bandage. And it felt like someone had stitched him up. His pulse thrummed. His other wounds were bandaged and stitched up, too. But his sword belt was missing. No weapon. No shirt. Someone had found him. Who? And why hadn't they killed him?

He had to get out of here and find the others. And his sword. A shirt would be nice, too.

He wrapped his throbbing arm around his sore middle and pushed off the floor with his left hand. As his eyes adjusted, he noticed three cavern walls surrounding him. This was some sort of alcove. A glint on the cave floor near the opposite wall caught his attention. That could be his sword. He just had to get over there and get his weapon.

He made it the few steps to the opposite wall and braced himself against the hard rock. Where was that glint? Stacks of books, a blanket, and—a soft tapping sounded behind him. Like footfalls. Ethan froze.

"You probably shouldn't be moving."

He'd recognize that voice anywhere. Kara. The assassin who'd led him straight to the palace and the clutches of his enemy. She sounded close, but with the sound bouncing off the curved wall, he couldn't pinpoint her location.

He inched across the stone floor, hoping to bump into his sword. Nothing. Not even a rock to throw. His Blood Moon talent didn't pulse a warning that Kara meant to harm him. Well, not yet anyway. If she did, his protective talent would kick in and cover up the pain. Hopefully then he could summon enough strength and speed to defeat her.

"What do you want, Kara?" The roughness in his own voice surprised him.

She rounded the corner, stepped into the alcove, and crossed her arms, her smirk visible. "Hello to you, too, soldier. Couldn't tell which direction I was coming from, could you? Can you hear anything out of that ear?"

Breath left his lungs in a rush as he recalled Scarface's fist repeatedly pounding into his left ear. Over and over. "Come to finish me off?"

"And waste my stitch-up job?"

"You?"

"I expected more gratitude."

"I'd thank you if I thought you did it for my sake."

She moved closer to the books and kicked the blanket aside. Ethan spotted his sword. He lunged for it, but Kara beat him to it and held it up to his neck. "Is that any way to greet a friend?"

Ethan backed away from the blade, regretting all that quick movement. "We aren't friends."

"We should be." She leaned against the wall next to him, still holding his sword, but she lowered the weapon from his neck. Cinnamon permeated the air between them. A sultry smile spread her lips as she leaned an elbow on the tunnel wall just over his left shoulder. "Except you did poison me."

"We're even."

"Hardly."

"Where are Jayden and Ryan?"

"Your friends got out thanks to my sister and me."

"You're the reason we were here in the first place."

Kara pushed off the wall and circled him like a cat with prey. "You were headed here either way." She stopped in front of him, tempting him with the sword just out of reach. "I can't believe you were willing to die for her."

She chuckled and the sharp point of a blade pressed against his stomach. No burn pulsed across his chest, nothing warned him of her ill intent. This threat was a farce.

He looked right into her eyes. "Go ahead."

She cocked an eyebrow. "Calling my bluff. Brave. There will be a day it won't be a bluff, but for now, I still need you."

"I won't help you."

"I don't need your compliance. You'll do what I want without my bidding." She withdrew the blade from against his stomach, propped his sword against the wall, and stood between him and his weapon. She stepped closer and handed him something else, hilt first. "Your knife, I think. I pulled it out of Nora."

He clutched the stolen weapon's handle as the memory of him accidentally killing the poor serving girl seared his mind. "It *was* yours."

She shrugged. "You earned it."

Ethan grabbed her shirt collar in his left hand and pulled her close. He pushed the knife up to her ribs. Angled it to puncture her lungs. "*I* don't need *you.*"

Her eyes hardened. "Your death wish." A prick of pain spread into his skin, the same position he held a knife to her. "Maybe you'll be quicker, but you'll also be dead. Right now your little Softheart is in trouble. Are you really willing to abandon her for a shot at revenge?"

Softheart. Wasn't that the name Kara and her sister, Thea, called Jayden? Betrayers, both of them. Revenge might be a flame that constantly tempted him, but not now. Not if it would take his attention from Jayden. Ethan retracted the knife. Kara pulled her knife back, too, her gaze still glued to his.

A flash of heat spread across his chest a moment too late. Kara's fist connected with the healing gash in his side. He doubled over, and she slammed him sideways into the tunnel wall. The hard rock grated against his injured arm, and a flash of white light shot through his skull as his head hit the stone. His knees weakened, and he leaned against the wall to remain upright—and to breathe. Stupid to get her angry when he was in no position to defend himself, let alone fight.

She rounded on him and held his sword up to his stomach. "Don't threaten me, soldier. I can always find a different pawn." Her eyes were hard this time. A hint of heat pulsed across his skin. This threat was real.

She lowered the weapon and stepped away from him. "You're lucky I needed you. Connor knew nothing about stitching a wound. You would've bled out under his care. Now, are you willing to cut the games and accept that you need my help? Or are you still contemplating that death wish?"

Connor? He was supposed to know that name. "Do you know where Jayden is?" His voice was strained.

Kara propped his sword up against the wall—out of his reach again. "Sort of. I know she isn't far. Besides, I think you can find her. You're bound to her somehow. An oath maybe?"

His oath scar would help him find her, of that he was certain. "If I can?"

"That's what I need. For you to protect her."

"I still have to get out of here. While you're being so helpful, perhaps you can arrange an escape." Ethan pushed off the wall, but found himself much weaker than anticipated. He nearly fell over, but Kara caught his right elbow and steadied him. His injured arm throbbed under her grip, and he flinched.

"Sorry," she whispered.

His eyes snapped to meet hers. He caught her eyebrows drawn together.

All the soft lines left her face, and her eyes glittered in the torchlight as her smirk returned. "You'd better sit down before you fall over."

She was probably right. His pulse pounded in every wound. "I'll be fine. Are you going to tell me how to get out?"

"Yes. But not during the day. Prince Franco has men searching for your friends. The forest is swarming with soldiers. I can get you out at night."

"Tonight." He really had no idea what time of day it was.

Kara cocked an eyebrow. "You're more chopped up than a fighting dummy. You won't make it far before you're buzzard food."

He couldn't have Kara following him. If Franco had men out looking for Jayden . . . "Did you say Franco?"

Kara nodded. "Softheart killed Idla. Who knew she had it in her? Blew the queen's eyes from her sockets."

She had? Good for her. The room started to look a little blurry. He reached behind himself with his left hand and guided himself back to sitting, closer to his sword. "Yes, tonight. No later."

"That I can arrange with little trouble." She shook her head. "Provided you don't keel over on the way out. Two days is hardly enough time to come back from the dead, soldier."

That choice of words made his heart miss a beat. Still, two days for him would be about four days' worth of healing thanks to another of his talents. Plenty of time. "Like I said, don't worry about me."

She crouched next to him. "You'll want my horse. She's faster, and she'll return here when you let her go. Connor can't go as far as I can. He's a bound prisoner to the palace. I'm not. Oh, and . . ." She smiled and leaned next to his left ear. Cupped her hands around it.

Hot breath heated his ear, but he didn't hear a thing. Not even her breathing. He didn't have time for her games. "Where will you leave the horse?"

"You didn't hear me?" She reached to touch his ear.

He grabbed her wrist. "Just tell me."

"Temper, Ethan. I like it." She pulled her arm free. "Take a left out of the alcove and follow the scent of rotting flesh until you see the crack of moonlight. It's a door. Just push. I'll be waiting outside with Javelin, my horse."

"What time of day is it now?"

"Midday." She stood to leave, stopped, and turned. "Oh, and it's too bad about that ear, soldier."

Ethan swallowed and stilled his hand from touching his ear. Useless, all because of Scarface.

He watched Kara slip soundlessly out of sight before he moved to get his weapon.

Ethan finally reached his sword. He should really get going— before she came back—but the thought of standing made him queasy. He groaned and leaned his head against the wall. He'd be in a lot better shape with another day to heal, but he had to get to Jayden.

She could be anywhere by now. When he pictured her face, a small twinge hit his heart—as if directing him toward a pull. He squeezed his hand in a fist and pressed his fingers into the oath scar, feeling the twinge to find Jayden in every pulse. First problem to solve: getting out of here unnoticed.

He braced his hand against the ground to push himself up, but his finger brushed against something small and solid. It was smooth and cold, like a polished marriage stone.

He picked it up. It warmed to his touch, and as he gazed at the stone, it glowed. A picture appeared. A small girl, about the same age as Wren, sat against jagged rock, dirty and alone with her knees pulled up to her chin. A chain encircled each wrist and bound her to the rock formation.

Trails through grime on her cheeks revealed a path for tears. She pushed up her torn, threadbare sleeve and Ethan gasped. Red, angry blisters covered her skin.

Her eyes, hazel and hopeless, connected with his through the stone—as if she felt him watching. She opened her mouth. He heard nothing, but her lips formed two words.

Help me.

The desire to protect her fanned in his chest.

Two eyes, blue like hot flame, appeared in the stone. *"Who is watching?"* The voice thundered through his being, though he was sure it wasn't audible.

"Put that away!" Someone snatched the rock from Ethan's hands. "She could have seen you."

Ethan stared at the young man who stood in front of him, and held up his sword as a warning.

The intruder jumped back and stood against the opposite wall. He wrapped the stone in a handkerchief and stuffed it into his pocket. "I see you got your sword."

"Who are you?"

"My name's Connor."

That name again. Who—oh, yes. The woman Logan had fought in the tunnel had been calling for a Connor. Ethan steadied his sword, wishing he was standing but not willing to attempt it and risk showing how weak he was. "What do you want, Connor?"

"At this point? To keep you alive."

"Why?" Ethan studied the young man's face. He'd never seen someone with golden eyes.

Connor crossed to the other side of the alcove. He picked up a satchel and tossed it to Ethan, staying just out of the sword's reach. His movements were wary, like a curious wild animal. "I imagine you're thirsty. Don't worry, your friends made it out."

Ethan peered inside and saw food and water. Just the thought of water made his tongue stick to the roof of his mouth. Dare he trust this Connor? It all depended on what Connor wanted from him.

"Drink first and I'll get you more." Connor chuckled. "It'd be extra work on my part to take care of you, then poison you."

Good point. "Thank you." Ethan drank like a horse refueling. "Why are you helping me?"

"I don't want you dying before you get where you're going."

"That makes two of us, and I was just on my way out."

"You nearly lost an arm. The sword that hit you cut into your bone." Connor winced. "The holes in your chest and stomach—I'm told—missed everything vital, but the puddle of blood I found you in was pretty big. Whoever stabbed you wanted you to suffer as long as possible."

"General Balton. Friend of yours?"

Connor's lower eyelids twitched. "If he were, why would I risk saving you?"

"Good point. Who was that? In the stone."

"I can't really say. Anyone who has one of these could—"

"Okay, then what kind of stone is it?"

"Piece of a seeing stone. Half of my piece, anyway. I want you to have it, but keep it covered when it's not in use."

Ethan had touched the thing. No rough edge revealed that the stone had been cut. "I don't like being lied to."

"I'm not. Seeing stones are a little tricky." Connor moved to the wall next to Ethan and sat down. "This one is a chunk of an untraceable stone. When you cut a piece with a special object, the stone takes on a smooth shape so you can't trace where it's been cut from. That's how you know it's untraceable. Those with clear-cut marks, they're traceable. Still, you can always see others who are watching in their stones, traceable or not. They appear, eyes first."

Ethan looked at Connor's golden eyes and motioned to his own brown eyes. "I see why you're being secretive. Brown eyes are hardly rare, though."

Connor smiled. "I suppose my eyes are the first thing people notice. But be careful. The Mistress of Shadows has a stone. And if she looks long enough, she'll see your face, your surroundings. She'll hunt you down."

"How do I put this? I don't know how long you've been locked up, but here's a little update for you. The Mistress, as you call her, has been dead a long time."

"Not dead. In prison. This time she's been in there for three thousand years or so, but her prison is breaking. She's escaped before. The Deliverers are born every so many years so they can rise up and prevent her escape."

Ethan leaned closer. "You're saying she can get out?"

"Why do you think Idla wanted the Deliverers? Why do you think the Mistress wants them? All four of them together can unlock enough of the Creator's power to banish the Mistress forever. A lot of people would kill for that power, the Mistress included. But if she were to get her hands on it, she'd be unstoppable."

A shiver shot through Ethan. So the fight was far from over. Jayden and three others would have to make sure the Mistress of Shadows stayed in her prison. "There are others who want the Deliverers?"

"The Mistress has many spies. Idla was one, but Idla wanted the power for herself. I can only assume she's not the only one greedy enough. Franco was aware of his mother's plans. If he can free the Mistress, the first thing she will destroy will be the Feravolk."

Ethan's stomach twisted. "How do we stop Franco?"

Connor pulled out the handkerchief-wrapped stone and offered it to Ethan. "You saw the girl?"

Ethan recalled those pleading eyes and the protective pull in his chest ached. He didn't reach for the stone.

"She needs a rescue. I can't go. I'm bound here by a trace spell. The Mistress wants her for a spell—I think it has something to do with breaking the prison. That's enough for me to want her rescued."

"Who is the girl?"

Connor looked right into Ethan's eyes. "I don't know. I just know she's important to the Mistress's escape. They move with her every day. I'm not sure where they're going, but I can communicate with you through the stone."

"They?"

Connor shrugged. "Powerful women. The ones who torture her."

"Why should I trust you? The enemy was looking for you the night my friends escaped."

"Not the enemy. Rebekah. My mother."

Ethan's pulse raced. "You're Logan's son. The one he's looking for? You're a Deliverer."

"Shh." Connor brought his finger to his lips and stalked to the edge of the alcove.

Ethan picked up his sword. He braced himself against the wall and slowly stood. Everything still throbbed. He held his breath to listen but didn't hear anything. Stupid ear.

Connor looked over his shoulder. "Are you well enough to leave? Because Captain Jonis is headed this way. He wants to make sure a certain 'dog' is dead. He doesn't mean me. No one else knows my secret save Rebekah."

"Jonis?"

Connor drew his finger over his cheek in the pattern of a crescent-shaped scar Ethan knew well.

"Scarface." Ethan all but growled the name.

CHAPTER 6

A BORROWED WEAPON

What does Captain Jonis want with you?" Connor asked. Ethan tightened his grip on his weapon's hilt as he recalled Scarface slamming a fist into his ear. "He wants me dead."

"Okay. That's not good." Connor started rummaging through his things. He handed Ethan a shirt and Ethan's own sword belt to go with the satchel of food and water. "I'll take you as far as I can toward the stables. There should be a horse waiting for you. I picked it because it will return here." Connor smiled. "It's Kara's. Her name's Javelin."

Trust or not, Ethan had to get out of here before Scarface could track him. And leaving before Kara came back was precisely what he wanted to do. He strapped on his belt.

Connor winced. "You're bleeding again."

Thanks to Kara. "Do you have a needle and thread?"

"Yes." Connor put the items into Ethan's sack. Then he held out the handkerchief-wrapped stone.

Ethan stared at it.

Connor placed it in the satchel, which he handed to Ethan before snuffing the torch. Thankfully, other torches hung sparsely on the rocky walls. "I can see. I can lead you out." He touched Ethan's elbow. "Put your hand on my back."

Ethan complied, but keeping Connor's brisk pace was more excruciating that he'd expected.

Connor stopped and looped Ethan's arm over his shoulders. "You're not as healed as you let on."

"I'm also not as dead as Scarface is hoping."

Connor chuckled. "All right. I guess there's no choice but to get you out of here."

"You should come with me. I'm sworn to protect the Deliverers. That includes you."

"Don't worry about me. I've been surviving here so far. I'll be fine for a little while longer."

"We need you to stop the Mistress, don't we?"

Connor stared at him for a moment. "Yes, but not yet. I'm bound here by a trace spell. It's more urgent that you find the others first."

Ethan didn't feel the pull of protection he thought he would. Perhaps Connor was right. He'd be safe here for now. Not that Rebekah seemed trustworthy. "I'll be back for you."

"I believe you."

They headed through the tunnels the way Kara had told Ethan to go. The scent of death and fire permeated everything. Light grew brighter as they neared the exit. And sounds grew louder. Stomping. Shuffling. Scarface drew nearer, and he wasn't alone.

"He was right here," one voice said. "I see blood."

Great.

"Well, he isn't anymore, is he?" Scarface's familiar snarl resounded behind them. "Find him."

Connor froze. "I think I'm going to have to head them off. Will you be able to make it out of the tunnel? The horse is just out that way."

"Kara visited earlier. I know where to find her horse." Ethan slipped his arm from Connor's shoulder. "But I don't think you can—"

Connor's face changed and Ethan had nothing more to say. It was like looking into a mirror. And boy, did he look banged up. He swallowed. "He'll kill you."

"He'll have to catch me first."

Ethan's talent urged him forward—his oath scar pulled him toward Jayden. It didn't make sense. If he'd taken an oath to protect the Deliverers, that included Connor. Did that mean Connor was safer here? Maybe for now he was. And Ethan had no idea how to break a trace spell. Perhaps taking Connor would put him in greater danger.

"Go." Connor nudged him.

Ethan nodded. "Thank you. For everything."

"Don't—well, don't get yourself killed." He darted back down the tunnel and Ethan headed out.

The scent of burning flesh seeped from the walls. Had Idla been killed here? His shoe kicked something and it skittered across the floor. A white horse charm. Hadn't Jayden said this was all she had left of her mother? He clutched it in his fist. She'd better be alive. And all right.

The tunnel let out, and Ethan squinted in the daylight. The scent of horse rode on the wind. He turned left. Kara's horse stood tied to a sapling. Ethan clicked his tongue. Javelin's nostrils flared as he got closer. She likely smelled blood. But she calmed. Perhaps it was normal for her.

He reached to pet her nose, then sighed with relief as he noticed the boulder just behind her. Good. He didn't have to jump into her saddle after all. He hefted himself onto the rock. "Okay, girl, this might be a little sloppy. Just don't move on me, huh?"

Javelin let air through her lips and dipped her head to graze on the long grass.

He pulled himself onto Javelin. She didn't seem to mind his sloppy movement at all. How many times had Kara mounted her while injured? He patted the horse's neck and clicked his tongue as he guided her with the reins. With a steady gait she complied, heading off the palace grounds.

A pull tugged his heart and his oath hand echoed.

Jayden. She'd better be okay.

CHAPTER 7

A PERSUASIVE OFFER

Connor headed back toward Captain Jonis and his men. He wouldn't be able to hold the illusion that made him look like Ethan for long, so he stayed in the shadows until he'd need to change.

What he'd told Ethan was true—both that they needed him to defeat the Mistress and that he was bound to the palace. He hadn't said that he planned to help them remotely. Ethan likely wouldn't have understood anyway.

Connor stalked near the tunnel wall, listening. His wolf hearing picked up the scuffle of footsteps headed his direction. He'd touched Ethan, so he could morph into a flawless representation of him. He focused. Changed. Stepped out of the shadows just in time to head down another corridor.

"There he is!" one soldier shouted.

"You won't get away from me again, dog." Captain Jonis's voice resembled a low growl.

Dog? Connor smiled. If he only knew.

This corridor led back toward the palace. Connor knew it well. He'd spent a lot of time down here. A lot of time in the shadows.

Four soldiers rounded the corner after him. He ran his fingers along the cool, rough stone wall in front of him. A small indentation. There. He faced the wall and changed back to himself, then he pressed the lever.

With a grating rumble the door opened, and Connor shot through into a sweltering kitchen. And it smelled divine.

Cooks manned the three ovens, and four women in brown dresses faced the tables, rolling and kneading dough or chopping vegetables. No one faced him except a young girl holding a basket of bread. Flour dusted her cheek and she nearly dropped the basket, but Connor recognized her. Cecilia—she often gave him an extra piece of bread or fruit when no one was looking. Would she help him now?

He reached forward and caught the basket for her. As she steadied it in her hands, he held his finger up to his lips. She clamped her mouth closed and nodded once. She leaned toward one of the girls chopping vegetables. "That pot is boiling over."

With a sigh, the girl left her station at the table and handed Cecilia the knife. "Finish chopping, will you?"

Cecilia nodded and waved for Connor to hide under the table, the servants making a wall of dresses to shield him from those who would come into the kitchen the way he'd come.

"Cecilia, there aren't enough loaves in that basket. You know how King Franco likes to—"

The hidden door grated open again, and the cook stopped and stared at it. So did Cecilia. Connor peered between the skirts hiding him.

Three soldiers and Captain Jonis broke through. "Where is he?"

"Beg your pardon?" The head cook placed her hands on her narrow hips. "You'll not be in here to take my staff, I hope. Wait until after supper at least to perform your beheadings."

Jonis's chest swelled and he stepped up to the cook, but she walked right past him, back to the stone wall. "How'd you get that to open?"

"Did you see a man run through here?"

"No."

"Quickest way out of here?"

She pointed. "Get. You're likely to make my cake fall. If you do, it'll be *your* head. Y'hear?" She called after him. Then she grabbed the bread basket from Cecilia. "I don't want to know a thing, child. Just put the bread on the king's tray."

When her back was turned, Connor crept out from beneath the table. Cecilia hurried with him toward the door and handed him a loaf of bread. "Why is the captain looking for you?"

"He's not. He mistook me for someone else. It's dark in there."

"And you didn't reveal yourself? Your friends are lucky, Connor."

He held up the bread and winked as he headed back into the tunnels. "So am I."

Bread eaten, Connor reached the corridor leading to the bard's gate. Luc, the smithy, was already there. The torchlight betrayed relief in his green eyes. "What kept you, friend?"

Connor shrugged. "The less you know, the better. Do you have it?"

Luc handed him a flask with the initials "T. A." Perfect. Now Connor would be able to successfully impersonate the guard. He pocketed it. "All right, head back to the smithy. Make sure someone sees you around the time the prisoners go missing." He clutched Luc's shoulder. "I can't have anyone thinking you're involved."

Luc nodded. "And you be careful. I'm sure Lieutenant Tobias will be here to take his post soon, especially if he thinks his flask could be here. You haven't much time."

"Don't worry about me. I'll be gone before he gets here." Connor tipped his head to the side and smirked. "Just make sure you're at the entrance to the tunnel when they get there."

"I will be." Luc patted Connor's shoulder and passed him the key. "The wooden plank has been moved." He took his torch and headed out the bard's gate but called over his shoulder, "Just don't forget to put it back."

Right, because then the loose bricks in the wall would move and the escape would be uncovered. Connor turned on his heel and walked through a different corridor, his wolf senses making it easier to get around in the darkness.

At last he made it to the guard's station. Before he turned the corner, he made sure to look just like Tobias.

The other guard eyed him. "It's time to change already?"

Connor shook his head and stumbled, acting drunk. "Any peep from the prisoners?"

"Nah. The potion is supposed to be ready today. Make sure you're not asleep on the job this time."

Connor rapped his knuckle against the hidden door in the wall. "It's solid." Then he pulled out the flask and offered the other man a drink. He couldn't recall his name, but Luc said the man loved his drink.

He chuckled and took a swig.

Connor smiled. Waited. The man's eyes rolled back into his head, and he slumped to the ground. That tangle flower worked every time. He chuckled and spilled out the rest of the drink and left the flask. Then he unlocked the secret door, morphed into his true form, and picked up the man's torch. "Thank you." He stepped inside and the door locked behind him.

Fourteen faces looked up at him.

He held up a knife. "Turn around so I can break your bindings. I'm here to rescue you."

One young man stood first. "She told me the man with amber eyes would come." He smiled. "I was starting to lose hope."

Connor sawed through the ropes on the young man's hands. Amber eyes, huh? He'd seen eyes that color in his nightmares, and they certainly weren't his own. "Whoever she is, I hope she saw this plan succeeding. Help me untie them." He handed the man his knife and walked to the wall opposite the one he'd entered. The bricks in the left corner slid out of place as he pushed.

"What are you doing?" the young man asked.

Connor faced him, pressing a finger to his lips. "I've made a few adjustments to the holding cell. Do you like them?"

Soft murmurs spread through the group of prisoners, and more bindings fell to the ground. Connor instructed them to pick up every rope. When the space in the bricks was big enough to fit through, one by one they filtered through the hole.

Once on the other side, Connor gave his torch to the young man he'd first freed. "Lead them down the tunnel until it splits. Then go right. You'll head up into the smithy. My friend will be waiting there to take you to the escape tunnel."

"You're not coming with us?"

A small tug on his leg told him Franco was pulling the trace spell binding him to the palace since he'd arranged to meet Franco for some sparring this morning—an alibi and a leash all in one. "I would that I could. But I'm bound here. For now."

The young man clasped his shoulder. "Thank you."

As they took the torchlight with them, Connor rebuilt the wall and said a prayer for their escape.

Rebekah woke as the sun spilled across her face. She jolted to a sitting position, then cupped her head in her hands.

"Headache?"

The voice from the other side of the room made her pull her blanket up to her chin, thankful that her nightwear was not revealing. "General Balton. What are you doing in here?"

A tight bandage covered his right hand, revealing a missing thumb, and he held a saucer out with his left. "I brought you some tea. You were complaining about a headache before you went to sleep two nights ago."

She stepped out of bed, still clutching her sheet. "Two nights?" Why had she slept for so long? And why couldn't she recall being anywhere near the general two nights ago?

"I carried you to your room, and you asked me to stay." He handed her the tea cup and Rebekah let her blanket fall to the floor as she looked into Felix Balton's eyes. Dark and brown and hard. Nothing like Logan's.

Balton chuckled as he bent to pick up her blanket and threw it on the bed. "It's all right. I didn't sleep here. You were obviously feeling ill, and Connor was doting over you. I felt no reason to stay. I just thought I'd check on you again. You look better." He reached out to touch her cheek, and Rebekah brought the tea cup to her lips to deter his hand.

She swallowed. "I don't even remember being ill."

"But you do recall being in the assassin's way tunnel?"

"Assassin's way?" She did not remember. Her heartbeat quickened. Balton smelled like a lion ready to pounce. She stepped back from him and tucked her chin toward her chest. "I'm not feeling very well. I think I'm going to sit down. Perhaps you could send a nurse—"

Balton grabbed her wrist. "I found you, Rebekah. I know what you were up to."

"What makes you so sure?" She took a seat at the table, trying desperately to remain calm.

He released her arm and sat across from her. "I found you in the assassin's way right after the prisoners escaped. Tell me, how would they know to go through the secret underground tunnels? Only a select few in the palace know of the assassin's gate." His eyes narrowed as if he could ferret a confession out of her. "Franco would be very displeased to find out you had a hand in the escape of that girl Deliverer and Logan. He would have your head, I think."

Logan? Logan had been here? Her throat tightened. "Franco?"

"Yes. Idla's dead, after all. The Deliverer killed her. Don't worry." Felix's voice grew softer and his finger slid across the back of her hand. "I'm the only one who knows you were there. I'll keep it a secret."

Her heart pounded. "Connor?"

"Connor doesn't know. He was out sparring with some of my soldiers."

"How did you find me?"

"After Logan escaped with the others, I found blood outside the entrance of the tunnel. You were in there, unconscious."

"I was trying to stop them."

"You had the prison keys in your pocket."

She felt like a dove in a trap. It was some sort of spell. It had to have been. Her hands were sweating. She put them on her lap and pretended to smooth her nightgown.

"Logan framed me." How she spoke his name so calmly amazed her.

"I believe you, but do you think it will make a difference to Franco?"

"What do you want?"

Balton chuckled. "You on my arm. Perhaps the throne. I have my own plans to take it from Franco. I hope you will reconsider my offer of marriage. I'll give you another chance." He placed a ring on the table. Gold with a diamond.

Rebekah stared at it.

"Make me the happiest man in the kingdom, and you'll never have to worry about your secret slipping out. Think on it, because if I become king, you'll be my queen or you'll die." He stood and showed himself to the door.

She remained still as a frightened doe until she no longer heard his footsteps echoing down the hall. What had happened?

A knock pelted the door. Connor. She pocketed Balton's suggestion. There was no reason for her son to know about this now.

Connor entered and raced over to her. "What's wrong? How long have you been up? I saw the general leaving."

"Logan was here?"

Connor leaned back. His eyes met hers with a hint of fear in them. "What do you remember?"

So it was true.

"I—I don't . . ." She looked at the cup on the table. "Tea. I remember Oswell bringing me tea."

"Right after I was ordered to go sparring and hunting off palace grounds with Balton's men?"

"Yes."

"Idla spelled you."

Of course. "You?"

Connor shook his head. "She just sent me out of the palace."

"But you didn't leave?"

"I did. I brought Luc. The two of us may have feigned getting lost while tracking a wild boar. Whatever secrets I have are safe."

"What happened to Logan?"

"Balton captured him and three Children of the Blood Moon and brought them here. They escaped. The Deliverers are being drawn to him."

"How did they escape?"

Connor's eyes darted to the floor. "I can't tell you."

"Balton says he found me in the assassin's way."

Connor's head shot up. "That's how . . ."

"He says I had the prison keys in my pocket."

"The keys?" Connor growled. "I know who planted the keys on you." He stood, hands fisted, and walked to the door.

"Connor, what are you not telling me?"

Her son looked over his shoulder. "Enough to keep you safe from Belladonna's prying."

CHAPTER 8

THREE LITTLE THINGS

Thea smirked. So the softhearted Jayden had a temper after all. Interesting. And good to see a little bit of fire in her eyes. She'd need it. "I do want to talk to you, Softheart. Alone."

Ryan stepped between them, his stormy gray eyes boring into Thea with a glare. "No way am I leaving you two alone together."

"I agree, kid." Logan looked at Jayden and his eyebrows rose slightly.

Was he asking Jayden what she wanted? Good. Maybe Thea could convince Softheart into that one-on-one conversation after all. Being able to see the future was one thing. Not being able to pick and choose what she saw was something else entirely. Thea needed this conversation; she just wasn't sure which cards to play to get it. Sometimes it was in the future visions. Other times it wasn't.

"Don't be so overprotective, Charmer." She winked at Ryan. "Tie me up first. I don't care. I have something for her ears alone." Her eyes bored into Jayden, and she guarded her emotions. It wouldn't be good if Jayden used her talent to sense Thea's uncertainty.

Jayden sheathed her weapons. "I'll leave her alive."

Thea silenced a laugh. Yes, this new fire would do nicely.

Logan lowered his weapon but didn't put it away. "She's a liar, Jayden. Don't let her create false hope."

Too late. Softheart wanted so badly to believe her soldier was alive, it shone in her eyes. That ray of hope was foreign to Thea, but it fueled her endgame.

Jayden straightened her back. "I'll never forgive myself if I don't hear her out."

Logan nodded. "All right. We'll secure her and you can talk, but if she says anything you don't like, just walk away."

Perfect.

○

Jayden approached the tree they'd tied Thea to. The assassin sat on the ground with her ankles bound together. Rope secured her waist and shoulders, pinning her arms close, but her hands were tied behind her, just like when Jayden's brothers used to tie Geoffrey, the family scarecrow, to one of the apple trees for target practice. Jayden stopped just far enough away that she could still hear what Thea had to say. The perfect distance to throw a knife between the assassin's eyes.

Thea looked right at her. "You don't really want to hurt me."

"You'd be surprised." Jayden clutched her weapon but didn't pull it out. Something about Thea's presence stoked her anger in a way she'd never experienced.

"I wasn't lying about Ethan, but he is in danger. You all are."

"Please." Jayden opened her talent. "The fact that we're in danger is hardly news."

She reached forward into Thea's heart. Feelings pulsed there, like strings connected to a heartbeat. Jayden mentally strummed them, and for the briefest moment everything rushed into her. Fear, anger, hatred, worry, regret, love. Nothing that could tell her whether or not Ethan lived. Why couldn't her talent be discerning lies? Much more helpful than feeling stupid emotions—not to mention less distracting. How on Soleden was she supposed to defeat enemies by understanding their feelings? She probed anyway.

"You're stronger than I thought." Thea's voice was quiet. "I guess I shouldn't be surprised. You did face the queen and survive. I knew you would, but when I met you, I had my doubts."

"What do you mean, you *knew*? That I would defeat her or that I would live?"

"Both."

"How could you possibly know?"

"I know a lot of things. You saw my birthmark. I have talents, too. I've seen things. You killing Idla. This moment. Your death."

Her . . . death? Jayden's heart choked her, but she kept her expression steady. "Is that supposed to scare me?"

Thea shrugged. "It shouldn't be news. Deliverers don't usually survive. You should know what they're up against. The history of the Deliverers is recorded in the library of Erinecath. You can see for yourself. Learn from past mistakes. Maybe you'll make it out of this whole thing alive. Sometimes the future changes. I'm rooting for you."

"You lie."

"Sometimes. Not this time. Let me show you the source of much of my knowledge. Maybe then you'll believe me. It's in my pocket."

Jayden didn't move closer.

Thea's emotions remained the same, as if she always felt this way regardless of what she was doing. "You'll have to reach it for me."

"Just skip to the message. Or don't you have one?"

"Yes. But I need the stone in my pocket to tell you."

Of course she did. Jayden straightened her back and crossed her arms.

Thea shrugged. "It's a seeing stone. It will show you things that other people with seeing stones can see. Right now Franco is looking in the stone. What he's saying will be of interest to you."

Jayden bent to eye level. "I don't trust you."

"You'll regret it if you don't look."

A taunt, but it worked. If a chance existed that Ethan was alive, he deserved to have her look for him. Especially if he was somewhere dying. A lump formed in her throat, and she pulled a ball of fabric from Thea's pocket. Evil seemed to permeate the fabric.

Thea watched her intently. "If you give it back to me after you use it, it won't tempt you further."

The sense of urgency bled through Thea. No hint of malice. The hatred beat in her heart, but not toward Jayden. That emotion was just a ball in the center of Thea's being. Sad that it would have such a permanent hold on her.

Jayden unwrapped the trinket. It had a sharp, jagged edge and a flat side. The other side was smooth. A flame seemed to burn within the surface. Then hard blue eyes appeared. Eyes she remembered. Franco's.

"I need that Deliverer," Franco said into a stone he held. Jayden watched him as if she were a spider hanging from the ceiling. "If you can't find her, then draw her out. I'll destroy everything she holds dear. Then I'll have her. And then I'll take her power."

His growl made her recoil. She recalled how he'd crushed her neck with uncanny strength. How he'd pressed her onto his bed and attempted to poison her with a goblet of spelled liquid. "Who is he talking to?"

"Careful. He'll hear," Thea said. "To see in his stone, just think about it."

Jayden focused on the stone in Franco's hand. The picture swirled and seemed to suck her inside of it. Then she was the spider on a different ceiling, staring at a different man. That face. That scar. She recognized him. The man who'd punched Ethan in the ear over and over and called him "dog."

This time hate poured into her. Some of it was hers, but some of it was his. It choked her like thick tar in her mouth.

"Don't worry, Your Highness. I'll personally kill everyone she holds dear, starting with that man who's nothing more than a dog." Then his green eyes looked into hers. "I see you."

Something invisible seemed to grip her throat. Pull her closer. She tried to wriggle away but couldn't. Finally, she dropped the stone.

"Cover it!" Thea shouted.

Jayden placed the cloth over the stone.

"Didn't you hear me calling you?" Thea's eyes widened.

"No."

"That was close. He could have seen where your camp is. Your surroundings."

"How do you know he didn't?"

"He'll likely know you're in these woods. And he's sworn to kill you."

Jayden stared into Thea's eyes. "You just endangered everyone I love. I should kill you now." She raised her dagger.

"You can, but I still have some messages to deliver."

"Enough." Jayden pressed her blade against Thea's neck, right under her chin. "Your cryptic messages don't cloak anything from me. You're scared, Thea."

"Yes. But Ethan is alive. He's looking for you. If no one finds him in time, he will die."

Somehow she held her dagger steady. "I told you, I don't trust you."

"You will."

"Never."

"Haven't I proved that I know future things? I'll tell you three things that will come true. Then you'll trust my words."

Jayden reluctantly dropped her weapon from Thea's neck.

Her gaze seemed to entrap Jayden, and all emotion disappeared from Thea again. "Franco intends to free the Mistress of Shadows. If you don't stop his plan, all of Soleden will perish. Do you understand?"

Jayden nodded, wishing she didn't care suddenly about what Thea had to say.

"Good," Thea said. "Then heed my words. I don't know what Franco's plan will be, but I do know how to get the information. I don't see everything. It comes out in pieces, like a puzzle. I've gotten good at putting it together.

"First, you will come across a man with a muzzled dragon tattoo. He would rather die than help you. I do have good news in the second vision. You will also come across a man wearing a broken arrow. He will tell you what you need to know about Franco's plan. Third, your search will lead you to a woman who can't see, but who will see right through you. Listen to her."

Jayden wanted nothing more than to wring Thea's childish neck. "Is this supposed to be helpful?"

"It will be." Her familiar smirk curved one side of her mouth. "Here's something for you alone. A frog and fox will show you your heart's desire."

"That's the stupidest—what do you know about my heart's desire?"

Thea just looked at her with an infuriatingly unreadable expression. "I don't recommend you pursue your heart's desire, Jayden. Not unless you want to risk the heartbreak."

"You don't think I can handle heart—"

"He can't."

Jayden stared into Thea's unblinking gaze. "Because I die." She tried to say it with as much venom as she could, but the breathless words slayed her heart even so.

Thea nodded. "I wish I hadn't seen it. But for his sake, heed my warnings. I've helped you all along."

"Helped me? Helped? You got Ethan killed." Jayden picked up her weapon, pressed it against Thea's chest, and pushed.

CHAPTER 9

NOT ENVIED

Jayden!" Ryan wrapped his arms around her waist and pulled her back.

If he hadn't heard Jayden's voice carry so much hate, he wouldn't have believed her capable of killing Thea.

She pushed at his arms. "Let me go!"

He guided her around to face him. "Why don't you let me talk to her while you cool off?"

"Cool off?"

"I might be able to get her to open up."

Jayden blinked and shook her head. "I—I don't know what came over me."

He breathed a sigh, because it seemed like his Jayden—the one who didn't jump at the chance to kill her enemy—was back. "It's okay. Come here." He opened his arms and she fell into his embrace. This. Comforting Jayden. With everything else going on, this made him feel more normal. He could almost believe everything was going to turn out all right.

"You can't have this."

Almost.

Jayden let go of him and stepped back. "I'm sorry."

He smiled. "For getting mad at Miss Nickname-for-Everything?"

"No," she whispered. "I wanted to kill her."

Ryan's heart stalled. Was that what killing did to someone? Made them believe it was an acceptable answer to problems? If so, maybe he never wanted to kill. Never wanted to have that—that hatred.

"Hate can be an effective weapon."

Ryan sucked in a breath. Red colored the clouds. Red on the bottom, white on top. Just like the white lion. He shuddered.

Jayden's eyebrows pulled together. "Do you think that makes me evil?"

"No." He cupped her elbows in his palms and looked right into her round eyes. "Never. You did what you had to, and you're still trying to protect your friends."

"Thea is dangerous."

"I remember."

Jayden smiled. "Thank you." She touched his arm gently before she headed back to camp.

Ryan approached Thea and crouched down in front of her. Pretty, but venomous.

She smiled. "I hoped you'd come."

"Listen, what you did back there, firing Jayden up like that? I won't stand for it."

"You tell her."

Ryan stopped short and swallowed. He really needed to get used to that voice before anyone noticed him reacting. "And I'll skin you if you lay a hand on her or my sisters."

"Your sisters are all redheads."

"Am I supposed to be impressed by your observations?"

She shrugged. "Your brother's hair is dark. Soldier's not your real brother, is he?"

Heat flared in Ryan's chest and he held up a knife. Of course Ethan was his real brother. As real as any brother who shared blood. "Don't you dare mention him."

"Even to tell you I left him in Kara's care? Alive?"

Ryan evened his breathing. He couldn't hope it. Couldn't not. "You're a liar."

She nodded. "No. I'm an assassin. He would've died if I hadn't told my sister to care for him. I figured it was the least I could do."

"The least? What are you talking about?"

Her blue eyes, dark and expressionless, seemed to offer a hint of emotion. "I know what it would be like to lose my sister. I couldn't bear it if you had to go through the same."

He laughed even as the hope inside him clawed to be set free. Too dangerous for that right now. "Because you're so accommodating?"

"Not particularly. But for you, I could be."

"For a price." He held up the knife. "I'm going to get answers out of you one way or another."

"You don't have to torture me. I'll tell you."

Incorrigible woman. Ryan stared right into her eyes. He wasn't sure if his talent worked when he wasn't making direct eye contact. "Tell me, what's this big news you've been *dying* to share?"

"You people really don't know how to treat a guest, do you? Take a girl's cloak, don't even offer her water."

This he'd anticipated. He draped the cloak over her shoulders. "Would you like some water?"

"Please."

Ryan crouched in front of her and held the water skin up to her lips. She drank deeply, then her blue eyes met his. "You really don't need to keep me tied up. I'll stay for as long as I want and leave when I'm ready anyway."

He sat back and propped his left arm over his left knee. "So confident."

"I'm an assassin. It comes with the territory."

"So does lying."

A sly smile touched her lips. "You don't believe me?"

"Shall I go over our history for you?"

"You are the one who would pick up on the lies. They're your territory, too, aren't they?"

Did she know about his talent? That he could persuade her to believe his words even if they weren't true? "What do you mean?"

"Does it bother you yet?"

He glanced at Thea askance, not willing to let her know how curious her comments made him. "Games are no fun for the other team if you don't explain the rules."

"Come now, this act isn't you. The Charmer, that's more your style.

Put on that cocky, winning grin and let's talk like old friends. Unless, of course, this new solemn face has more to do with the hallucinations."

Ryan tried to control his breathing, but it was too late. Judging by her smile, Thea had noticed his surprise.

Her eyes narrowed like a cat with a mouse. "She's in your head, isn't she?"

"What are you talking about?" He'd wanted to ask, "Who?" but that would give too much away.

She leaned as close as the bindings allowed. "You've figured out my secret already, I'm sure."

"That you're clairvoyant?"

"Yes." The ropes around her shoulders and chest fell away, and she rested her elbows on her knees. "Don't look so surprised. You already know I'm a step ahead."

More like three. "Why are you here, really? Who do you work for, if not Franco?" He offered her some dried meat.

She took it. "That's the trick, isn't it? Finding out my motives. See, you've already figured out what I am, even though I've never told a soul. I'm not surprised, though. I know to what you will bond."

"What does that have to do with anything?"

"Everything. Think about the Deliverers. What do you think gives them their powers? The animals they'll bond to, of course. Just like any Feravolk. And here we are, in an age when that which was extinct is returning. Forgotten powers are emerging. Forgotten creatures re-surfacing. Of course, Deliverers can't have all the fun. Any Child born the night of the Blood Moon could be blessed to bond with one of these returning creatures."

Did any of this really make sense? Forgotten creatures? Like what? Dragons? White lions? "How do you know this?"

"You showed up in some of my visions." She shrugged. "Can't think of a prettier face, actually, but you—I don't envy you."

Perhaps her talent was making people want to strangle straight answers out of her. "What are you talking about?"

"Your future, of course. Your road isn't an easy one. Neither is mine. I am glad to have met you, Charmer, but like I said, I don't envy you. Your role in all of this will break you. I can give you something that will help with the hallucinations and the voices, if it's gotten that far already."

"Excuse me?"

"Here." She held out her hand and a strange root rested in her palm. Ruddy brown with several branching pieces. "This will help."

A hiss echoed in Ryan's mind as he stared at the root in Thea's palm. Good sign or bad one? "You know I don't trust you."

She cocked one eyebrow and one corner of her lips curved up. "Yes. I also know you'll use it eventually."

She reached out and took his hand. He watched as she uncurled his fingers and placed the sprig in his palm. The hiss thundered, then died away.

He met her eyes. "Why do you pity me? What will I bond to?"

"I can't tell you. The path you're headed down is too important for me to alter with needless details."

Perhaps he could deceive her into telling him.

"Break off a small piece like this." She snapped off the tip of one of the twiggy branches and held it up to his lips.

"Doesn't look like it'll last long." He chuckled, though it felt more forced than any other fake chuckle he'd ever delivered.

She smiled, and he glanced at the herb in his hand. Of course the missing piece had grown back. It was spelled. Or poisoned. He gripped her wrist with his free hand.

She sighed. "You have to eat it right after it's been broken off."

A voice thundered in his brain, *"Do not eat it."*

"I'm not planning—"

She flicked the piece into his mouth. Before he could spit it out, the piece of root dissolved, leaving a residue of cinnamon on his tongue. The cloud in his mind dissipated, and the thundering whisper with it. Gone.

He let her go. "How did you—"

"Clairvoyant, remember?" She touched his arm, and her normally haughty eyes looked soft. "It's temporary, but you'll figure out how to get rid of her."

Her? Ryan stared at Thea. Dare he ask what she meant now?

Thea ran her fingers over his forehead and down the side of his face. Something about her touch was actually tender. More games?

"The Mistress has a hold on you, Ryan. Don't give her more than she's already taken. But right now, she isn't your immediate danger. Now that Idla is dead, Franco has rallied soldiers. He wants the Deliverers because they have the keys to the Creator's power. Until they unlock it and relock the Mistress's prison, they are in danger from anyone who wants the Creator's power. Don't you understand? Franco won't rest until he gets them. A group of his men has picked up your trail. They're on horseback. They'll be here by midmorning. The best thing you can do is head east."

"Are you mad? That's toward the palace."

"You're wasting time." She motioned to something behind him. He didn't look. She frowned. "I'm sorry. You're going to lose that one. Too bad I won't be around to mend your broken heart. I would have liked to be."

He glanced over his shoulder. Ah. Of course Jayden would be waiting to hear what he'd found. And his sister Chloe. And of course Thea would use that to distract him from the conversation at hand. "Jayden won't break—"

"No. You're too strong now for that to break your heart. But you'll wish it had."

What did that mean? His sister headed toward the water while Jayden walked down the other side of the hill. Soon she'd be back in view on the top of this hill.

She really shouldn't be letting Chloe go alone to the lake. He'd have to persuade Jayden to follow his sister. He pocketed Thea's gift. "You're pretty good at the distraction thing, I'll give you that, but—" He turned back and Thea was gone. Of course she was.

He scanned down the hill but didn't spot her. She had one of those Feravolk cloaks on. Unless one of the animals was out that way, she was gone. And he had a mind to just let her leave. She knew what was coming anyway. There was no catching her unless she intended to be caught.

A soft hand rubbed his arm, and he turned toward Jayden. "Are you okay, Ry?"

He breathed deep. Before he could say anything, Jayden knelt by the tree and picked up the broken rope. "Thea's gone?"

"Yes."

"You don't seem very concerned."

"She said there was danger headed our way."

"And you just let her go?"

He rubbed the back of his neck. "She was already unbound and got the jump on me." Admitting that was harder than he'd thought.

"Are you okay?"

"I'm fine."

Jayden bowed her head and worried a loose thread on her clothes. "Did she tell you anything about . . . about Ethan?" Her eyes met his.

His next breath hurt. "She's a liar, Jayden."

"What if she's not?"

"What did she tell you?"

"That if we don't find him soon, he will die. I think we should at least look. I—"

He touched her shoulder. "I know you want to."

"You don't?"

"I do. Heavens, Jayden. He was my brother." If Thea truly could tell the future, why didn't she tell him where to look? His heart dropped. She had sent him toward the palace.

"You will go with me?"

"With you? It's a trap, Jayden."

She backed a step away from him, an incredulous look in her eyes. "I guess I don't care."

He stood there, rooted. But if she was going, he was going. "I guess I don't either."

She leaned in and hugged him so tight. "Thank you."

Perhaps Thea was counting on that.

A scream pierced the air. Ryan's heart jolted. Chloe.

CHAPTER 10

TESTING THE LIMIT

Ethan followed the pull anchored in his heart deeper into the forest, and it grew stronger. According to the sun, he'd been on the horse for at least the rest of the day and all night. Everything hurt worse, and new blood seeped from the wound in his stomach. And his arm.

He stroked the horse's neck. "Where are we?"

One of Javelin's ears trained on him, but the other flicked around, trying to pinpoint a sound, no doubt. Ethan strained to listen, but he got nothing. Well, plenty of sounds, but they all amounted to nothing. "What do you hear, girl?"

He covered his right ear and everything muted.

He rubbed the mare's neck. "It's up to your ears now."

She stopped and he scanned the woods. There. Behind a tree, Ethan thought he saw movement. He drew his sword. "Who are you?"

A young woman stepped around the tree, hands up in surrender, but she held a bow and carried a full quiver at her hip. Her Feravolk cloak rippled in the wind, hiding her, but she seemed to want to be seen. "Are you him? Stone Wolf?"

Ethan narrowed his eyes. How did she know him? And how many others surrounded him?

She drew in a deep breath and bent, slowly, to place her bow on the ground. Then she stepped toward him. Javelin shifted her weight.

Ethan stroked her neck. "Easy, girl. What is it?"

The young woman lowered her hood, brown hair cascading over

her shoulders. Her eyes, green like jewels, studied him. "I need your help."

"Who are you?"

"My name is Morgan. And if you help me, Stone Wolf, I will take you to Jayden."

Ethan's heartbeat spiked. She had Jayden? He dismounted and placed his sword against Morgan's neck, backing her against the nearest tree and pinning her there with his blade. "Where is she?"

"Ethan." Morgan's breathing turned ragged, and tears glimmered in her eyes as she looked down at the weapon mere inches from her throat. Her gaze flicked to meet his, but no threat pulsed there. Only pleading. "Please. Help me. I need to save my friends."

A familiar tug pulled at his insides and he sucked in a breath. Danger. Not for him. For someone he knew. He had to move now. Chest heaving, he released her and stepped back. "I—I can't. I have to—"

"Help the redhead?"

Chloe. Yes. The threat was for Chloe. He lunged at this Morgan again, this time pinning her to the tree with the threat of his blade against her stomach. "Tell me what I have to do to get Jayden and Chloe back."

Her eyelids fluttered. "Ethan, I want to help you. And in turn, I need your help." Slowly she lifted her arm and he watched as she pushed up her sleeve. A Blood Moon birthmark. She was a Child. "I can see things. Future things. I don't have your friends. But I know how to help them."

He stepped back, sword tip faltering. Honestly, he didn't know what to believe.

"Is—is that your blood?" She neared him and shook her head. "In my vision, I see you helping me. I—the things you did—I don't know what changed." Her eyes met his now, hope draining. "In my vision, you fought like ten men, but you're clearly injured. There's no way you can—"

If she saw him fighting like that, she was telling the truth. There was no way she could know how his talent worked. "Am I to do this thing you ask of me in order to save . . . the redhead?"

"Yes. I'm sorry. Maybe I should have tried to find you sooner. Before . . . what happened to you?"

"Never mind that." He sheathed his sword. "Tell me what you saw. Tell me how to save my friends, and I will become the man you saw in your vision."

○

Ethan huddled near Morgan at the base of a fallen tree. The exposed roots proved a good hiding spot. The hike had drained him of much of his energy, so he rested his head back against the wall of dirt and roots.

Morgan looked at him askance, but the worry in her eyes was clear. How would he explain that his talent would take over when the time was right and turn him into . . . well, a monster?

"You're bleeding still. Let me—" She lifted his shirt and winced. "Oh." Her gaze snapped up. "When did this happen?"

She pulled a clean bandage out of her quiver and offered a soft smile. "I thought I'd need this to bind your wounds after you helped me rescue my friends."

"You might."

He closed his eyes and tried not to groan as she packed the wound, too exhausted to argue. Then she wordlessly took care of the gash in his arm and hole in his chest.

"I hope you hold together."

He chuckled and opened his eyes. "You and me both."

But the burn crossed his chest in a faint flicker, and he knew he'd be numb to the pain soon.

Morgan's wide-eyed gaze met his. "They're headed out to find your friends now. Help me rescue mine, and we'll have the numbers and knowledge to beat them."

He nodded.

The sound of hoofbeats touched his ear. He couldn't tell which direction they came from. Leather creaked. No chainmail in the wood—not when they were tracking quarry.

She pressed her finger to her lips and peered between the roots. He watched with her. Soldiers of the Royal Army came into view. Then more. Two units meeting less than a bowshot from where he hid. He held his breath as he saw—tied to a leash like an animal—a giant.

He would never be able to fight a giant and all these soldiers. Not in this condition. What did Morgan expect of him?

One of the soldiers brought his horse forward and Ethan's blood boiled. Scarface. "Take the giant to the river. He will find their scent. We will have King Franco's prize. As for the redhead, bring her to me."

Ethan's talents rushed into him.

He waited, quivering like a coiled spring, as half of the soldiers left with the giant.

"Not yet," Morgan whispered as one man muscled a bound and gagged prisoner toward Scarface. Chloe.

What had she gotten herself into? And where were the others? Were they okay? They were still this close to the palace, which meant at least one of them had to be injured pretty badly. That thought tightened his stomach. According to Kara, Jayden was okay. If Ryan—he couldn't even finish the thought. Ryan had better be okay.

Morgan placed a hand on his uninjured arm. "Be still. My friends will be here soon. They will have a few weapons. The one with golden eyes will have supplied what he could."

"Golden eyes?" Connor.

She nodded. "He rescues as many kidnapped Children as he can. Then I come here to meet them and take them to my camp." She smiled. "They will be here soon. My owl delivered my message this morning."

He regarded her. Must be a nice talent to possess.

She shrugged as if she'd heard his thoughts. "I came to get you this morning. If I didn't bring you . . . well, it wouldn't have been a rescue. None of these men can know of our exit point." She chewed her lip. "I'll need you to draw them away from here. So they think we've come out of the woods."

He nodded. A solider held Chloe tight while Scarface rolled out a map. He had twelve men with him. There was no way he'd take down all of them, but Morgan would know that. He'd trust her reinforcements. He could make a diversion, no problem there.

Morgan looked at him and nodded once. "Go now."

A flare of warmth spread across Ethan's chest, and he shot forward. His talent dulled the pain from his wounds, but not like before. Apparently there was a limit to how much he could handle. It would be really nice if he still had his bow. Looked like he'd have to do this in close quarters. He rushed in, sword ready. One of the soldiers let go of Chloe and pulled out his sword. That gave Chloe time to kick him.

Unfortunately, that just made the guard slam her into the tree. The threat for her heated, and she fell. Now the other soldiers were alerted. Ethan focused on his talent. He had to take care of the man in front of him first.

The twang of a bowstring and scream of a man told him Morgan had his back. Speed was his ally. He called it and dodged his attacker's swing. Then he buried his blade into the man's stomach. Pulling his weapon free, he whirled around. A second attacker reached him. Ethan swung his sword, ripping that man's stomach open.

Two men raced toward him.

He stood in front of Chloe and faced the oncoming threat with his reddened blade.

The clash of steel on steel rang through the air as his sword met the first attacker. Ethan pivoted. Leaf-cluttered soil made his feet slip. Gaining purchase here wasn't easy. Speed fueled him in a burst and he slashed the man's neck open. As soon as that man fell, the other attacker had made it within fighting range. Ethan faced him. He blocked a blow. Another. This guy moved faster than the last.

Ethan sliced low through the air and his blade sunk into the attacker's thigh. The enemy stumbled back enough for Ethan to dodge the blade aimed for him.

He felt as though he moved in slow motion, his speed slipping away. His talent had reached its limit. He wouldn't be able to keep this up much longer. He blocked one blow, pushing the soldier's sword aside. The man stumbled back. Ethan called one last flare of speed and pierced the man through. Red coated his blade and the man fell, lifeless.

A shudder of pain ratcheted through him. His talents draining.

Come on, Ethan. You're stronger than this.

Reinforcements headed his way; so did more of the enemy. He just had to hold out long enough.

Morgan had reached Chloe and started to cut her bindings.

Ethan yanked his sword out from another soldier, but the forest started to spin. Arrows thwacked the ground. Ethan's talents didn't die away slowly this time. They were just gone. Pain and weakness washed over him and he clutched his arm. Fell to his knees.

Chloe hunched over him. Tears wet her eyes, but she scowled at him. "You're more cut up than the log Father stores his axe in."

"Chloe?"

Morgan handed Chloe a knife and touched Ethan's shoulder. "Thank you." She smiled. "Only one got away. We'll have to move from here before he comes back."

"One? The one with the scar?"

Morgan's mouth opened, but she didn't speak. Didn't have to. He knew it. Scarface still lived. Still hunted Jayden. He tried to stand.

"Easy there." Morgan gently pushed him back. "Let me tend to those wounds so we can get you out of here."

"Jayden."

"Yes. Then we'll find Jayden. I promise."

"Ethan?" Chloe grabbed his shirtsleeve and pulled him to look at her. "They told me you were dead." Tears streamed down her face. She wrapped him in a hug.

"Easy, Chloe." He hugged her gently. She might not admit to being his sister, but she clearly loved him.

"Sorry." She pulled back.

"You should get out of here with the others. I'll—"

"No." She shook her head so that her hair flew in front of her face. "I'm not losing you again."

"You won't." Then he closed his eyes. She was calling his name, and he was trying to answer, but he couldn't. He didn't even have the energy to grip his sword.

CHAPTER 11

A GIGANTIC PROBLEM

Ryan's heart stalled at the sound of the scream. Chloe.

Jayden's hands flew to her mouth. "I let her go alone."

The quiet certainty of Thea's voice filled Ryan's mind as he recalled her statement. *I'm sorry. You're going to lose that one.* An ache tightened his chest. Chloe. He'd thought Thea meant Jayden, but it was clear now. How had he not seen her meaning in the first place? He fisted his hands and ran down the hill in the direction his sister had gone. Jayden followed, her apologies lost in the wind.

"How dare she let your sister walk into danger? She wanted to know about Ethan. That's all she cared about. Now Chloe could—"

"Just stop!"

"Sorry." Jayden's soft voice cleared his mind, but he didn't stop running.

It wasn't her fault. Chloe probably didn't want to wait. It was a decision she'd made. The voice. It wanted to tear him from those he loved. No matter what, he wouldn't let it.

"You think you're stronger?"

He picked up speed. At the bottom of the hill, Logan, Gavin, and Melanie caught up with him.

"Where is she?" Logan asked.

"At the lake." Jayden's voice broke into pieces against the wind.

"We'll get her. You stay here." Logan's gaze held intensity Ryan was certain his matched.

"That's my sister."

"So are they." Melanie motioned behind him.

Kinsey and Wren stood, wide-eyed. That was enough to make him comply. No more stupid decisions. He wasn't trained yet. With Ethan gone, who would they have if he died?

He faced Jayden, and her wet eyes melted his heart. "It's not your fault."

She nodded. "I left her alone. I—I should have—"

"No. You didn't send her off alone." He hugged Jayden close.

She gripped his shirt and buried her face in his neck, and a hiss shot through his head. He held tighter to Jayden. If the white lion wanted him to start a war with his loved ones, it didn't know a thing about him. Jayden had his heart as much as any of his sisters. He would not lose her. Not over something so stupid.

Not over anything.

He smoothed her hair. "Chloe will be fine."

"I should have known. I should have gone with her."

He pushed her back and wiped a stray tear. "Chloe's a mule. You can hitch her to the cart, but it won't make her pull it."

A smile lit Jayden's face and made her eyes sparkle. He wanted to kiss her. Now. In the middle of worry. Surrounded by uncertainty. She grounded him. Chased the voice away. He needed her.

The sound of something breaking through brush caused Jayden to turn. Her fingers curled around the dagger at her waist. Ryan gripped his borrowed sword and hoped what little skill he had would be enough.

"I found more of them." A voice carried through the trees.

Ryan glanced at Kinsey and Wren and pulled the sword free. "Run."

Bushes crunched as a foot stomped them flat. Ryan's eyes trailed up, up, up. Legs like tree trunks. Arms like branches. He had to be twice as tall as Ryan and twice as wide. A giant. He carried a poleaxe in one hand and dragged a heavy-looking chain in the other. Ryan had no desire to find out what the end of that chain attached to.

Jayden ran in front of Ryan and glanced over her shoulder. "Run."

"Not happening."

"Ryan, someone has to—"

The giant fixed tiny eyes on Jayden and laughed, deep and booming. He pointed a thick finger at her. "I found you."

Ryan tugged her arm and tried to shield her, but she remained beside him. "Go with my sisters." He gripped the old sword Kara had given him in the palace. Worn leather wrapped the hilt. Its previous owner had likely died. Ryan swallowed and tried to calm his shaking nerves as he looked up. "I think it's your turn to hide."

The giant's bushy eyebrows pulled together like a flock of angry crows. "My orders are not to retrieve you, dragonbait. That means you die."

"Dragonbait? I like that one. It means I'm fast and smart."

The giant's beefy arm swung forward and the sound of a chain clinked. A Morningstar. Ryan uttered a curse and pushed Jayden down. Together they fell against the dirt. Air whooshed as the spiked ball sailed over them, just missing Ryan's back.

He looked at Jayden. "Remember what you said about running?"

"Ryan!" She grabbed his sleeve and scrambled to her feet.

Then she ran, herding Wren and Kinsey farther into the woods.

Ryan skidded to a halt and turned.

The giant lumbered after them. Ryan was no match for that monster, but that wouldn't have stopped Ethan.

"You're not Ethan. Don't throw your life away for this. You're not strong enough."

That voice certainly knew how to burn his straw. Not strong enough? No. Not Ethan. Certainly not. But that didn't mean he couldn't take Ethan's place as a protector. He could learn to be a hero. And didn't all the real heroes overcome because they were brave and smart?

Then again, maybe this wasn't a smart choice.

"Ryan?" Wren's panicked voice reached him.

He couldn't look. Instead, he faced the giant. One thing was certain. Ryan Granden wouldn't die a coward.

The giant roared as he ran, his poleaxe high.

Ryan stood rooted.

The giant stepped closer. Close enough for Ryan to watch drips of sweat trickle over the beast's bare, pockmarked arms. Arms that crashed down.

Ryan lifted his sword and the crack of steel meeting wood pierced the air.

A jolt of force shot through his limbs, but he pushed back. The giant pulled his weapon back, and his body angled to the other side. He was going to swing the Morningstar.

Ryan rushed to safety beside a tree, eyes on the spiked ball. His heartbeat raced in his throat. The tree shook and splinters flew into the air. Ryan fell to his knees and scrambled up in time to see Jayden coming to his aide.

No. He'd been trying to avoid her involvement.

Jayden raced up behind the giant and sank her dagger into the giant's meaty thigh. She pulled her reddened blade free, and the giant spun toward her.

Okay. A little help wasn't a bad thing.

She darted around like a mouse past a fat cat, and Ryan took the opportunity to get closer. He swung his sword. It bit into skin. Sliced through flesh. Blood gushed out of the giant's torso, stained fabric, and tainted the blade.

Ryan shook his head. He didn't want to kill.

This wasn't a man.

It was a monster.

A monster.

"Keep telling yourself that."

"Ryan!" Jayden's voice cut through the fog, and Ryan looked in time to see the Morningstar headed his way. He jumped back, but spikes caught his leg. The force knocked him backward and he slammed into a tree.

The earth seemed to shake and he squeezed his eyes shut. The sound of his breathing drowned out everything. The burn of pain clouded everything else.

He opened his eyes.

Focus.

Blood seeped through the edges of his ripped pants, but the cut wasn't too deep. He could still put weight on it. He stood, but his hands were empty. Where was the sword?

There, on the ground where he'd been standing.

"Ethan would never have lost his sword."

The giant's roar filled his ears. He glanced up in time to see Jayden race between the giant's legs. Her daggers cut deep into the beast's inner thigh. But he caught her cloak and pulled. She fell flat on her back. The giant stepped on the material, anchoring her to the ground. She squirmed like a lost worm in a bird's shadow.

Ryan glanced around him. His bow. He picked it up and grabbed four arrows. Nocked one. Held three others in his hand. Line taut. Eyes locked on his target. He released an arrow. It sank into the giant's ear. The monster snarled, and Ryan stalked to the side. As the giant turned, his foot shifted off Jayden's cloak. She rolled out of the way.

Ryan focused. Let out a breath. Shot the second arrow. It lodged in the giant's eye. Everything seemed to stall as the beast fell to his knees.

Jayden scrambled to find her weapon on the ground.

The giant, even dying, picked up his Morningstar and aimed it at Jayden. He'd kill her.

Now it was time for the sword.

A cry escaped Ryan's throat as he raced forward. He swung. The blade glinted in the sun, drying blood mixed with something so pure—like sunshine. He couldn't stop it now. Couldn't change his mind. Momentum stole that choice. He had to own the fact that he'd chosen to make a killing blow.

The blade sliced into the giant's neck and cut clean through. His grotesque face contorted then spun in circles as his head left his neck, a stream of red flowing out after it. The head landed near Jayden.

Ryan's knees gave away as the headless heap crashed to the ground. He'd . . . he'd killed someone.

A purr thundered in his skull.

CHAPTER 12

MUZZLED DRAGON

Jayden screamed as the giant's head hit the ground beside her. Her breathing quieted and she clutched her injured arm. That enemy couldn't hurt her anymore. As the body of the giant collapsed, she caught sight of Ryan on the other side.

He sank to his knees, staring at the dead giant.

Oh no. He'd been forced to kill. She picked up her weapons and raced over to him. Knelt beside him. Crimson trickled down the side of his face, and the ripped fabric in his pants revealed a huge gash. But he was okay. Physically.

"Ryan?" She gingerly touched the side of his head. He winced and pulled away from her hand.

His eyes focused on her, and at once his mask of a smile returned. "I might have a headache for a whole season."

He was joking right now? Something about that calmed her quaking.

His eyebrows knitted together and he touched her cheek. "You okay?"

She wrapped her good arm around him and buried her face in his chest. "If you weren't here—"

"I was." He hugged her. "But Logan and the others aren't back yet."

The words "with Chloe" lingered unspoken on the end of his sentence.

Westwind raced up to them, blood staining his muzzle. Ears back, he scanned her body and whined.

"I'm fine." She touched him. "Are you okay? Where are—"

Her question died as Logan, Melanie, and Gavin returned. They brought someone with them, but it wasn't Chloe. It was a soldier, and judging by the sword tip in his back and rope around his wrists, his presence with them wasn't by choice.

Logan pushed the man, who stumbled to his knees with a thump. "We caught this one fleeing. It seems someone else joined our fight. We don't know who, but a group of Franco's men was ambushed."

"Chloe?" Ryan's voice cracked.

Logan pressed his blade to the captive's neck. "We'll get information out of this one."

Jayden gasped when she saw the tattoo of the queen's crest on the back of the man's hand. A muzzled dragon. The first of Thea's warnings rang clear in Jayden's mind: *He'd rather die than talk.*

Logan leaned closer to the captive, his sword tight to the man's skin. "How did you find us?"

The man laughed, a deep, wicked sound that gave Jayden gooseflesh. He looked right into her eyes and chilled her bones.

"He wants you. You can't stop him. If he can't have you, he'll kill everyone you love. He'll make sure the Feravolk are destroyed."

Jayden stepped toward him. "Franco." His name emptied her lungs. Would she never be rid of the man who had the ability to spread fear into her veins?

The prisoner's unflinching gaze bored into Jayden. "You know what to do." Then he thrust his head forward, and Logan's sword punctured his throat.

Blood pooled out, black as pitch, and his head fell back.

Jayden turned away. How could anyone do that to themselves?

Ryan pulled her away from the body. "His blood is black."

"Clear out of here." Logan held out his hands to tell them to stay back. "I don't know if it's magic or sickness. And I'm not sticking around to find out."

"Logan," Gavin said. "Callie and Glider found more soldiers headed this way. We need to backtrack."

"How will we find Chloe now?" Ryan's voice seemed so small.

A tingle prickled behind Jayden's ears—a warning that someone's emotions were too strong for her to block on her own. Ryan's. She looked up at him, and his pain and worry crashed into her. She clutched her daggers. Breathed deep. Now was not the time to let emotions ruin her ability to focus. She touched his arm, hoping that would help.

His return glance bled gratitude, but the worry hadn't lessened.

Gavin gripped Ryan's shoulder. "Glider thinks he spotted Chloe down by the lake. She's not alone."

Logan faced Ryan and Jayden. "Let Melanie take care of your wounds, and we'll rescue Chloe."

Ryan stepped forward. "I'll—"

"Stay with Jayden and your sisters." Logan's gaze didn't flinch, and Ryan finally conceded.

○

Jayden tried not to wince as Melanie sewed the last stitch on her arm.

Melanie wrapped a makeshift bandage around it. "Unfortunately, it'll leave a scar."

Jayden let her sleeve fall over the gash. Scarring was not her main worry. Why weren't Gavin and Logan back yet? And where was Chloe? "Have they found her?"

Melanie shook her head. She looked unruffled, but Jayden opened her talent. Her stomach seemed to tie in twice as many knots. She closed her eyes and turned away from Melanie. The herd of galloping horses in her stomach didn't thin. She pulled out her dagger and held the hilt. Channeled everything she felt into her bond with the weapon. The thunder of hooves on her heart seemed to lessen.

Melanie's hand covered Jayden's, not in comfort. She was stiff and still. This was a warning. She stood. "Callie says the men are surrounded."

Jayden grabbed her pack and sprang up. "Are they okay?"

Everyone else grabbed their supplies and stood. Echoes of their worry returned, and she could hardly breathe. She glanced at Ryan, and the hope in his eyes sent a ray of warmth through her. Even so she tried to turn her talent off.

"Follow me." Melanie covered her blonde hair with her Feravolk cloak and headed the way the men had gone. Her boots barely made a sound. Jayden tripped on too many sticks to count. They followed in silence until Melanie stopped. Finger to her lips, she faced them. Movement in the trees had Jayden reaching for her weapon until a familiar face rounded a tree.

Logan lowered his hood.

Jayden glanced into his emotions. Wariness. Typical Logan. But did she also detect a hint of deep regret? "Chloe found a group of Children escaping from the palace. She ran into some of the Royal Army, but helped the Feravolk fight them off. They brought her to their camp."

"A Feravolk camp out here?" Melanie asked.

Gavin came up from behind them and lowered his hood. "Apparently Children have been escaping from the palace and building an army right here by the palace. They call themselves the Dissenters." He held his arms out as if showing them something, but Jayden saw nothing but trees.

Melanie sprouted a smile. "Yes. I see it. Very well done."

Saw what? Jayden saw no people. Smelled no cook fires.

Gavin disappeared.

Jayden stared at the trees in front of her. Then Gavin's head peeked out from behind some invisible wall, and he motioned for her to follow. She complied, moving toward what she thought was a dense clustering of trees.

A whole town unfolded out of the camouflaged covering of tents arranged between the trees. Jayden stopped in her tracks and stared in wonder at the world she would have walked right past.

Fires blazed. The aromas of stew, potatoes, and sweet bread filtered toward them once they stepped past the camouflage. Gavin led them through a maze of trees and tents until Jayden was certain she'd be easily lost. People mingled everywhere. Animals, too—slinking through the shadows, curled up in the sun, or lurking in the trees.

"How?" She turned in a circle.

"This is how the Feravolk use camouflage." Gavin smiled.

Logan's eyes met hers, and worry siphoned into her so that her heart squeezed. He swallowed. "There's something you should all know. Chloe is fine. She was rescued . . . by Ethan."

"Ethan?" Jayden's knees turned to water. Hope dared to rise, and it sparked a part of her heart to life. The part she'd tried so hard to keep numb. "Thea was telling the truth? How is that possible? I thought you said—" She stopped when his sadness grew. Oh. Logan must feel terrible.

"He's hurt pretty bad." His voice cracked. "Most of the bleeding has stopped, but—"

Kinsey grabbed Logan's arm. "Where is he?"

Scout bolted past her, and Ryan and his sisters ran after him.

Jayden forced her leaden feet to follow. They followed Scout into a tent, and she went inside, too. The Grandens clustered around someone. Blood covered his clothes. Scratches and dirt marred his face, but it was him. Her Ethan.

Scout whimpered, his whole body quivered, and he lay down and rested his chin across Ethan's chest.

It was really him.

Kinsey and Wren knelt near him, holding each other.

Ryan fell to his knees next to his brother, and his shoulders shook.

Jayden cupped her hands over her mouth. Tears flooded her eyes. She blinked them back as she sank to the ground next to Ryan. Gripped his hand in hers.

He looked up at her, his eyes red-rimmed. "I didn't—Thea was right."

"It's okay now," she whispered as much for him as herself. "He's going to be okay." She hugged him until his breathing evened and he wiped his eyes.

"Sorry," he whispered.

She released him and touched his shoulder. "No need to be." With her other hand, she grabbed Ethan's. He didn't stir, but he was warm. Ethan was alive. She memorized the feel of his hand. Pressed it against her cheek.

Melanie checked Ethan's wounds.

"How is he?" Jayden's voice held a tremor she didn't expect.

Melanie's eyes softened. "His pulse is weak, but it's there. Let him rest. They've taken good care of him here."

A redhead entered the tent, and the Grandens sprang up to greet her.

"Chloe!" Wren reached her first and smothered her in a hug.

Chloe sported a few new scratches and bruises but looked otherwise fine.

"You okay?" Ryan asked, his voice rough.

"Thanks to him." She motioned to Ethan.

"And those Children are all right thanks to him."

Jayden finally let go of Ethan's hand and stood as a young man—tall like Ryan, but lanky—entered.

"I'm Richard. Welcome to the Dissenters camp."

Melanie said, "Gavin tells me you're all escapees from the palace?"

He nodded. "We have spies inside. They help as many of us Children escape the palace as possible. Idla was building an army—using some sort of spell. We're not yet sure how, because none of us have been infected with it. But there are people in the palace who are on our side. It's best to assume Franco is continuing his mother's work. We want to build our own army to fight him."

"How is it you keep safe in the palace's shadow?" Melanie asked.

"We'll move soon, and we move often, but we have to stay close for the escapees. And we have special talents among us that help us to guess when and where the Royal Army will enter these woods."

"Clairvoyants?"

Richard simply smiled. "If it weren't for our Morgan, I think Chloe, Ethan, and the Children they rescued would have been taken back to the palace. She saw it coming and rescued them."

"I'd like to thank Morgan, then."

Richard shook his head. "I'll pass the message along. She's already left to find her sister."

"Richard." A young woman with reddish blonde hair entered the tent. She had fresh blood on her sleeve and a cut beneath her eye. "As ordered, we brought a prisoner."

"Good, let me talk to him."

"He's asking for someone named Jayden."

Jayden's heart skipped a beat. "What's his name?"

"Calls himself Rune," the young woman replied. "Do you know him?"

"No. How does he know I'm here?"

Richard's eyes narrowed. "He doesn't. I'll talk to him."

"I'd like to come." Jayden touched her dagger's hilt to still the rising emotions battling to get inside of her. A tingle behind her ears told her it wouldn't be easy to keep them at bay.

Richard motioned for her to follow. Logan and Melanie walked beside her, but Ryan stayed with Ethan.

They approached a young man with a large, hooked nose and skinny arms. Jayden had never seen him before. "Is that the prisoner?"

The young woman nodded. "You recognize him?"

"No." But perhaps Thea knew him. Maybe she'd sent him. "But I'm not afraid to talk to him."

They held him with his hands and ankles bound. "I want to speak with Jayden. I have a message for her from King Franco himself."

He turned toward her, and she noticed a small charm tying his cloak together. A wooden arrow. And it was broken. Thea's second warning stared her in the face. She'd said a man wearing a broken arrow would tell her what she wanted to know about Franco's plans.

She didn't want to admit it, but this time she hoped Thea was right.

CHAPTER 13

A BROKEN ARROW
AND A WHITE HORSE

Jayden stood behind Logan as they approached Rune, but Rune's gaze found her. Unnerved her. His smile brought no light to his eyes. She fought the urge to recoil.

"You're Jayden, aren't you?"

In three strides, Logan was close enough that his sword blade bit into Rune's neck. "The message?"

Rune's eyes opened as wide as a frightened horse's, and he tried to pull back from the sword, only to find two men restricting his movement. His back arched like a startled cat's. "I—I w-won't tell you."

"You will if you value your life." Logan's voice was quiet but hard.

"You can threaten all you like—"

"It's not just a threat. You're no use to me if you won't talk." He pressed the blade deeper, ready to slice the man's throat open.

Jayden held her breath.

"Wait!" Rune's knees knocked together, and he sank lower to the ground. "I'm no soldier. I'm a palace bard."

Logan didn't answer, didn't even move. Rune's eyes flicked to Jayden, and her ears tingled. His fear was attempting to control her.

She stepped forward. "What's the message?"

"Franco says he never finished things with you. He says if you return to him, he'll spare your friends, but if you don't he'll kill everyone you love. If you don't return with me within four days, he'll hunt down your loved ones and kill them. H-he'll let the Mistress destroy Soleden."

Jayden's heart squeezed until it hurt. Why always her family? Her people?

She fisted her hands. "When I face Franco, it'll be on my time and my terms. And if he doesn't surrender to me, I'll kill him."

"I'll be sure to let him know."

Logan grabbed Rune by the shirt collar and nearly lifted him off the ground. "How does Franco plan to find everyone Jayden loves?"

"He has ways."

"How?" Logan raised his voice and Rune trembled.

"I don't know."

Logan slammed him against the ground and lowered his sword to Rune's chest. "What does Franco have planned?"

"I truly don't—"

"A palace bard always knows more than he should." The blade pushed harder, through clothes, and the tip sank into skin.

"Stop. Please! He's planning to free the Mistress. All he needs is blood from a female Deliverer, a Whisperer's tear, and . . . an untraceable seeing stone. Then he has to put them into a Feravolk's heart to complete the spell that will break her prison open."

"Where is he performing the spell?"

"I truly don't know."

Logan's shoulders sagged. "You've been very helpful. The Creator give you peace."

Rune's eyes widened. "I don't know! I'm telling the—"

Logan thrust his sword through Rune's heart. "I know you are."

Jayden turned away, a shaking hand covering her mouth.

Logan touched her shoulder. "I'm sorry. He had to die. He'd seen the camp."

"I understand."

"Gavin, will you send Glider to Moon Over Water? I think it's time we bring Reuben, Beck, and Samantha in on this." Logan sheathed his sword.

"Perhaps they can meet us halfway?" Gavin said. "I looks like we're running out of time. We have to stop Franco from freeing the Mistress.

That's what the Deliverers have come for. 'A sorceress will rise' and all that. They are the keys to the Creator's power. You know we aren't the only ones looking for those keys. Franco can't be, either. As soon as she's free, though, she'll be after the Creator's power. We have to find the Whisperer and female Deliverer before he does. Soleden's existence—our existence—depends on it."

"Agreed."

"When do we leave?"

Logan was quiet for a moment. "I am not leaving Ethan again. He's too valuable in protecting Jayden. We will wait here for three days, then we leave." Logan looked at Jayden. "I'm sorry. This is far from over."

Jayden nodded. She knew the prophecy. It hadn't always made sense to her, but now that she knew Idla wasn't the sorceress—and who truly was—she understood one thing clearly: she had to stop Franco from unleashing a greater evil. "I won't let the Mistress escape." Even if it killed her.

○

Jayden opened her eyes. Wind blew outside, rippling against the tent flap. An electric taste in the air told her a storm wasn't far off. This storm churned in the distance like the worry in her stomach. Storms like this were wild.

She sat up and pulled her knees into her chest. Lightning flashed, brightening her surroundings. This storm would be drenching. She breathed deep. Franco wanted her. Wanted to use her. Bed her. Logan warned her that he wouldn't allow her to sacrifice herself like that. They'd find a different way. But it wasn't just her. He threatened everyone she loved. Why hadn't Thea told her how to defeat him or get out of this mess? That would have been helpful. Instead Thea had spoken of Jayden's death. She'd seen Jayden's death.

Thunder rumbled low and treacherous like a growl.

So Jayden had been right all along. She wasn't going to survive this destiny.

She breathed in the sweet, rainy scent. The static charge in the air still had the ability to calm her. So did Ethan's presence. She'd placed her bedroll near his, per Melanie's request, so she could check on him in the night.

Scout had curled up beside him, unwilling to leave Ethan's side.

Unable to help it, she touched his hand. He gripped back and squeezed with more strength than she expected.

Her heart caught in her chest and she sat up. "You're awake?"

"I don't sleep well during storms." His smile was evident in his words.

Scout whimpered, trying to bury his head under Ethan's hand to be petted.

"Hey, boy. I missed you, too." He touched the dog and only then did Scout's whining cease. He curled up near Ethan's leg and sighed contentedly.

Jayden watched them, smiling. How she'd missed his voice. Wetness collected in her eyes and she sniffed.

"Hey. Don't cry."

"I'm not. I'm—" Every emotion she'd been holding back burst forth. The relief, the fear, all of it. And the rain broke through. Just a sprinkle that spattered the fabric above them and stopped as quickly as it started. As if the clouds meant to contain it, but some leaked out anyway. "I thought I'd lost you."

He rubbed his thumb over the back of her hand. "You didn't."

A sob caught in her throat.

"Jayden." He tried to push himself up.

She pressed her hand against his chest and shook her head, unable to speak.

His fingers wiped away her tear, brushed the hand she'd laid on his chest. Tugged her sleeve. "Come here." He opened his arm and motioned for her to lie next to him.

She needed no more coaxing. Fears about Thea's prediction faded. Right now, if only for a moment, she could be his. Or at least pretend. She cuddled into him. Let his warmth melt the chill in her heart. She breathed in his scent that the raindrops had made stronger. Pine. Leather. His gentle grip pulled her close, and she closed her eyes. A tear dripped onto his shirt. Then more. He didn't say a word. Just hugged her tighter.

When every last silent tear had quelled, she noticed the wet spot they'd left on his shirt and wiped her hand over it, as if it would do any good. "I'm sorry."

"Don't be."

"We—I thought you were dead. I never would have left if I knew you were alive in there."

"I know."

She pushed herself up to sitting and stared at him. The darkness muted many of his features, but she could still make out his outline. She wished to see him—look into his eyes, the doorway of her talent. As if in answer, the clouds shifted and moonlight peeked through.

Ethan's gaze entrapped her. His brown eyes were unfathomably dark at night. The hum of electricity crackled between them again. Heat lightning echoed it. Holding her breath, she leaned closer.

He reached up, pushed a stray strand of hair behind her ear, and smiled. "I heard you killed the queen."

Idla's burnt face filled her memory and she glanced away.

"Sorry, Jayden. I—"

"It's okay."

He tried to push himself up again and, rather than argue, she helped him sit.

Lightning flashed in the sky, giving her glimpses of his face. Illuminated the bruising around his ear. Pictures of Scarface punching him pulsed through her mind in tandem with the storm's light.

The thought of losing him again stabbed her heart with a deep ache. "I don't want to lose you." *I can't lose you.*

His chest stopped mid-breath for half a heartbeat, and she realized she'd spoken her fear aloud. He took her hand in his, and the current of electricity surged between them again. He placed something into her palm and gently closed her fingers around the object.

She looked down, opening her hand. Air rushed out of her lungs when she saw the tiny white horse from her mother's necklace. "Ethan, how did you—"

"Anything for you, Jayden. Anything."

"Thank you." She clutched the charm close to her heart and leaned toward him.

He didn't move away. His eyes grew softer and his emotions didn't slam into her like normal. Instead they lapped against her heart like calm waves against the sand, pulling and pushing at the same time. So many emotions tightly wound together that she couldn't unravel. She pulled one of the strings. Fear. Another. Regret. Still another. Hope. She stopped.

Her stomach squeezed and she remembered Thea's words.

She couldn't have this. Not if she was going to die. It wouldn't be fair. Yes, she needed love. The kind that made her fight for her people and protect them—that's what she would embrace. This kind of love—desire for a life she could never have—was going to have to stay locked tight in her heart.

Moonlight slipped away again, and the storm seemed to swell. Rain remained in the clouds like emotions unable to escape. She knew exactly how that felt.

CHAPTER 14

PURE MOTIVATION

Connor crept into the library and breathed in the aroma of old parchment. Thousands of books packed the hundreds of shelves in the arched-ceilinged room. A few tables and leather armchairs lined the floors. Not that anyone used them save him.

Sunlight spilled in through the high window, illuminating a wheeled ladder that rested against the shelves on the west wall. Connor aligned the ladder with a mosaic on the ceiling of a gryphon, then he plucked a book from the fourth shelf, seven books in.

The ladder wiggled as he scaled thirteen shelves high and counted seven books over. Dust motes sparkled in the sun as his fingers ran over spines of books rarely touched. He stifled a sneeze and pulled a thick volume from the last place he'd hidden it and replaced it with the other one he'd picked. He chuckled as he read the title: *A History of Feravolk Dance.*

Cradling the book he needed, he climbed down and sat at one of the tables. As a boy, he'd attempted to take this book from the library, along with a stack of others. Idla had found him and had him given a switching that Rebekah likely never forgave her for.

He laid the book on the table farthest from the entrance of the room and sat down so he could see the door. Something in this book might have answers. He'd read the whole volume several times, but much of it still didn't make sense.

One prophecy in particular always seemed a good place to start.

And though he knew each word already, he opened to the well-worn page and read it again:

A sorceress will come with power to destroy all the Creator has built.

She'll break the land and the people's hearts and bring death to those who'd oppose her.

But hope will be found when the Deliverers rise through flame, through ash, and heal the heart of the land.

Through blazing fire and torrent of rain, the Forest shall fall and rise again.

Those who will deliver the land will summon the Creator's power.

They will work as one, each having different talents: the heart of one, soul of another, the mind of one, and strength of her brother.

No matter how many times he read it, he didn't know enough to unravel the real meaning. But he was certain it was the key to stopping the Mistress. Or to finding out her true plan to obtain the Creator's power.

"Studying again?"

Connor's hackles rose at the voice in the doorway, but he didn't look up. "Why are you here, Kara? You don't seem the reading type."

Kara sauntered toward him and walked around the table, taking her time. She leaned over his shoulder. "*The Book of Prophecy.* I think this one is your favorite, you choose it so often. You must have it memorized by now."

He turned toward her, his nose nearly bumping hers, and refused to back away. "The picture books are on the east end."

She touched the tip of his nose with her finger. "I like the one with maps in it. Something about thrones and corners meeting, strange things that would sail right over your pretty little head."

Maps and thrones? Connor glanced toward the east end. One of the prophecies rang clear in his thoughts: *They shall sit on thrones of life and there find the Creator's power.*

It was likely true. He had most of the book memorized. The problem lay in deciphering what everything meant. But if there truly was a book that told him the location of these thrones, he needed it.

Kara chuckled and slid into the chair next to him, crossing one leg over the other. "You didn't know about it?"

He just stared at her. Maybe if he didn't respond, she'd go away. Not that it had worked in the past. He pulled his book closer. She'd already seen him with it anyway, so might as well keep reading.

Her fingers touched the top edge. "Can't you share? I like this one, too." She slid the book away from him and opened it, thumbing through the well-worn pages. "My favorite part is this passage: 'When the four Deliverers join their talents, the Door of Death will be opened.' Arcane, isn't it?"

She pushed the book back toward him and tapped her finger over the passage. Connor didn't need to read it. He read it every time he entered the library. Not that this prophecy made much sense, either.

Kara searched his face with narrowed eyes. "What do you suppose it means?"

He glared at her.

She leaned away. "No reason to get ferocious, Wolfy."

"Wolfy?"

She leaned uncomfortably close. "I like your eyes. They match your temper. Ferocious."

He leaned back in his chair and crossed his arms, hoping to convey a nonchalant attitude. If Kara knew his secret, that could really change things. Then again, Kara's games might be tedious, but playing along usually resulted in useful information.

He shrugged. "I'm not ferocious."

Kara laughed and it seemed authentic, not just one of her agenda-driven, annoying laughs. "Really? Because I've seen you get pretty—"

"I can be." He glared.

She tapped the book. "What's your take on the passage?"

"The Doors of Life and Death are part of the Afterworld. Only the Creator has the power to open the door to the Afterworld. It must be the moment the Deliverers obtain the Creator's power. When they take the thrones."

"That's a fine theory, but there are others who have the power to open the door to the Afterworld."

So Kara knew more than he'd thought. He'd studied the *Old*

Custom as much as the *Book of Prophecy.* One other—the Mistress—had the power to open those doors, but only the Creator had the power to open the Door of Life and the Door of Death simultaneously. Besides, she didn't have those powers anymore. They were taken from her and given to two others. "The Creator has banished her to a life of imprisonment. She was stripped of her powers."

Kara placed her elbows on the table. Her eyes darted around the room. "Only stripped of the ability to use them. Once she is freed, her powers will be within her reach again. She will be free soon. Her spies have been hard at work. And she seeks the Deliverers."

Connor examined Kara's face. "She wants the Creator's power."

Kara nodded. "There are those who would free her. Franco is one of them."

"Are you?"

Kara's sultry smile returned.

Connor smirked. "You carry a seeing stone. It's an ancient weapon of the Mist—"

Kara placed a finger on his lips. "Don't say her title in my presence." She cocked her head. "You know about my stone? It seems I am not the only one who has been spying in secret."

"You and your sister want to help my mother. Why?"

She smiled. "And you. Don't exclude yourself, Wolfy."

"Don't call me that. Answer the question."

"Franco plans to use the Deliverers before taking them to his master—the one we have been speaking about. I can't have that."

"Because the"—he'd almost said *the Mistress of Shadows* again—"*she* . . . is your master, too?"

"Thea seems to think you're thick. I don't, but you do mistake one thing. I have no master."

"And you would give your master the Creator's powers?"

Kara stared at him, a glimmer in her blue-green eyes.

Connor leaned closer. "You would take me to your . . . employer?"

"Perhaps. But what do I stand to gain if *she* wins?"

"Doesn't *she* claim to want to give her followers power over the land?"

Kara licked her lips. "I am an assassin. I have all the power I need already."

"Then whom do you work for, really?"

Kara's lips slid into a smile. "The highest bidder."

CHAPTER 15

ALTERING THE PLAN

Thea slipped through a secret passage from the tunnels into an empty hallway. She knew those tapestries with the hounds chasing the fox. She was on the sixth floor. The south stairs were open to her, but she'd have to pass the kitchens on the way down to the spell chamber if she went that way. If she took the north staircase, she would pass Belladonna's room.

She breathed deep, clearing her head, and listened to the pictures in her mind. A red ruby. Blood. A silver blade. Death.

If she didn't go to the spell chamber now, everything in that vision could be avoided. She wouldn't have to die. Kara would. Kara couldn't die, not while Thea could help it. Spell chamber it was. And sealing her fate. She breathed deep and headed toward the north staircase.

She'd only ever truly loved two people in her lifetime. Both were sisters to her—one by blood, the other by circumstance. She could think of no better reason to die than to save both of them.

Thea descended to the ground floor. Then she walked through the corridor, letting no one see her, and headed outside. The sun shone on her back, warming it as she stopped in front of the palace's secret way, the bard's gate.

Different heat warmed her. She peered into the blacksmith's hut. The steady thud of the hammer clanking against metal easily hid the sound of her soft footsteps as she sneaked behind the blacksmith. She picked up the wooden plank in the floor just enough to slide through. The man never moved as she put the plank back in place from beneath.

In the dank corridor, she leaned against the wall until her eyes adjusted. Rats skittered along the dusty ground. She stalked forward and opened the secret door. On the other side, illuminated with the glow of torches, stood the stone door to the spell chamber. Thea walked up to it and slipped the key from her pocket. She slid it into the lock. It clicked open and she stepped inside. The pungent aroma always twisted her stomach. Today, it wasn't the only thing knotting her insides.

The spell book sat on a pedestal in the entryway, tempting anyone who entered to touch it. Wouldn't Franco just love that? The first time Thea had reached out to touch the book, the pictures in her mind warned her that Idla would be alerted. It was the reason Thea had learned to make her potions from other sources. Idla might be dead now, but the price for using the Mistress's spell book was high. Idla would have had to blood-will a successor to take her place as the Mistress's host—the book held her power. Only one chosen by the Mistress, or, in the case of death, the person blood-willed to take her place, could touch the book without tripping an alarm. Who had Franco blood-willed to take his place if he died?

Thea's mind filled with pictures. Her talent would answer that question. She stopped to listen. She saw Franco and Belladonna slice their palms. Blood dripped into a bejeweled goblet, and they both drank. Thea's stomach turned.

Belladonna? Odd choice.

She gasped. Everything made sense now. The way things would end. The things she needed Kara to do. She'd better get to making those potions then. She'd need some of Idla's ingredients.

She pulled the piece of paper from her pocket and set in on the wooden table, smoothing it with her fingers, careful not to smudge any of the writing. A resurrection spell. The most powerful of all the potions. It was said that anyone who made such a spell would surely die within months.

This time it would be true.

The other potion she needed to make was a recipe she knew by heart. She searched the long rows of shelves for her first ingredient: dried dragon embers.

Once she'd collected everything she needed and laid it out on the table, she read the instructions again. She could afford no mistakes. The dried ember fit in the palm of her hand. She crushed it, singeing her fingers in the process.

When she finished creating her final potions, she tucked the two vials safely in her clothes. If she exited now, Belladonna would find her.

But it had to be now. Images of Kara's death played in her head every time she considered the alternative. Thea's heart squeezed. She opened the door and took two steps into the tunnel.

A quiet sniffle punctured the silence.

Belladonna. The wicked woman was here to set everything in motion.

Thea breathed in. Her father had said she could never tame the future, but by accepting that truth, she had. Or at least made it less scary.

"Thea, I am surprised to see you here." Belladonna's voice echoed in the stone corridor.

"I could say the same about you."

Belladonna held up the key to the spell room—the very one Idla had always worn around her neck. "I am here on the king's business. Whose business are you here on?"

"An assassin knows never to reveal all of her secrets."

"Franco doesn't trust you or your sister." Belladonna took a step closer.

A bold move if Thea could kill her. There were only two ways to kill a Healer. Thea matched Belladonna's movement. "No one really does."

"Do you know who helped Logan escape?" Belladonna narrowed her eyes.

"How should I?"

"Answering one of my questions with one of your own only makes me suspicious."

Thea shrugged.

Belladonna narrowed her eyes. "So, do you know who helped Logan escape?"

"I do not."

"Your heart betrays you. I sense a lie. You are no dragon that you can hide the truth from me. Was it Kara?"

"No."

"Was it you?"

"Logan got himself out."

"True, but how do you know it?"

"An assassin knows never to reveal all of her secrets."

"I suppose she does." Belladonna sneered. "Did you help Logan?"

"Of course not."

A greedy smile parted Belladonna's lips. "I see."

Now the woman would go tell Franco that Thea had let Logan escape. Thea turned and walked away. Her heart sank to her knees, but she kept them from buckling beneath her until Belladonna was no longer watching.

CHAPTER 16

A HUMBLE WIZARD

Purple smoke dissipated, leaving Belladonna in a valley of rock formations. Orange stone arches and pillars as far as she could see, and a small, lopsided hut hidden among a grouping of pillars.

Amazing. This magical potion Franco had given her had transported her from the palace right to the strange hut. Maybe she'd been wrong to be skeptical. Too bad he'd given her the last bottle that could bring her to this place, although maybe the wizard here could make her another one.

She touched the other vial of purple liquid in her pocket. Franco had said the potion would only take her back to the place where it was made. That meant this one would take her back to the palace. When the time was right.

Her boots made imprints in the sandy soil as she walked toward the hut. What kind of wizard was this Rubius? And why did he live in the middle of nowhere?

"Who goes there?" a voice echoed in the cavernous valley.

Unable to tell which direction it came from, Belladonna placed her hands on her hips and looked at the empty space right in front of her. "One who seeks the council of a wizard."

"Wizard? You flatter me."

A humble wizard? Please. Why must men put on such an act?

A man wearing a tattered brown cloak appeared from behind some invisible wall. So she had guessed right on his location. Hopefully he'd noticed her confidence.

The breeze ruffled his long, stringy white hair. He clutched a staff in his hand and seemed to lean heavily on it. "I watched you appear from thin air, yet you call *me* a wizard?"

Belladonna eyed the stranger. "It seems you've done the same. I've heard you know all about the old ways because you're old enough to remember them." And hopefully not too decrepit that he'd forgotten.

"Who sends you here?"

She checked her fingernails. "Queen Idla of Soleden."

"She's dead."

Oh good, he did know. He must have some powers for that news to have made it out here. "Her son approved my mission."

He hobbled closer. "And what do you come for?"

At least the look in his eyes was spritely. He might just be what she needed. "I was banished from my Healer camp for breaking the code. I wish to take vengeance on those who left me for dead. I wish to take something from them."

Belladonna's whip lifted from her belt. She didn't flinch as it floated over to the wizard and stopped in front of him. He fingered it and lifted a bushy eyebrow. "You embellish your weapon with fine jewels? Bones. And teeth."

"I only want what is best for those I torture. Is there anything harder than a diamond or a dragon's tooth?" Belladonna couldn't hide her growing smile.

"I am Rubius. Come in. I think I may be of service to you."

CHAPTER 17

THE FOURTH DELIVERER

The forest smelled older here.

Gnarled branches spanned above, with bark so black it looked wet. Leaf cover was thin on the odd-looking trees, like something diseased them long ago and they'd never recovered. Never grew again. No birds or squirrels made their homes in these dead trees. The farther they walked beneath the decaying branches, the closer the limbs grew together. Logan sniffed the air thick with fog. It smelled odd.

"Animals don't pass through here." Westwind flattened his ears. *"I don't blame them. Something happened here. Death of some sort. Fear stains the ground, old and potent."*

Scout whined and dropped back so that he walked next to Ethan. Aurora loped with her tail low, her confidence wavering.

Fear, huh? Logan couldn't smell the emotion, but he wasn't really good at that anyway. Rebekah had been. He quickened his pace as if he could leave those thoughts behind him. Perhaps they should move out of the area quickly.

"No argument from me." Westwind chuffed.

The others followed his lead and walked at the brisk pace for hours without complaining.

At last the cover above thickened with green leaves. Chirps and chatters filled the air again. Golden light replaced gray and the fog dissipated. It was almost as though they'd walked through an invisible wall to a new place.

"That's more like it." Westwind looked over his shoulder and winked.

The wolves loped up ahead, but Scout didn't join them. *"You okay, Scout?"* Logan asked.

The dog whined. *"My human is limping."*

Oh no, the kid. He shouldn't have pushed Ethan so hard. Logan patted Gavin's shoulder. "What do you say we stop here for a little while? You want to give Ryan a few lessons?"

He glanced over his shoulder in time to see Ryan perk up.

"Maybe I'll just watch." Chloe practically flopped onto the ground.

"You'll do no such thing." Melanie gripped Chloe's hand and towed her up. "It'll be good for you. Jayden will help, won't you?"

"Of course." Jayden dropped her pack and pulled out her daggers.

"How about we throw knives?" Chloe pulled out her belt knife. "I have one of those, thanks to Gavin."

"Oh, come on, Chloe. This will be fun." Kinsey practically clapped her hands.

Chloe put a protective arm in front of Wren and smiled at her sister. "If Kinsey is holding a weapon, I think Wren and I will be way over there."

Wren rolled her eyes. "I'm not scared, and I'll learn faster than the lot of you." She swung at the air a few times and Logan watched her. He nudged Gavin with his elbow. "You might want to start with that one. She shows promise."

Wren brightened.

Ryan laughed and shook his head. "You have no idea."

Wren's fists flew to her hips and she jutted out her chin. "I know how to hold my own."

"No one's doubting that." Ryan tussled her hair, and she practically glared at him. Then her lips curved and she winked at him.

A pang hit Logan's heart. He'd never seen his children at this age. *"We're stopping, Westwind."*

"It's as good a place as any. Aurora and I will get you some rabbits, unless Scout wants to join."

Tail-wagging, the dog took off.

Logan approached Ethan, who sat with his back to a tree. "How're you holding up?"

Ethan chuckled. "Pretty well. But I admit, I was a little nervous that you were going to ask me to spar."

Logan smiled. "Maybe later."

That got another laugh. "I wanted to talk to you, too." He paused. All trace of smile left his face. "I would have died down there if—"

"Ethan, I'm sorry." He hoped the kid saw how sorry he truly was. This guilt would likely never leave him. He'd left one of his own. "I thought you were dead, but that was no reason to leave you behind. I wouldn't have if the cave hadn't been collapsing." If he hadn't been injured and wondering if Jayden was okay. He closed his eyes. "I should never have left you, no matter what."

Ethan stared at him, quiet for what seemed like an eternity. "I'm not angry with you. You did what you had to, and I understand. You're forgiven, Logan."

More than he deserved. "I'll never leave you again. I hope you know that."

"Hey, we protect Jayden first. Then each other." He held out his hand and Logan clasped it.

"So, sparring now?"

"I hope you're kidding."

Logan couldn't help but laugh. "I am."

"Good." Ethan took a deep breath. "What I wanted to tell you is that I met your son. He saved my life."

All the air left Logan's lungs. "My . . . son?"

"Connor. The wolf. He's your son. There's no need to worry about how he turned out in there. He saved us all."

Logan cupped his hands over his face. It all made sense. But why? Connor. His name was Connor. Rebekah had always liked that name. Logan swallowed, his voice seeming so far from reach. He wanted nothing more than to go for his son, but Connor had said he wouldn't go with Logan. Then he'd protected Rebekah. It didn't all make sense. It was still going to be tricky to get him out of the palace. Even so, Connor would have to wait. First duty was to get his daughter. And the Whisperer.

He didn't know where they were. The taut rope in his chest seemed to draw him closer to the Forest of Legends. Something he almost heard, but not quite, seemed to whisper in his soul. And it was telling him to look for his daughter there, that she needed him first. He hoped it was right, because Franco was looking, too. And Franco had scores of men to help him search. All the more reason Logan needed to see his people. He was counting on his friends to help him find his daughter and their Whisperer.

Finally finding words, Logan glanced at Ethan. "Thank you."

"I just thought you should know. I was going to bring him when he helped me escape, but he's bound by a trace spell. He said he's in no immediate danger. I told him we'd go back for him."

"And we will." A trace spell. That made sense. Connor had to save face with Rebekah, and it was too dangerous for him to leave. As soon as he had his daughter and the Whisperer, Logan would go in himself. The wolf. His heart shattered. Then it mended. His own son had protected him. He breathed deep, stood, and patted Ethan's shoulder. "Get some rest, kid."

After they were fed and rested, Logan got them moving again. "Gav, how far?"

Gavin paused, no doubt listening to Glider. "Not far now."

"How was Ryan?"

Gavin's smile was bright. "Chloe's as green as a sapling, but Ryan has obviously spent some time with a sword in his hand. The fact that he's a blacksmith works in his favor."

"Good." Because One Eye would help shape him into a fighter, and Logan figured they'd need all the help they could get.

Westwind loped near Logan. *Do you smell that?* He slowed and his head lowered as his hackles rose.

CHAPTER 18

IN PLAIN SIGHT

The warmth of a threat spread over Ethan's chest, and he pulled arrows from the new quiver he'd received from the Dissenters. He held his new bow, ready to pull the string back, and nudged Ryan, who quickly did the same.

Scout lowered his head and growled.

"Logan?" Ryan's voice sounded shaky. Ethan glanced at his brother. It wasn't like Ryan to sound scared, and his face had gone pale. Not normal at all.

A sharp hiss punctured the air, but Ethan couldn't tell where it came from. As for the source of the danger, it was potent in every direction.

Logan tapped Ryan's shoulder. "It's just Callie, kid. Put your weapon away."

Ethan scanned the trees, bow still in his hands, but he saw nothing aside from the mountain lion. "Not just Callie, Logan. We're surrounded." And he had too many to protect.

The trees rustled. Hundreds of cloaked people crouched in the branches and crawled across the limbs, bows in hand, stalking them.

Ethan aimed his arrow up and tapped into his talent. Hopefully he could trust it with this many to protect at once.

"Ethan, put your weapon away." Logan's voice was a whisper.

The growing threat receded, but the inkling remained. Whoever they were, they would fight back if provoked. He lowered his weapon, but didn't put any arrows back.

A massive grizzly bear lumbered toward Logan and stood on its rear paws, towering above Logan.

"Logan," Kinsey whispered.

But Logan smiled. "Berne, it's a long way from Moon Over Water. Tell me you brought Reuben."

A man, taller than even Ryan, stepped out of the cover of the trees near them. He dropped the hood of his cloak and looked at Ethan first. Everything about him seemed sharp. His features, the look in his eye, and his many weapons.

"Reuben." Logan rushed to greet the man.

Reuben's movements were much more calculated and calm. He wore his cloak so that the fabric didn't even seem to ripple. Stealth seemed to be his talent. Reuben clasped Logan's hand and pulled him in for a hug. "It's nice to see Gavin brought you back in one piece." He reached to give Gavin and Melanie the same greeting. "Looks like you've doubled the size of our camp."

No more feeling of umbrage from the people in the trees, but they hadn't put away their weapons, either. Ethan returned the arrows to the quiver, but kept his hand close, just in case.

Kinsey had gravitated closer to him. "They're Logan's friends. Don't you trust them?"

He moved closer to her and lowered his head. "I don't trust anyone who could hurt you."

She smiled. "I feel the same. Only about people who could hurt you."

He chuckled. Leave it to Kinsey to try to ease the tension. So like Ryan.

Reuben tilted back his head and cupped his hands to his mouth. The distinctive call of a blue jay escaped his lips. The other cloaked people began to pass the call along, and it echoed deeper into the woods. How many of them were hidden among the trees?

"I see you brought an army." Logan laughed.

"Only twenty of my best men and women from Moon Over Water. I like to be prepared."

"Twenty-one!" A man with a scarred face and pronounced limp

stepped out from behind a tree and lowered his hood. His smile was broad.

"I didn't ask you to come, Beck." Reuben slapped the man's shoulder, and a wolverine growled and lurched for Reuben's arm.

Beck's huge hand pushed the animal away. "Now you've insulted Cenewig. That's never a good idea. Even Berne leaves him alone."

"Of course he does." Reuben laughed. "He's a smart bear."

"Logan! Gavin!" Beck grabbed Logan's hand and pumped his arm. "It's been too long, my friend."

"Beck." Logan held his hand out to slap the man on the back, but a threat loomed. Before Ethan could react, the wolverine charged at Logan, hissing and spitting.

Beck's thick hand pushed the animal away. "Cenewig, leave Logan alone. You silly beast." His rich laugh boomed. "Temperamental thing."

The threat vanished, and Logan's laughter joined Beck's. *Great.* Ethan breathed deep. Looked like he'd be stuck on edge this whole time.

Logan turned his attention to a third person who joined their group. She had tight, dark curls and a hooked nose. Her smile practically beamed. A falcon perched on her slim shoulder. Logan opened his arms wide. "Samantha."

She hugged him tight. "Stranger. Did you find them all?" She motioned to Jayden and the others. Ethan walked closer to the group, still standing behind everyone. Logan might trust these three, but Ethan didn't—yet.

Logan tipped his head to the side. "Let's talk where it's safe."

"Yes." Reuben put his hand on Logan's shoulder and led him under trees infiltrated with camouflaged Feravolk. "But just so you know, Alistair insisted on coming. He wanted the update from you himself."

Whoever Alistair was, the name made Logan's shoulders tense. Ethan glanced at Jayden and Ryan.

Ryan shrugged.

Jayden looked up as she passed beneath the archers.

Ryan bumped her shoulder with his. "Don't worry. If they wanted us dead, we'd be on the ground already."

"How can you make jokes like that?" Chloe whispered. She stuck as close to her brother as Jayden.

He smiled and glanced at Ethan. "If I don't, who will?"

Ethan chuckled as he put away his bow. "Too bad they aren't funny."

Reuben disappeared in front of them.

"Another Feravolk camp. Is it Moon Over Water?" Kinsey grabbed Wren's hand and a giddy gleam lit her eyes.

"No." Logan smiled. "But it's a number of people from there. And I imagine they've made the place feel like home. Follow me." He stepped forward into the invisible wall. No threat loomed there, so Ethan didn't follow. Instead he waited to be sure everyone made it through.

Jayden stopped next to him and held out her hand toward the invisible wall. "I don't see a thing. How do they do it?" Westwind brushed her hand and she looked down at him. "It's amazing."

His eyes seemed to smile. He tipped his head toward the opening and together they stepped through. Logan and his friends followed.

Ryan stopped at Ethan's shoulder. "How are you holding up?"

Ethan kept his voice low. "I don't trust them yet, but I don't expect anything to happen. If it does, I'll be ready."

"That's not what I mean. How are *you*? Seven days isn't much time to heal. I don't care how fast you mend." Ryan's look held concern.

Ethan touched his injured arm. "I'm still sore. But if anything comes up, I'll be ready. I promise."

Ryan shook his head. "You won't be alone."

"I know."

Ryan's throat bobbed. "Take care of yourself. I already thought you were dead once. I'm not going to lose you again."

"Hey, I don't plan on getting lost."

Ryan chuckled. "I'd punch you if you didn't have as many stitches as Kinsey's old favorite doll."

Ethan laughed. "Do I really look that tattered? Besides, I only gave you two free hits. You'd better make sure this last one is a good one."

"It will be." He motioned toward the invisible wall. "You headed in?"

Ethan nodded and scanned around again. Ryan turned to leave.

"Hey, Ry?" Ethan's word's stopped him.

He turned back, eyes expectant.

"I trust you at my back."

Ryan's eyes widened slightly, then his familiar crooked smile slid across his face and he nodded once. He slipped past the camouflage door.

With one more glance behind him, Ethan followed.

The Feravolk world unfolded. Tents lined up between trees, perfectly placed so that those looking at the trees wouldn't see them. Men and women in camouflaged garb walked between the tents. Black bears and coyotes trotted beside people. A fox licked its paw. A lynx turned its head toward him. The scent of fire and cooking rabbit filtered through the air, and his stomach growled. The Dissenters camp was crude compared to this. He really needed to learn this art of camouflage.

Everyone seemed to be walking toward the center of the camp. Ethan stopped to get a sense of his surroundings. Scout stuck close to him, never leaving him alone when things were uncertain.

Chloe leaned closer to him. "You look ready to lead us into battle. Smile, Ethan, or they might find you threatening."

"Only if provoked, Chloe."

"I know." She touched his arm and walked away, following the others. The gesture left his feet planted. Was Chloe finally forgiving him for leaving?

He caught Kinsey's smirk out of the corner of his eye and turned toward her. "You going to tell me to stop being so serious, too?"

She walked up to him, shaking her head. "No, brother. I can't stop you from being you." Her smile still shone of innocence. If he could do nothing else for her and Wren, he hoped he could at least spare them from having to lose their innocence in this terrible war. She stopped in front of him and tilted her head. "Be safe, Ethan." Her eyes glistened.

"Hey, Kinny." He pulled her into a hug. "Don't worry about me."

"I always do."

He nudged her back so he could look into her lime-green eyes. "You know I'd never let anything happen to you."

"Yes." She smiled now. "And I trust that you'll protect Ryan with the same fervor."

"Absolutely."

She nodded. "Good. We both know he needs it. He's as headstrong as Wren."

"Oh? Not you?"

"No one's as headstrong as me. I'm just smart about it."

He narrowed his eyes. "Right. You always have a plan. A reckless plan."

She shrugged. "I can't help it if I'm two steps ahead." She paused. "Just . . . Ryan will want to help. Make sure he's trained. Make sure—"

Ethan placed his hands on her shoulders. "Ryan is lucky to have a sister like you."

She nodded, chewing the inside of her lip. Ethan chucked her chin as he turned to follow the others, but her soft, confident voice stopped him. "So are you."

He closed his eyes as her words warmed his heart, then glanced over his shoulder and sent her a wink. He'd miss her. She'd been his little sister even when his parents were still alive. Yes, he'd strive to keep her innocence, her unwavering hope, alive.

When Ethan reached Logan and his cluster of friends, Samantha asked her question again, "Have you done as Alistair asked and found all of the Deliverers?"

"Not all the Deliverers. Only Jayden." Logan introduced all of them, including Scout. "And this is Ethan. He's taken the vow to be one of the Protectors." He squeezed Ethan's shoulder, gently. "He's good at it."

"He took a vow?" Gavin regarded Ethan. "It all makes sense now." He turned his attention to Logan.

"The Deliverers were meant to have four Protectors."

"Why four?" Jayden asked.

Logan looked at her and his smile faded. "The Protectors were to be your parents. It's clearly not possible with yours dead, and . . ."

With Logan's wife working with the palace.

"Well, you're two protectors short." Gavin was silent for a moment. "I'd like to pledge myself as one."

Melanie touched her husband's shoulder. "I'd like to pledge myself, too. It's what Loralye would've wanted."

Jayden stared at Melanie. "Why would my birth mother have wanted this?"

Gavin's gray eyes grew softer. "Because she was my sister."

Jayden gasped. "I have an uncle?"

"Yes. Your father was one of my best friends."

"And your mother was mine," Melanie said.

"And Rebekah's." Jayden grabbed Melanie's hand.

Melanie bowed her head and her blonde hair hid her face. "Rebekah is my sister."

Ethan looked at Logan, who nodded slightly. Well, that made sense. They were all tied together. "Perhaps the Creator planned it this way." Ethan knew all too well that the Creator had planned this for him. A shiver shot through him at the memory he wanted to keep buried.

"You accept us as Protectors then?" Melanie's smile was warm.

Ethan smiled in return. "Who am I to turn down help?"

"Then let's make it official." Gavin removed his belt knife and handed it to Logan.

One by one, the four of them surrounded Jayden. Her eyes, large and worried, met his. She was going to have to get over that. He'd protect her until death. The oath would extend his obligation to the other Deliverers, once they found them, but he would do anything for Jayden—oath or no oath.

Logan sliced his hand, then passed the knife to Ethan. He stared Jayden in the eyes as he drew the blade across his palm, over the old scar. The feel of the binding seemed to tie his blood to the open wound. His skin seemed tight, like a constant reminder. A reminder he didn't need. He handed the blade to Gavin. He didn't look away from Jayden while Gavin and Melanie joined the oath. He felt it. A tie between them, binding them all to the same purpose.

When Jayden's eyes, wet and round, met his again, he mouthed the words, "Anything for you." And he meant it.

CHAPTER 19

WOODEN TOKENS

Jayden tore her eyes from Ethan's gaze. *Anything for you,* he'd said. And his devotion scared her. She'd already witnessed loved ones dying so she could live. She stared at the drops of blood seeping into the ground. Remnants of a promise. For her and the other Deliverers. She'd take their sacrifice to heart. No one else would have to die for her. She wouldn't let them down.

"Logan." A strong voice rose up from behind them.

Everyone stiffened. Jayden turned to look at the newcomer. He was an older man. Gray adorned his temples and peppered his short, curly hair. He carried a staff, and a black wolf stood near him. The way everyone bowed their heads in greeting told her this was the man they referred to as their leader.

"Alistair." Logan approached the man and bowed to one knee.

Jayden blinked. Strange to think of Logan having superiors.

Alistair touched Logan's head with weathered fingers. "Rise. I see you brought the Deliverers. Your discussion with the Whisperer must have been fruitful." Alistair's cool, dark-eyed gaze slid over Jayden and the others, then gently back to Logan. "It seems your bargain has been more than fulfilled. Bring them by my Council tent, and we can relieve you of your duties. We have chosen those who will see these four to safety."

Jayden's heart tripped on a beat at the older man's words.

Logan stood tall. "I haven't found all of them. Only one. Nathaniel and Loralye's daughter."

"Yes, I see her." Alistair's dark eyes latched onto Jayden's face again.

Her insides chilled to the core. She wouldn't let this Council, whoever they were, take her away from Logan. She was tied to him.

Alistair's brows pulled together. "I suppose there is a reason for all the others to be here?"

"Yes." Logan nodded. "But I wanted to talk to you about being renamed Protector."

Alistair's eyes twinkled and a smile deepened his wrinkles. "You've had a change of heart, I see."

Logan chuckled. "I suppose you could say that."

"Embracing your Destiny Path?"

"I wouldn't go that far."

"Well, destiny or no, the Council will have to decide if it's right for you to take the Deliverers under your wing." Alistair looked at Logan with narrowed eyes. "After all, you did pass the responsibility on."

"I understand."

Jayden stepped forward. "I don't."

She squirmed under Alistair's gaze. They weren't exactly cold eyes, but they weren't warm, either.

He regarded her and she opened her talent. His emotions remained closed off, even as she pushed.

"The Council is the governing system for this camp," Alistair said in his calm, quiet voice. "You think it unfair for them to be involved in such an important decision simply because one of our own has a change of heart?"

Sweat beaded on her forehead. What was she doing? The last thing she wanted was to make enemies, especially with him, but trust was too important and those sworn to protect her now were people she trusted. "No. It's unfair to make Logan go before the Council alone. Don't I have a say in those who will protect me?"

"We made the decision before you were involved."

Her voice trembled. "I was involved the day I was born. The day my father died to make sure this man would survive to protect me." Jayden pointed at Logan. She stepped closer to Alistair, meeting his phlegmatic stare. "So no, you did not make the decision before I was involved. Will your Council continue to keep me out of decisions that directly impact my future?"

Alistair rubbed his finger across his lips. "You would like to face the Council?"

"I would like the Council to hear from me."

Alistair looked fleetingly to Jayden's left. Logan stood there. Jayden wouldn't turn. She felt Logan's unease, but she couldn't handle seeing his face just yet.

"Very well, you can plead your case to the Council. We'll be assembled in two hours."

"I'm pleading my case to you. Now. Logan, Gavin, Melanie, and Ethan have sworn to protect me. I trust them."

Slowly Alistair turned. "And you make this decision for the other three Deliverers?"

"No. They did. I simply accept with humble gratitude. With fear that they will be hurt because of me. With determination to make their sacrifice count. These are people I will not fail. People I will not defy. People I love."

The wrinkles around Alistair's eyes deepened, but a small smile formed on his lips. "Your request is granted, Jayden of the Feravolk, one of the Tribe of Moon Over Water. Your courage rivals your birth mother's. It's refreshing."

Then he turned to Logan. "I'm glad she changed your mind."

His gaze stopped on Ethan.

Ethan tensed as the man regarded him.

At last Alistair said, "You trust this one, Logan?"

"With my life."

Alistair nodded once, then turned and walked away, his black wolf following.

Jayden released a breath as soon as Alistair was clear of her sights. Behind her, Ryan whistled. She turned to see him staring at her with his eyes wide. All of them stared at her, most of them with open mouths.

Chloe started clapping. "Well done. There's a leader in you begging to be released."

Jayden's knees weakened. "Oh." A thousand thoughts fluttered through her head, but words evaded her. She breathed. "You think?"

"Absolutely." Logan winked at her.

Jayden watched as Reuben clasped Gavin and Logan's shoulders. "Brave to take on such a responsibility, my friends. And I'll make sure our whole camp is rallied behind you." Then he looked at her. "And your courage is certainly commendable."

Jayden's face flushed.

"Thank you, friend," Logan said to Reuben. "Now I have much to tell you."

"My tent is open." Reuben motioned toward the crude, green tent.

Logan glanced at Ryan and his sisters. "No need for anyone to hear more than they should. Can I trust you four to stay put while we talk?"

Chloe huffed and crossed her arms.

"Of course." Ryan eyed his sister. "Besides, I'm dying to arm wrestle some of these warriors."

Chloe called Ryan incorrigible while Logan patted his shoulder, then Logan followed the others into Reuben's tent.

Jayden walked close to Ethan as they entered the tent, thankful she didn't have to do this without him. Right now she needed familiar. He glanced at her, his eyebrows pulled together. As soon as their eyes met, he gave her a soft smile. Something swelled in Jayden's heart. Pride? Not hers. It made Ethan feel proud that she sought his protection? She smiled back and he gently touched her elbow to steady her as she stepped into the tent.

An oblong table rested in the center. A cluster of rolled up maps and a few sword-sharpening leathers and stones sat atop it. Reuben grabbed one of the long rolled-up parchments and spread it across the flat, smooth surface, setting a polished stone in each corner.

Logan placed his palms on the table and leaned over the map. "I still have two of the Deliverers to find, and we need an army to go after Franco. Unfortunately, we need to do it more quickly than originally thought. Franco plans to free the Mistress, and he knows how."

"Idiot." Beck snorted.

Logan glanced at his friend with a faint smile, but it fell fast. "If he frees the Mistress, that sorceress will destroy Soleden."

Beck's face grew serious. "Then we can't let him."

"Agreed." Samantha's eyes met Jayden's. "You're so young. When the prophecies started coming true, I was your age. I didn't feel young then, but now I look at you . . ." She reached across the table and grabbed Jayden's hands. "May the Creator protect you. Our fate lies in your hands."

A heavy weight pulled against Jayden's heart as she stared into Samantha's eyes. "I won't let you down."

"You and the other three are the only hope we have to defeat the sorceress."

Jayden shook her head. "How much more powerful will she be than Idla? I've already defeated her. Idla is dead."

"Idla?" Samantha released Jayden's hands and smiled ruefully. "You are more powerful than you seem. But the Mistress is much more powerful. Idla would have gotten her powers from the Mistress. The prophecy states that the Deliverers shall save Soleden from the sorceress. She wants to break free. She's been trying for thousands of years. If she does, she will try to bring the Deliverers to her. She's trying even now. Be wary. She uses darkness to shroud evil. Her creatures are roaming this earth. Black lions. Kelpies. Black leather vines. They are all attempting to draw the Deliverers to her."

"Why?" Jayden asked as she stifled a shiver.

"Because you hold the key to the Creator's power. You can banish her back into her prison. Back into the Afterworld where the Creator banished her. If she's freed, she will destroy the Feravolk and attempt to take the Creator's power for her own."

Reuben rubbed the stubble on his chin. "I thought black lions were legend."

Beck leaned toward Logan. "What does Franco need in order to free her? We'll make sure he doesn't get it."

"Deliverer blood from one of the girls, a Whisperer tear, and some kind of untraceable seeing stone. That means we have to find my daughter and our Whisperer before he does."

"I thought Alistair sent you to look for the Whisperer?"

"I found Anna, but she wasn't our Whisperer. That means there is another out there."

Samantha leaned forward. "I thought only one Whisperer could be alive at a time."

Logan shrugged. "Anna told me my Whisperer was out there. That she'd seem young, but mature before my eyes."

"Where is this Anna?" Reuben asked.

"With her Creator now." Logan's voice grew quiet.

Samantha touched his hand, and Jayden felt the friendship between them like warmth in a fireplace. "Maybe that means the Whisperer's talents pass to another once they die."

"How do you plan to find this new Whisperer?" Beck asked.

Logan scratched his chin. "Finding the Deliverer is one thing." He glanced at Jayden and smiled. "I think I can feel her presence—like a pull in my heart. But the Whisperer is trickier. I don't know where to start. We utilized all our leads in finding Anna."

"Try a library," Samantha suggested. "Salea has a large one. The history of the Deliverers of ages past will be there, or at Erinecath. Perhaps even Nivek. But Salea is closest. The histories might have information you can use to decipher where you're supposed to meet your Whisperer."

It was a good idea. Aside from the palace or ancient and lost halls of healing, Salea and Erinecath were the other homes to a wealth of books on every subject. Jayden had always wanted to visit an ancient library. Not that she would have thought of it.

"And the Deliverer?" Gavin asked. "Where do you feel . . . pulled?"

Jayden leaned close to Ethan and whispered, "Do you feel a pull, too? I mean, to someone else?"

He locked gazes with her, and the small smile that pulled the corner of his mouth didn't dim the intensity in his eyes. "Are you doubting my ability to protect you?"

"Of course not. I just mean—"

"The correct answer is 'never.'" The way he stared into her eyes pierced her soul. Did they all feel such a strong tie to her?

Logan's deep voice severed her eye contact with Ethan, which was just as well. It was starting to get very warm in the tent. Logan placed his finger in the middle of the map. "Something Anna said leads me to believe my daughter may be in the Forest of Legends, the Forest of Memories, or the Forest of Old. I know the Forest of Old is closer to Meese, where she's supposed to be, but I feel pulled back to the Forest of Legends. Since Salea is on the way, I'll take Ryan and Chloe there to be trained." Logan's fingers traced the locations on the map. "I'll stop in the library at Salea to see if I can find anything about the Whisperer that could help me. Samantha, I trust you can train and protect the younger siblings?"

She smiled, accentuating the beauty mark on her cheek. "You can count on me, Logan."

"Good. I need the rest of you to help me."

Beck slammed a heavy fist onto the butt of his axe. "You can count on us." The others murmured their agreement.

Gavin motioned to himself and Melanie. "Let us go to the Forest of Old."

"We can travel to the Forest of Memories." Beck motioned to himself and Reuben.

Reuben met Logan's eyes. "A war is coming. I hope we find the other Deliverers before it starts."

"We leave tomorrow. I can't waste any time," Logan said, and Jayden felt a sense of kinship flood through him. This was his family. "Thank you, friends."

"You have more news, don't you, Logan?" Beck squinted at his friend.

Logan smiled. "Yes. More of a riddle."

"Riddle?" Beck rubbed his hands together, and a smile spread across his scarred face.

Logan held out a small velvet bag. With a clatter of wood against wood, its contents fell to the table. Eight tokens rolled across the smooth surface of the map.

One stopped in front of Jayden, vibrated on the table, then lay flat in front of her. The picture carved into the wood was beautiful—a horse's head. Unable to take her eyes away, she reached for it. Five stars congregated around the horse's profile. Her finger nearly reached the token, almost touched the smooth-looking wood. Though it wasn't possible, it almost felt like the wooden token was reaching for her with . . . an emotion? A strange type of nostalgia.

Logan's hand bumped hers. He scooped it away before she could grasp it.

"These are the tokens the Whisperer gave me." Logan's deep voice interrupted her thoughts—her thought. She had just the one thought: touch the token. Jayden blinked and shook her head. She needed sleep.

"Souvenirs?" Reuben chuckled.

"Messages. She called them keys to be used when the time is right." Logan passed around one of the wooden tokens and shared what Anna had told him.

There was a carving on one side of two wolves howling together at the moon. Jayden felt emotion pulse through the wood. Sadness and hope mingling together, as if she was getting pieces of what Anna's husband, the Wielder, had felt when he carved the tokens.

"This one signifies the Protectors," Logan said. "Anna said it was the key to my protecting the Deliverers. That I would know when to use it."

"This next one represents our Whisperer," Logan continued to pass around the tokens and relay to them what Anna had said.

It was a tree on fire. Jayden touched it, and the feeling of sadness and pain pulsed into her. She passed it along quickly.

Logan continued, "And this one represents our Wielder."

It was a picture of a man surrounded by animals. His right hand rested on a wolf, and a beautiful bird like nothing Jayden had ever seen perched on his left arm. "What do the Whisperer and Wielder do? Why is it so important that we find them? Will they be . . . together?"

Melanie answered, "According to history, they unlock ancient secrets of the prophecy to help you defeat the Mistress. They know where to find the four thrones and how to obtain the Creator's power, which will help you keep the Mistress of Shadows in her prison. All records of what kind of power the Wielder possesses are lost, but stories say the Wielder can destroy the land. He can bring fire or turn water to blood. Many of the tales are embellished, but we know he's powerful.

"The Whisperer has an opposite, symbiotic type of power. She can heal the land, call memories from the trees. The Feravolk were born of the first Whisperer and Wielder. We get our connection to the earth through that lineage. Their powers directly fight the Mistress's ability to destroy the land. The Whisperer can tell you where to find the

Mistress's prison, the other Deliverers. I'm not sure how, but she has always had these answers."

Strange. But Jayden knew she had a link to them—the emotions in this wood. If it was any indication, the Whisperer was scared, innocent, familiar with pain. The Wielder was ashamed, confident, reluctant. They didn't sound like a very powerful team. Then again, Jayden was certain she didn't appear powerful, either.

Logan passed the next token around.

It was the one she'd seen before. "This is one of the Deliverers. Anna said she could sense the moods of others and calm them. She desired peace. Fast, resilient, and an ally in storm and water."

Ethan smiled at her. "Pretty accurate, huh?" He held the small object in his fingers. The horse-head token.

Someone had carved this for her before she'd been born. She touched it. And intense hope filled her. A strength. It felt like a congregating storm and fueled her desire to persevere. Breath left her lungs in a rush.

Ethan nudged her shoulder and his eyes met hers. "You okay?" he whispered.

She was supposed to be the one in tune with everyone else's emotions, but he seemed to be able to read hers. Did her talent affect him that way?

"Yes, thank you." She tore her gaze from him and passed the token along. Then she picked up the next one. The carving depicted a spiraled horn sprouting from the center of a plant. Not just any plant— *the* plant. The one that had healed Ryan from the black lion venom. "White alor."

Reuben took the token from her. "What's white alor?"

Melanie stole it from Reuben's hands. "It's an old-world plant with special healing qualities. I've never seen it. It is said that unicorns really like it."

"That's certainly a unicorn's horn in the picture," Ethan said.

Melanie looked closer at the coin. "How can you be sure?"

"I've seen one. Up close."

Melanie tapped her lip with her finger. "What did the Whisperer say about this Deliverer, Logan?"

"She's a Healer. Fierce and beautiful. She can sense the pure of heart and be aware of the truth of things. Difficult to tame, not trusting of men."

Melanie set the token down in front of her. "It all makes sense. A Healer's bond structure is for a unicorn. If you narrow down which animals are depicted on these tokens, I think they'll have the same attributes as the Deliverers the tokens represent. These pictures are the animals they'll bond to."

"I'm not sure all these animals exist." Samantha set the wooden trinket she held down on the table. "I have never heard of an eagle with ears. These are as big as a horse's."

Jayden looked at the center of the table at her token. "Mine's a horse. Can they predict storms better than other animals?"

"Do you have other Blood Moon-given talents?" Reuben raised his eyebrows.

Jayden looked at her lap. "Yes, but I don't see what they have to do with a horse. Except . . ."

Beck leaned closer. "Except?"

"I'm fast. And I can . . . I can tell what people are feeling. Emotionally. Horses are very good at that."

A bolt of surprise shot through her. Ethan's. His worry churned her stomach. She really needed to get her involuntary connection to him under control.

Jayden didn't look at him. "I rarely use it. But what about storm predicting? You really think that comes from an animal? I'm not even bonded."

Reuben folded his hands and set them on the table. "All those marked by the Blood Moon are Feravolk, and all Feravolk are born with gifts. After we bond, those gifts grow, mature, heighten. But they're there from the beginning. Children of the Blood Moon are just now reaching the age to bond in the last couple of years. We don't know what they're capable of. I personally think Children have extra talents."

"If they bond to the animals on the tokens, we'd best be careful." Beck set the token he held on the table, and with one thick finger pushed it back toward the center. "This one is a dragon." He rolled up his sleeve to reveal a scarred arm. "Fire does that."

Jayden looked at the coin. A ring of fire surrounded a scaly eye. Beck was right; he had to be. "I thought dragons were dangerous." She glanced away from Beck's mutilated skin.

"Oh, they are." Beck pulled his shirtsleeve back down and chuckled. "But so are wolverines."

Melanie picked up the token with the dragon's eye. "What did Anna say?"

"Secretive until he gets to know you, then intensely loyal. Wise. A friend of fire," Logan said.

She nodded. "I think we've figured it out. That means Beck's right. Better be careful."

Beck grunted. "I hope he's not the one Franco has."

Tension flared in the room again. Jayden concentrated on not letting it affect her. She uncurled her fists.

"Samantha is right." Gavin set the other coin on the table with a snap. "This is no eagle."

Ethan reached over and pulled the token close so Jayden could see it. This one bore the head of a golden eagle with tufted ears like a horned owl. "What did Anna say about him?"

"Strong, fast, and cunning. Protective of what is his—his family, his friends, his quest—things that are important to him."

"It's a gryphon," Ethan said. "My sister was always obsessed with them. Always trying to prove that they really existed."

"Makes sense," Melanie said as she looked at the carving.

Reuben picked up the one token Logan hadn't yet explained. The one carved with the picture of a snake. "What about this one?"

Logan growled like a wolf. "That one represents the traitor. The one who would hand us over to the Mistress."

"Traitor?" Reuben's eyes shifted back and forth. "I'm sorry, Logan, but don't you think we already know who the traitor is?"

Tension swelled and Jayden pressed her arm against Ethan's. He didn't pull away from her.

Beck narrowed his eyes. "You mean Rebekah?"

Logan glared at Beck. "I think we all know about Rebekah."

CHAPTER 20

TEACHING LOYALTY

Belladonna could hear the man's screams reverberating off the walls even after he'd stopped. He was weeping now. Broken. How perfectly marvelous. He feared her.

"Unshackle him," Rubius said.

Belladonna did as the wizard ordered, and the prisoner fell to the floor. Free of his chains, he tried to crawl across the floor toward her, slipping in his own blood. In the seven days she'd spent beating him, today he'd taken the worst.

"Please," he whispered. "Please, mistress. I'll do anything. Just—just heal me."

Belladonna glanced over her shoulder at the wizard, and he nodded once. It was time to complete the training.

"I'll heal you." She bent down next to the man. He moaned when she touched his back. She took the pain from him. Her own back burned as the whipping she'd given him passed into her body. She clenched her jaw tight.

Seven days of torture, and she had never once healed him completely. Today Rubius instructed her to do so. She dug deep with the healing, reaching to even the oldest of the wounds she'd inflicted. Her bones cracked and mended, her skin felt as though it tore open and healed from the inside out. She used all the strength he still possessed to aid with quicker healing.

When all the pain receded from her body, she towered over him. "Do you think you can serve me?"

Still trembling on the floor, he lifted his head. "Yes."

"Good, because there is something I want you know about me." Belladonna crouched near him and pushed his chin up with her finger. "I am more powerful than you."

"Yes, I know you are."

"You know?" Belladonna cocked her head. Then she chuckled. "I don't think you know. See, I am not just a Healer. I am an Originator. Do you know what that means?"

"No."

"It means I can do things against Healer code. Things Healers would die for if they tried. Would you like to see my great power?"

"Yes."

"Good." Belladonna gripped his hand and helped him to his feet. Then she placed her hand on his chest. "I have taken much pain from you, haven't I?"

"Y-yes, mistress, and for that I give you my allegiance."

"And in case you ever try to take your allegiance back, I just want you to know what I can do to you."

Belladonna released the pain—just a trickle of it at first. The wizard had been right. It felt magnificent, like power. It coursed through her like a rushing wave and crashed into the man's body. He screamed. She sent more pain through—whippings, burnings—all the things she had healed him of. The pain poured into him until the blood thundering in her own ears seemed as loud as his screams. The man fell away from her, breaking the connection, but the pain was still unleashed inside of him. She watched him writhe.

If the Healers of old had used their full range of powers, men never would have imprisoned them. Never would have taken them to bed against their will. Never would have used them as human shields.

"Enough." Rubius's haggard voice interrupted her thoughts.

She bent down and stroked the writhing man's ear, turning the pain off. He lay shaking on the ground.

"Very good," the wizard said. "Come, have some tea with me. We'll let him rest; then you can test his loyalty."

"Haven't I done that?"

"No. But I'll show you how."

Belladonna joined Rubius at the table and sipped her tea. "So I can give him that kind of pain any time?"

"Yes."

"But not to others?"

"You can only take pain they've experienced and use it. That is why, when you find one you want to break, you torture them first. You make sure they know what pain is. Then you heal them. Not fully at first. Just enough to take the edge off—until they begin to beg you to heal them. They'll profess their love to you because you alone set them free of the pain. That is your weapon. That is how you gain allegiance. Love."

Belladonna looked at the shivering man on the floor. He lay curled in a ball, whimpering. He did not look like he loved her. "He looks broken to me."

"It is the breaking that makes them yours. Now you know how to do it. Shall we see if he loves you?"

Belladonna cocked one eyebrow. This should be good. "Yes."

Rubius snapped his fingers. "Mario." An older man stepped forward from his position behind Rubius' chair. Rubius held a sword in each hand. He gave one to Mario. "Take this sword and lay it next to the man on the floor, please." Mario did so. Rubius held up the other weapon. "Now come and get this sword." Mario obeyed. "Now, kill the lovely Belladonna."

The chair scraped against the stone floor and clattered to the ground as Belladonna stood.

Mario raced at her with his weapon held high. She reached for her daggers, but Rubius had made her remove her weapons for torture sessions. He said it was in case the prisoner tried to get hold of one. The whip she'd used earlier was out of reach, but she had her hands, and she had every intention of using them.

The man she had been torturing grabbed the sword next to him on the floor. He charged Mario. Mario didn't stand a chance against this trained fighter. He drove Mario to the wall and stabbed him through. Mario got one good swipe and cut the man's stomach open.

When Mario slid down the cave wall, dead, the man turned to Belladonna. Holding in his entrails, he knelt in front of her, placing the sword tip on the ground and resting his other hand on its pommel. "Did I please you, Mistress?"

Rubius clapped slowly and stood. "Well done."

Belladonna stood open-mouthed. "You did please me."

"Good." The man groaned and fell to his side. The sword crashed against the ground next to him.

Belladonna knelt near him and placed her hand on his open stomach. Pain ripped through her as she healed him.

No one had ever saved her from anything. No one had ever taken a blow for her. She self-healed. Why would someone protect her? His hand curled around her wrist and she looked into his dark eyes. "What's your name?"

"Cain." His grip loosened as he closed his eyes in sleep.

"That," Rubius whispered behind her, "is how you teach loyalty."

Belladonna glanced at Mario's still form on the floor. Blood leaked out from him, a puddle of crimson seeping into the wood. Did Rubius not care that one so loyal to him would so willingly die? She regarded the wizard. If he cared so little for his own pawns, what did he care for her? For Cain?

She would not allow him to hurt her subjects.

If the time ripened, she would kill the wizard and take his power and knowledge. Then she would use it to take the Creator's power. After she freed the Mistress of Shadows.

CHAPTER 21

SUMMER'S END

Feravolk took their feast days seriously. Even out here in a temporary camp with only a few, they decided to celebrate Summer's End. Ryan was glad Logan had decided to stay the night. They needed a little fun in the midst of all the other heaviness.

There was music, fire, and the animals had caught enough food. The cinnamon-flavored root Thea had given him was working. And soon there would be sparring matches and dancing. The bonfire, as they called it, blazed almost as tall as him, but those who had built the camp assured him no one would see the light. It crackled and popped and snapped louder than the music sometimes. The glow showed everyone's happy faces. Ale flowed readily, adding to the cheery, loud mood, and the smell of wood and smoke was joined by pipe tobacco and cooked apples. Perfect night to forget about worries. If the night continued this well, maybe he'd challenge a few burly men to an arm wrestle.

Beck sat beside him on the downed log and slapped his hand against Ryan's back. "Logan tells me you mean to help protect the Deliverers?"

"Yes, sir, I do."

Beck's laugh was harsh and rough, like the man's hands. And his personality. His wolverine nosed around Ryan's boots. "No sudden movements. He's created a few well-intended scars." Beck pulled a piece of cheese from his pocket and gave it to the wolverine. "Here you go, Cenewig." He patted the beast's head.

Well-intended scars? The man was certainly blinded by loyalty.

That could be a good thing. Still, the wolverine made Ryan a little uneasy, especially when it stuck its nose in Ryan's lap and started sniffing. He waved his hand to shoo the wolverine away. A heavy paw slammed into Ryan's leg. He froze.

Cenewig eyed him askance, and a guttural sound rumbled in his throat. Those huge claws pressed without cutting, but Ryan got the message. His heart jumped into his throat as the wolverine opened his mouth. But Cenewig simply licked a stray breadcrumb off Ryan's pants, then ambled away.

Ryan released a breath and glanced at Beck.

The man just smiled, which distorted his puckered scar. "Cenewig won't take food from anyone but me. He likes you."

"Is that so?" Ryan's voice felt more strained than he'd hoped, but that only brought out Beck's booming laugh. He slapped Ryan's back once more, stood, and winked. "Here comes your pretty lady."

Ryan glanced over his shoulder. Jayden and his sisters all headed toward him.

"I like redheads, too," Beck said.

"Red—no, that's my sister."

Beck nodded, something of a gleam in his eyes. "Aye. Was teasing you is all. I'll leave you kids alone."

Jayden sat down next to him with a cooked apple and winced as she took a bite. Chloe, Kinsey, and Wren filled up the rest of the log.

"Burn your tongue?" Ryan chuckled. "You never wait long enough."

Jayden smiled and her nose crinkled.

"Where's Ethan?" Chloe asked.

Jayden tried not to seem interested in that question, which did nothing to boost Ryan's confidence. He'd lost her. And to his brother, no less. Part of him fumed. The other part . . . well, he'd seen how broken she had been when they thought Ethan was dead. How could he stand in the way of what she truly wanted?

Ryan tossed a stick into the fire. "Probably arguing with Melanie about whether or not he can participate in the sparring matches this evening." He shot Chloe a sideways look. "Or at least dancing."

Red colored her cheeks. "If you can't dance, what's the point of a feast day?"

Kinsey grabbed Chloe's arm and gave it a little shake. "Give Ryan his gift." Her eyes sparkled.

Wren plopped down next to him and beamed. "You'll love it. I can't wait to see you open it."

"Gift?" Ryan sat up straighter. "How on earth did you manage gifts? I didn't get you—"

"Relax." Chloe's smile brought a rare glitter to her eyes. "It was in the bundle Father gave me." She handed him his father's flute.

Ryan froze, staring at the instrument.

"Play something." Wren clapped her hands.

The flute felt so heavy in his hands. Worn where his father's fingers, shorter and stubbier than Ryan's, had rested when he played. He didn't know what to say. "There's already music."

"Play next, then." She beamed.

Ethan and Scout approached them. Scout nuzzled up to Wren first, wiggling his whole lithe body as she patted his golden head.

Ethan nodded toward Ryan's instrument. "It's about time you had one of those in your hands."

"Yes. Now you need a lute," Ryan said to his brother.

Ethan smiled, but this time there was a hint of sadness to it.

"Don't tell me you no longer play."

Ethan shook his head. "I'm sure I could."

"You traded music for fighting?" Chloe nodded to his sword.

"Something like that." Ethan's face became unreadable.

Kinsey bumped his shoulder with hers. "So? What was Melanie's verdict? Are dancing and sparring in your near future?"

His return smile was crooked. "Of course. And what makes you think I asked permission?"

Jayden seemed interested in her lap. Ryan curled his arm around her shoulders. "You okay?" He squeezed and she flinched.

She touched her arm and he remembered the gash from their fight with the giant.

His wound had already healed. "I'm sorry."

"Don't worry about it. You didn't do any harm." She smiled, but the look in her eyes gave him pause. Guarded. She was going to push him away. If she chose Ethan, would he lose her friendship?

"Play something." Wren's voice broke his thoughts.

The music had stopped for a moment. He brought the flute to his lips and played the first tune that came to mind. Jayden's favorite.

The instrument on his lips, his fingers against the holes, the sensation of music in his ears all flooded his senses as if he'd never experienced playing an instrument before. Surreal. It was just like the newness he'd experienced after waking from being poisoned with black lion venom.

Just thinking about that awful black lion venom made him shiver. It had been like burning from the inside out. After he'd been healed, it was like experiencing life for the first time.

Jayden touched his knee, offering comfort. Always in tune with his feelings.

A couple out dancing paused for a kiss. A kiss. Now his first kiss after waking from the venom was sure to be amazing. If Jayden's heart wouldn't be in it, then he'd save it for someone else.

Ethan held out his hand to Chloe. "May I have this dance?"

She looked at his extended hand and blinked. Crossed her arms. Did she have to be so predictable? *Oh, Chloe, just dance with him.*

Chloe persisted. "You want to dance with *me*, Ethan *Branor*?"

"You're welcome to dance by yourself, but it's easier with a partner."

Kinsey tipped her head toward the group of young Feravolk on the other side of the fire. "If you're so embarrassed to dance with your brother, ask one of those nice Feravolk archers."

Chloe placed her hands on her hips. "I'm not embarrassed. Besides, I'll tow at least one of them out there before the night is over. And Ethan is not my brother."

"Chloe." Kinsey nearly whispered her name, but Chloe felt the full disapproval—her flinching made that apparent.

She faced Ethan, her face flushed. "It's just that you were a friend first. It's hard to think of you as anything different. I didn't mean anything by it."

"It's all right, Chloe." Ethan's forgiving smile didn't falter.

Her eyelashes fluttered rapidly, and she cupped her hands together under her chin, as if Kinsey's admonishment embarrassed her. "I—I didn't mean anything by it," she repeated, looking so small standing in front of Ethan.

He smiled and held out his hand. "Prove it."

Her deep breath spoke of relief, and she stood tall and grabbed his hand, her green eyes sparkling. "If I must."

Ethan led her out by the fire. Kinsey and Wren joined them.

Ryan welcomed the gentle summer wind on his face. Music mingled with the popping and crackling of the bonfire, becoming part of its harmony. The joyful faces of his family caressed by the warm orange glow and the softness of Jayden's dark hair against his arm were enough to bring contentment to this last moment before he took his life into a new direction.

A direction he wasn't ready for.

He'd had his first taste of a fight, and it wasn't anything like the guts-and-glory stories Norm Grotter, the crazy old man with a missing ear, told. The metallic tang of blood still wet his tongue when he thought about lifting a sword. Still, there was no other choice. He had to protect his sisters. If only his father had prepared him for this instead of refusing to talk about his role in the wars. Then maybe Ryan wouldn't have sought old Norm's tales.

When his song ended, one of the other Feravolk men played something. The tune was familiar. Perhaps they played the same songs in Moon Over Water as the city folk. He glanced at Jayden. "Would you like to dance?"

"Are you sure?" Her gaze flicked to his leg, where the Morningstar had sliced him.

He stood and waved it off, then extended a hand. "Of course."

"Then I'd love to." She practically beamed. Maybe he still had a chance after all. He led her out among the other dancers.

The night grew older, the fire warmer, and the dancing slower. Jayden and Ryan finally returned to their seats. His sisters must all still be out there. Chloe was. If music was playing, she was dancing. He spotted her on the arm of a tall fellow.

Jayden's head rested on his shoulder. He looked at her, but her eyes weren't on him or the dancers. They'd found Ethan, and he was talking to Logan and Gavin. Disappointed, Ryan fingered his flute.

Ethan joined them all too soon. He sat down stiffly on the log next to Jayden.

"Too much dancing?" Ryan asked.

"Listening to Melanie might have been a good idea." He shrugged. "But Chloe needed this."

"They all did." Ryan agreed. His poor sisters. Torn from everything they'd ever known. All of them had lost so much.

Oh no. No dwelling on the sad stuff.

"Listen, Ethan. What Chloe said: she doesn't hate you. She loves you like the rest of us. She just—"

"I'm used to it by now." He smiled at least. "She's one of those conundrums."

"I can't argue with that." Ryan lifted the flute to his lips. He played a lively tune this time.

The music went on, and the bonfire was nothing more than a small cook fire when Wren and Kinsey returned, slumping together on the log, Wren with her head on Kinsey's lap. It was just Chloe out there now.

Ethan nudged Kinsey's shoulder. "You have fun with Dalton?"

Kinsey sighed. "Chase. I danced the night away with Chase."

"Oh, my mistake." Ethan chuckled.

"What about you? Have fun with that pretty brunette?"

"Sure. She's a good dancer."

"Did you kiss her?"

Ethan laughed like someone caught off guard. "No."

"No?" Ryan faced his brother. "Ethan, what's wrong with you? She's beautiful."

Jayden looked at him askance and heat crept up Ryan's neck. "I—that's—I mean—"

She just laughed and the sound was lyrical.

"I know what's wrong with you, Ethan." Kinsey wagged a finger in his face. "You're too shy to ask the girl who caught your fancy." Kinsey pursed her lips and crossed her arms in a typical Granden sister pose, daring Ethan to prove her wrong.

Next to Ryan, Jayden tensed.

Ethan dropped his head, but it didn't hide his shy smile.

"Someone caught your eye?" Ryan hoped against the odds that it wasn't Jayden.

Ethan laughed nervously. "No."

Kinsey pointed her finger at his nose. Ethan's eyes crossed as he looked at it. Her arms flew up. "How would she even know you're interested if you never look at her?" She was getting a tiny bit fierce, and her voice was starting to carry.

"Kinny." Ethan cocked an eyebrow at her. "Have you been drinking ale?"

She shook her head wildly, then put her hands on Ethan's shoulder to steady herself. "Who spun the log?"

Ethan looked at sleeping Wren and sighed. "I think you both have."

Kinsey put a finger to her lips. "Shh."

Ryan groaned. "Kinsey, really? You gave some to Wren? If Chloe finds out—"

Kinsey shook her finger back and forth. "She won't. Besides, Wren gave it to me."

Now *that* he believed.

"Off to bed, I think." Ethan stood and scooped Kinsey into his arms. She yelped and held tightly to his neck. Ethan looked at Ryan and smiled. "I'll be back for the other one."

Jayden's eyes lingered on Ethan's retreating form.

Ryan tucked a stray hair behind her ear. "I'll take Wren to bed so my fool brother doesn't pull out his stitches carrying both of them."

"I can take Wren."

"No. You shouldn't be carrying anyone either." His ability with a sword was lacking. The others were picking up too much of his slack and getting hurt for it.

Her forehead wrinkled. "You okay?"

"Just worried about tomorrow," he lied.

"You'll be fine."

"I know." He scooped up Wren.

Jayden smiled sadly. "I'll be fine, too. I've got Logan and Ethan."

"I've seen them fight, but it doesn't douse my worry."

"You haven't seen anything. Ten men were after Ethan and me. He killed them all."

Killed. Ryan swallowed. The picture of the giant's head flashed in his memory again. The ugly pockmarked face flying off the man's neck with a stream of red following from it. The sickening way his sword hitched against the man's neck bones before slicing through. Every night that vision haunted his dreams. Would he be able to kill again? Would it come to that?

"It will."

"Ryan?" Jayden's voice tore him away from his thoughts.

He smiled at her; another lie. "Still, I'll feel better when I'm with you."

"Me, too." She kissed his cheek, and he took Wren to the tent.

After he dropped his sister off, he headed away from everyone else and breathed the cool night air. He pulled the root from his pocket and snapped off a piece. That voice had to stop surprising him.

The fire dwindled, and wolves howled a welcome to the deepest part of the night. Ryan wasn't ready for it to end. Morning would bring change. Change he wasn't sure he was ready to embrace. He popped the tiny piece of root into his mouth and someone behind him coughed. He whirled around. Logan.

Ryan stood straighter.

"You'll be ready in the morning?" Logan asked.

Ryan nodded.

"Good. If you change your mind—"

"I won't."

CHAPTER 22

LOVE YOU MOST

The sky was gray and cold. Ethan picked up his sack and nudged Ryan's bed with his foot.

Ryan rolled over and grumbled something.

Ethan chuckled. "You deciding to stay after all?"

"I'm up." Ryan sat up and rubbed his eyes. "You realize it's not even light?"

Ethan tossed his brother a shirt. "Logan will be looking for ways to leave you behind, I'm sure."

"Are you?"

Ethan stopped, hand almost to the tent flap. He faced Ryan, who was pulling on his boots. Why in all of Soleden would he ask that question? Of course Ethan would want his brother trained. Of course he would want Ryan to have the ability to defend himself. Of course . . . oh, of course.

Jayden.

Apparently he hadn't done a very good job of hiding his feelings.

Ethan cleared his throat. "I think you need to learn to protect your loved ones. I wouldn't take that opportunity from you."

Ryan finished lacing his second boot and stood. He picked up his satchel. "Good. Because you need someone to protect you." His lopsided grin filled his face. "You have this . . . thing for sacrificing yourself."

Ethan tried to laugh, but Ryan was more right than he probably knew. He lifted the tent flap and walked out. "Only for very special people." Or as Jayden called them, *very good friends*.

Ryan followed. "And I didn't make the cut?"

Ethan squeezed Ryan's shoulder and smiled his best teasing smile. "Sorry, brother."

Ryan's face turned serious, and he slapped his hand over Ethan's, anchoring it down. "I never thanked you. For saving my life. Twice."

Ethan shook his head. "You don't need—"

"I know. But thank you." He patted Ethan's hand, then walked forward to meet Logan and a couple of slump-shouldered redheads.

Ethan swallowed. At least they would be safe here. And Ryan and Chloe would be safe with One Eye. Soon he'd have only Jayden to protect, and he'd protect her with his all.

Saying goodbye to his sisters was harder than expected. Wren buried her face in his neck and hugged him tight. Kinsey stood in front of him, lips twisted in a half frown.

He touched her chin. "Hey, what's that for? Keep your head up."

Her lips quivered. She took a deep breath and steadied her breathing. "I love you most."

Ethan's heart hitched when he heard the words their father had said to each of them every time he left for weeks to go to a different town for market.

"You're quite mistaken." He offered the next line in the ritual.

"It must be true. You've shed no tears." Now she held the hint of a smile.

"Oh, but inside my heart is breaking."

Her breathing quivered and she threw her arms around him. "I wanted to come with you."

"I'm sorry, Kinny." He squeezed her close. "It's too dangerous. But Samantha will train you. And you'll be here."

"And you'll come back?"

How could he promise such a thing? "Of course."

He tilted up her chin again and her wet eyes met his. "Good. Because I never want to lose you again."

"You won't." Not if he could help it. "Now, you take care of the others, okay?"

She nodded and wiped away her tears. "And you take care of Ryan and Chloe."

"Always." He smiled, and that brought out the sparkle in her eyes. Then he turned to go. The others were already waiting.

The sun had reached its zenith now as they trudged through the forest. Ethan didn't mind the slower pace Logan kept. He'd said it was because he was waiting to hear what the wolves and Scout saw up ahead before walking into it, but Ethan had the feeling Logan was taking it easy on him. Every movement still ached, but not nearly as bad. His wounds would be nothing but scars soon.

He was far enough behind that he thought it might be safe to pull out the stone Connor had given him in the palace. Just to have a peek.

Maybe Connor had some news for him on the whereabouts of that poor girl. Not that he wanted to add another person to rescue. He just couldn't stop thinking that he had to. If not him, then who?

The girl appeared in the stone first.

Her eyes were so big and round. Something clearly had her frightened. A fire burned in his blood. The need to rescue her grew. If only he knew where she was.

A pair of cold, green eyes appeared. *You? I can see where you are.*

Heart pounding, Ethan covered the stone and pocketed it. Who was that?

"Ethan?" Jayden's voice startled him.

He looked up. "What's wrong?"

She eyed him askance. "I was just about to ask you the same thing. Are you all right? Do you feel something?"

He shook his head, trying not to look like a young boy holding a slingshot near a fallen bird. "You seem worried."

"Me?" She fell into step with him.

"Yeah. Ryan told me you had a run-in with Thea."

She looked at the ground. "Oh."

"Is she what has you all shaken up?"

She looked up at him and he trapped her gaze. Her eyes squinted, as if she wanted to bolt, and she shook her head really fast.

"Are you seriously lying to me right now? Don't you trust me?"

Her chest hitched on a breath. "I do. I just . . ."

Clearly she wasn't going to tell him. Just as well. She should probably be talking to Ryan about it. "Hey, don't let her get to you."

She frowned as she nodded, focusing on the ground in front of her. Even so, she tripped on a tree root. He caught her arm.

Pink flushed her cheeks. "I'm good at that."

He laughed. "You are."

It finally brought a smile to her face. Ryan glanced over his shoulder at them, and Ethan stared at his brother. Twice now he'd been caught with that "slingshot."

The smallest twinge of heat flickered in his chest. A threat? For whom? And why did it seem so far off?

Ethan picked up the pace, hoping to get everyone walking closer together. Maybe whatever this dim threat was, it would dissipate if he put more distance between whatever it was and the people he was trying to protect.

The low pulse of heat remained, though. Strange.

Then the heat exploded.

A muffled scream came from behind him.

Ethan spun around. Shielded Jayden.

A twig snapped loud enough to betray that whatever stepped on it was no squirrel. Ethan set down his satchel and pulled out his bow. He removed three arrows from the quiver at his waist and held them in his right hand.

"Ethan?" Ryan's voice seemed hazy as his senses sharpened around the trees. Movement. Noise. He searched for them. Heat shot through his chest. The threat loomed.

"Ethan." That voice was Logan's, demanding information.

His mind raced to recall his surroundings as he kept his gaze trained on the trees to the north. Something was there. The threat pulsed from that direction.

The heat in his chest grew. Another threat. Jayden was in danger. Ryan was in danger. Chloe was in danger, but there was someone else. Who? And how was he supposed to protect all of them?

"We're surrounded," he whispered.

Logan stood just behind him. "I called Westwind back. He says he smells the queen's filth riding on the wind."

That jolted his heart to beat faster. How was he going to react to his instincts, bark orders for them to follow, and save everyone? He couldn't. And which threat was he supposed to listen to first? He couldn't trust his talent now, not if he wasn't sure which person he was protecting. It hadn't worked when his parents needed him, and it wouldn't now.

Ethan closed his eyes and listened. A muffled whine drew closer. The heat pulsed in his chest. "There's no time to run."

The queen's men stepped through the trees to Ethan's left. He'd been wrong pinpointing the sound, but not wrong about the threat. His heart dropped to his stomach as Scarface walked into view with his sword at Kinsey's throat.

Ethan would recognize his enemy's scarred face anywhere, but he hadn't remembered the man's green eyes. Green. The same as the eyes in the stone. How could he be so stupid? Because of him, Scarface had found them. Found Kinsey.

His heart was like a smithy's hammer.

"Let's be reasonable, shall we?" Scarface smiled.

"Kinsey!" Chloe screeched.

Soldiers closed in from all around. The threat pulsed. Ethan listened.

Scarface hollered and ripped his hand off of Kinsey's face. Ethan saw blood on his palm.

"I'm sorry, Ethan," Kinsey whimpered. "I wanted to learn to fight. Please forgive me. I—" Scareface's hand clamped over her mouth again, cutting her off.

Ethan's heart choked him. "There's nothing to forgive, Kinny."

"Turn over the Deliverer, and I'll give you this little pup back, dog." Scarface snarled. "I saw her red hair and thought she was the one I saw you with before, but I see you're attached to more than one."

Hand over Jayden? Never. Ethan raised his new bow, thanking Morgan for her gift. "Let her go."

"Or what?"

His insides screamed at him to do something. Part of him was being pulled to shoot the man holding Kinsey, the other part wanted him to spin around and take out another.

"Put down your weapon or she dies," Scarface said.

"No." Chloe's voice was wild.

"You can't have her." Ethan made his voice hard.

"If that's the way you want it." Scarface pressed his knife into Kinsey's throat. A trickle of blood wet the blade, and her muffled cry leaked through his fingers. "You move, she dies."

Ethan looked into Kinsey's eyes. So big and wide and bright. Tears pooled over her eyelids and dripped onto her captor's hand. Ethan nodded once. She blinked in response. She understood. She'd be safe. He'd rescue her.

Heat pulsed. He needed to take out the man with the knife, Scarface, and the archer trained on Jayden. Which one first?

Another drip of blood trickled out on Kinsey's neck where the blade pressed.

"You can take me." Jayden walked forward.

"No!" Logan's deep voice overpowered Ethan's with the same answer.

"Then you've made your choice. Franco promised to take those you love."

Ethan's talents surged. He tuned in. Spun and shot the archer behind them. That man fell and he turned toward the pulse. His talent pulled him right. He fired his arrow and a man with an arrow aimed at Chloe fell. The new burning pulse wanted him to take out Kinsey's captor, but someone aimed an arrow at Jayden.

Jayden's attacker was closer. He could get both. He shot his arrow at that man first, then he grabbed another arrow.

Ethan turned.

A smirk curved the scar on Scarface's cheek, and he looked right into Ethan's eyes. "Say goodbye." He stabbed Kinsey clean through the middle.

Red bloomed on her clothes.

Blood dripped off the blade.

The loudest sound in Ethan's ears was her sharp exhale.

Not Kinsey. His heart wrenched.

Chloe's pained cry dulled in the air.

Ryan's yell echoed as if in a distant cave.

"Take the Deliverer; kill the others!" Scarface's voice drowned out everything.

Then nothing. Ethan heard nothing else as he raced forward to catch Kinsey's falling body.

She crumpled into his arms. So light. So warm. So limp.

"Kinny? Talk to me."

Scout shot between him and another man. The canines had arrived too late.

Logan's sword clanged above Ethan's head. A threat for Jayden still pulsed, but the heat didn't burn. She could have taken care of herself. His talent had failed him. Too much to listen to. He couldn't protect them all.

He lifted Kinsey's body up to his chest. "Kinny."

"Love you most . . . brother." She fell limp in his arms, unseeing. Her chest didn't move.

"No!" His scream scorched his throat. This couldn't be happening. Couldn't be real. Not Kinny. She was so young. And he'd promised to teach her to defend herself.

The sounds of fighting grew silent. Ethan stood. Only three soldiers remained. Westwind had one pinned to the ground. The other one clashed his sword against Logan's. Scarface stood, waiting.

Ethan rushed at his enemy. Heat pumped through every vein now, not just his chest. He'd tried to keep it quelled, though the embers were always there, waiting to be fanned into flame. This was no threat taking over. This was the familiar heat of revenge. And Scarface would die.

Ethan faced his enemy. "You killed an innocent child."

"I killed her? You knew the price. You weren't willing to pay."

Ethan clashed his weapon against Scarface's. Pushed. His strength fueled him. He kicked the man into a tree and Scarface's arms spread to break his fall. Ethan brought down his blade and it sliced into Scarface's stomach. Deep. He screamed.

Now he would die. Ethan swung his sword, but Scarface's look changed to a smirk. He held out a glass vial filled with dark liquid and dropped it. Purple smoke rose from the ground like a funnel cloud.

Ethan's sword cut through it, hit something hard and sent a jolt through his arms.

The smoke cleared. Nothing. No one. Ethan's sword imbedded into a tree. He yanked it free and turned to see the remaining soldier. Logan held his sword up to the man, but Ethan didn't care. He walked up to him and swung his weapon. The soldier's head thudded to the ground.

CHAPTER 23

AN OLD FIRE

Jayden turned away from the gruesome death in front of her. Ethan had become that killer she'd seen on the hill. The red hill. That's what she called it in her memory. He'd killed ten men without blinking. But this man hadn't been a threat anymore—he'd been a prisoner.

This kill had been from rage. Hadn't it?

Chloe pressed her hands over her gaping mouth. Her wide eyes framed her fingers. Ryan had cringed, squeezing his eyes closed. The same horror and surprise pulsed through them.

Jayden peered back over her shoulder at Ethan. He stood there, chest heaving.

The skin behind her ears tingled. Sorrow with the strength of a tornado tore into Jayden. It joined rage, like a tide pool filling. She tried to choke the emotion away, gripped her daggers tight.

"Jayden." Logan touched her elbow, and she realized her knuckles were white. She released her weapons.

Ethan dropped his sword and fell to his knees next to Kinsey's body. He pulled her onto his lap.

Chloe rushed to his side. She wrenched his shoulder. "Is she—?"

Ethan's wet eyes looked into hers. "I'm sorry. I—"

"No." Ryan dove next to his sister. He scooped Kinsey into his arms, pulling her body from Ethan. Eyes blazing, he stared at his brother.

"Ryan, I'm sorry. I thought I could protect her. I thought—"

Ryan curled Kinsey's body into his chest, shutting Ethan out. Chloe cupped Kinsey's head in her hands. Tears dripped off her face.

"Ethan." Jayden touched his shoulder. "It's not your fault." A rock sank into her stomach, pulling her heart with it. All of this was her fault. She hadn't turned herself in to Franco.

Ethan pulled away from her as if she'd burned him, and his guilt hit her like a lightning bolt. "It *is* my fault."

He walked away.

Jayden started to follow but Logan caught her, shaking his head slightly.

She wanted nothing more than to comfort him.

Ryan stormed past her.

Jayden pulled her trapped arm. "Logan, please let me follow Ryan. I—"

"Let them be." He released her, and she knelt next to Chloe who hunched over Kinsey on the ground. A tear leaked out of her eye. "Westwind says there are more soldiers." Logan's voice was firm, quiet. "You stay with Chloe. I'll send Ryan back your way."

Jayden stood. "Logan, Ethan is in no shape to go with you for a fight."

"Ethan can keep it contained. You stay with the others." Logan stalked off.

Jayden placed her hand on Chloe's shaking back. So he'd noticed the emotions playing with her. Or at least noticed that she wasn't herself. She had to get it under control. Bury her emotions. Be a warrior. Be stone. Like Ethan.

"It's not fair." Chloe sobbed. "She was so young."

Jayden closed Kinsey's eyelids over those lifeless eyes. It wasn't Kinsey anymore. No warmth of emotion emanated from her. Just a cold nothingness. A void where so much life should be.

A rustle in the brush caused her to turn, hand on her dagger's hilt.

"It's me." Ryan put his hands up.

She replaced her weapon and ran to him, wrapping her arms around him. He held her so tight she could barely breathe. He stroked her hair as he held her.

"I'm so sorry," she whispered.

"It wasn't your fault. It was Franco's fault. We all did everything we could."

She pulled back and looked into his eyes. The storm raged, though he looked nothing more than sad. "Ethan?"

"He won't listen to me." Ryan's eyes scanned her face.

A pang hit her heart—Ryan's. Why?

Ryan's throat bobbed. "He'll listen to you."

Ethan ground his teeth together. He didn't need more people coming after him telling him it wasn't his fault. He turned, ready to tell someone off, but Logan approached.

"Westwind says there are three more." He motioned west.

Ethan grabbed his bow and stood. "Not for long."

He followed Logan into the woods to where the scent of smoke filtered through the trees. Three more. He took three arrows from his quiver and pulled the bowstring back.

Logan stood next to him, hand on his sword hilt. "I've told the wolves to stand down."

Ethan stepped out of the trees into full view. The three men stood.

He called on his speed. It shot through him with such electricity the pulse made his heart trip through a beat. Fire fueled it. An old fire. Revenge. He embraced it. His talent urged him to protect himself from the man on the right first. Ethan ignored it and aimed his arrow at a different target.

One arrow flew. Smacked into the man's chest. The man fell, limp. The second arrow shot through another man's eye. The third soldier ran at Ethan—the one his talent had warned him to take out first.

The quiet throb of a threat in his chest warned him. Revenge said let him come. Revenge said relish a fight. Revenge burned. He wanted this. Needed it. This man would die. Ethan dropped his bow.

"Ethan?" Logan's voice was distant.

The enemy drew his sword. Ethan spun. Slashed. His blade hit bone and he called his strength. It fueled him. He yanked out his weapon and buried it into the man's heart.

But Kinsey's blood was still on his hands. Another dead body hadn't changed the fact that he'd failed to protect her. He'd failed because his stupid talent gave him too many orders at once. How was he supposed to listen?

But he'd been the one to endanger her in the first place. Scarface had found him because of that stupid stone.

Someone touched his shoulder.

Ethan spun, sword ready, but it was Logan.

He'd backed up, hands in surrender. "Can I count on you to hold it together, Ethan?"

Could he? The fire of revenge had taken over his talent. He couldn't let that continue. He shook his head, trying to push back all the anger. Then he took a deep breath. "Yes."

"Good. Let's get out of here."

They made it back to where the others were, and Ethan choked when he saw Kinsey's body again. Jayden rushed up to him. Hugged him so tight. Seemed to hold his sadness with her arms.

Chloe's wet eyes met his. "How did he get away?"

"I've seen that trick before." Logan touched the shard of broken glass on the ground with the tip of his sword. "This was nothing but bottled magic. They aren't talents. I've seen Idla create a funnel cloud with the same purple smoke."

Jayden turned toward him, but left her arm around Ethan. "Spells? Aren't those dark magic?"

"They belong to those associated with the Mistress of Shadows. Those who follow her." Logan clenched his jaw.

"Then there's no way we can predict what power he can wield at any given time. No way to tell who he's given spells to."

Ryan looked into Logan's eyes. "Or how long the spell lasts."

"Unless we can find a way know what types of spells—"

"A Whisperer would have these abilities to discern," Chloe said.

Logan nodded. "More reason to find her before Franco does."

He picked up Kinsey's limp form and Ethan's heart squeezed. Killing only took the pain away for the moment. When everything rushed back to him, his head seemed so clouded. And an ache ripped through his chest. He wanted to let his knees buckle. He wanted to fall to the ground and curl up into a ball. He wanted to be done with all of this.

Jayden rubbed his back, then she turned and followed Logan, hugging Chloe.

Scout leaned against his leg, eyes round and ears laid back. Ethan patted the dog's head. "I'm coming, buddy. I just need a second to cool off." His dog stayed with him, as was Scout's way. He never left Ethan alone if he sensed any distress. Ethan smiled and crouched down, letting Scout nuzzle into him—something he didn't know he'd needed until right then.

He took a breather leaning against a tree, and Scout settled next to him, head on his paws, eyes closed. Ethan reached into his pocket and curled his fist around the stone before he even realized what he was doing. He pulled the object from his pocket and drew his arm back to throw it. But it seemed to whisper his name. He stilled his arm and unwrapped the stone. Two round, blue eyes peered back at him. Then he saw a familiar face. *"Took you long enough, Soldier. Don't say his name."*

How could Thea know he planned to seek out Connor?

Her smile was sleek. *"You look terrible."*

"I'm not in the mood." He almost said her name but stopped himself.

Golden eyes appeared in the rock followed by Connor's face. *"I don't know how she does it. Are you going after the girl?"*

"I don't need anyone else to protect." Ethan's voice broke on that last word.

"Well, she needs you." A picture of the poor girl surfaced in the stone. Her hazel eyes met his through the stone. Did she know he was there? She sat curled in a corner, dirty. Scars covered her arms. Every protective instinct swelled in his chest. He had to find her. The pull started yanking his heartstrings.

"I can't protect anyone else. If I do, those in my care are in trouble."

"Her name is Quinn."

Quinn. She had a name now. Ethan closed his eyes.

"You need her," Thea whispered.

Ethan covered the stone. No. He couldn't even keep those in his care safe. How could he add another? But he looked at Kinsey's blood on the ground. Another innocent girl didn't deserve to die. "I'll do it."

Connor stared back at him. *"She's at a place called Castlerock. Do you know it?"*

"The old ruins. I thought that place was fiction."

"It's just well hidden."

Something warm and soft brushed his hand. He fondled Scout's ears and snuck the stone back into his pocket.

"Thanks for sticking with me, buddy. Tell Logan I'm catching up now."

"Ethan?" Jayden's soft voice sounded behind him.

He didn't want to face her. He'd seen how she looked at him after he'd killed that man. He'd scared her. All of them. He'd made a decision. Scarface had a potion that took him who knew where. He couldn't risk another person who'd seen them getting away. He—it didn't matter.

"Ethan?" She touched his back.

He swallowed and faced her. Dried blood from a scrape on her face reminded him of the battle. Of Kinny. He squeezed his eyes shut, but her lifeless expression still stared back at him.

That ache crushed him from the inside.

Jayden's warm hand cupped his cheek. Creases marred her forehead as she stared at him. She pulled him in and hugged him close. "I'm sorry."

He hugged her tight, but the words "thank you" got caught in his throat and never made it out.

CHAPTER 24

LIFE AND DEATH

Serena moved a moss-covered vine and stepped through a cluster of trees, eyes scanning her surroundings. No one would see her coming, of course, since she walked in her invisible form, but if anyone was watching, they might notice random vines swinging. This very spot had been the foundation for a healing house sometime in the past age. Now it was a group of abandoned stones stacked in the center of a copse of trees.

But that didn't stop the people from coming.

She didn't sense anyone else. It seemed all those who had come here for healing today had left, but there were more than there had been last time. It seemed word had spread that this healing house had a guardian Healer again. Hopefully word would not get back to the leaders of her clan. She stilled a shudder. If her Circle found out, what would they do? Ban her from coming?

At least this place was far from the Forest of Legends, making it more difficult for word to get back there.

Dash sat beside her and nuzzled her. *"You need a moment? I can make you invisible so you can rest."*

She snuggled into his silky fur and stared at the ruins, recalling the first time she'd ever been here. It wasn't that long ago. A few months. Dash had also been with her then. The house had called out to her, sensed her somehow. When the people came here, the remains of the house had reached out to any willing Healers in the area. Like a seedling growing beneath a stone, searching for the light, these people hoped a Healer would come to their aid.

And she and Dash had answered the call.

"I found them." Dash's voice had carried over her bond.

"How many?"

"Serena, I don't know how you're going to help them all. I'll have to help you."

"No. Dash, people finding out that Healers still exist is one thing. But unicorns? I don't think they're ready to keep that a secret. Your kind was just as hunted as mine." She followed the pull of his bond up a hill and looked down to see the group of people camped below. There had to be two dozen. And the pain inside her throbbed. Some were sick, others injured. They had come here looking—no, hoping—for a Healer.

Had any Healers visited these poor people in the last hundred years? Not likely. And yet they still came here, seeking hope.

The Circle might have her head for this, but she wasn't about to back down. *"Maybe I should build another healing house here."*

"The Circle would keep you confined to a cell if they knew this was your secret thought." Dash made himself visible. *"I'm going to help you."*

"Dash—"

"Someday you'll understand how much you mean to me, young one."

There he went calling her that again. She stared into the unicorn's wise eyes and made herself visible. *"You're the only family I have."*

He nuzzled her arm. *"You've gotten good at hiding yourself."*

"Your insistence that I can do everything you can has come in handy. At least the other Healers don't know about that trick."

"You'd think, since we reside in the Valley of the Hidden Ones, that they would have figured it out."

She smiled. *"Oh, the trouble I'd be in. All those nights in the kitchen after hours."*

"Not to mention all the books you've borrowed from personal collections."

"I gave them back." She suppressed a giggle.

Dash snorted. *"Come on, we have some travelers to heal."* He trotted down the hill and Serena followed him.

A few people looked up at his shimmering form and pointed.

Murmurs spread through the trees like a hushed wind through leafy boughs. Then gasps, pounding heartbeats. Women pressed their hands against their chests. Some approached Dash, others withdrew.

As they walked nearer, the people pawed at them, cried, touched Serena's cloak. Her hair. Her face. The hope in their eyes warred with the sorrow.

"We've come to help you, but we need you to keep this a secret," she said.

All of them seemed to agree. One by one, Serena and Dash healed the sick and injured women and children. One by one, they headed home with smiling faces and dancing steps. All vowing to secrecy. All with glimmering eyes that touched Serena's heart.

One cloaked figure seemed to back away from the clustering crowd of women and children. Serena tilted her head to try and get a better look. The person looked left and right, likely about to bolt. Serena moved closer.

"Serena, tread carefully." Dash's warning resounded in her head.

"I feel your pain," she said to the person. "Your wound is . . . older."

"I—I didn't expect to walk in on this."

Serena gasped. *"It's a man."* She stepped closer, her heart pounding. Nothing drew her to this man like she'd been drawn to Ethan, but the urge to heal was stronger than her fear of him.

"Serena—"

"I don't think he means to harm me. He's scared." She held out her hand to stop his retreat. "Please don't run. I can help you."

"No one can help me." He held out his hands. Both were wrapped in cloth.

She breathed deep. "I can."

"Please, don't come any closer."

They were out of sight of Dash and the others now. It could have been his plan to lure her out here. "Are you going to hurt me?"

"No."

Truth.

He shook his head and backed away another step. A stick snapped and he fell backward. One arm went back to catch his fall, the other he held tight to his body. A flicker of pain flared in the arm he'd used to catch himself.

Serena blinked back tears. Compassion flooded her. She risked another, closer step and held out her hand to help him up. "I *can* help you. But you have to let me." Or be unconscious, but that wasn't a detail she was going to share.

He let out a shuddered breath and removed the hood from his head. Serena gasped at the sight of him. Tight, scarred skin covered half of his head. Distorted his features. A patchwork of scarred skin and scattered clumps of dark hair covered his scalp.

Serena reached for the ruined limb. "You're not fully healed. Not everywhere, at least."

"What does that mean?"

Serena knelt next to him. "Your skin here isn't healing."

"But here?" He touched his face.

"That has scarred. Your body completed the healing."

"So you can't do anything about it?"

"We take a vow to never harm with our powers. If a Healer breaks her vow, her life is forfeit. In order for me to heal the effects of this wound, I'd have to reverse the damage. I'd have to make you feel it all again so I can take it away."

"That's considered using your power to harm me? Look at me. I lost my whole family. Fire nearly killed me, and you're worried that making me feel it all again will do harm? Not if it heals me in the end, it won't. So tell me, what makes you so different that you can help me?"

The truth of his words seemed to strike something in her heart that resounded like a plucked lute string. *Dash, I'm about to do something I've been told not to.*

"Wait for me, please. The last of these people are leaving."

She held her hand out for the young man. "What's your name?"

"Luc."

"Well, Luc, I'm not like other Healers. I tend to make my own decisions."

"I thought you would die if you broke your code."

"I will. But I think you're right. If you're willing to relive the pain, I don't believe I'll be using my powers to harm you."

He breathed deep, tightened his jaw. His eyes focused on something behind her, and Serena felt Dash's familiar presence. He pressed his nose against her shoulder. *"I don't know how much strength you'll need for this."*

"What if I'm sentencing us to death?"

"Is it worth saving his life? These burns won't heal on their own."

"It is."

Luc unwrapped his left hand and placed dark, swollen fingers in her hand. "Do it. Please."

Serena closed her eyes. She delved deep into the memory of the wound. Past the death and the crumbling. New skin started to regrow. Tendon and muscle began to repair. The infection blazed. Dash pressed his head harder into her back, filtering his strength into her. Heat seemed to course through her whole body. All around her. Luc's skin regrew as ugly, diseased, broken, and seared flesh.

Further back into the wound's memory she went until she felt two strings pulling her. One led to more pain, to the ultimate reliving of this terrible nightmare. The other led to a place she knew—healing. She'd reached it. But she felt so weak. Her strength waned.

Luc screamed. The pain filtered into him. That wasn't supposed to happen during the healing part. She was losing her hold on him. If she lost it, he'd be slammed with the full injury again.

"Don't let go now, Serena. If a Healer leaves someone unhealed, the damage cannot be reversed by anyone but you. He'll die of his wounds before you can get your strength back. You have to finish this now while you're here."

Here. As in the door of the healing.

It took so much energy to pass into this threshold. She had to keep her presence here, with the wound. She gripped tight to the string that pulled her toward healing, and the pain flooded into her. Luc stopped screaming.

All she had to do was hold on until she reached the end.

Bright light encompassed her. She . . . wasn't . . . going to . . . make it. The world snapped into a harsh reality. She was back in the forest, surrounded by the trees, and they spun. Then darkness.

Serena's eyes opened to a dusky sky. Red darkened to blue through leafy tree cover above. Where was she? The Forest on the way to Salea. She was supposed to be headed to Salea to . . . Luc! She sat up and saw no one. "Luc? Dash?"

"Whoa, it's okay." Someone crouched beside her and touched her arm.

She jerked back. "Who are you?"

"It's me, Luc."

Serena grabbed his hands. Both hands. His hair had grown back in, and his face was so different. No more heavy rasp plagued his voice. "You . . ."

A huge smile lit his face. "You healed me. I—I don't know how to thank you. I didn't know you were going to faint. Your unicorn friend seemed worried."

"Where is he?"

Luc shrugged. Absent the scars, she could tell how young he looked. Younger than her. She grabbed his hands again. "I didn't think I'd be able to do it. I thought it might kill me if I tried."

He stared at her with his eyes wide. "You thought you'd die? And you healed me anyway?"

She bit her lip.

"Really, I don't know how to thank you. I'm—I'm whole again." He stared at his own hands, turning them over.

"You can thank me by keeping this a secret."

"Absolutely. I have no home to go back to anyway. I'll keep heading east until I find a place to work. No one will ever know."

"Thank you."

"It's nice to see you're awake. This young one wouldn't leave your side. He kept pacing and worrying about killing you. I stopped him from taking you into town to see a physician."

Serena stood and walked over to Dash. *"Where were you?"*

"There are some Royal Army scouts headed this way. We need to move."

Serena's eyes widened.

"What is it?" Luc asked.

"Royal Army. Of all people, they must not see me."

"I have no qualm with them. Go. Hide. I'll make sure they don't find your trail."

"I can't ask you to—"

"Go." He touched her shoulder briefly and offered a smile. "It's the least I can do."

Serena mounted Dash, and he cloaked them both from view.

"I hope you can forgive me for performing such a dangerous healing." She stroked Dash's mane.

"There's nothing to forgive. You did no wrong."

"The Circle would not share your sentiment."

"No, and they can never find out what you've done."

The sound of hoofbeats reverberated against the forest floor. They were closer to Salea now. Out of the cover of the woods, it would be harder for Dash to remain invisible. She still wasn't at her strongest. But they couldn't remain here.

"You there." A deep voice boomed, and for a moment Serena's heart thumped.

"Yes, sir?" Luc asked.

"I've heard reports of a Healer in these woods. Have you seen anyone?"

"A Healer? You've got to be kidding me. Aren't they extinct?"

"He's very good at lying."

Dash didn't respond. He remained frozen, ears trained on the soldiers.

The soldier dropped off his horse and circled Luc. "Did you know that they feel pain? That they're drawn toward it?"

Luc touched the sword at his hip. "Have I done something wrong?"

"Where are you headed, boy?"

"To the palace, actually. I want to learn to be a soldier."

"Really?" The soldier lunged with his weapon, and Luc brought out his sword in time to block.

"I can't let this happen, Dash."

"There's more at stake than just our safety this time. The palace finding out about Healers puts too many lives at risk."

"Quick reflexes, boy."

"My name's Luc. My brother Daniel was slated to join the Royal Army this year. He was killed by Feravolk. I wish to follow in his footsteps."

Truth. Serena's heart shuddered. Who had she saved? The enemy?

The soldier narrowed his eyes and leaned back. "Healers are Feravolk. Did you know that?"

Luc's sword tip dropped. "I didn't."

Truth.

She held in a gasp. Dash's nostrils flared. Her heart wanted to explode. If the palace found out about her, every Healer in Soleden would be hunted.

CHAPTER 25

LOOSE ENDS

Thea crept down the hall to make her final stop—Kara's room. She stepped inside. Everything was in its place. Assassin neat. She approached the mahogany wardrobe against the back wall. Stopping and stilling her breath, she listened. No sound touched her ears. She was alone. The vial she lifted from her pocket was a weight in her hands. Not because it was heavy. She was leaving Kara on her own now.

Thea took the note she'd written her sister and rolled it around the vial. The heavy scent of wood rushed out as she opened the wardrobe. She ran her fingers along the rear inside panel and found the secret compartment. Here she placed the vial and note. Her final instructions. Farewell. Her apology for everything.

She began to close the compartment, but stopped and took out one of her knives. With it, she cut a lock of her long, blonde hair. Then she grabbed her dart shooter. These she laid in the secret compartment as well.

Warmth and wetness crept down Thea's cheeks. She wiped it away. When was the last time she'd cried? Kara would never understand. Never forgive her for what she was about to do. But she would never forgive herself if she let Kara die instead.

The fate of Soleden and the whole Forest Lands now lay in Kara's bloody hands. It was a lot to leave her little sister to deal with. Alone.

Forgive me.

Thea straightened. "I smell a wolf," she said without turning.

Connor was more dangerous than he let on. He carried one of the secret seeing stones. He knew who she worked for. But it was also true that his path and hers were the same, to a point. That fork might be soon, but Connor was smart. He knew how to get what he wanted. It was safer to have him as an ally than an enemy.

He moved closer and leaned his shoulder against the wardrobe so she could see him. "You're helping my mother, so I'm going to return the favor."

"Oh?"

"Belladonna thinks you helped free Logan. She's told Franco. Franco isn't really the forgiving type. I think he means to kill you."

Thea looked back into Connor's strange eyes. He wasn't smiling. He looked sad actually.

He shrugged. "Maybe you don't believe me, but I'm telling you—"

"I believe you." Thea let her satisfied smile fade in front of someone other than Kara. "If you want to return the favor, then watch Kara's back for me."

"Excuse me?"

"She's more reckless than I am."

"I think you mistake who I am. Why I'm here."

Thea stepped toward him and met his eyes. He straightened his back and looked down at her. She could almost sense his hackles rising.

"I'm one of the few who does not mistake your identity, wolf." She watched his eyes widen. "You may think you know things, but I can actually see the future. Our work is more the same than you might understand."

Connor eased back against the wardrobe, but his gaze remained hard. "Kara isn't exactly fond of me."

"She talks to you. That's about as fond of people as she gets." Thea smiled.

"I don't know what you're trying to get from me."

"You will when the time comes."

He narrowed his eyes.

She sighed. "I left you a note. You're not going to like some of the things I have to say."

"Like what?"

She shrugged. "Suggestions about waiting before you try to escape."

He crossed his arms. "You're the one who gave us—"

"I know, and I hope you will trust me when I say that you should really heed my suggestions. Pushing your mother out a window may seem strange to you now, but it won't. You will come to understand."

He backed up a step from her. "You're insane."

"Sometimes I wish it were that easy. Goodbye, Connor. Good luck." She turned to leave, then stopped and looked back where he still stood near the wardrobe, watching her with furrowed brows. She pressed her fingertip to the corner of her left eye, then her right, an assassin's silent greeting to a friend. "And thank you. For the warning."

"Why would Franco send you to Meese without me?" Kara crossed her arms.

Thea shrugged and placed a wrapped stone into the secret pocket at the small of her back. "Something about a Feravolk camp down there. He wants me to bring one of them back alive."

"Alive? Does he know what 'assassin' means?" Kara smirked.

Thea shared the smirk. "Fitting, isn't it?"

"What?"

"That I go to Meese without you. Again."

Kara cocked her head, no doubt trying to read Thea's expression. "May we never be separated like that again." She gripped Thea's arm.

Thea gripped back. "Don't worry. This will be a short trip, and this time I'm going in as a trained assassin, not a frightened child." But she was frightened. And she felt like a child.

"Still, I won't like being away from you for so long."

"I know. But rest assured, little sister, you will be fine on your own."

CHAPTER 26

AN INTERESTING
DEVELOPMENT

Connor's soft boots padded down the marble floors in the hallway. Torches lit his way—not that he needed them. And since he didn't look like himself, he didn't expect to be stopped. Impersonating palace guards was a good way to get out the front gate unnoticed. Not that he could go far before the trace spell would alert Franco. He headed toward the front gate.

"Maynard." A guard turned to him. "I say, Maynard."

Connor stopped. Though he resembled—what was his name? Maynard?—down to this morning's shaving cut on his chin, Connor knew nothing of the portly guard. "Yes?"

"I thought you'd gone home."

"Yet here I am."

"Well, you best be off so the king doesn't suspect a thing."

Now that was an interesting turn of events. "Right. I'll be just off then." Connor bowed his head and headed right for the door. His sleeve pulled tight around his arm. He stopped. "If you'd kindly release me."

"Kindl—Maynard, stop fooling around. Do you have it?"

Snare me. "Yes. Of course."

"I thought I was supposed to leave right after my shift and meet you."

"I haven't changed the plan. Just gotten myself detained is all." Connor looked at the guard's hand still gripped around his sleeve. He shook himself free. "Twice now."

"Right. I'm just nervous. If anyone notices it's missing before you leave—"

"Then you best let me go."

The guard dropped Connor's sleeve. Connor nodded tightly before he spun around and headed for the palace gates. Once free of them, he raced into the woods and morphed into his true form. He sighed. Holding the illusion exhausted him, but he wouldn't be walking around as Maynard again. Not unless he found out more about this mysterious trinket and to whom it belonged, which meant he'd have to find another guard to impersonate. That always proved worrisome. He stopped. That guard should be off shift soon. Maybe Connor would have to tail him and find out more about it.

Connor scaled the palace wall and dropped to the other side with a thud. He leaned against a young tree and pulled out the small, smooth obsidian stone. Resting it in his palm, he looked into it. The ice-blue eyes of the Mistress of Shadows appeared. Connor covered the stone before she could see him.

He waited, his head repeatedly tapping against the tree bark as he willed himself patience. When he deemed it safe again, he uncovered the stone and peered past the black surface into the core. The picture he was looking to see presented itself.

Quinn.

She lay curled in a tiny ball against a rocky surface. It was time to find out who she was. And why she'd called out to him in the first place. *"Cliffdiver?"*

"Yes, master." A creature with the head and chest of a bald eagle and body of a lion flew into view in the stone and folded his brown wings against his tawny back. Cliffdiver's head was covered in white feathers, but the other gryphon accompanying him had golden-brown feathers, like a golden eagle.

"How is she?"

Cliffdiver swished his tufted tail. *"In need of rescue. The beast doesn't seem very interested in her, and you were right. The birds have been feeding her. Bringing her water. But she isn't well. And the chains holding her are spelled with some sort of magic. I cannot break them. We've been keeping her safe from other predators."*

"Thank you for protecting her. Have you found out why the Mistress wants this poor girl?"

The gryphon shook his feathered head.

"All right. I may need you here, though. Will the other gryphon stay with her?"

"Yes, master."

"Please, don't call me master. I'm your friend. We're bonded."

He couldn't be sure, but he thought the gryphon may have smiled.

Connor peered past Cliffdiver to see Quinn's curled up form. Burn marks covered her arm. He ground his teeth together, unable to stifle the growl that rose from his throat. A slight hitch in the picture alerted Connor to another presence looking into the stone. He pocketed it so no one would see him.

Why did the Mistress want her? He stood. The night-watch shift was nearly over. Maybe he'd head back to the palace and tail a certain soldier. Maynard's secret could turn out to be useful.

He undressed, folded his clothes, and placed them in the cache at the base of his tree. Then he morphed into his wolf form. Nose to the wind, he found the scent of Maynard's worried friend and headed toward him.

The man paced from one tree to another, worrying his sword hilt. Harsh steps scuttled against the ground. Connor crept closer. The soldier stopped and looked up. "Finally, Maynard." His whisper was harsh. "Did you bring it?"

"Of course, I brought it. But you will tell Balton I was the one who secured it?"

Balton? What was that snared man up to?

"Of course, Trevor. Don't worry so much." Maynard thrust a meaty hand into his bag and fumbled around. When he lifted it, Trevor leaned closer, cutting out Connor's line of sight. He got up, careful to stay out of the torchlight, and moved deeper into the tree line, circling the unsuspecting men. Connor nosed the air as he moved closer. A glimmer caught his eye. It looked like one of the bracers archers and swordsmen used to protect their wrists, but made entirely of metal.

"It's not exactly pretty, is it?"

"It'll do."

Connor crept closer. A twig snapped under his paw. Clumsy. Trevor thrust the bracer back in his bag and grasped his sword. Connor crouched behind a tree.

"You are jumpy." Maynard chuckled.

"I heard something."

The men stood in silence, unmoving. Trevor replaced his sword. "Tell me how it works."

"When Balton puts this on, he will be able to use compulsion to control anyone not protected by the Blood Moon birthmark, *and* he'll be able to control those Children whom he's poisoned with the black blood. Franco doesn't know about his mother's ring. He will be Balton's servant."

"So will the whole army."

Connor breathed in. Compulsion? His breathing quickened. He had to think. Where had he read about compulsion? It was a power the Mistress had tried to create for herself.

And could he get his paws on that bracer? Franco was bad, but Balton could quite possibly be worse, especially if he was given unbridled access to Franco's spells. He had to get a look at that bracer. He crept closer.

Trevor clasped Maynard's shoulder. "Balton has just secured his place as the new king, and we are now his personal guards."

"Yes." The gleam in Maynard's eye told Connor there was possibly more to wielding that bracer than the chubby man had offered. He had to find out what, and steal it. And keep his eye on Maynard, who was quite possibly not Balton's real friend.

CHAPTER 27

THE PRIZED BULL

Rain fell steadily from the gray sky. Only five days had passed since Kinsey's funeral, and the blanket of sadness that covered everyone had not dissipated. Jayden touched her dagger's hilt again. Habit now. She couldn't stop sorrow from choking her when it came from all sides.

And no one would talk. Ryan had tried joking around a few times, but only got cold glares from Ethan, and Chloe had yelled at him to shut up. But Chloe wouldn't speak to Ethan either. The last thing she'd said to him was an accusation about how he should've shot the scarred man first. Thankfully, Logan had quieted her with harsh eye contact.

Scout had actually growled at her until Ethan looked at the dog and shook his head. Then he'd whimpered and nudged Ethan's hand with his nose.

Now they just walked in silence.

A chill skittered over Jayden's skin from the incoming weather. The drenching storm would last through the night and gain momentum. If they could stay in a tavern tonight, it would be best.

"Are you heading to Oaken?" Ethan said.

Logan nodded. "We'll never dry out otherwise. Besides, you kids need a warm bed."

Ethan's eyebrows popped up. "Have you been there recently?"

"That rough?"

"Pretty rough."

Logan patted the hilt of his sword. "We'll probably be left alone. Least we can do is try."

Oaken *was* pretty rough. No guards at the city gate, which was torn from its hinges. The scent of alcohol permeated the streets. Rats skittered between buildings. Men with scarred arms leered from the shadows. Knife blades glinted in their hands. Hoods shielded their features. Ethan kept everyone clustered close to Logan. Not that Jayden would have lagged back in this town.

All three of the men scanned their surroundings constantly, and all three kept their hands on their sword hilts.

Jayden made sure her daggers were visible on her belt and not hiding in the folds of her cloak. It deterred a few looks, but attracted others. Too bad the canines hadn't followed them into town. It might have felt safer.

Logan led them to a tavern with no sign, although the picture of a bull had been crudely scratched into the door. With missing shutters and splintering wood, the place didn't look like anyone prized it. Except maybe the local alcoholic.

The wind blasted into them, and Logan looked at Ethan. "You'll let me know if you feel anything."

Ethan clenched his jaw and nodded. As he did, Jayden realized the unease she'd been feeling wasn't just hers, but Ethan's, too.

They entered, and Logan approached a young girl who was wiping a cloth over a dented and worn table. "Excuse me, miss. We'd like a room."

She slapped the cloth over her shoulder and placed her hands on her hips. Her eyes narrowed in a way that made Jayden turn on her talent. "You're not from around here."

Logan chuckled. "That's why I need a room."

She cocked an eyebrow. "Oh? A clever one, are you?"

"Can you handle the request or not?" Logan's voice was a growl.

Tension, thick and bristling, filled the space between them, and Jayden didn't need her talent to read how boiled this woman's blood was. Logan must have been the final stick that burst this woman's satchel.

Ryan stepped around Jayden and faced the young barmaid. He

chuckled. "Listen, my friend is a little . . . shall we say, he's not used to talking to a pretty lady. He doesn't mean to be gruff and condescending. It's just that he *is* gruff and condescending."

The barmaid tilted her head toward Ryan, but her eyes remained slits. "He certainly is."

"My name is Ryan, and I must know yours."

She glanced over her shoulder. "Cora." Her previously harsh voice had turned soft.

"Pleased to meet you, Cora." Ryan held out his hand. She placed hers in his palm, and her lips parted when he kissed the back of her hand. "What is it?" he asked.

"It's just, I can't remember the last time someone did that."

Ryan's eyes widened. "No one gives you a proper greeting anymore?"

She just shook her head, totally transfixed on him. A small smile touched her lips.

"I've heard it said that when a woman smiles, it doubles her beauty. I didn't think it possible for you to be more enchanting."

Red flushed her cheeks. She glanced over her shoulder again. "Follow me."

Before she could move, a young man—whose shoulders were significantly wider than his hips—grabbed her arm and laughed. "Enchanting? That's the biggest vat of hogwaller I've ever heard."

Cora's face turned downcast, and she hid behind her hair as she turned her gaze to the floor.

Jayden gasped. How could he treat her like that?

"Let her go." Ethan's voice was hard but quiet.

The man puffed out his chest and dropped her arm. She scurried back to table-washing while the man squared his shoulders. "Or what? She's my wife. I can do whatever I want with her."

"Excuse me?" Ethan approached the man.

"Ethan." Jayden placed her hand on his arm. Normally, letting him do this might be beneficial, but right now the hatred that pulsed through him made her want to grab her weapons. "Let Logan take care of this," she whispered.

"This is *my* inn." The man placed his hands on his hips. His arms were as big around as a bull's middle.

Ethan didn't even move, just stared at the innkeeper as if he wanted to start a fight. "This piece of filth? That explains a lot."

What was he doing?

"Are you insulting me?"

Ethan glared. His hatred boiled. Jayden nearly wanted to rip the man's head off. She touched her dagger and quelled the rising emotions.

The innkeeper made a fist and waved it at Ethan. "You little—"

Before he could finish, the flat edge of Ethan's sword pressed against the man's stomach.

"Ethan." Logan raised his voice.

Ethan just pushed the man back into the bar.

The room quieted.

Jayden approached him and put her hand on his back. If Kinsey had been right, this would work. She tried to channel her calm into him. "He's not worth it, Ethan."

"She is." He motioned toward the woman, who now held a hand over her rapidly heaving chest.

"Yes. But he isn't. Just walk away."

Ethan's shoulder's relaxed. The hate in him seemed to crawl back into his heart and nestle there like a flame bound to a candlewick. It didn't snuff out.

The innkeeper pointed to the exit. "You've earned yourself a stay on the other side of my door. I don't take kindly to men who would rough up my establishment."

Ethan sheathed his sword. "Think twice before you hurt her again."

Jayden pulled Ethan's shoulder gently, still trying to calm him. He turned around and stalked out.

Once outside, Ryan rounded on him. "What was that?"

Ethan glared at his brother. "You could have gotten her in trouble with all that flirting."

"It was innocent flirting. Any woman—"

"Not her, Ryan. When you see a woman with bruises on her arms and a scar around her neck, you don't—" he shook his head. "You played with fire."

Ryan stood there with his mouth open. "I—I didn't notice."

Logan walked past them. "Word about us will spread in this small town. We'd best find shelter before the storm really hits."

Then he faced Ethan, eyes hard. "I'm trusting you to get your recklessness under control." His eyes flicked to Jayden. "For their sakes."

A cold rush of air shot through Jayden's chest, and Ethan closed his eyes. "I'm sorry."

Logan nodded. "Good." Then he led them out the city gate.

CHAPTER 28

PLAYING WITH FIRE

Ryan sat on the wet ground in his soaked clothes and turned the spit over the fire. After hours of taking the long way around Oaken through these bug-infested woods, the rain had finally let up enough for them to have a much-needed fire. Fat dripped off the meat and sizzled in the flames. The sound reminded him of the black lion he'd roasted from the inside out.

He fingered the scar on his arm. Flames had given that to him once.

Fire never hurt him again, even if he flirted with it often.

Flames.

Dancing. Whirling. Always susceptible to the wind currents. He touched the tops of the fire. His hand grew hot. This time the fire seemed to lick at his fingers. Over, around, under. Never singeing. Strange.

"Ryan."

He stopped. Jayden was staring at him from the other side of the fire.

"You're burning supper." Ethan pulled the spit off the fire and blew on the flames spouting off the rabbits.

"Sorry."

Jayden grabbed Ryan's hand and turned it over, inspecting his fingers. They weren't even blackened. She squinted and stared at him. "What were you doing?" she whispered.

He shook his head. Then he looked right into her eyes and let his talent fill him. "A little daydreaming never hurt anyone."

She blinked and shook her head. "Right." She dropped his hand. "I guess we should eat."

"If it's even edible." Ethan rolled his eyes.

Logan chuckled. "Clearly you haven't had any meat cooked by Gavin. You're lucky." He clasped Ryan's shoulder. "Westwind says he's not getting any more for you."

Ryan forced a laugh. He looked at his hand. Not even a blister. It was as if the fire hadn't touched him.

"Good. I don't want the fire to be able to hurt me. It will make it so much harder for them to kill me."

Ryan squeezed his eyes shut. *"Go away."*

"I like it here. You suit my purpose better than I could have dreamed."

"Are you okay? You haven't been acting yourself." Jayden's pretty blue eyes rounded.

Maybe because his sister had just died. Why did everything have to remind him? "I'm fine. I just need to go wash off this soot."

"There's nothing on you. Your skin isn't even red. Are you sure you're—"

"I said I'm fine." It came out louder than intended, and she shrank away from him.

Ethan shot him a glare.

That fanned Ryan's temper.

"Get angry."

He clenched his jaw. There would be no use getting angry now. Especially if whatever was inside his head wanted him to.

"I don't think it's a good idea for you to go off alone," Ethan said.

"No?" Ryan rounded on his brother.

"Look, Ryan, I'm just saying that—"

"That I can't take care of myself. I hear you loud and clear, Ethan. You're the better swordsman. You're the better woodsman. I belong in a smithy pounding things."

Ethan stood, held up his hands to calm Ryan down. "Stop getting all hotheaded."

"Oh, that's nice coming from you."

"What's that supposed to mean?"

"We were in a tavern all of three minutes, and you picked a fight with the innkeeper right as I was about to secure us a room. Probably a free one at that."

"Ryan." Logan's voice was a warning.

He couldn't stop. Didn't want to. Everyone was likely comparing him to Ethan. The better brother. Better suited for Jayden. Better at protecting Chloe. Better at cooking the bloody dinner. He pointed a finger at Ethan. "The reason we're out here in dangerous territory is your inability to keep your temper in check."

"So I should let you possibly endanger an innocent woman?"

"Endanger? That's you pulling out your sword every time someone looks at you funny. Are you trying to get us all killed?"

Ethan pulled out his sword. Logan just stood there, said nothing. Right. So Ethan could just challenge Ryan whenever he wanted, but Ryan was chastised for what? Yelling.

Ethan took a step closer. "My sword protects—"

"Right. Just like it protected Kinsey."

Ethan grabbed Ryan's shirt collar. "What's gotten into you?" A fire lit his eyes and he pushed. Ryan's back hit a tree.

"Are you going to let him throw you around? Punch you?"

Ryan shook. His fist connected with Ethan's jaw.

Ethan staggered back but kept hold of Ryan's clothes.

Ryan pushed Ethan with both hands, punched him again. They landed on the ground with a thud.

"Stop it!" Chloe's voice mingled with Jayden's, and someone tried to pull Ryan back. He pounded his fist into Ethan's face. Again. Again. Again.

"Ryan!" Jayden screamed.

Logan pried him off.

Ethan lay on the ground, blood streaming from his nose. He propped himself up on both elbows and spit.

Red on the soil.

Red on his shirt.

Ryan looked at his bloodied fist. No. Oh, no. No, no, no. He touched his forehead with his shaking hand. It spread blood. Ethan's blood.

Ethan hadn't fought back.

No. Ryan had imagined it. Ethan had been trying to calm him down.

Ryan stared at his hands and scrambled to his feet. Chloe glared at him with incredulous eyes. Wet eyes. Jayden stared at him with her eyebrows pinched together. She didn't understand. Of course she didn't. Ethan had never punched him.

Logan held out his hands. "Ryan, look at me."

He didn't. He looked at Ethan and noticed his brother's sword on the ground. Ethan had taken off his weapon. He'd never even pulled it out. Hadn't threatened at all. Did he know Ryan was going to lose it? Why was everything so clear now? Why didn't his memories match up? It was like two versions of the same story played in his head. Ethan had hit him first. Only his face didn't sting. Ethan had never punched him.

How was this happening?

You needed a push.

No. "I have to wash my h-hands." Ryan's own quaking voice surprised him.

"Let him go." Logan stopped Chloe from reaching for him.

They thought he was a monster. Maybe he was. All he knew was he got to the bank of the lake, plunged his aching hands into the water, and watched the red stream off.

After he'd gotten all the blood off, Ryan sat on the edge of the bank with his elbows on his knees and stared at the water. Watched the sun sink lower. Kiss the horizon. What had he done?

With shaking hands, he reached into his pocket and pulled out the root.

Footsteps on the loose gravel caught his attention, and he put the root back before he was able to use it. He didn't turn. Logan wasn't very like Ryan's father, but he imagined a lecture was coming. He deserved it and worse.

"Hey." Ethan's voice surprised him.

Ryan buried his head in his hands, not wanting to look at his brother right now. Not wanting to see what he'd done to Ethan's face.

"I'm sorry about Kinsey." Ethan's words were nearly inaudible.

Ryan wiped his hands over his face. "That's not your fault."

"We both know it was."

Ryan stood and faced Ethan. He had some swelling to his nose, the skin under his right eye was dark as a forest river and it was nearly swollen shut. "Ethan, I'm"—he closed his eyes—"I'm the one who should be saying sorry."

"I felt the threat for her and you know it."

"And you did everything you could."

"I hesitated."

"So I'm supposed to hate you now? Blame you? Because I don't. And I won't. I said those things because—because I'm angry, but not at you. I'm angry at myself."

"For what? You didn't do anything."

"Exactly. I didn't do anything. I left you to die in the palace because I'm not good enough with a sword. I asked you to help Jayden because I was dying. I couldn't even save my own sister because I was afraid that if I shot an arrow, I'd miss. I never miss. But with her head right there, by his . . ."

"Ryan, that shot wasn't—"

"It was easier to blame you because I didn't have to face the reality that I can't take care of them."

Ethan was quiet for a while. He scuffed the rocks with his shoe. Picked one up and skipped it across the water. "You'll learn. You'll probably be better at it than I am."

"You can bet on it." Ryan picked up a rock and skipped it, too.

Another stone skittered across the water, leaving ripples. They stood there for a time, skipping rocks as darkness descended.

Ethan put his hands in his pockets.

Ryan threw another stone. "I am sorry about your face."

Ethan laughed. "You're lucky I didn't hit you back."

"No. You're lucky. This face would have gotten us a free room if you hadn't messed it up."

"Luck had nothing to do with it. I had to keep your best asset intact. You can't charm your way into a free room with a black eye and a busted nose."

Ryan's rock slipped from his hand and sank instead of skipped. "I broke your nose?"

Ethan looked at Ryan askance and shrugged. "I heal fast."

Ryan chucked a rock this time. How could he have been so stupid? The damage was done. He'd told Ethan he blamed him for Kinsey's death even though it wasn't true, and that had to hurt worse than a busted nose.

Maybe his talent could be used for good. If he could use it to make Ethan believe—

"Yes. Use your talent."

He tossed another rock. It soared into the middle of the lake and landed with a massive splash for such a small stone.

"Nice throw."

"Ethan, I don't blame you. I said those things out of anger to hurt you, not because I believe them."

He nodded. "I know. You've already apologized, Ryan. Come on. The girls are probably waiting on a prickly bush wondering if I retaliated."

They turned to walk back together, but a soft, hissing laugh in Ryan's head made him glance over his shoulder. The water bubbled and something made him shudder.

"It's awake."

Ryan's step hitched and he nearly tripped. *"What's awake?"*

"You'll find out soon enough. It smells your brother's blood."

CHAPTER 29

BREATHTAKING PERSUASION

Jayden breathed in the wet air. There was a lull in the rain, but not for long. The trees, the ground, everything still carried the residue of heavy rainfall. Gray sky still hovered above them, but Logan had told them to rest.

Jayden dragged her satchel closer to Ethan. His right eye was still swollen shut. That cut above it looked awful. She grabbed water, a clean cloth, and some of her father's ointment. "Rough day?" She smiled.

A sad version of his boyish smile returned. Better than nothing.

"Let me help." She washed the cut and he winced. "You didn't hit him back."

"I didn't want to fuel it."

A lot of self-control for someone who had just pulled a sword on a complete stranger. She'd felt the hate then. When Ryan attacked him, she'd felt Ethan's sadness, regret, and self-loathing, but no hate. So what had sparked him at the tavern? She spread the ointment across his cut. "Better?"

He turned his head to look at her. "Thanks."

"Of course, but I should probably stitch it."

He nodded and she got out her supplies. He was much more compliant than the first time she'd met him. He'd had that awful rope burn around his neck from the soldiers. Oh. Her hands fell to her lap.

"Everything okay?"

"Yes. I just . . ." She started stitching the cut. "You said the woman had a scar on her neck. Like Logan's?" Like Ethan would have if not for the Healer.

Heat spread through her blood—from his anger. She had to get that under control.

"Her scar was thin," Ethan said. "But someone had used her marriage cord to—I don't know, choke her? Either way, it left a scar. Who knows, maybe he used it as a leash."

"How awful."

"When I saw that scar, I—well, I lost it." Now his regret lapped against her.

She tied off the last stitch. "It's understandable. I'm sorry that happened to you."

"Never again." He clenched his jaw.

She squeezed his shoulder and the tension left him. She hadn't even realized that she'd tried to calm him until that moment.

Everyone else was sleeping. She put away her supplies and looked at her bedroll. So far away from Ethan. She settled next to him. "Can I sit with you?"

"Any time." He smiled. "Are you okay?"

A moment ago, she'd been terrible. A moment ago, she'd felt heavy with the weight of everyone's emotions. The worry that Franco would find someone else she loved. That she wouldn't be able to stop him in time. But now, when Ethan looked at her as if he could see into her soul, she felt that she didn't need to bear the weight of everything alone. And that was a beautiful feeling.

"I am now." She caught herself staring at his hand. Wanting to hold it. She breathed deep. This was exactly why she should not be sitting so close to him.

The weight of his head landed on her shoulder and she sighed. Yes. Right now, she was okay. But right now, with everyone sleeping, emotions weren't seeping into her beyond her control. Ethan's were the worst. They came unbidden and strong. She had to get this under control before his emotions pulled her under like a riptide she couldn't escape. Children were always taught that their talents were blessings. Not hers. This feeling so much hurt, so much sorrow—she couldn't handle the burden.

A burden she had to control before it controlled her.

Jayden rolled over and noticed the others still sleeping. Ethan, too. Good. She'd worried that he might not with the thunderstorm. Even while sleeping, he carried a sadness that choked her. She looked away from him and started to pack up her wet things.

Tonight, if Logan got them as far as he wanted to, they'd be in Primo —one of two small towns just outside of Salea. The others began stirring.

Westwind and Aurora approached her.

She smiled at the wolves. "Morning. Come to escort us to the lake?"

Westwind nodded, and she fell into step with him. Chloe and Aurora walked right behind.

The more time Jayden spent with Westwind, the more she hoped to follow in her birth parents' steps and bond to a wolf. But there was Melanie's theory about the wooden tokens. That left her with a horse. Nothing wrong with that, but the other Deliverers would bond to magical animals. What would she gain from a horse? Speed, endurance, sensitivity—as if she didn't already have enough of that—and a ferocious kick. Now that she could use.

The rising sun showered everything in a soft, yellow glow. A fine mist rose off the water, parting near the shore. The whole place looked so perfect, almost magical.

A beautiful gray mare stepped out of the mist. Its eyes were large and dark and soulful. Jayden expected to see a horn in the center of the horse's head, but only wisps of deeper gray mane fell between the creature's ears.

"What's your name, girl?"

Jayden's heart thundered. "Are you speaking?" she addressed the horse.

The horse flipped her head. *"Yes."*

"Jayden," she whispered, unable to summon anything louder.

"Jayden." The horse repeated her name like a melody. *"What a pretty name. My name is Thunder."*

The horse stepped farther away and swished her tail.

"No. Don't go." Jayden put out her hand to try to beckon the enchanting horse to stop. "How can you talk to me?"

This was it. This had to be her horse.

"Does it surprise you?"

"Yes, actually." Jayden walked over to the animal and reached up to touch Thunder's nose. She felt like silk. And at once, all the residual sadness that had clung to her for the past few days lifted. Her heart seemed buoyant. Light. Floating. If her horse could help her contain everything, she wouldn't have to feel so much all the time. She could be free.

Jayden nearly faltered as her surroundings swirled around her like a dreamscape. When—at last—all was right again, she was no longer at the misty lakeside, but in a sunny meadow. The grass in front of her was long, and Thunder stood in the center of the field and frisked, buoyantly beckoning Jayden to follow her.

Grass slapped against Jayden's thighs as she waded through, but the grass weighed her down. It pulled against her clothes and made her legs feel as if they were dragging.

Thunder stood right in front of her now. She was so dazzling, so sublime, she took Jayden's breath away.

Jayden wanted to speak, but she couldn't. Everything felt heavier. Deeper. Darker.

Thunder reached out to comfort her, and the mare's soft nose was unbelievably smooth against Jayden's skin. Long streams of velvet began to encompass her, lifting the weight from her feet. Yes, that's what she needed. She let the silken strands overtake her.

Ethan stared at the red glow beneath the white dust-covered wood. His face still throbbed, but at least he could see out of both eyes today. He separated the fire-chewed timber with a stick. Something was wrong with Ryan, and it was more than Kinsey's death.

Heat flared across his chest. He stood and put his hand on the hilt of his sword.

"What's wrong?" Logan grabbed his knife.

Ryan stood.

"It's Jayden and Chloe. Something is trying to—to kill Chloe and steal Jayden."

Ethan took off running toward the lake, Logan and Ryan at his heels.

Logan's voice broke the heavy silence. "I can't talk to Westwind or Aurora."

Scout whined. Ethan swallowed, hoping they weren't already dead.

The clearing looked tranquil, like a painting. No birds chirped. No sound but running water touched Ethan's ears. Westwind and Aurora lay on their sides on the shore. Water lapped against their paws. Ethan scanned the area. There was no sign of Jayden or Chloe.

Something red floated down the center of the lake, a wake behind it. Chloe's hair. Was she underwater? Ethan tossed his weapons to the ground except for his belt knife. He raced toward the lake and splashed in after her.

Finding it deep enough to swim, Ethan put his knife between his teeth and plunged underwater. Kelp everywhere reached out toward him, inhibiting his vision and grasping his legs.

Jayden and Chloe walked along the bottom of the lake as if it were dry ground. What were they following? He thrust his body forward. Chloe was almost in reach. He reached for her arm. She turned toward him, her green eyes glazed over with a reddish hue. She resisted his pull and pushed his arm away with her free hand.

Ryan grabbed her, and Ethan and Logan swam ahead for Jayden.

Green tentacles of kelp reached out for him. They pawed at his clothes and arms and tried to wrap around his legs. He cut them with his knife and they withered back from him. Then he saw it.

Its head could have belonged to a horse if the rippling green colors of the water were a color of horses. And the red eyes. Its compact body was also equine, but its rear legs were a sinewy braid of kelp. The kelp wrapped around Jayden. She was being strangled and she looked so serene.

Ethan surfaced to take a deep breath, then he plunged toward Jayden. Logan swam toward the creature, knife ready.

Ethan grabbed Jayden's wrist. The horse screeched. The water seemed to boil, then the horse pulled back and Jayden slipped from Ethan's grip. The creature separated Ethan from Logan, and its deafening hiss exploded, pushing Ethan back through the water. Red clouded everything. He lost track of the surface.

Where was Jayden? He closed his eyes and listened to his talent. It urged him forward. He followed. Opened his eyes. There she was. Ethan swam forward and grabbed her hand.

His lungs ached. Everything seemed darker. The blow of a hoof hit his cheek. Then his arm. Another blow hit his shoulder. The horse was pushing him toward its entrapping tentacles. He dove deeper to avoid the horse's kick. There she was, tangled in kelp. He sliced through the seaweed. Blood muddied the water.

Ethan reached blindly to where he saw Jayden's form sink. Her skin slipped through his fingers. He dove. Caught her. Hefted her closer and wrapped his arm around her waist.

Jayden spewed water on the ground. Air filled her lungs. She couldn't get enough of it. Ethan knelt next to her. She was lying on the ground, on her side. The last thing she remembered was the horse. She coughed out more water onto the ground. Everything hurt.

"You're okay." Ethan cradled her head. "You're okay."

"What . . . happened?" Her voice was so rough. She sat up and Logan was there with the wolves and Scout. Blood cascaded down his shirt. She reached out to touch the gash in his shoulder.

"I'm all right."

Ryan sat beside a shivering Chloe. "What was that thing?"

"It was a kelpie," Logan said.

Jayden shuddered. "A kelpie?"

Logan glanced over the water. "They sing to their prey to lure them close so they can drown them."

Chloe shivered. "The s-song was haunting."

"Song?" Jayden shook her head. "It spoke to me."

Logan's eyes widened for a heartbeat. "You could talk to it?"

"Is that bad?"

He glanced at Ethan. "You said it wasn't trying to kill Jayden."

"It wasn't. It wanted her," Ethan said.

"The dark creatures belong to the Mistress. She's trying to lure the Deliverers to her."

Chloe's teeth chattered. "Will it c-come b-back?"

Logan scanned the water. "Not that one."

CHAPTER 30

UNLIKELY HERO

It was his doing. Ryan glanced up from his boots at Jayden and Chloe, who both walked ahead of him. They'd already walked far away from that pool in the woods, but their long hair remained wet, though hours had passed since their swim with the kelpie. That creature had to be the same beast the white lion had warned him about.

The blood he'd washed off his hands in the water had called to it. His stone had awoken it. The lion had probably wanted him to throw it so the Mistress's creature would wake and lure in Jayden.

His being here, with them, was endangering everyone.

He looked back at Ethan scanning the forest as they walked, and his stomach clutched. Ethan's eye was no longer swollen shut, but the skin beneath both eyes was still dark. His nose was still puffy and his jaw bruised. Ryan fisted his hands and his knuckles throbbed. He'd done that. Punched his own brother.

Hurt them all.

Those he loved were no longer safe with him.

"They never were."

A slow burn spread in his gut at the sound of that voice. He almost expected it now.

"Day by day my reach gets farther, thanks in part to you."

"It's not willing participation." He hoped his thought conveyed the growl he wanted to put in his voice.

"Mostly true."

Mostly? No. He squeezed his eyes shut. She was just trying to get to him. He fumbled in his pocket and pulled out a piece of the root. Popped in in his mouth and immediately, as the cinnamon taste dissolved on his tongue, he felt better. And worse. The more he relied on the herb, the less that voice was under his control.

Jayden hung back and stepped in line with him. "You okay, Ryan?" Her eyes searched his face.

He shrugged. "Why wouldn't I be?"

The pity eyes would be the death of him. Then she bowed her head, and her hair hid her face. Why did he push her away like that? If that wasn't bad enough, Chloe shot him a glare. For what? For not talking to Jayden? Fighting with a voice inside his head was hardly a topic he wanted to bring up. And talking about his worries revolved around that.

There was no one safe to talk to.

"There's me."

"You're not safe."

A purr vibrated in his skull. He needed to stop talking to her. It. Whatever. The library of Salea was close to Primo. Maybe this One Eye character would let him go over there. He had to figure out how to stop this voice before he hurt anyone else.

By evening, Logan stopped and passed out rations. Westwind and Aurora broke off from them, staying in the woods, but Scout stuck near Ethan as they approached the city limits.

Primo was alive. The door to a tavern opened and a couple spilled out, laughing, staggering. Ryan shook his head with a smile. Some people didn't know when to stop with the ale. Drowning in some seemed a good idea right now. It might silence the voice. Then again, it might make her more chatty.

Logan led them deeper into town. They strayed into the back alleys. The moon was behind the clouds, and the streets were dark but surprisingly crowded. Ryan kept his hands curled around the straps of his pack.

They finally reached a small hill on the outskirts of town with a house sitting on top. A deep bark sounded and a huge, black animal raced down the hill. It had to be as tall as a wolf. Taller. White teeth stood out in stark contrast to the dark fur.

Another creature of the Mistress come to hunt Jayden? Ryan's heart beat fast. He pulled out his knife and braced himself, standing in front of everyone.

"Ryan?"

Ethan's voice sounded distant.

Logan wrenched Ryan's knife free of his hand.

The animal lunged toward him. Heavy paws slammed into his chest and wet slobber soaked his face.

Jayden and Chloe stood above him, giggling.

Ryan pushed the dog's chest. "Get off me."

A huge man, with a patch over his left eye and a puckered scar that peeked out from the bottom of the patch, stood over him. Yeah, he was intimidating all right. The man looked like he could grab a branch right off a tree, or wrestle a mountain lion with his bare hands. "Tried to kill my dog, did you?"

The man held out his hand to help Ryan up. He took it and stood, dusting off his clothes.

Jayden raced forward, arms open. "Uncle Percy!" He nearly swallowed her in a hug.

Logan nodded. "One Eye."

So this was One Eye. Well, the nickname made sense, at least.

"You all must be hungry." The man watched them with his one good eye. "Estelle will have a goose on the fire faster than your stomach can growl." One Eye's rough voice fit nicely with his smile.

Logan clasped One Eye's shoulder. "We shouldn't make Estelle feed all of us. I have coin."

"Nonsense. You know how Estelle is. Grumpy as ever." One Eye laughed. "She cooks better when she's got something to complain about. Come. We'll eat, and you can tell me what brings you all together. And here." One Eye's gaze rested on Ryan and then his sister behind him. "Neither of you look like you're ready to take down the world in search of a single wrongdoer."

Maybe. Maybe not.

Logan laughed. "All right, let's pay a visit to Estelle."

The dog bayed.

"Shut up, Stag. Good ol' boy." One Eye patted the huge animal's head. Loose skin hung from its jowls. It sniffed Ryan and left a huge, wet mark on his pants.

Ryan sighed. This day could not get worse.

"Old Stag remembers your Scout." One Eye slapped Ethan on the back.

Then he walked past the watch dog, and everyone followed him up the hill and into the hut. It was quaint. Stuffy, but homey. The main room opened to a kitchen area, and there was a small loft near the rear. The fireplace took up one half of the southern wall. Wide chairs, made from wood left almost as natural as if they were just found on the forest floor, littered the other two walls. One half of the kitchen area was filled by a sturdy oak table with matching chairs. Blankets—piled in a lopsided ball—sat near the fireplace, and Stag took a seat on them.

The rear door opened, announcing the arrival of a woman who only came up to One Eye's chest. Her graying hair was curly, not brushed since the morning—or perhaps the morning before.

"Percy, you brought me visitors?" Her voice came out sharp and abrasive. *Grumpy* seemed the appropriate word to describe her. "Logan, Ethan, and what's this? Jayden? How did you come to be with the likes of these? And who are you? More subjects, I imagine."

Heavens. Was this woman always so loud? Ryan flinched when she came over to him and spoke just as thunderously in his face. "Well?"

"I'm a—"

"Speak up, dear. I can't hear a mumbler."

"She can't hear anything, really." One Eye stood behind her and laughed. "She can see like a hawk, but she can't hear a blasted thing." He put a hand on her shoulder, and Estelle turned to see her husband's smile.

"Talking about me, huh?" She elbowed his gut. "Sit down, all of you."

One Eye led them to his sturdy table, and Estelle busied herself around the kitchen, humming. Blaringly.

"So, tell me the story." The chair groaned as One Eye slid into it.

Logan was discreet with his information. He said that he'd rescued all of them from being captured by the queen, and that Ryan and

Chloe were also Feravolk but not yet trained to fight. Then he set a bag of coin on the table.

One Eye crossed his arms. "You think you can pay me to train them?"

Logan pushed the coin closer to the burly man. "I'll pay you if you agree to train them."

One Eye drummed his thick fingers on the table. He looked at Ryan and Chloe. Sizing them up, no doubt.

His single-eyed gaze locked on Ryan. "Can you wield a sword?"

"I've practiced with one a number of times, but I'm not very good at it. Yet."

"You ready to learn to fight?"

Ryan straightened his back. "Yes. I want to be able to defend my family and friends, sir."

"A hero, huh?" One Eye scoffed. "We'll see about that." He turned his head so that his blue eye could rest on Chloe, who had been unbelievably quiet so far. "And what about you, Missy? Aren't you afraid?"

"I'm not afraid of anything."

"Nothing?" One Eye removed his gaze from Chloe and cut off a thumbnail with his knife. "Brave girl, huh, Missy?"

"My *name* is Chloe. And yes, I'm a brave girl. I've seen enough to make me fearless."

One Eye lifted his eye to look at her, still cutting his nails without watching what he was doing. "Enough to make you fearless?" His tone was no longer light. "Among other things." That would be enough to burn Chloe's straw and likely light a flame she'd fuel for days.

One Eye pointed his knife at Ryan. "I'll train this one for the coin."

Chloe slammed her fists on the table and stood, barb in mouth and ready to shoot it at this three-hundred-pounds-of-muscle swordsman.

One Eye put his knife back in its sheath and blew his fingernail shards to the floor. "The sprite I'll train for free."

Chloe simply stood there like a fool, a gaping fool. She sat slowly.

"Thank you, old friend." Logan pushed the bag of coin to One Eye. The other man just nodded. Then he looked at Ryan and smiled.

Ryan's stomach clenched.

CHAPTER 31

FROG AND FOX

With a growling stomach, Ryan watched as Estelle cut the goose open. Juice spilled out across the wooden plate, and she hurried to pass out the slices. Ryan soaked the juice up with his bread. It tasted amazing. Conversation flowed easily. He glanced at Jayden and saw her staring at Ethan.

"*She should be yours.*"

That was it.

Ryan curled his fingers around his bread and squeezed. Jayden wasn't his. Her heart didn't belong to him, and if the voice wanted him to fight with Ethan, he'd do the opposite.

Jayden glanced at him, lines forming on her forehead. He set down his battered bread. Maybe he hadn't quite lost her yet. She seemed to care about him.

"*She does. Your brother is in the way.*"

Ryan closed his eyes. "*It's her choice.*"

"*Keep telling yourself that.*"

"*I'm telling you.*"

Silence now? Oh, really? Now that he was actually talking? Nice.

Jayden touched his hand. "Are you all right?" she whispered.

One Eye pushed his chair back from the table, and the screech broke their eye contact. "Ethan, why don't you take Hero here and fetch some wood from the woodpile out back. It wouldn't be a proper night of dancing without a fire, now would it?"

Hero? Ryan winced. Hopefully that nickname wouldn't stick.

They stepped outside, Scout following. The wind hit them. It was changing, cooling. Ryan followed Ethan toward the back of the barn. "So tell me, what should I expect? From this One Eye, I mean."

Ethan chuckled. "If anyone I know can make it through training with One Eye, it's you."

"I'm being serious."

"Me, too. It won't be easy, but he has a way of understanding people. Helping them beyond the art of the fight. He'll help you find your strengths, but also your weaknesses. Then he'll help you overcome them."

They reached the woodpile. It was almost as tall as Ryan's chest. Ethan scratched the back of his head and laughed. "I believe I put most of this wood here."

Ryan chuckled, too.

Scout sat beside Ethan and seemed to smile as he looked up at him. Ryan patted the dog. "Do you remember the last time we met at a woodpile?"

Ethan froze for a heartbeat. "Of course. I recall you dragging me home to your family's shed, promising you'd never tell your mom about my hiding there."

"It's a good thing I broke that promise, isn't it, Scout?" The dog licked Ryan's chin. "See, he agrees."

Ethan smiled. "So do I."

Ryan scratched behind Scout's ear. "This dog wouldn't leave your side during the storm, even when it poured on both of you and I tried to coax him into the shed with a piece of meat."

Ethan bent to pet him. "He's a good dog. Never let me go through anything alone." He looked up at Ryan. "And you're a good brother, making your mother drag me out of the rain. Thank you."

"Thank Scout. He's the one who helped me find you in the first place."

Ethan stood. "He always seems to know what I need before I do."

Ryan outright laughed. "That's because you're the last to know what you need."

That caused Ethan to roll his eyes. He turned to the woodpile.

"When I'm finished with my training, you'll have room for another Protector?"

Ethan put his hand on Ryan's shoulder. "Of course."

Ryan stared at his brother's black eye. His face seemed to be healing faster. "Good."

Ethan plucked some of the wood from the pile. "Jayden would rather have you around anyway."

Ryan froze for a heartbeat. "You sure about that?"

"Well, she does worry about you getting hurt, but I told her to let you decide."

"You told her that?"

Ethan's eyebrows pinched together. "I thought it appropriate."

"Of course. I just mean . . ." Ryan sighed. "You'll take care of her for me?"

"You have my word."

"And if she falls for you—"

"She won't." Ethan interrupted with a smile. "She loves you."

"If—"

"She won't."

"I'm just saying, you'll be spending a lot of time with her."

Ethan faced Ryan and narrowed his eyes. "I would never do that to you."

"I know." Ryan had to chuckle, which lightened Ethan's face slightly. "But I see it, Ethan. She has feelings for you."

"Ryan, she's your betrothed."

"Not anymore."

"How'd you get out of that?"

Ryan shrugged. "It's not like our parents are alive. Her heart belongs to her, and if she chooses you—"

"She won't," Ethan repeated, his face as emotionless as stone.

"You know, she's never admitted to loving me." Ryan paused.

Ethan grabbed more wood. "That's not really my business, Ry."

"Just know I won't be angry. That I would rather it be you than anyone else. And I hope you'll still let me help as a Protector."

Ethan just clenched his jaw and stared at the woodpile. "Of course."

He looked Ryan in the eyes. "And she won't." He walked back toward the house.

Well, he'd get no more out of Ethan on that subject. It didn't matter. Ryan had said what he needed to say. And the voice hadn't interfered.

When he made his way back to One Eye's, arms full of chopped wood, everyone else had gathered outside. Before long the fire was tall and lively. Ryan let the flames that flickered back and forth, licking the logs, mesmerize him.

"The dance is just as important as the fight," One Eye said. "When you dance, you feel your partner's movements. You will visit the tavern every night until you can fight like a dancer."

Was he serious?

"A tune then." One Eye sat on an old soot-stained stool with his lute. He strummed the instrument. "Partners."

Estelle was not shy about grabbing Logan's hands, and Ethan offered to dance with Chloe. She narrowed her eyes, hands on her hips. "I suppose you'll do."

At least it got him to laugh.

Jayden smiled at Ryan. Sure. One more dance before he officially told her she was free of him seemed fitting.

Except her hands fit so perfectly in his, and she followed his lead with such ease. Letting her go wouldn't be easy.

One Eye gave them no break when the next tune played. This tune, "The Frog and the Fox," was animated. Dancers had to flee from their partners, like a frog running from a fox. They only ever touched their partners for a moment before zigzagging between other dancers. It was a good one for parties, especially where the ale was flowing. Each round the music would go faster and faster. When a pair messed up, they sat out, until only one pair of dancers remained.

One Eye was relentless as he sped up the song, but Ryan and Chloe came from a family that liked to dance. They flew each other back and forth, not missing a step. Estelle must have been able to hear One Eye's lute, for her steps were flawless.

Ryan let go of Jayden's hand, but he watched her ankles cross. She stumbled into Ethan's arms and pushed him down. Laughing, she put her hands on the ground on either side of Ethan's body.

Ryan stood motionless as he watched her brush grass off Ethan's shirt. The laughing stopped as she pulled a stray leaf from his hair. She froze. Stared into Ethan's eyes. Her laughter faded and she just stayed there. Their faces were so close, almost touching.

Ryan's insides squeezed together. A painful lump settled just below his heart.

"Well, kiss her already." Estelle clapped her hands together.

Jayden and Ethan tore their eyes away from one another and scrambled to their feet, beating dirt and leaves from their clothes.

"Shy, are we?" Estelle tilted her head coyly.

"What? No. No, no, no." Ethan was shaking his head.

Eyes wide, like a rabbit in a snare, Jayden gravitated away from Ethan.

Estelle put a hand up to her mouth. "I am sorry. I thought you two—I didn't mean to cause such a ruckus."

"Perhaps that's enough dancing for one night." One Eye rose and stretched. Then he handed Ethan the lute.

Ethan took it, wandered closer to the fire, and sat down on one of the log seats surrounding it. One Eye took out a pipe and joined him. Stag rested his slimy jowls on One Eye's lap. The rest of the huge dog's frame was on the ground.

Ryan walked over to join the others and let his thoughts drown out everything but the music and the feel of warmth from the fire.

Ethan started with a happy tune, but after a while his songs grew sad. Ryan thought those tunes more fitting for his mood. He watched the flames sway in rhythm with the music. Jayden sat next to him, eyes were fixed on Ethan. Of course.

Ryan tucked her hair behind her ear.

She looked at him and smiled. Her brows furrowed as she searched his face. "I wish you would tell me what's troubling you."

His heart cracked a little more. But he hadn't pledged his heart to her, even if he planned to—expectation or not—and if he wasn't the one to make her happy, how could he make her feel like she was supposed to honor tradition? They weren't in Tareal anymore. No one here, except maybe Chloe, expected them to marry. He couldn't tame someone so free. He wouldn't, not if it meant stealing Jayden's absolute happiness. He would have to let her know she was forgiven.

"Forgive? You are weak. Fight for what's yours."

He took a bigger piece of the herb and popped it in his mouth while pretending to stifle a yawn.

Then he pulled out his flute and waved it. Ethan smiled. His fingers changed the tune. Something familiar. One of Ryan's favorites. They played as the night grew older. Colder. When the moon peeked through the breaking cloud cover, Ethan set the lute aside.

Logan rose and stretched. "We will leave in the morning before first light," he said to the four of them. "You two will be fine here."

"I know," Ryan said.

"Good." Logan patted Ryan's shoulder. "And you'll sleep in the barn, if you know what's good for you."

Estelle sat on One Eye's lap, looking rather cozy, staring into his eye. He whispered something in her ear and she giggled. Then he scooped her up and headed toward the house.

The barn seemed like a great idea.

Jayden's soft touch on Ryan's shoulder lured him away from the others. He steeled his heart. She led him off a little way toward the edge of the hill. The cloudy cover was starting to dissipate, and the moon peeked through once in a while.

"We don't have to say goodbye, you know." He smiled, though only half his heart was in it.

"I just thought that since this is our last night together, at least for a little while, that perhaps—"

"Stay."

"What?"

"With me. You would be safe here, and Logan will be back soon. You could stay just while they look for the other Deliverer."

She stared at him with her mouth open for so long that he decided to nudge her.

"I—I can't, Ryan. I can't." She reached for his arm, but retracted her hand before she touched him. "We would have been happy if things had stayed the same. But I'm a Deliverer." The moonlight hid, making her pretty face look pale in the dark. And so forlorn.

"Jayden, that doesn't mean you have to be alone."

"Yes. For now it does."

He touched the side of her face, and she leaned into his palm. Her blue eyes met his. "I'm sorry. I can't have anyone."

"You're wrong, you know. But I understand."

CHAPTER 32

MAGIC, SACRIFICE, AND PAIN

The sun rose into the gray morning. Belladonna looked south toward the tall trees that marked the Forest of Legends. She would head that way after twelve more sunsets. Rubius had promised to give her a special power, and she wished to accept it.

He approached her and placed a hand on her shoulder. "Are you ready to become a Healer's worst nightmare?"

"Yes."

"The Mistress of Shadows has sent you a present."

Belladonna tilted her head. Really? Wizard Rubius must have a seeing stone.

"She is pleased that you've decided to unlock your full powers by learning the dark side of magic that Healers deny. She wishes to give you something that can make you even more powerful."

"What could make me more powerful?"

"A creature to bond to."

"My bond structure is for a unicorn. I do not wish to be inhibited by one of those creatures ever again."

Rubius waved her inside. "This bonding is a bit different. It involves magic. Sacrifice. And pain. It requires that you be strong enough to survive."

"And you have the secret to my survival?"

He smiled. "Yes. Follow me. But hurry—this creature is hungry."

Belladonna followed him into his chambers and over to a bowl of some crushed substance such a rich green that it stained the sides of the bowl. Belladonna wrinkled her nose at the smell. Her pulse raced. She knew that smell. "What's that for?"

"I'm sure you know what bandy root does to Healers."

"Of course. It stops our healing powers from working."

"Momentarily."

Belladonna crossed her arms and thrust out a hip. "With a dose that large, it would be much more than a moment."

"We need the venom to take hold of most of your heart."

"Venom?"

"It will make your heart harder to slay. It will make you venomous. It will make you irresistible."

"Will it allow me to lie to a Healer?"

"No. But it will make them instinctively fear you."

"Where is this beast?"

"Drink first, then I'll let you through the door. The bandy root will allow your heart to stop regeneration for a time—long enough to absorb the poison. Then your heart will begin to heal, but the scarring will already be complete. This other potion"—he handed her a vial—"can only be taken once your healing powers have returned."

Belladonna tucked the vial in her pocket. Rubius handed her the bandy root. The awful taste slid over her tongue and down her throat. A strange void filled her middle as her powers drained away. Like she'd been stripped from the inside out. No way to turn back now. Not if the Mistress of Shadows was secretly watching. Belladonna held her head up and met his gaze.

His crooked teeth flashed in a smile and he reached to the floor. His fingers curled around something unseen, but as he pulled up, the wooden door revealed itself.

She strode over to the secret passage. No steps led into the darkness below.

He pointed a long, curled fingernail toward the entrance. "Your oubliette awaits."

Belladonna plunged into darkness. Her heart raced as she free fell to the ground. It was hard. Slate. Pinpoints of light bled through the cracks in the wooden door above her, but her eyes could see nothing of her prison yet.

She stood from her crouch. Her heeled boots clicked against the ground. A soft purr resonated behind her. Her eyes began to adjust, so she stepped back. Whatever was down here and hungry would have to step through the light to get to her.

The scent of lavender filled the air. Belladonna squinted into the darkness. Furry, black wings extended. By the Blood Moon, it was massive. Belladonna scanned the room. No weapons. No rocks. Nothing for her to use in defense.

The black lion leapt toward her.

Her scream echoed as teeth pierced her chest.

CHAPTER 33

WIELD CAREFULLY

Rebekah placed her brush on her dresser and pinched her cheeks. Someone tapped against her door three times. Silence. Three more raps. Then nothing. Her stomach twisted. Balton's summons. He wanted her in his bedchamber. Her time was up. She had to decide and tell him whether or not she'd marry him. Everything in her chest tightened.

She braced her hands against the dresser as her knees weakened. If no one would tell her what had happened the night she'd helped Logan escape, she had to keep her secret safe. Pretending to be Balton's betrothed was her way out. Answering his summons had to be part of the act. And since he knew she was no longer a virgin, waiting would not be an option he'd want, but she'd try anyway.

She plucked the ring out of a dresser drawer and placed it on her finger. Such a strange custom. This trinket would never mean to her what her marriage stone meant. *That* she still wore under her clothes. Hopefully Logan would understand if Balton . . . had his way with her.

Rather than risk angering Balton, she placed the marriage stone in her drawer and noticed the bag of crushed tangle-flower seed Thea had given her what seemed like ages ago. Tempting. She picked it up and let it sit in her palm, weighing it. Wondering if the powder was worth using. Certainly not yet. Balton would realize what she'd done, and there was no way out today.

No plan. She desperately needed a plan. She lowered the bag back, but noticed a small vial sat atop a folded piece of paper. That was new. She picked it up and opened the paper.

> *I thought you might reconsider my offer.*
>
> *Take this vial and drink half. Give the other half to Wolf. Then that terrible trace will be broken, and you'll be free to leave as you please. If you can get out.*
>
> *The trace spell was bound by blood and passed to him upon Idla's death.*
>
> *The trace is like a web, and when Franco mentally pulls on the string connected to you and there is no resistance, he will know you've broken the spell. So make sure your timing is perfect or it'll be for nothing.*
>
> *If I were you, I'd leave that pretty ring behind.*
>
> *Thea*

The paper shook in Rebekah's trembling hand. Thea had left her a way out? With new courage, Rebekah put the paper in the fireplace. Now she had to pick the perfect time, because if Franco found out the trace spell was broken before she got out the front gate, all could be lost. She—and most importantly, Connor—might be stuck in the palace forever.

She breathed in, straightened her shoulders, and headed toward the door. Just before her hand touched it, another knock resounded. She pulled the handle and let her son in. His eyes were wide and his hair windblown.

"Connor? What's wrong?"

He closed the door behind him. "What did Thea give you?"

Thea must have left Connor a note as well. No use keeping it a secret from him then. "I'll show you." She pulled out the tangle flower and vial and shared with him what the note said.

He paced in front of the dresser, tapping his finger against his cheek. "You know we can't trust her and her sister."

Rebekah stared at him with her arms folded. "For this to work, I don't have to trust them."

"You do if everything in your plan hinges on this potion. It could change us into . . . well, the Creator only knows."

"It will remove the trace, Connor."

He stared at her with his eyes narrowed, intent on willing her to see his side. "That's trust."

"Fine. Do you think she's lying?"

His shoulders sagged. "No, I don't. But those two are up to something. And they're using you."

"Me?"

"They want you out of here so the Deliverers will be drawn to you. It will draw you right back to Logan. They will follow. They want the Deliverers."

"Connor, Logan is my husband. I do belong with him. And I am sure we can take care of those two once we are with him."

Connor scrunched his nose. "The last time you were with him—"

"What?" Rebekah closed the distance between them. "The last time I was with him, what?"

"It is probably best that you know nothing."

"Tell me."

"You—well, you were spelled."

She crossed her arms. "I know. Something you've conveniently left me out of."

"I was supposed to be off castle grounds with Luc and some of Oswell's handpicked men."

"Which I am sure you did anyway to cover your tracks."

"Yes."

"Well, then, what's the problem?"

"The problem is telling you what went on between you and Logan. If Franco suspects you remember something—"

"Then we leave. I can't stand the secrets any longer." Rebekah searched her son's face. "Including whatever this new thing is that you're keeping from me."

Connor grabbed her hands and towed her to the table. He sat. Rubbed his forehead. "Balton is about to receive a very special gift I can't let him keep."

"Tell me what it is. I may be able to get my hands on it."

"How?"

"I have just been summoned to his bedchamber."

Connor sat up straight, his fisted hands on the edge of the table. "What? Why?"

She placed her hand on the table and showed him the ring. "Probably to give him an answer." She choked on a breath. "And so he can *claim* his prize."

"Claim . . ." Connor's eyes flashed a brilliant gold and he stood, his jaw tight.

"Connor," she touched his tense arm. "I may be able to keep him from . . . defiling me . . . but not forever." A tear leaked from her eye.

"Mother." He knelt beside her. "You can't go in there. This gift— he'll use it to compel you."

She pulled back from him. "What?"

"It is a tool of compulsion. That's why I have to take it from him."

"I'll help you." She stood tall. "I'll go, and I'll seduce him so he need not compel me. Then I'll take this *gift*."

Connor stood, shaking his head. "Too dangerous."

"More dangerous than letting him tell me what to do?" Rebekah smiled. "I have an idea. And we'll make him forget this trinket ever existed."

Rebekah glided down the hallway. All she had to do was get the man on his bed and slip the bracer off his arm. Easy, right? She almost licked her lips, but stilled herself. She stopped in front of Balton's door and raised her knuckles, hovering them in front of the wood.

Breathe. She rapped on the door.

"Come."

A shiver crawled over her skin as she pushed the door open and stepped over the threshold.

Balton stood inside, shirtless. A thick, white scar trailed over his abdomen. A dark pink one tainted his shoulder. And he wore a golden bracer. Only one. Rebekah stifled another shudder and closed the door.

He poured red wine into a cup and turned toward her. A smile spread across his face. "Rebekah." His gaze trailed from her chest down and back up before meeting her eyes. "You look beautiful."

She dropped into a curtsy, head bowed. "Thank you."

He strode over and offered her the wine. She stared at the bracer as she took the drink. The relief in the metal was a coiled dragon that looked like a snake ready to strike. "What's that?"

"A gift. I never remove it. That's not a problem, is it?"

She set the glass on the table. The currant-red liquid sloshed as she trembled. A drip slid out of the cup and over her fingers. She dared not put them to her mouth. Instead, she wiped them on her dress. The crimson had stained her fingers as if she'd sliced them with a knife.

Balton cleared his throat. The sound startled her. He was closer than she realized. He lifted her left hand, the stained hand, and stared at the ring. "Have you considered my offer?"

"I have." She calmed herself and looked into his icy eyes. A smile spread across her lips that she hoped was seductive. "I have been holding on to a dream for too long. Logan is never coming for me. I might as well be dead to him. You, on the other hand, have always been kind to me. You're strong and powerful. I shall accept your offer and want for nothing."

A smirk slid across his cocky face. "I am so pleased to hear you say that. Now . . ." He set down his glass and gripped her arms in his strong hands. Pinching skin. "May I suggest—"

"That you kiss me?"

His grizzled eyebrows rose, and he grinned. "I'm glad to see you're so willing."

She placed her hand on his scarred chest and his breathing quickened. "May I call you Felix?"

"Please."

She stretched her neck. Closed her eyes. Choked back tears. "Kiss me, Felix."

Hot arms squeezed her close. Pivoted her toward the bed. She opened her eyes as she slammed against the mattress. His moist lips hit hers with a brutal force, as if he were claiming something, and she wanted to scream.

Connor's fingers curled into fists as he paced in front of Balton's chamber. His mother had asked for five minutes. That was all she'd get. No more. The tangle flower should work fast. Thea better not have been lying about that. Doubtless it would knock his mother out, too, since she wore it on her lips.

He stopped walking and leaned against the wall, his wolf-sharp hearing tuned in to the conversation in the other room. She was accepting his offer. Connor tapped his head against the wall behind him as the time passed excruciatingly slowly. If that man had done more than kiss his mother, he'd personally rip out the general's throat.

"Connor!"

He sprang off the wall and raced toward Balton's room. He pulled out his dagger and slammed his shoulder into the door. It flew open. His mother lay slumped on the bed with a half-naked Balton on top of her. Neither of them moved. Connor checked the hall before he pushed the door closed. Then he scratched the back of his head. Well, the stuff had worked—and fast.

He hefted the man off of his mother and removed the bracer. Slipped it onto his arm. He stared at the gold piece. An intricate design of a dragon's head circled the metal. Two eyes stared back at him and he pulled his sleeve over it. The bracer didn't feel right sitting there all cold against his skin. And heavy.

Connor scooped Rebekah up and gently placed her on the duvet. Then he hefted Balton over, careful not to wake him. Connor pulled the rope from beneath his tunic and tied Balton's wrists and ankles to the bed frame. That should hold him in case he didn't stay out long. Then he shoved a handkerchief into the general's mouth.

Now Connor just had to wait for him to wake.

Rebekah stirred first.

He raced to her side. "Mother. Are you okay?"

She nodded, lips drawn into a tight line. "Did you get it?"

He pulled up his sleeve to show her. "You might want to leave."

"I'm staying." She gave him that hard-eyed look that reminded him he was still her son.

Balton jolted up. Muffled shouts came from beneath the handkerchief. Connor towered over the bed and looked down at the general. Even tied up and gagged, the man was menacing.

Connor's hackles rose. He pressed his fist against Balton's chest, just below the man's sternum, so that Balton grunted. "Quit screaming and thrashing. You don't need guards." A throb pulsed in Connor's head.

Balton lay quiet and still.

Connor removed Balton's gag. "Keep quiet."

Pain stabbed through his temples and he staggered back a step.

Connor closed one eye but caught Balton staring at him intently. He couldn't show weakness.

"Connor?" Rebekah sat up.

He put out his hand to stop her from getting up. Maybe he could ask the questions without using the compulsion. Maybe Balton would just answer. Connor pulled up his sleeve and pointed to the bracer. "Who told you about this?"

Balton chuckled.

Connor braced himself against the bed frame and kept his voice calm. "Answer me."

The throb pulsed like a heartbeat of pain in his head. He clutched the bed frame, his knuckles white.

Balton tipped his chin up. "Idla. She got it from a wizard named Rubius. I'm the only one who knew she had it."

"Rubius what?" His knees weakened. The room started spinning. Sweat trickled between his eyes.

"Deltine. You don't look so good."

"Delti—" He knew that name. "You will forget about the bracer. You will forget I was here. You will remember that my mother is going to be your beautiful bride—" The pain warned him to stop. Everything spun, but he kept Balton's eyes in his gaze. "But you won't defile her. You will wait until after your wedding."

Connor pressed the heel of his hand into his temple and groaned. "Do you understand?"

"Connor?" Rebekah touched his back.

Balton nodded, his eyes cloudy. "I do."

"Good." Connor pressed his palms against his eyes. They wanted to pop out of his skull. Then his pounding head hit the floor.

CHAPTER 34

GOOD DAY TO SEE
THE FUTURE

Jayden stood in front of the domed building. The library of Erinecath was like nothing she'd ever seen. It towered as tall as the trees. Beautiful reliefs covered the building. People exited the library with their noses in books. They said "Good day" to every person they passed. One tall man with a bald head had even said "Good day" to her shadow.

Logan had decided to come to this city, which lay north of Salea, before going to the Forest of Legends to find his daughter. He needed the book that would tell him where the Whisperer was. Hopefully Franco hadn't sent someone here for it.

She touched her daggers so often now, turning off the emotions, it had become habit. She caught herself holding them without even realizing she'd touched them. Every time she replaced them in their sheaths, she reminded herself that warriors didn't let emotions get in the way. And she wouldn't let the others down by allowing that to happen to her.

The library's domed building towered over her in the sunshine, and her stomach fluttered as if a swarm of hummingbirds lived inside. Did answers await inside?

She clutched her daggers to calm the fluttering, but it didn't seem to work. Everything else Thea had told her had come true so far. Her death seemed imminent now. Maybe she could just look in the book of Deliverer history and see if they had all died.

Thea said the future could change. And one thing she'd predicted hadn't come to pass yet—something about a person who couldn't see being able to see right through her. Absurd.

Thea had also said that the frog and fox would show Jayden her heart's desire. She swallowed. When they'd danced to "The Frog and the Fox" at Uncle Percy's and she'd tripped, fallen on top of Ethan—her skin warmed just thinking about it—she'd wanted nothing more than to kiss him.

But Thea had warned her to stay away from her heart's desire.

Just as well. Jayden had decided not to let emotion rule her—she just wasn't very good at it yet.

Logan walked up the library's steps and Jayden followed, trying to leave her worries at the bottom.

Floor-to-ceiling shelves of books and scrolls lined the walls inside the library of Erinecath. Jayden scanned the titles. Dare she look for the book? What if looking drew attention to herself as a Deliverer? She should just leave it be.

Unless she could find it.

Just take a peek.

A new wave of anxiety rippled through her. The toe of her boot brushed against the ground, causing her to stumble. A gentle grip on her elbow steadied her.

"Careful," Ethan whispered.

She smiled. "I can't very well walk through the library tripping over my own feet, can I?"

That boyish grin overtook his face, distorting the fading bruise beneath his eye. "I don't know how you can walk anywhere very well if you're tripping over your own feet. But you manage just fine."

"I manage?"

"It surprises me, honestly, the amount of things those dainty boots of yours get caught on."

"You think I'm dainty?"

"Roots, sticks, stones, the normal things. But they also get caught on obscure things."

"Obscure th—"

"Your left foot often catches on your right."

It was true, but did he have to notice?

He chuckled. "And sometimes just the mere presence of air sets them off kilter."

Air? What was he, some teasing brother? He laughed. She couldn't help but join him. She was rather clumsy at times.

Then his face softened. "There's your smile. I've missed it."

Jayden's breath snagged on that stumble-inducing air. He missed her smile? To think that he even noticed it.

"This way." Logan's voice broke their eye contact, and Ethan followed.

Jayden remained rooted. When Ethan glanced over his shoulder, she pulled a book off the shelf so fast that three others fell with it. Her cheeks felt as though she'd kissed a fire. She couldn't look at him. Just picked up the books.

One of the books on the shelf had toppled over, and she righted it. Then she saw the title. *History of Deliverers of the Second Age.*

Her heart seemed to stop.

"It seems the book you're looking for has been checked out already." That voice—a distant echo in her thoughts—belonged to the librarian who spoke to Logan.

She stared at the book in her hands. Dare she open it?

Look inside?

Allow it to dictate her own future?

"Go ahead. Look inside." A warbled voice caught Jayden off guard. A woman with milky-white eyes stared at her. Dead eyes.

"Have I frightened you? I can't tell. I don't see. Well, not in the way most people see." She held out her hands as if she wanted the book.

Jayden handed it to her, and Thea's warning came flooding back: A woman who could not see would see right through her. And Jayden was supposed to listen to her.

The woman ran her fingers along the pages. Feeling the letters. "What is it that you want the book to tell you?"

That she would survive. "Is it true most of the Deliverers die?"

"Everyone dies."

"I mean, trying to defeat the Mistress."

"It's not a safe quest, but don't worry your heart about it. The Creator always chooses the right Children."

She'd heard that before. Perhaps it was the only answer she was going to get. The right Child. "Then the Creator lets them die."

"I told you, we all die. I don't know when and neither do you. Don't let that rule you." She handed the book back to Jayden and patted her cheek. "You are the right Child. And you have the right talents, too."

Jayden gasped. "What do you know of my talents?"

The woman seemed to stare into a void. "They scare you. You think they rule you. But it's less about ruling and more about embracing."

"What does that mean?"

The old woman placed a wrinkled hand on Jayden's shoulder. "Stop running from what you're capable of." She patted Jayden's shoulder, then tapped her cane on the floor and walked away while Jayden stared at the book in her hands.

Capable of? Did everyone speak in riddles? What was she capable of? One thing was certain. She could protect her loved ones. And she wasn't running from that.

Heart thundering, Jayden turned to slide the book back onto the shelf, but a piece of paper stuck out of the top. She opened the book and the paper fluttered to the floor. Strange. There was writing on it.

Softheart,

The stone of Ishkar will help you find your Whisperer. It's in the Forest of Legends in the camp of Healers. You're headed there anyway. And I think you believe me now, so I have another warning for you. It's the hardest for me to see clearly, but after you find the Healer you're looking for, go through Balta. You don't have to trust me, but heed my warning. One of you will find something you need at the Winking Fox.

I don't think you need my signature to know who this is.

Thea. Jayden wanted to crumple the paper. How did that woman have her hands in everything? If she was just leading them into some elaborate trap . . . Jayden paused. Wouldn't Ethan notice? Besides, what did Thea really know? They weren't looking for a Healer. She pocketed the note and closed the book so hard that a smacking sound echoed through the library.

Clearly her outburst with the book had ruffled the librarian because he looked at her with his eyebrows mimicking a line of flying geese as she approached.

Then he cleared his throat. "I remember. The book was checked out by a young woman wearing a black leather mask. She called herself Swallow."

Ethan pulled Logan and Jayden aside and whispered, "I know her. She's Serena, the one who healed me. She's in the Forest of Legends."

"A Healer." Jayden's words escaped in a wispy breath. "I—the book I was just looking in—about Deliverers—said something about the stone of Ishkar helping to locate Whisperers."

Logan regarded her. "Did it say where to find the stone?"

Should she trust Thea? She glanced at Ethan's expectant face and recalled the frog and the fox. She swallowed. "Healers guard it."

"Then it's settled," Logan said. "We go to the Forest of Legends for my daughter and the stone. No time to lose."

CHAPTER 35

WINKING KNIGHT

The sun was still high enough, shedding light on the hazy dust cloud that perpetually surrounded Salea. Serena's bones seemed to hum with a sense of adventure. Oh, that cities could be something a Healer visited regularly. If the Circle ever found out about her using her trips to pick up white linens to venture to Salea, they would have her hide switched twenty ways, and then they'd strip her of her freedom.

That thought sent a cold shiver through her veins. Freedom. May no one ever try to take that from her again, or they'd see what Swallow's blades were really for.

She approached Salea's Blind Pig Tavern. Lively music filtered out through the still-opened windows. Rowdy shouts accompanied. She'd come at the right time. The men were starting to get frisky from drink—something Serena would never understand. Apparently the ability to self-heal kept one from becoming inebriated. They would start with the more reckless fights soon. Those were the ones she preferred to win.

She stopped at the dusty road in front of the tavern and glanced at the water trough. The last time she'd been to the Blind Pig she'd met Ethan—or as the locals called him, Stone Wolf. The strange bond she'd felt with him still nagged at her mind. Stronger recently, almost as if he were near again. Perhaps that was what had led her here again tonight. The books she'd read had her convinced she was bonded to him somehow. Now she wanted to know why, and if he felt the same way.

Worn wooden steps led the way up to the tavern's back door. Serena opened it, stepped inside, and breathed in. The scent was a mix of drink and wood and people and food—not an offensive smell. Instead, it was strange and familiar at the same time, almost like a piece of her childhood.

The part right before everything else she'd just as soon forget.

As she neared the bar she listened to snippets of conversations. One in particular caught her attention.

"Have you seen him? I heard he's here tonight."

"Who?"

"The Knight. He's the new sport fighter from the Winking Fox."

"Haven't heard of him. He must not be any good."

"Oh, he's not. Not yet anyway. He's green yet. My daughter is already begging him for a dance."

"I guess he's come here to see how the real men fight."

A new fighter from the Winking Fox? Stone Wolf trained there. Best fighter since Lone Wolf. Able to make himself as calm as a stone and then strike hard before you even saw it coming. That was how word had reached her anyway, but Serena had seen Ethan rescue a young woman that night. He was a gentleman if there ever was one.

How did this Knight stack up?

A pig of a man wagged his eyebrows at Serena and reached to touch her bottom. "What's with the mask?" he asked.

She drew a dagger and placed it against his hand, inhibiting his touch.

His eyes narrowed. "If you're going to draw those, you'd better know how to use them."

"I'm looking for the Knight."

The man scoffed. "If he's in your fighting class, you'd better take more lessons."

Serena kept walking.

A hand tugged her arm and she spun, dagger ready. The same pig of a man stood there, eyes hungry. "You sure like that blade. They aren't to be used as toys."

"I don't like to be touched."

He chuckled. "Well, you'd better get used to it, missy. There's a lot of men who'll want to touch you. And a toy sword won't keep them at bay."

"Then they'll be sorry." She lifted her chin.

"Is there trouble, miss?"

Serena turned to the voice behind her and had to look up. His serious face sprouted a smirk, and she realized she'd been staring. First at the way his tunic stretched over his chest. Then at his incredible gray eyes. Regaining any dignity at this point might be useless, but she tried. "I have it handled, thank you . . ."

"Ryan." His smile was charming, and he bent to take her hand. She let him, and he kissed the back without tearing his eyes from hers. Heat crept up her neck. Was she seriously blushing? When was the last time she'd blushed? Well, to be fair, when was the last time she'd seen anyone so handsome, let alone coming to her rescue? At least the mask hid her cheeks. But it was certainly getting warm.

"Swallow." She introduced herself.

"I seem to have scared your last suitor off. Can I buy you a drink, Swallow?"

This question came up often. Every time she entered a tavern. But for the first time, she wanted to say yes. "Please."

His smirk returned and so did the heat in her face. He led her to the bar and ordered a drink for each of them.

She turned on her stool and faced the crowded room. The music was louder this close to the musicians, so she couldn't hear the patrons' conversations, but she could read a few lips. So many conversations going on at once. Fascinating.

"Do you visit taverns often?" He held a full cup in front of her, and she realized her mind had wandered.

"Thank you." As she took the drink, her fingers grazed his.

His smile deepened, showing his teeth.

"What's so funny?" she asked.

"Nothing."

Lie. But she knew that already. He must be laughing at her. She looked down, her face warm for a different reason. The ways of the world made her so naïve. She just wanted to fit in here, but maybe she never would. She shyly met his gaze again. "Something made you laugh."

"Yes. I just figured out you didn't want a drink so that you could talk to me. You must have just been thirsty. Clearly someone else has your attention."

"Oh. No. I just . . ." His earlier question finally registered. She angled her body so she faced him instead. "I don't get to come to taverns often. This whole place is fascinating. But so are you."

His eyebrows rose, hiding further beneath bangs that seemed both perfectly placed and carefree at the same time. "I'm fascinating?"

"Now that's funny." A different voice—distinctly female—joined the conversation, and Serena looked around Ryan to see a redhead ordering a drink. She looked at Serena. "If my brother has you believing he's fascinating, he's probably telling you lies."

"Only one." Serena smiled.

"Ah, well. I tried to save you from a huge mistake—letting him dance with you."

"Dance?" Serena looked out at the dance floor.

Ryan set down his drink. "Do you want to dance?"

"I'm not very good at dancing."

"I'm an excellent teacher." He held out his hand.

She bit her lip and stared at it. What would the Circle say if they found out? Then again, how would they? She set down her drink and hopped off the stool. "All right."

"Two things first."

"Two?" Her hand stopped, hovering above his, and she looked up into those gray eyes.

"First, I need your real name."

Her heart beat faster. If the sisters of the Circle came to town and found out she'd been frequenting here—

"And no mask. I have to be able to read your face."

A talent? Her pulse galloped.

"Unless you're not willing." A crease formed between his eyebrows. "I assure you, I mean no ill will."

The truth of his comment registered so plainly in her heart that she felt silly for even doubting. Why did Healers have such a hard time trusting men? Maybe they just hadn't run into any of the right kind.

Could she be Serena here, instead of Swallow?

She stared into those eyes and reached with her talent to see the purity of his heart.

Unbidden, it beat beneath a surface of charm and good humor—his heart was wary, untrusting, unsure. Like hers. He certainly put on a good show. But his heart was so pure. Except one small sliver. A taint. Like one bitten by a black lion. How had he survived?

And how had he fought to keep the taint so tightly locked up? Only someone so pure of heart could do that.

She unlaced the mask.

"Serena." She laid the mask on the bar and took his hand. "I'm Swallow when I'm fighting."

His smile didn't ooze the self-confidence and charm she'd gotten used to from him. This smile was pure, innocent, and it accentuated the sparkle in his eyes. "Thank you for trusting me enough."

Her heart thrummed as if it were a lute he'd just strummed, and she froze as he tugged her onto the dance floor. His eyes rounded as if to ask if she was okay, but she smiled and joined his steps, letting him lead her in the dance.

"Just finding everything fascinating?" He smirked.

She looked deep into his eyes. "Absolutely."

Dancing with Ryan seemed to last one eternal, warm, delightful moment. And yet it ended so soon. As the candles bore longer drips of wax than wicks, she realized how late it was getting.

"Serena?" Dash's voice filled her mind. *"We really should be heading back."*

She gripped Ryan's hand, trying to memorize the feel of it. Strong, calloused, warm, rough. "I should go."

"Was it something I said?" His lazy smile made her feel all the more warm inside.

"Of course not. I just need to get home."

He walked her back to the bar and handed her the mask. "Do you live near? I can walk you."

"Oh. No. Thank you." She caught the look on his perplexed face and didn't want him to get the wrong idea. "Do you come here often?"

"I just came here this evening to see the sword fights." His eyes brightened. "But I do visit the Winking Fox every night. It's in Balta. They have great dancing."

She smiled. "Perhaps I'll see you again. Next time I'm in the area."

"Bring your sword, Swallow."

Of course. "You're the Knight?"

His eyes popped open wide for a moment before that smirk formed again. "You've heard of me?"

She laughed.

"Oh." His eyebrows pinched together. "Not good things. I hope that won't deter you."

"What I've heard doesn't matter. I've met you. That's all I care about."

Now the real smile broke through that tough outer shell. And her heart did something she'd never felt, ever. That's when she knew she'd have to see this Ryan again. The sooner the better.

CHAPTER 36

YELLOW MOON

As they hiked higher up the mountain, Ethan scanned the area. On one side treetops swayed just below the ledge. On the other side a craggy rock wall rose to the sky. Plenty of boulders littered the ground—perfect for hiding behind—and hundreds of crevices in the rock wall offered shelter. The rock formations made it difficult to see what was up ahead, though.

Logan handed them rations as they walked. There'd be no fire when they reached camp tonight. It was getting dark. And fast.

Hopefully they could make it as far as the Valley of the Hidden Ones tonight. After all, the black lions were near here. Not a creature Ethan ever wanted to meet again. Healers seemed safer to stay with than black lions.

"Westwind says camp isn't far."

Too late. A burn shot through Ethan's heart.

Darkness blanketed them as if a thick cloud covered the moon.

A soft purr vibrated through the blackness. Another echoed it. Ethan looked up as four yellow-beacon eyes dove toward them.

"Get down." He pushed Jayden to the ground and lay on top of her as the winged beasts swooped past, wind eddying around them, leaving the scent of lavender in their wake.

Jayden gasped. "A black lion."

He rolled to his feet. "Two."

Logan raced over to them, scanning the dark expanse above them.

He held his sword in one hand and a wooden stake in the other. Ethan recalled that weapon from their first encounter with a black lion.

Both lions landed.

A pair of eyes locked on Ethan. Scout rushed to his side. A low growl rumbled the ground. These lions made the last one they'd fought look like a juvenile.

Ethan gripped his sword and pulled out a knife. Shadows seemed to trick his eyes. The lion's shoulder twitched. He braced himself as it lunged.

Scout darted around the beast and grabbed its wing in his jaws. Good. Scout had remembered how they'd kept the last one down. Ethan prepared to swing his sword. The lion stopped advancing. It snarled at Scout and snapped its wing. Scout flew into the air and slammed into the rock wall with one yelp. Limp, he fell to the ground.

Ethan's chest squeezed. He stared at his dog, waiting to see his side rise with a breath. Waiting for some movement. *Come on, Scout.* Nothing. His eyes burned, but he pushed the emotions away.

A tingle of heat spread across Ethan's chest, and he moved just in time to deflect the lion's paw with his sword. It snarled and lunged for him.

Ethan slashed. It whirled out of the way. He lunged forward again, rocks crunching beneath his boots. Airborne, it backed away. Dust billowed toward Ethan. He drove through the cloud. Heat throbbed in his chest. Revenge for Scout.

Every muscle tensed. Ethan gripped his sword tighter. This beast would die today. "Don't like it when your prey fights back?"

The purr descended all around him.

The big cat crept closer along its belly like a snake.

"Look out!" Logan darted next to him, Jayden right behind. She motioned up. The other black lion hovered above them. Ethan stood ready. The aerial creature dove at the same moment the land snake snapped.

Ethan charged toward the lion on the ground. Westwind joined him—good, the wolves had made it. Ethan raised his sword and the lion moved to avoid a blow, but Westwind clamped his jaws into the cat's neck. It shrieked and Ethan stabbed his sword where the beast's heart would be. It shrieked and writhed.

"Ethan!"

He turned to see Logan toss him something that landed on the ground at his feet. The stake. He scooped it up and turned to the beast. It still lay on its side, but its wound was healing. Ethan plunged the stake into the black lion's heart.

With one final shriek, it turned to dust and blew away in the wind.

A scream split the thick air and Ethan turned. Aurora clung to the other lion's wing. Westwind raced to help his mate. He jumped and grabbed the other wing. Logan stood under the beast and motioned for the stake. Ethan tossed it, but the lion snapped its wings.

The wolves were tossed into the air. They landed on the rocky ground. Yelps and then silence.

"Get that thing to hunt you!" Logan's voice rang out.

Ethan clenched his jaw. He hesitated, and blackness moved closer to Jayden. Two-handed, he chopped through the air with his sword. The blade connected with flesh. A jolt resonated through Ethan's arms. A roar punctured the night. The creature chased after him.

A heavy paw batted Ethan down. He kept his head from slamming into the earth and positioned his sword above him. Yellow irises moved minutely, focusing on prey.

Logan raced to the beast's side, wooden dagger ready to strike. The lion turned on Logan.

Jayden screamed as she buried her dagger into the lion's flank. Too late. Its teeth clamped onto Logan's arm and its blood-red claws buried into his chest.

Ethan raced toward Jayden and pushed her away in time to stop the lion from hurting her. But Logan fell to the ground, blood spreading across the ground from his wounds.

He didn't move.

"Jayden, get the stake. I'll distract it."

"No. I'll distract it." She darted in front of it before he could stop her.

Why wouldn't she just listen to him? Ethan raced behind the creature, his talent fueling speed. He had to do something before it hurt Jayden. He lifted his sword high and brought it down with all his strength, aiming at the beast's tail.

Blade sliced through flesh and bone. Half of the lion's tail thumped onto the ground. The beast screeched. Mighty wings flapped, kicking up dust. It ascended and whisked out of sight.

Jayden ran to Logan. Ethan joined her. Logan was breathing but unresponsive.

The venom. Ethan clutched his shirt. He couldn't breathe. Heavens, it was like something was sitting on him. He took the wooden weapon from Logan's hand. "Will he . . ."

Jayden moved him aside. Her fingers slid calmly across Logan's neck. "He's alive."

Ethan drew in a long breath. How long did Logan have? The wounds in his arm and chest were gaping. Black liquid bubbled out of them. If Logan died—

"We need to get him help. Fast." She looked so calm.

Ethan's chest burned. "It's coming back."

A dark form dove toward Jayden like a black lightning bolt. White prongs of teeth exposed. Yellow eyes locked on him. Good. This thing wouldn't get away again. Not if he could help it.

His talent seemed to whisper an idea and he knew how to get out of this, but he had to act now.

"Jayden, duck inside that cave."

"I can help you."

He looked at her, eyes pleading. If she didn't move now, he'd have to push her out of the way and—well it wouldn't be good for him. "Please! Trust me!"

"No, Ethan, I—"

He pushed her and dove on top of her.

Claws dug into his side, deep. Piercing. Too strong. So much pressure. Then pain. He screamed. The claws ripped through him so easily. Picked him up and tossed him off of Jayden. Red and sharp, they dripped with his blood.

He tore his eyes from the lion and found Jayden. She stood, sword ready.

He tried to move. Heat throbbed through him. Jayden was in danger. His body shook. Revenge wanted death, but revenge didn't mask the pain. *It'll consume you like a raging fire.*

He remembered One Eye's words. Remembered thinking how revenge felt the same as a threat. How would he know the difference?

It controls you. One Eye's voice rang loud and clear.

So did his talent.

It controls you because you're too afraid of something. What are you afraid of?

Losing Jayden.

Revenge masks fear, but it's only a mask. Fear is the true fuel of revenge. Remember that.

It was true.

The black lion's paw extended claws and swiped at Jayden. She jumped. White claws left red slashes on her legs and swept them out from under her. Midair, her body jerked sideways and her head slammed into the rock wall.

She slumped to the ground, limp.

No! The word echoed in his mind like a thundering whisper.

He focused on his talent. It covered up the pain in his side, told him there was a threat for Jayden. That meant she was alive.

He could still save her.

With renewed strength he stood, waved the wooden dagger for the beast to see. "You die today."

He ran. The earth thundered as the lion bounded after him.

A hiss.

He sank to the ground, clutching his middle. Red drenched his shirt. Black spots clouded his vision. He gritted his teeth. He had to save Jayden first.

The lion jumped at him. He dove under it. Dirt and tiny rock shards stabbed through his shirt and clung to his skin.

He gripped the stake in both hands. The beast descended, and he plunged the weapon into its heart.

The ensuing shriek ripped through the dusky sky. Thick blood—so dark it looked black—oozed down Ethan's arms. The mask of lavender faded into the scent of decaying plants.

The beast erupted into a cloud of black dust. And another black lion descended. *Help me, Creator. I have nothing left.* He couldn't leave Jayden unprotected. *Hear me, Creator. Send help.*

CHAPTER 37

BLACK LION
TERRITORY

*T*ry again." Dash touched his soft, white nose against Serena's hand. She huffed and lifted her hand up in front of her again. *"You're a unicorn, I'm a human. Just because you can do it doesn't mean I can. I don't even have a horn."*

"I understand. Humor me." Dash stretched his neck forward and his long, spiraled horn glowed. A ball of light burst on the end, shining like a star. *"Did you feel how I did that?"*

She did. He let this surge of energy that stemmed from a warm memory fill him, then somehow channeled it into his horn. That didn't mean she had the same power. But she focused on her outstretched hand. She latched onto a feeling of something wholesome and true— her friendship with Dash—and tried to push it through her arm.

A small sparkle of light glittered in her palm. She opened her mouth. "Do you see that?" She kept pushing the thought and the ball of light grew, like a star in the center of her palm.

Light surrounded her. "Do you see it?"

"I see it." Dash nuzzled her.

She stroked his long nose. "You were right, my friend. I'll have to tell Rochelle. We should—" She stopped and doubled over. Searing pain stabbed her side.

Dash caught her with his nose, pushed her up. *"Where is it?"*

She stood, clutched her middle. The pain always came as an explosion all at once, letting her know the intensity. Then it began to wick

-223-

away and settled into a tight knot pulsing within her. Letting her know someone had entered the Valley and was in need of healing.

Then her head felt as though it cracked open.

Dash dipped his head for her to get on his back. *"Someone entered the valley? I don't feel the pain."*

She jumped on his back. "Not in the valley. Close. On the border. It's someone . . . Ethan."

Dash's hooves pounded into the soil as he carried her toward the border.

"No, stay here. The black lions are out."

"I feel the pain now. There's too much for you to heal alone. I'm going with you."

The pain continued to throb in the tiny knot inside her. She held onto it. As long as she still felt it, Ethan was alive. *"Hang on, Ethan. We're coming for you."*

Dash galloped over the threshold of the valley and into black lion territory. One of the beasts flew through the air in a dive toward two bodies on the ground. Dash didn't slow. He charged the beast. Red claws extended, it dove right for Ethan.

Red claws meant it was going for the kill. Serena's heart clutched. She hung tight to Dash's mane. He lowered his head.

A jolt knocked Serena from his back as his head rammed into the creature of darkness. His horn passed easily into the skin and the lion shrieked. It clawed at Dash's face, but it had already been dealt a killing blow. Black dust rained down on Dash's white fur. He shook his head and looked at Serena, dark blood dripping down his horn.

She released a breath she didn't know she'd been holding. *"Thank you."*

"Heal them if you can. Before any more of these beasts come," Dash said. *"I got lucky with that strike."*

Serena raced over to Ethan. He dropped to his knees next to a young woman. It was her head injury Serena had felt.

"Serena?" He clutched her arm with his blood-covered hand. The pain in him pulsed into her and she wanted to retch. "Can you heal her? C-can you heal Jayden?"

She knelt beside him and hovered her hand over Jayden. Neither she nor Ethan had been poisoned with the lion's venom. Strange, because the gaping holes in Ethan's side looked to be claw punctures.

Jayden was moments from death.

Serena laid her hand against Jayden's forehead.

Oh. There was a lot of damage in there. She was fading fast. Serena's hand shook. If she healed this wound, what would it do to her mind? Would she be able to keep focused enough to keep the healing energy flowing? She looked into Ethan's pleading eyes. She breathed deep. Creator help her, she had a gift and she was meant to use it.

Her bloody hands pressed against Jayden's head.

Shooting pain pulsed in her skull.

At last Jayden opened her eyes.

Ethan sighed. "Thank you, Serena."

Jayden stared at her with wide eyes, then she turned her attention to Ethan. He'd lost a lot of blood and started to fade out of consciousness. He pitched forward, but Serena caught him and laid her hands against his wounds.

Blood soaked her sleeves. Her insides felt like they ripped open. Everything burned. Her eyes squeezed tight. After what she'd just done for Jayden, she might not be strong enough.

Dash touched her back. She pulled strength from him, funneled it into the healing. "Come on, Ethan."

He sucked in a shuddering breath and opened his eyes. "Serena?"

She touched the side of his face with her bloody hands. "Almost lost you there." A lump got caught in her throat. "You all right?"

He pulled her in and hugged her tight. "You said you'd come if I needed you. I didn't think—thank you."

Then he turned to Jayden. "You okay?"

She nodded, eyes welling with tears.

Dash's voice filled her tired mind. *"Serena, there are others in need of healing."*

She turned to Ethan. "Dash says there are others."

"Yes. A man." Ethan stood, towing Serena with him. Jayden followed.

Serena slowed as she felt those who were injured. There were so many. Two wolves lay on the rocky ground. The larger of the two lay in a puddle of blood. His foreleg was slashed open, and a shard of bone stuck out of it. The other one rose, unsteady on her feet due to the gash in her side, and bared her teeth.

"It's okay." Ethan held out his hand. "They're friends."

Dash strode closer to them, his hooves silent on the gritty ground.

Serena got down to the wolf's level. "Dash will heal you and your mate."

The wolf nodded.

Dash followed Ethan's gaze, lighting the area with his horn. Oh. A large farm dog lay on the rocky ground. She touched Ethan's shoulder. "He's alive. Dash can heal him, too. Take me to your friend." She felt the sting of black lion venom spreading in her veins. Whoever it was didn't have a lot of time.

Jayden led them to a man on the ground. Deep puncture wounds in his chest oozed blood. It was as she feared. Venom infected him. "I cannot heal him here. He has to come to the Tree of Wisdom. The venom is spreading, but it has not infiltrated his heart yet. If we can extract it before it does, he will have no lasting effects. But we must hurry. Dash will carry him. Help me."

○

The air was warmer and the breeze gentler the moment they stepped into the valley. Serena noticed that Jayden stayed close to Ethan, and both of them stumbled often. She'd had to use much of their strength to heal them.

"Don't worry, Serena. They'll be able to rest soon enough. You saved both of them from the brink of death. That would make anyone feel weak."

A silence hung over them as they walked into the dark woods beyond the meadow. Once beneath the boughs, the darkness fled. Silver leaves shimmered when the wind touched them.

Serena and Dash halted in front of the largest silver tree in the valley. The Tree of Wisdom. The two healers she most trusted, Miranda and Rochelle, stood outside with their unicorns, waiting for people to come for healing. Not that anyone ever did. Tonight would change that.

The massive tree's thick trunk rivaled the width of some houses. The breeze tickled the silver leaves. Was a storm brewing?

Miranda stepped forward. "Serena?"

"Miranda." Serena bowed. "Venom from a black lion runs through this man's veins."

"You've healed the rest." It wasn't a question.

"They were not . . . bitten." Serena's gaze flicked to Ethan.

Miranda's hand hovered over Logan. "I'll get some other Healers to help you. There is much venom in him. Let's get him inside."

CHAPTER 38

RED RUBIES

Thea had not gone to Meese. Not even made it off the palace grounds. She'd been ambushed before entering the carriage, just as she'd foreseen. Now she waited inside, bound and gagged, for Franco to show himself. To stab her while she watched.

The door opened and Franco entered, wearing the same blood-red cloak he'd worn in her vision. She knew the words he'd speak before he even spoke them, and her heart sputtered in her chest.

"I thought you might want some company." Franco sat on the bench across from her and lowered the scarlet hood. He smirked, lazy and dangerous.

Thea stared right into the prince's eyes. She'd never consider him a king. He was some kind of wolf having a power play.

Thea's fingers carefully found the object hidden in the pocket at the small of her back. Now she just needed to shift her weight and bend unnoticed so she could place it on the bench.

"Still struggling, I see." Franco sneered.

Something hit the outside of the carriage. Franco shifted his gaze. It was all Thea needed. She placed the tiny object on the seat of the carriage uncovered. Its black form blended in to the dark leather seats.

Franco dipped his hand into his breast pocket and fished out something. Thea slid over slightly so the seeing stone she'd placed on the carriage seat could catch everything. The Mistress of Shadows would know what her pawn, Franco, was up to. But more importantly, Connor would see everything.

Franco held up his right hand, a small object between his thumb and forefinger. A ring. Thea's ring—given to her by her other sister, the one not related by blood. She always wore it. He'd stripped her of it when he tied her up.

"It's pretty." Franco inspected it. Then he let it fall into his fist. "What I like most about it is how I'll be able to use it. Once you are disposed of, Kara will seek vengeance against your killer. Pity she won't know it's me."

Franco had a terrible laugh.

"You've been a good assassin, and I thank you for getting my mother out of the way. I didn't even have to ask." He leaned forward, closing the distance. "But the truth is, she was my mother. I never would have killed her. And I can't tolerate those who try to get me killed." He stood and pried the gag from her mouth. Then he leaned down, face close to hers. "Why did you free Logan and the Deliverer?"

Thea glared. "*Prince*, I hope you know my sister is more dangerous than I am. You're lucky she won't know you killed me. I'd pity you if she did."

Then a vision hit her. Melted her heart. She gasped. Some of it was the same, the way things would go from here: Jayden lying bloody in the snow, eyes open and unfocused. General Balton stabbing Logan in the chest. Connor pushing Rebekah out of the window.

But one thing was new—Kara drinking a potion made by Franco. Her heart ached. She hadn't seen everything. And she couldn't fix it now.

Franco tipped his head and arched an eyebrow. "Losing your tough demeanor?"

The plans Franco had for Kara formed in her mind. This couldn't— this wouldn't—she glared at the prince. "Never. And Kara will never submit to you."

"She'd better, or she'll find herself dead."

Thea forced back tears. Perhaps this was for the best. If Franco did this to Kara, she wouldn't have to worry about him killing her. Thea's father's voice echoed in her mind, comforting her: *The future is always changing. Hang onto the threads that are firm. The ones that dance around can change at any time, with any decision. Be careful you don't try to hang on to those threads, daughter."*

Franco lifted a vial with clear liquid and shook it. "I'll have Belladonna's power for the next half hour." He drank it, then faced her with a wicked smile. "Is Kara to be trusted?"

Thea laughed. "Kara trusts only me."

"Did she have a part in your plan?"

"Kara has no idea what I have planned. I wish she did. That way she would never believe the lies you will tell her."

"Who do you work for?"

"The Mistress of Shadows does not trust you. She planted me in your palace."

"You and your sister?"

"Kara is unaware of the plans I have been making with the Mistress."

Franco studied Thea's face. Half-truths like that could muddle a Healer's search for truth, but Franco didn't seem to notice. He finally spoke. "I think your carriage is about to catch fire. Pity you'll be in it. But as I said, you were a good assassin. You won't feel the burn. You'll already be dead. Any final words?"

She'd already said them. "Did I complete my mission?"

"Worry not, your sister will see you as the heroine who died performing her duty. And she will never know you betrayed me." Franco stood and held a small dagger in his hand. Red rubies gilded the hilt. "Feel free to scream." Franco placed the dagger's tip against Thea's abdomen.

It was just like Thea had seen play in her head time after time. The silver penetrated her jerkin and thrust into her lung. Her breathing hitched. The vision had been void of pain, but this didn't hurt as badly as she'd expected. Mostly she felt pressure.

So much pressure.

Then the pain filled her.

Crimson tainted her clothes. It was warm at first, then cold. Very cold.

CHAPTER 39

JUSTICE IS SERVED

The inside of the tree seemed different than Jayden expected. And larger. Candles adorned the curved walls, lighting the whole room and filling it with the scent of roses. Three pallets lined the walls, and one long table sat in the center of the room. A cabinet with a pitcher of water and wooden bowls rested against one wall.

Reliefs of unicorns and elegant women adorned the tree's peach-colored wood. Jayden caught herself staring at the designs. Many were of Healers laying hands on people, but some depicted Healers with daggers.

One picture showed a unicorn thrusting its horn through a black lion. Jayden shuddered. The black lion's pained face was just above one of the candles on the wall, and the resonating light of the flickering flame distorted its gruesome face even more.

"Set him here." Serena's voice called Jayden back to the urgency at hand.

Ethan lowered Logan onto to the table.

She ripped his shirt, where it was already torn and bloody, and exposed the wounds. He flinched when she applied the water to the black, oozing punctures. "Awareness is a good sign."

"You two must be exhausted. Please, rest." Serena motioned to the pallets. "The other Healers will be here soon. I'm going to go with Miranda and make sure they're aware of the urgency of the situation."

Ethan moved toward Serena and stumbled.

She steadied him. "Easy there. I had to use quite a bit of your strength to heal you and Jayden."

Jayden straightened her back. "You used his strength to heal me?"

Serena nodded. "You didn't have enough of your own left. You almost didn't make it. Both of you." She looked into Ethan's eyes.

"Thank you," he said.

"I wasn't going to let that happen." She squeezed his arms once more before she left.

Jayden bit back her jealousy. It was stupid, really. This woman had just saved them. She should be feeling grateful. Happy. And she was. But too many emotions wanted to rise to the surface right now. She gravitated closer to Ethan.

He rubbed a finger against her arm. "Hey, I'm sure Logan will be fine."

His emotions lapped against her. Push, pull, push, pull. They mirrored hers.

Everything from the black lion battle rushed back to her. He'd told her to run, but she hadn't. His fear had spiked, and she'd ignored it.

She'd thought it weakness to let his fear in. To let her own fear—the thought of losing him—in.

He'd asked her to trust him and she hadn't. Because of that, he'd been in the path of the lion and then it went after her. All because she didn't want to lose him. Because she was afraid to let him protect her.

But it was his job—not hers. His choice. He'd taken over where her family could not.

If she kept trying to stop him from protecting her, it would only make things worse. It *had* made things worse, more than once. She needed to accept that this was what he'd do. That last thought pierced her heart like an icicle. But she'd have to accept it. Honor the fact that he'd taken an oath.

But losing him would crush her.

Yes. The emotions would cripple her, but only if she let them. They weren't to be controlled, they were to be embraced. But how?

Perhaps the first step was to stop trying to become her idea of an emotionless warrior.

She looked into his eyes. "Thank you for protecting me."

He stared at her, and his relief rushed into her like a dam breaking. It was as if he finally felt that she understood him.

He leaned in close, intensity deep in his eyes. "Anything for you. Anything."

His soft smile melted her. His eyes searched her face. Her heartbeat quickened. He leaned closer. So close she could—

The door to the tree opened. Serena and Miranda, followed by two other women, slipped in. The first was a dark-haired, dark-eyed woman who looked much older than Serena, though not exactly old. The other woman had white hair.

"Lydia, Tabitha." Serena introduced the newcomers.

These women also wore white, flowing gowns that rippled as they strode over to Logan. The white-haired woman jerked away from him. The dark-haired woman placed a hand over her mouth.

What did that mean? Was he beyond healing?

"We cannot heal this man," the white-haired woman spoke.

Jayden's heart clutched.

"What do you mean?" Ethan placed a hand on his sword hilt.

"This man"—the white-haired woman faced Ethan—"is a danger to Serena. We cannot heal him. Justice has been served."

"Justice?" Ethan's eyes narrowed.

"Yes." She arched an eyebrow.

Ethan ripped a candle from the wall with his blood-stained arm and handed it to Jayden. "Jayden, take Scout and Aurora and find one of the plants. Westwind and I will bring Logan to you." The wolves bounded to Ethan's side, teeth revealed.

"We cannot allow this." The two women barred Jayden's way.

Ethan began to pull out his sword.

"Ethan, don't." Serena's voice stopped him.

"Ethan?" Miranda's wind-chime voice broke in. She looked at Serena. "This is your Ethan?"

"Yes. This is the Ethan I healed." Serena's eyes pleaded with the other women.

"We still cannot—" the white-haired woman began.

"How can you make this judgment, Tabitha?" The dark-haired woman interrupted her.

"He is evil, Lydia."

A fire lit in Jayden's chest. "He is no such thing."

Tabitha glared at Jayden. "Are you bonded to unicorns, Child?"

She recoiled from the old woman's cold stare.

Serena stepped closer to the older Healers. "It's the evil of the venom you feel."

"No, child," Tabitha said to Serena. "He will try to take you. I cannot allow that."

Serena's eyes widened. "Logan? This is Logan?" Her voice came out as a whisper. Her hand pressed against her throat, and she staggered a step back.

Tears coursed down Jayden's cheeks now. "If you won't heal him, then let me save him. We'll take him far from here, if you're worried."

Serena's gaze met Jayden's. "Do you trust him? Logan?"

"He's like a father to me."

Serena glanced at Ethan. "And you?"

He released his sword. "With my life."

"Then I'll heal him myself." Serena rolled up her sleeves and placed both hands above Logan's leg.

"Serena, no. You're not strong enough." Tabitha charged toward her.

Ethan blocked the white-haired Healer.

"She is," Miranda whispered.

"Serena, the Hall will form a Circle if you decide you must heal this man," Tabitha warned.

"Form your Circle. He has no time left." Serena dropped her hands to Logan's thigh.

"So be it." Tabitha whirled around.

Lydia followed her out. The two women brushed by Miranda as if she wasn't there.

Serena cried out as if in pain.

Ethan jumped toward her, but Miranda put her arm out to stop him. "You can go to her, but don't touch her until she falls away. That will mean she is done."

"Falls?"

"You must not break her concentration. She is absorbing the poison."

"She's absorbing it? Snare me. She'll die."

Miranda shook her head. "She is very strong."

Serena swayed visibly. Sweat beaded her forehead. Ethan dashed over to her, hovering behind her.

Logan convulsed. His back arched and his whole body shook.

Jayden pressed her hands to her mouth. Ryan thrashing on Anna's couch, the black lion's poison in his veins, returned to her memory. The pounding from Logan's thrashing mimicked Jayden's erratic heartbeats. She dropped beside Westwind and touched his shoulder. He leaned into her, and she pulsed emotion into him: sorrow, love, and hope. He turned his eyes onto her for a brief moment, and in his gaze she felt his sincere gratitude.

At last Logan's body fell against the bed with a lifeless thud.

Serena trembled. Her eyes rolled back into her head and she collapsed. The only thing to hit the floor was her golden hair as Ethan caught her still, limp body in his arms.

CHAPTER 40

RELATIVE TRUTHS

Jayden pressed her fingers over her mouth. She couldn't tell if Logan was breathing.

"Are they okay?" Panic edged Ethan's voice as he held Serena's limp form in his arms.

Miranda placed her hand on Jayden's shoulder and gently moved her aside. She then rested her fingers on Logan's temples. "He'll probably sleep for a week—black lion venom is very potent—but he'll suffer no lasting effects."

Miranda then touched Serena's temples. "She'll also be fine. She's even stronger than I thought." The Healer motioned to one of the pallets. "Set her here."

Ethan complied, but he didn't leave Serena's side. A pang fluttered through Jayden's chest. Was it his job to protect Serena now, too?

Miranda picked up a blanket. "It usually takes at least two Healers for what she did. Serena is the strongest Healer I know." Miranda brushed a hand over Serena's golden hair and forehead, covering her with a blanket. "It's why Tabitha and Lydia want to protect her. Sometimes I wonder if their protecting is more inhibiting." She motioned to Logan. "Help me move him to a bed."

Ethan helped carry Logan to another pallet, and Miranda draped a blanket over him. Westwind jumped onto the bed next to his friend and placed his head across Logan's chest. Aurora curled up on the floor near them.

Miranda laced her fingers together. "The Circle will be in session soon, if they aren't already. I'll keep them out of here at least until Serena wakes, but once she does, there is no doubt that they will storm in here uninvited."

"What will they decide about Logan?" Jayden asked.

"Logan has been a threat to Serena since the day she was put into hiding. They will at least banish him from here, along with the rest of you. Or they may hold him prisoner."

Heat flooded Jayden's blood. Rage, but it wasn't her anger. She grabbed Ethan's arm. Heavens, he was tense. "She's helping us."

"Is she?"

Miranda straightened her spine and walked up to Ethan. "You and your sword don't scare me. Your heart is pure and Serena trusts you, heaven knows why. Healers seldom trust men."

Ethan clenched his jaw. "I would keep Serena safe."

Miranda let out a deep breath. "When Serena came to us, her adoptive family sent her with a letter. It warned us that if Logan were to ever find her, he would turn her over to the queen. If you wish to protect her, you won't let Logan get his hands on her."

"Who wrote the letter?"

"Her mother."

The door to the tree opened, and Jayden slipped her hands onto the dagger hilts at her waist. The brown-haired, hazel-eyed young woman who had been standing watch with Miranda entered. She had to be no more than fourteen.

Miranda faced her. "What is it, Rochelle?"

"Dash would like to hear how Serena is." Her voice was soft and meek. She bowed her head and clasped her hands in front of her. When Jayden looked at Rochelle, the young Healer's worry churned her stomach.

Miranda nodded. "Serena will be fine. As will Logan. Any news from Tabitha or the Circle?"

"Not yet." Rochelle grabbed her white skirts in her fists. "Is it true? Has Logan come to take her?"

Jayden gasped. "Serena is Logan's daughter, isn't she?"

Miranda's eyes narrowed. "You knew that when you came here."

"No." Jayden shook her head. Miranda and Rochelle both stared at her, echoing one another's shock so loudly, Jayden's head hurt. She closed her eyes and turned off her talent. "You don't believe me?"

"They do." Ethan didn't take his eyes off the Healers.

Rochelle's smile was warm. "Healers can tell if you lie."

Oh. This changed everything. "Then you know Logan wouldn't hurt her. He came here to find his daughter, to protect her. He's her Protector."

Miranda sighed. "Whether or not Serena is permitted to go with you is a decision for the Circle."

Again the burn of anger fanned out across Jayden's chest, but it wasn't hers. She tried to catch Ethan's arm again, but he shrugged her off. "Because she can't choose for herself?"

"If Serena is truly Logan's daughter, she'll choose to come with us. She won't be able to resist the . . . connection," Jayden said.

"Connection?" Miranda raised her eyebrows. "To what?"

"To *whom*." Jayden bit her lip. "Deliverers feel connected to their Protectors. And apparently to one another. At least I do. If I were separated from my Protectors, I'd still be able to find them."

Rochelle gasped. "A bond to another person? Is that possible?"

Miranda narrowed her eyes. "If there is truly a bond between a Deliverer and their Protectors, something in the *Old Custom* may change the Circle's opinion of what is necessary. I'll go to the library and see what I can find. Rochelle, you stay here. I'm not certain Dash will trust anyone else guarding the tree."

Miranda lifted her skirts, exposing the toes of her white boots. She stopped and looked over her shoulder at Ethan. "If you leave, you'll be hunted." She turned on her heel and opened the door. The outside wind pushed her auburn hair behind her as she strode out.

The breeze reached Jayden's face, and a tingle skittered over her skin. The storm. Currents of its power swirled in the air and brushed up against her. Filled her like a battle cry ready in her lungs. It would be over them soon. She closed her eyes and relished the fresh, outdoor air until the door sailed shut. These Healers wouldn't contain her any longer than she wanted to be here. A whining creak sounded above them.

Ethan looked up, but Rochelle didn't seem to mind. She shot Jayden a warm smile. "The tree is quite safe."

The young Healer walked over to Serena with Ethan's eyes tracking her. She touched Serena's temple and smiled. "She's so strong."

"How can you tell?" Jayden asked.

Rochelle's eyes sparkled when she smiled. "The temple radiates to Healers how the person feels. How tired or hungry they are, things like that. When I touch her, I can tell that she's regained much of her strength. Like this." Rochelle reached a hand toward Jayden's temple. "You are weary as well as hungry and thirsty. I can get you some fruit."

"You can *feel* that?" Ethan asked.

"Yes."

Rochelle held her hand out toward Ethan's temple, but he backed away from her.

"Could you heal it?" he asked.

Rochelle's eyebrows pinched together. "I could, to a degree. But I won't. Using our gift drains us and those we heal." Rochelle walked over to the cupboard and returned with a couple apples and some bread. Jayden took some of both, but seeing as Ethan wouldn't, she put the apple in his hand.

Rochelle continued, "Serena is my friend. If she weren't so young, I'd be her apprentice. The Circle has rules about how old you can be before you can take an apprentice. Miranda has taken me as hers, but Serena still teaches me things in secret."

Jayden pulled Ethan's sleeve and sat on one of the pallets with her back against the tree.

He followed her, sitting so close his arm touched hers. "Serena teaches you?" Scout curled up next to her and stared at her apple. She gave him a piece.

Rochelle's eyes grew round as she knelt near them. "Yes, she found me. You won't tell the others she teaches me?"

Jayden smiled. "Of course not."

Thunder rolled. Jayden breathed deep and let the sound relax her. Soon the tree was filled with the sound of gentle patters slapping against the protective bark. Ethan's head touched her shoulder and she glanced over. Even during the thunder's lullaby, Ethan was asleep.

Rochelle giggled. "I knew he couldn't stay awake much longer." She sat on the pallet across from Jayden's. "Still, Serena said he was very strong."

"When did she say that?"

"He was Serena's first heal. She told me all about it."

Jayden's mouth fell open. "Serena never healed anyone before Ethan?"

"No. When a Healer first heals, it is usually someone they love. Family, or a very close friend, or a lover." Rochelle let the list spill off her tongue like it was common knowledge, but Jayden's heartbeat hitched at the words *love* and *lover*.

Rochelle continued, "I healed my younger brother first. He tripped over a log and broke his ankle. We were far from home, and I wanted to help him. It was like this ball of warmth filled me. I placed my hand over his ankle to tell him I'd get him home. But I felt the pain in my own ankle as if it were my own. It didn't last long. My brother pried my hand from his ankle, and we both stared. The bruising was gone, and he could put weight on it with no pain. He asked me how I did it, but I didn't know."

"You can feel what you are healing?" Jayden looked at Logan's still body on the bed. The rise and fall of his chest was his only movement.

"We take the pain or sickness and heal it in ourselves. When we stop feeling the pain or sickness, we know the healing is done."

"You must hate healing, then."

Rochelle shook her head. "It's our duty, our purpose. That's what Serena says. I agree. Knowing that you can take someone else's pain from them—someone you love, so they don't have to endure it anymore—makes everything else worth it."

The thunder rolled.

"It's not without cost." Rochelle looked at Serena's sleeping form. "Using our power drains us because our bodies overcome it. But we can take more than pain from those we heal. We take strength, too, if we need it, only for Healing purposes."

"That's why you didn't heal Ethan's tiredness?"

"You grasp this better than most non-Healers, but Serena says you are a 'kin' to her."

"What does that mean? And how do you know that?"

Rochelle beamed. "Dash told me. He thinks Serena is right. As for what they mean by 'kin,' you'll have to ask Serena."

"What does Serena teach you?"

Rochelle paused and her eyes darted around the tree. "She does what many Healers won't. She goes into cities. Healers are afraid to leave their forests because of the Imprisonment. But Serena says our people need us. We should stop being so afraid and go out and do what the Creator puts us here to do. War is coming again. All the signs point to it, and the Healers should be on the battlefield with the other Feravolk. I agree with Serena, and that's why I mean to come with you when you leave."

Jayden stared at the young Healer; her glance flickered first to Logan, then Ethan. She'd almost lost both of them today. Maybe having a Healer around wouldn't be a bad thing. "Imprisonment?"

Rochelle shuddered. "Healers are considered valuable. We've been taken prisoner during times of war for armies to use not only to heal their soldiers but also as human shields, and even to breed other Healers." She looked at her hands. "If war is coming, the Healers will hide even better than they do now. More of the old Healing houses will be abandoned. We will cease to serve our purpose."

Then Jayden had to stop Franco from starting a war. She felt it now more than ever. It was time to go after him. Before he came after her.

CHAPTER 41

DUTIFUL PENANCE

Stretching arms of yellow contrasted with the still-lingering night sky. Light quietly overtook the dark, and it looked so effortless. One of the reasons Ryan loved sunrises.

This morning, the beauty in the sky couldn't banish the tug he felt in his chest. A strange sense of urgency. It had started last night. Woke him like a hammer hitting the lunch bell.

"You should follow it."

The voice hissed in his mind. Seared his thoughts. He stared at the trees in the valley. Behind them, shadows stretched long against the dew-crystallized grass. Blackness on the land that the sun couldn't quite reach. A stain.

"You think I'm a stain in your mind?" Her laugh was always a hissing chuckle. *"Wrong. The root is here in your heart. Dark as night and pulsing with each heartbeat. Your blood cannot escape my work. Soon I'll begin the transformation again. Soon. No prison can hold me forever."*

"Enough!"

He pressed his palms against his ears, tried to make it—*her*—go away. But he couldn't. Slowly he pulled the root from his pocket and turned it over in his hand. Such a small thing. But Thea was right. It helped. The problem was, it seemed to be helping less each time he took it. He'd started taking bigger chunks, and it seemed smaller sections took their place. It could be just his imagination. He broke off a piece and stared at it. There had to be a way to get rid of this voice.

"There is. Cut out your heart."

He tossed it into his mouth. Quiet overtook his mind. It was his alone. For now.

Good. He needed it. And one thing was certain: he wouldn't go following that strange tug anywhere. Not if she—*it*—wanted him to. He'd wait for Logan and the others to return as promised.

Time to head back. Ryan stood and stretched, making sure his sword was still secure, and headed back to the barn where he slept. And there was Chloe, making her way from the kitchen to the stable, mop in hand, scowling. Ryan rolled his eyes. If Chloe would just learn to stop talking back, she'd have much less penance.

In the month he'd been here, he'd been the perfect student. He learned fast. Mastered the lessons. Practiced with every free minute. And everything he'd known about sword-fighting before One Eye had been what One Eye called "good form." Plus, he was a pretty good dancer.

He didn't talk back like Chloe. Didn't verbally challenge everything One Eye said like his fiery, redheaded sister. And he helped Estelle with supper without being asked. How on the Creator's green soil could Chloe—flame-eyed, fiery tongued, hot-headed Chloe—be the easy one to train?

Stag's heavy baying announced One Eye's departure from the house. The day was beginning. Ryan ran to the barn for some training before breakfast. Breakfast that Chloe was helping to make because of penance. Ryan greeted Stag, and a string of slime clung to his sleeve when the dog moved his head. Gross.

"Up early again." One Eye spoke in his gruff voice. He had a perpetually happy face, even though it was scarred.

Ryan nodded.

"You like the sunrise. I'm more of a sunset person myself."

Darkness was never better than light. Even in the dark Ryan would have a fire or full moon, if he could. Then those yellow-moon eyes, dark like the amber stones Norm Grotter used to sell, shot into his memory, and he stilled a shudder. On second thought, fire trumped a full moon.

One Eye chuckled. "You seem to be making quite the name for yourself at the tavern. All the girls want a dance, sure, but now you're starting to be recognized by your talent."

Well, that was good news.

One Eye's eye narrowed. "You certainly have a lot of ambition."

He did have a brother who was always pushing him to give his best.

One Eye scratched his chin. "You don't say much."

What was he supposed to do with that? Agree? That wouldn't be true. Disagree? That would just be disrespectful. Okay, there hadn't been a lot of talking. Except for the cursed voice in his head, and no one needed to be tipped off about that.

One Eye scratched his bristly chin and leaned against the gnarled apple tree outside the barn. "You're a conundrum, you are."

Hardly. "I beg your pardon, sir?"

He pointed a thick finger at Ryan. "You're the most guarded human being I've ever met."

Guarded? Now wait just a minute. He talked all the time. Not during chores, maybe, and never during training. But dinner, sure. There should always be a solid conversation with that many people at the same table.

And at the tavern. There were a lot of pretty faces there to engage in conversation with. He hardly shut up. In fact, Tessa, the tavern owner's daughter, had told Ryan she wanted his sword-fighter name to be the Jester, not the Knight. Because the jester never stopped talking. Hardly behavior for one as guarded as One Eye claimed.

"How do you mean, guarded? I believe I've been an open book, sir."

"Open, sure. Just not to the chapter I want to read."

Oh. Well, those chapters were likely private. "Ask me anything."

One Eye crossed his arms and stretched his spine along the tree. "Ethan. You call him brother?"

"Yes."

"Why?"

"He's family to me. To my sisters. He would do anything to protect us."

"So you value loyalty."

"Of course."

The way One Eye stared as he shifted, like everything moved except his eye, made Ryan uneasy. Where was this going?

"You call Chloe sister."

"Of course."

"Same reason?"

"Well, no. I mean, she was born my sister, but yes. She'd protect every one of us with the same ferocity."

"And do you deserve to have them call you brother?"

Ryan shifted his weight to his other leg. "Are you asking if I'd be willing to give my life for either of them?"

"No. I was asking if you would protect them, but it's interesting to know how deep you feel that protection goes."

"Of course I would."

One Eye nodded, his gaze drifting to the ground. Then, like lightning, he drew his sword.

Ryan stumbled back. Stupid for not being ready. He met One Eye's sword with his own blade, barely.

One Eye pushed. Ryan pushed back. Whirled out of the way.

There was always so much to remember, and Ryan felt his movements were sloppy, but he managed to stop One Eye's sword from slicing into his arm. He watched the man's every move. One Eye's feet showed weight shifts, his arms and his torso told Ryan where the sword would be aimed. Problem was, he had to read the intentions fast enough. And react faster.

His foot landed on a hard root, and Ryan lost balance just as One Eye's weapon slapped into his. Ryan's ankle rolled. His shoulder hit the tree. An old nub from a broken branch pressed into his arm. A sting slashed his finger and his sword fell to the ground.

One Eye disarmed him.

Again.

"Snare me." Ryan kicked at the offending root.

"Again." One Eye pulled back his sword and stood ready.

Ryan's bleeding left hand clutched his sword hilt again. He'd lost track of the number of healing cuts on his fingers. When he got his own sword, he'd opt for a bigger cross guard.

The weapon flew out of his hand three more times before he finally ended with his blade against One Eye's chest.

The man smiled and patted Ryan on the back. "Well done, as usual. You're fast to learn and quick to imitate. You learn like a dragon."

He learned like a dragon? Now that was a compliment and a half.

One Eye nodded once. "You're a conundrum because I've seen you at the tavern. It's not the same boy who stays here. When you fight at the tavern, you win sometimes. When you fight me, even the trees slip you up." One Eye winked. It was the most unnerving thing the man did.

Ryan cracked a smile. "I suppose I'm just having fun there."

"I suppose so, too. But you're always in control, aren't you?"

Control? What did having fun have to do with being in control?

One Eye chuckled. "You use your charm and winning smile to hide the fact that you're guarded and untrusting. You make everyone else relax and trust you. Then, when their guard is down, you decide who's worth trusting. It's a good strength to have. But your weakness is always wanting to be in control. You can't control others. But you can control your response. That is what the dancing is for. Lead them to the direction you want them to go, but if that fails, be ready anyway." One Eye pulled out his sword. "Again."

By the time One Eye left, Ryan was breathing hard, sweating through his shirt, and his hand was bleeding with fresh cuts. But not from the last two rounds. He'd finally bested One Eye twice in a row. He sheathed his sword.

The man's obsession with dancing as the key to learning to fight was frustrating. Sure, Ryan enjoyed dancing. It was as good as any other way to spend an evening. Besides, the girls flocked to him like winter pigeons on a baker's roof. That didn't hurt his self-esteem. But if dancing was the key to unlocking his inner sword fighter, Ryan needed a way to pick that lock.

Evening finally came, and Ryan grabbed his sword and nicest shirt. Chloe met him at the house.

Estelle patted his cheek. "You two have fun and learn a lot tonight." Then she caught sight of his sliced-up fingers and stopped him from leaving. "This won't do."

So they'd cracked open again.

"My husband worked you hard this morning, did he?"

Ryan cringed as Chloe hid a smile.

Estelle placed some ointment on the cuts. Heavens, that stung. She brought out a bandage.

Ryan put up his hand to stop her. "I don't need—"

"There'll be no blood on those girls' dresses. Y'hear?"

"Yes, ma'am." He gave her his hand back.

"Such a mumbler."

Ryan let her tie the bandage, then waved as she went inside. He turned to Chloe, who stood there, smug smile still on her face.

"Bleeding again?"

"It's not like you had time for practice this morning, queen of penance."

"Honestly." Chloe linked arms with him and towed him away from the house toward the Winking Fox. "I don't know how Estelle hears half of my back-talk."

"Why are you whispering?"

"I think the only thing wrong with that woman's hearing is that she doesn't miss a thing."

They finally arrived at the Winking Fox and entered though the back door into the kitchens. The owner, a wide woman with friendly eyes and a red face from cooking, let them in.

"Good evening, Martha." Ryan always greeted her with a smile.

Martha wrapped him in a smothering hug. He chuckled when she let him go and smoothed the new wrinkles from his shirt. Chloe was already gone, so Ryan headed straight to find Tessa, Martha's daughter. But first he threw away the bandages Estelle had insisted he wear.

He caught up to Tessa and helped her clear away some dishes and crumbs that guests had left for her to clean up.

"Good evening, Ryan." She greeted him with a smile like her mother's, but no smothering hug. Not that he would have minded one from her. "You don't have to help me, you know."

"You'll be saying that to me all night, but you'll still appreciate the help."

The door opened and Tessa looked to see who came in. "Here come your first callers."

Ryan's gaze stopped at a pretty girl with long brown hair. She wasn't whom Tessa had been speaking of, but she was the one to catch his eye. Her gaze met his for a shy glance as she descended the stairs.

A redhead with bouncy curls and enough cleavage to swallow a man's head stepped into his line of sight. Francesca. "I hoped you'd be here tonight, handsome."

Ryan wasn't supposed to turn down a dance, but this was one woman he might like to say no to, at least once. She was a bit too persuasive for his taste.

"Hi, Francesca. I was thinking we could dance to 'Fiddle for a Bride.' That one is fast and bouncy." She always giggled when he winked, so he indulged her.

"I'll be ready." She wagged over to the musicians, no doubt to request the favorite.

"You really shouldn't encourage her." Chloe laughed.

"Maybe I like her."

"Let's not tell lies. There's a cute little brunette standing over there. She's been eyeing you."

"I'm getting there."

Too bad she wasn't Serena. He'd hoped, after telling her that he was at the Winking Fox every night, she might visit. Every night he watched the door, but she hadn't come back yet. She probably wouldn't.

Tessa moved into his line of sight, balancing a full tray. "Well, I'm still working, so if the two of you will excuse me."

Ryan faced the door and leaned on the bar. A couple girls looked his way and he shot them a half smile. They sure were giddy.

Chloe smacked his shoulder. "You're such an—"

"What? They came here to be swept off their feet. I'm just living up to the expectation."

Chloe snorted. "We'll see." She grabbed her mug and slipped off her stool. She handed a drink to her brother. "Which one are you going to sweep up first?"

His gaze found a pretty green-eyed girl. The only one in the tavern who wasn't overtly trying to get his attention. A little bit of a challenge was always more fun. Besides, she seemed more his type. Pretty, but not trying to be noticed. A little shy, but by the way she stood straight and tall, hands on her hips, she was confident.

"Her."

Chloe patted his shoulder. "Good luck, brother."

"Luck has nothing to do with it."

"Come to think of it, she looks familiar."

"Don't stare, Chloe. You'll ruin my chances."

She cocked her eyebrow at Ryan and leaned on the bar. Then she whispered, "She looks like that young woman from the Dissenters camp. The one who could see the future."

Ryan shot Chloe a glance, hoping she'd take his hint and be quiet. Talking about things like the Dissenters or Blood Moon talents here was beyond dangerous. As quickly as he'd shot the warning look, he sprouted a smile. "She looks like she needs a dance partner." He set down his drink and headed over to the where the green-eyed girl stood by the dance floor.

She glanced at him and quickly looked away. A little pink flushed her cheeks. Good sign. He closed the gap between them. "No dance partner?"

"No." Her smile captivated him.

"Well, I'd be happy to step in."

She tilted her head and bit her lip.

He extended a hand. "I'm Ryan."

"Madison." She let him take her hand and kiss it. Her palm was calloused. Like someone who fought with daggers and fought with them often. Definitely still his type.

"Well, Madison, what do you say?" He hung on to her hand a little longer.

She glanced at their joined hands and pulled hers back. Her gaze darted to the floor, smile remaining. "I don't know how to dance."

"Really? Well, it just so happens that I'm an excellent teacher." He bowed.

She giggled. He took that as an invitation and grabbed both of her hands this time. As he led her onto the dance floor, she worried her bottom lip again.

"There's nothing to be scared of, Madison."

Her eyes widened. "Who said I was scared?"

He held back a laugh. "Put one hand here." He pressed her right palm against his shoulder. "And the other here." He held out his right hand.

Her lip slid from her teeth and she placed her left hand in his. Now those eyes looked up at him, round.

He placed his other hand on her waist. "Now breathe and let me lead."

She took a deep breath, and her smile returned as she exhaled.

He couldn't take his eyes off the sparkle in hers. "That's right. Ready?"

The music started, and her grip on his hand tightened. The music picked up speed, and she clutched his shoulder as tightly as if she rode behind him on a startled horse in the woods. She smelled wonderful.

He whispered into her ear. "Relax. I've got this."

Her hold loosened as the song continued. Her smile returned and she looked into his eyes again.

He smiled. "That's right. You've got it."

That made her miss a step and her cheeks turned bright red, but he just led her on, didn't even mention the misstep, and she relaxed again. But this time she held him closer—just not as tight.

The music slowed. He pulled her to a stop.

"You're good at this," she said.

"So are you."

The blush returned. "I think not."

"A lot of women resist a man's lead on the dance floor. It causes more missteps than you'd think."

"Oh. Well, I think you're a fine leader."

"Leader?" He chuckled. Interesting choice of words. He never led a thing. Except in dancing.

The tune of the fiddle struck up faster, and Ryan recognized the next song. "Fiddle for a Bride."

"Are we going again?" Madison looked up from beneath her eyelashes.

"I'd love to, but I promised—"

"There you are." Francesca sauntered over, her red curls bouncing. "You going to let someone else have a turn, Knight?" She batted her eyelashes.

"Knight?" Madison tilted her head and searched Ryan's face with narrowed eyes.

"It's just a nickname." A stupid one at that.

"Really? Do you fight for sport?"

Not yet. Not really, anyway. But how could he say that to her without losing all credibility?

"Of course he does." Francesca grabbed Ryan's arm and towed him toward the dance floor.

Madison's look became a bit more guarded.

"Please save me another dance?" he asked her.

She crossed her arms. "We'll see, Knight."

That was that, apparently. Leave it to Francesca to ruin a perfectly good time. When the song ended and the music changed, Ryan finally caught sight of Madison sitting at a table, paying no attention to him and too much attention to the dark-haired, bearded man sitting across from her. Someone grabbed Ryan's arm and spun him around.

"Dance with me, Knight."

He sighed again. The next seven songs had him switching from one bright-eyed young woman to the next, all of them swooning, stepping on his toes, and resisting his lead. Ah well, some of them never learned. Although, he was starting to get good at moving his feet so they didn't step on him.

"Knight?"

"I'm going to sit this one out, Francesca. But have fun. It looks like Blade is open." He nodded toward the sport fighter tilting his head back with a tankard of mead, then he slipped away.

Madison stood alone in her green dress, gazing over her shoulder toward the door.

Breathless, he reached her. "Care for another dance?"

She smiled brightly and stared at his outstretched hand. "Should I call you Knight?"

"Please don't."

Madison tipped her head and studied his face. If she didn't take his hand, he'd have to give it to another, and he really, really didn't want to.

Her eyes rounded into that innocent look again and she grasped his hand at last. "Why not?"

"It's a silly name. I don't know how it even got started."

"I do."

She did? It wasn't really his best moment. "How do you—I mean, I don't recall seeing you here before."

Her warm smile brought out the dimple in her cheek. "You've been nothing but chivalrous to me tonight."

"Very funny."

"I mean it. You're sweet, Ryan."

Sweet? What exactly did that mean? Wasn't that what pretty girls called the boys they thought too young or too old for them? Or worse, the boys they thought only good for friendship and nothing more?

He lifted an eyebrow. "Uh . . . thanks?"

That dimple made its way back on her cheek. "You're welcome. Now, how about that dance?"

He led her onto the dance floor. "Just one?"

She placed her hand on his back and pulled him closer. "How many are you offering?"

"As many as you'll have."

She smiled, and he nearly forgot to start dancing. Three songs later, she had completely relaxed and let him lead her around the dance floor. Effortless. If he hadn't met her in a tavern, he'd have thought she'd grown up in the palace, such was her grace and confidence. When the music ended, he brought her in and dipped her.

She looked up at him, chest heaving, smiling that enchanting smile.

"Would you like to step outside?" He set her back on her feet.

She nodded, but her eyes flicked around the room.

Ryan followed her gaze. The bearded man stood in the corner, watching. He moved toward the door as they did.

As soon as Ryan had her outside, she breathed in the night air. "You're a very good dancer. I had no idea I'd be the center of attention with you out there, or I might have declined."

He chuckled, but it sounded forced to his ears. The bearded man had followed them out and lurked in the shadows beside the tavern window.

"Excuse me one moment?" Ryan asked.

Madison nodded.

The bearded man watched him head for the door, making his

way closer to Madison the farther away Ryan stepped. With one fluid motion, Ryan pulled his sword free and advanced on the bearded man.

Before he gained two steps the bearded man pulled out his weapon and faced Ryan, back to Madison.

Ryan tightened his grip. "What do you want with her?" He circled closer to Madison.

"I could ask you the same thing."

Ryan glanced at Madison. "He followed you out here."

She giggled. "He's my bodyguard." Madison put her hand on the bearded man's shoulder. "Stop, Torin. He's fine."

"What?" Ryan sheathed his sword.

Madison's smile was rueful. "I trusted you. He didn't. But I think he does now."

Torin just mumbled and walked back to his dark post under the window.

Ryan stayed rooted to the porch. "You need a bodyguard?"

She rolled up her sleeve and the red, raised birthmark of a Blood Moon stared back at him. She lowered her sleeve, but Torin was already voicing his concern.

"Don't worry." Ryan pulled is collar aside and let her see the identical mark on his chest. He didn't let her gaze linger, though. His mark had been changed.

"Wait." She rushed up to him and moved his shirt. He tried to stop her, but she placed a hand on his. "I've seen this mark before. My sister told me that a man with this mark was going to help me."

"Help you? How?"

Laughter and the creak of an opening door interrupted them, and Madison stopped talking. She pulled him aside. "When can I see you again?"

This had just taken a strange turn. "I'm here every night."

"Good. I need to talk to my sister again, but I'll come back to see you. Promise you won't forget me?"

Easy. "Okay."

"You might just be the missing piece we need." She grabbed his left hand and touched the cuts from One Eye's sword. Her fingers glided over the wounds and a trickle of heat skittered over his skin. He looked down as a cool breeze chased the warmth and left the skin healed. He looked up at her with wide eyes. She smiled, dropped his hand, and kissed his cheek. "You truly are a knight." Then she stole into the shadows with her bodyguard. Gone. Just like that.

His mother had always told him the women worth chasing were mysterious. Boy, was she right.

CHAPTER 42

DANGEROUS
AND BEAUTIFUL

Serena's eyelids fluttered open. The familiar reliefs on the walls and the gray woolen blanket tucked around her told her that she was still in the Tree of Wisdom.

No pull in her chest let her know that people had entered one of the Healer's sacred places to request healing, so Logan had either died or was no longer in need of a Healer's touch.

Hunger pangs gnawed at her insides. How long had she been recovering from the sting of venom in her veins? Many Healers slept for up to seven days. Powerful ones, like Tabitha and Lydia, had been known to only sleep for a day or two when they worked together. Three and a half days if they healed alone.

The candles, dispersed all over the walls of the tree, were lit and the rose petals used to make them gave the room a comforting smell. Slowly Serena sat up. The blanket fell to her waist. The reddish wolf who had stuck close to Logan jumped down from the bed and silently padded over to her. His mate followed him.

They were graceful animals, wolves. Serena had never really thought of them as such. Large and intimidating by their very presence. Stealthy to the core. But also graceful. These two were beautiful. Like dragons.

If any Healer ever knew she'd even had that thought about dragons, they'd surely switch her arms until the gash was deep enough to remain open for more than a moment.

Dragons. Healers called them kin of death. But they weren't. At least, she didn't think so. They were made by the Creator during the days of creation. Formed with light and love. Blessed with gifts like all creation. How could something like that be considered evil? How could something like that be lumped in with the vile creatures that were made after the days of creation had ended? Born of shadow and malice and envy. Creatures of the Mistress of Shadows, born to destroy and kill.

History stated that the Mistress had created a dragon of her own. Her personal mount. But surely that creature could not compare to the animals the Creator had made.

Serena's gaze turned to the man on the table. Logan.

Her father.

All her life, she had been told he was dangerous. That he would take her to the queen if he ever found her. All her life, Serena had feared this man.

She rose. The edge of her white silk skirt fell to her feet. The wolves walked with her the few steps to where Logan lay.

She placed her fingers on his temples. He felt weak, but his strength was quickly returning. When it finally did, how would she face him without trembling?

"Will he be all right?" Ethan joined her at Logan's side, his faithful dog following.

She smiled. "He is gaining strength as we speak. How long have I been asleep?"

"It's evening."

"What day?"

"The same day. Or the next day, depending. I mean, it hasn't been a full day since—"

Serena turned to face Ethan, heart hammering. "Not even a whole day? Are you sure?"

"Yes." Ethan's eyebrows furrowed. "Are you okay?"

Blood still stained his arms and clothes, his shirt was torn in various places. Of course it was the same day.

"I'm fine. How are you?" Serena raised her hand to touch Ethan's temple. He held perfectly still. The black lion had sunk its claws into him, yet no venom had tainted him. Strange. Perhaps the beast's claws weren't red when they cut him. That would mean venom wasn't being pulsed into him.

Serena looked into Ethan's eyes. The strange pull tugged between them even stronger than before. Could he feel it?

His eyes rounded. "Please, pretend you're sleeping. The dark-haired woman said she could only keep the Circle out of here until you woke up. I don't know what they'll do if—"

The door opened and Ethan whirled to face it, sword ready.

Rochelle came through the opening. "I brought some supper."

"Any news?" Serena put a hand on Ethan's bloody arm and he put his weapon away.

Dash's head entered the tree. *"Glad to see you awake."*

"It hasn't even been a day!"

"Didn't you think you could do it?"

"I wasn't sure, but I should still be asleep from the venom."

"You're more powerful than even Tabitha and Lydia thought."

Dash's words resounded in Serena's thoughts. They knew she was powerful, but *this* powerful? They'd never let her leave now. Let her do the good that she could be doing out in the world. But that was a whole different matter.

Rochelle closed the door when Dash left. "The Circle is still in a meeting. They won't come out until everyone is in agreement." She moved close to Serena. "Dash said you were awake, but I was surprised." She leaned in and spoke for Serena's ears alone. "I wish to come with you."

Serena's thoughts raced. Did they all expect her to leave with Logan?

It was true—something connected her to Ethan and Jayden. But to leave? This was the only home she'd ever known. Not family, perhaps. But could she, a girl abandoned by two families, ever hope to belong?

"Serena? Have I upset you?"

She touched Rochelle's hands. "No." Having Rochelle with her would ease her worry with Logan, but if Rochelle remained here, that could be good for other things. Possibilities flooded her thoughts. "Right now, let's sort out this mess with the Circle."

"Of course." Rochelle set a tray of biscuits and fruit on the table. "Miranda has gone to the library to look up something in the *Old Custom* that might let you be free to go with them."

"Really?" Why was Miranda so willing to help? "What kinds of things?"

"About bonds. Perhaps I should check on her?"

"I think that would be wise."

"I won't tell anyone you are awake until I am asked."

As if that would delay things. Serena sighed. "Thank you, Rochelle, but the Circle will demand an update as soon as they come to a convenient conclusion."

Ethan rubbed the hilt of his sword. "We'll leave. We'll take Logan and leave before they come."

Jayden gravitated closer to him. "You sense something?"

"Nothing helpful."

Jayden put a hand on his shoulder. "You need to relax."

"Relax?"

"Jayden's right." Serena's comment bought her both of their attention. "I think the best thing to do will be to wait and see what Miranda finds. Then we can plan what we'll say to the Circle."

"Why are you still wearing your bloody clothes?" Rochelle blinked. She was staring at Ethan. She motioned toward the back door of the tree. "There is a brook right out back. And I imagine I could find you a shirt. That bloody, shredded linen you're wearing is not fit for clothing."

Ethan turned his arms over and picked at his shirt, inspecting it for what looked like the first time. "I have a different shirt."

Rochelle smiled at him. "I'll fetch one for you."

"I can fetch my own shirt."

"Ethan." Jayden extended her hand. "Give me that sorry excuse for a shirt, and go wash."

Ethan clenched his jaw, pulled the shirt over his head, and tossed it at Jayden. "Sitting around here isn't doing any good." He headed out the door.

When he was gone, Serena turned to Jayden. "He's right, you know." Serena tried a smile. Clearly she was tied to Jayden, too, but more than that, Jayden was a kin to her. She could not help but like her immediately.

Jayden simply raised an eyebrow. "You have some sort of plan?"

Perhaps Jayden did not return the same immediate affection. Serena cleared her throat. "I am still working on that."

Jayden walked over to Logan. "He's not dangerous to you."

A tight ball formed in Serena's throat. Men had been responsible for the Imprisonment of the Healers. Only women could be born Healers. Something about bonding to unicorns. "For centuries, Healers have tried trusting men. There isn't one story in the history books that tells of a Healer who wasn't betrayed by the man she trusted. Used. Raped. Imprisoned to make more Healers." The only man she'd ever known, the one she'd called father, had betrayed her, too. And Logan had been the one to choose this other man to raise her.

She looked over at Jayden and saw the horror she felt mirrored in her sister-kin's eyes. "We don't generally trust men."

"Perhaps they don't tell the good stories."

"Perhaps there aren't enough worth mentioning." But Ryan and Ethan were. Surely there were others out there like them.

"I can assure you, Logan is different."

Serena composed herself. "There was a letter, written by my mother, saying he would take me to the queen."

"That's a lie. How do you not see it?" Jayden fisted her hands. "Logan's son, another of the Deliverers, was taken by *your* mother to the queen. Not by him. Logan will protect you from the enemy. Can't you see I'm telling the truth?"

"I can. But if Logan lied to you and you believed him, you could be telling me the truth and it could still be a lie."

Jayden straightened her spine and crossed her arms. "Then when Logan wakes, you can ask him yourself."

The fire in Jayden's voice made Serena smile a little. "It does comfort me that you trust him so much."

"Good." Jayden's eyes narrowed. "But you trust Ethan, don't you? How does that make sense?"

"Ethan is . . . different."

A flush of red dotted Jayden's cheeks. "Really? How?"

The door creaked open and Rochelle returned with a shirt for Ethan. "I found this and had to tell Mary that it was for Ethan, but I did get a shirt for Logan as well, since his is ruined." She set the clothes down. "Did I interrupt something?"

Something Jayden said sparked a thought cycle. "Rochelle, I need you to go to my room. Take this key." She handed Rochelle the cord she wore around her neck. A metal key dangled on the end. "There's a box under my bed. This will open it. There's a letter inside marked with the red wolf-head seal. Please bring it to me?"

Rochelle took the key. "Of course."

She'd have Logan read the note when he woke. Then she'd learn the truth.

And why had no one else thought to test the letter? Oh, right. Of course it was true because Logan was a man. By his very nature, he meant to harm her.

The door opened and Ethan returned shirtless, his dark hair wet. He sat next to them, one hand propped on his bent knee. "Have you given any more thought to how we're going to get out of here?"

Serena's stomach clenched. Going with them meant trusting them. All of them. "When you say 'we' . . ."

Jayden put a hand on Serena's shoulder. "You mean to come with us, don't you? You have to—"

"She doesn't *have* to, Jayden." Ethan's eyes met Serena's gaze.

She wanted nothing more than to throw her arms around him. He had no idea how much it meant to her that she would actually have a choice.

Ethan's eyebrows drew together. "Hey, it's your Destiny Path. No one can walk it for you. Besides, we aren't going to force you to do anything. Okay?"

How did he do that? Understand her so easily. He had to feel the connection.

"I—" She wanted to say she'd go with them. She wanted to go with them. If Ethan left this place, she'd follow this time. She'd trust him with her life, and she'd protect him with hers. "I need to talk to Logan first."

Ethan nodded.

"Ethan, she's one of the Deliverers. If she doesn't come with us and Franco gets his hands on her—"

"I know, Jayden. But don't you remember how unwilling you were to take up this Destiny?" The lopsided smile he gave her was so different than the one he showed Serena.

Jayden faced Serena. "I was reluctant. I thought the Feravolk killed my family. Helping them was not something I was willing to do. I know you don't trust men, but you do trust me?"

Trust. Such a heavy word.

Serena closed her eyes and breathed in.

Jayden's voice was quiet. "Strange. I thought I felt connected to you. I thought we were bound together somehow."

"I do feel it." Serena opened her eyes. "I feel connected to both of you." She glanced at Ethan and he smiled back.

"Good." Ethan leaned back against the inside wall of the tree. "So I guess that means we wait here until Logan wakes up?"

Serena's gaze fell on a thick, red scar on the right side of Ethan's stomach. The Healer's compassion in her grew like a white-hot fire. The scar appeared healed, but a dull ache still emanated from it. She stood and plucked the shirt Rochelle had brought off the table and gave it to Ethan. Then she leaned closer.

"What happened?" She motioned toward the scar.

"It's already healed."

She hovered her hand over it. Opened a different door of her talent. Not the door for Healing, but for probing. A dangerous door, but not for what she wanted to do. Besides, if she was about to follow these two into the unknown, she should really check to see how much of her talent she could control. How much of the forbidden parts. *Forgive me, Dash.*

A stabbing sensation filled her middle and sliced through her. She wanted to retch, but she probed deeper. She needed to know what had happened to Ethan when he'd receive this injury. If it was possible that the legends were true. The pain churned her stomach, forced tears to her eyes.

A strong grip curled around her wrist, broke the connection.

She stumbled to the ground, Ethan still gripping her arms. The wild look in his eyes told her that she'd scared him more than herself.

"What's wrong?" he asked.

She caught her breath. He might have broken her connection before she was done, but she'd seen enough to know what was possible for at least one Healer.

"You—you could *feel* it, couldn't you?" Jayden stared at her with her eyes wide. "His scar. You could feel what happened to him?"

Serena trembled. "Yes."

Ethan narrowed his eyes. "Feel?"

Serena stared at him. "Ethan, how are you alive?"

He released her arms and shrank away from her, a cornered-gryphon look in his eye. "What are you talking about?"

Oh, he knew very well what she was talking about. "A sword stabbed you through."

He was quiet for a while. "I remember."

Jayden gasped. "How did you survive that?"

Serena cocked an eyebrow. "My question exactly."

Ethan glared at Serena, then looked at his lap. "Obviously someone knew what they were doing when they took care of me."

"Obviously," Jayden whispered.

It looked like he wasn't going to give her the information she needed right now. There was time. Serena turned to Jayden. "How did you know I could feel it?"

"I spoke with Rochelle last night. She told me how you feel what you're healing."

Ethan ripped the shirt from Serena's hand. "I told you, it's healed. And what do you mean *feel* what you're healing?"

"Legend says we can feel things from scars. They don't teach that here. Healers don't exactly have scars, so I was curious."

"Curious?" Ethan's eyebrows shot up. "Serena—"

"I just want to know what I'm capable of. The things they don't teach here. Why would the Creator give us these other powers if He didn't intend for us to use them?"

Dark powers.

Ancient powers that play with fire.

Like a dragon, unicorns were beautiful and dangerous.

Ethan made hard eye contact with her. "If you can feel what you are healing, then let's get one thing straight—"

"Ethan, healing is my job. I'll heal whom I choose when I choose, and asking me to refrain is nothing short of insulting." She locked eyes with him.

His jaw clenched several times before he nodded. "You're right. I'm sorry." He pulled the shirt over his head.

The shirt was a brilliant white with laced cuffs and a wide collar that hung to his shoulders. Serena pressed her fingers to her lips to hide a smile. Even Jayden giggled.

Ethan looked down at himself. "This isn't my shirt. Where'd you get it? The palace?"

Jayden's laughter exploded. "The frilly sleeves are quite becoming."

He gave Jayden a wry smile. The three of them laughed together and Serena sighed. Something about this moment. It was almost how she imagined it would be to have a family. A strange lump formed in her throat.

Jayden glanced at her. "Are you all right?"

Serena nodded. "So, you think I'm a Deliverer?"

"You most certainly are."

"So I'm supposed to help keep the Mistress of Shadows from escaping? I know she's close. The black lions have been back hunting unicorns since before I was born. But how are we to do this?"

"We need to find our Whisperer. She will guide us."

"Whisperer. You've come to the right place. The Healers of the Forest of Legends guard the stone of Ishkar."

"What's that?" Ethan asked.

The stone. Healers were supposed to protect that stone with their lives. That and the sword . . . she shook her head. They didn't want the sword. Besides, they needed the stone to find their Whisperer if they were to defeat the Mistress. "I'll take you to it."

CHAPTER 43

THE STONE
OF ISHKAR

Jayden bit her bottom lip. Was it really that simple? Could Thea really be trying to help her? She'd been right about the woman who couldn't see and now the stone of Ishkar. And, as much as Jayden didn't want to admit it, Thea had been right about "The Frog and Fox."

Did that mean she couldn't have Ethan?

Of course it did.

Because Thea was also right about Jayden's death.

Letting Ethan know how she felt would only end in heartache—his heartache—assuming he'd grown to feel the same way about her. Jayden looked at Logan's still form. He breathed easier, as if he were just sleeping. As soon as he woke, she'd tell him what Thea had said about heading to Balta after meeting their Healer, because she wasn't about to lead them all into capture.

"You coming?" Ethan touched her shoulder.

She tore her eyes from Logan and followed Serena out the back door of the tree. Once outside, Dash approached them, his nostrils flared.

Serena stroked his nose. "Keep watch. Tell me if anyone comes."

Then she motioned for Jayden and Ethan to follow her. "There's a passageway in the library, but Miranda is in there. I know another way in, but we'll have to be quiet."

She led them through the silver-leafed trees to the trunk of a white tree and pulled out her dagger. The blade glistened in the sunlight as she held it over her palm.

Ethan grabbed her wrist. "What are you doing?"

"It only opens with blood." She sliced her palm and pressed the wound against the left side of the trunk. The blood absorbed into the wood. A door appeared like etchings of light within the bark, and Serena pushed. It opened to darkness. Serena motioned for them to go in ahead of her. "The door opens both ways. Only the left will take you down. Below the library." She closed the door behind them.

Darkness enveloped them. Jayden reached out and touched Ethan's arm. He surprised her by grabbing her hand.

A soft sparkling glow, like a shimmering opal, lit the path in front of them. The source of the light came from the palm of Serena's hand.

Jayden gasped. "How are you doing that?"

"Dash taught me. He seems to think I can do whatever he can." She led them down.

Made sense, from what Melanie thought about the talents being linked to animals. Jayden shuddered as she recalled the kelpie. How had she thought that would be her horse?

The steps were hard beneath Jayden's shoes. Stone. The air grew colder and damp as they descended. At last they reached the bottom. Serena's shimmering light illuminated a small room. Tree roots spread out above them like a ceiling and draped the walls like the canopy of a willow tree. Wooden cases of all shapes and sizes lined the walls. Leather trimmed their hinges and corners, but none of them seemed to have locks.

Jayden looked up. "Won't it collapse?"

"The white alor is a protective plant. It grows into a tree, if old enough, and protects whatever lies beneath it. The stone of Ishkar is here. It will tell us where the Whisperer is."

"Tell me you know where the stone is." Ethan scanned the walls.

Serena stood in the center of the room and turned in a circle. "I am not sure which one holds the stone. I've never seen it."

Ethan touched one of the trunks and snapped his hand back with a hiss.

"Are you okay?" Serena asked.

"Yeah. It seems these are being protected."

"Maybe I can open it." She reached forward. A lock appeared as she touched the trunk. But it wouldn't open.

"It didn't burn you?" Ethan asked.

"It did, but I heal. Pain is something we're taught to handle. I can't open it, though. I imagine the Circle has the key. Getting that from them will be impossible."

The Circle. Why did they have the power to keep the stone from those who should have it? Jayden crossed her arms. "They know what the stone does and that the Deliverers need their Whisperer to find the Mistress's prison. They should gladly hand it to us."

"They should." Serena nodded. "But you don't need her to find the Mistress's prison. The Mistress is locked tightly beneath the ruins of Castlerock."

Jayden had heard of Castlerock, of course. The castle was said to be built under the rule of the Feravolk kings and queens from the first age. The ruins were supposedly in the Forest of Woe.

"Where's that?" Ethan asked.

Serena's eyes widened. "Someone is coming down here. We can't be caught."

Ethan drew his sword.

Jayden reached out with her talent. She couldn't see who was coming, but with the way the emotions had been building lately, she didn't always need to make eye contact anymore. Something flooded into her. Hot. Violent. "The person who is coming is very angry."

Serena's eyes widened. "Do they know we're here?"

Ethan shook his head. "I don't feel a threat for you. So whoever they're angry with, it's not us."

"Not yet." Serena tugged Jayden's sleeve. "They'll have my head for bringing you two down here. Hurry. The back way. It'll take us to the library." Serena led them toward the other stairs.

"Go." Ethan motioned for them to leave while he stood watch at the door.

Serena stopped. "Ethan."

Jayden gently pushed her to keep going. "He won't come until he knows we're safe."

Serena picked up her skirts and headed up the stairs. Jayden followed. They came out through a relief in the wall of the library's south side.

Serena smoothed her white dress. "Follow me." She froze. "Where's Ethan?"

"I'm here," he whispered, coming out of the tunnel.

"Did whoever it was see you?"

"No."

"I thought I heard something." Miranda approached them. "Serena?"

"We wanted to know if you've found anything." Ethan motioned over his shoulder at Serena. "She's awake."

"I can see that." Miranda crossed her arms. "Go back to the tree, Serena. The Circle can't know yet. Ethan and Jayden, come with me. I think I've found something."

CHAPTER 44

TIE THAT BINDS

Ethan followed Miranda and Jayden through the labyrinth of shelves. The scent of books and parchment hung heavy in the air. Stacks of books covered every available space in the high-ceilinged room. Lit candles revealed where Miranda had been. She led them past worn and tattered tomes and scrolls and parchments that must have been more than one hundred years old.

Then she stopped near a pile of books on the floor near a few lit candles. Miranda sat down and hefted a huge book onto her lap. She dragged her finger down the page. "Every work that has anything to do with the bond is missing." She sighed. "Curious." She motioned for them to approach her. "When I looked up bonds in the *Old Custom*, this was what I found."

Ethan and Jayden peered over her shoulders.

Bond: Something that brings two or more beings together in a form of mental, spiritual, and emotional unison. Feravolk often bond to animals this way. To accept a bond, one needs only to accept the offering of the bond. Often the beings are drawn together by the longing of the bond.

To break a bond is much more difficult; you must denounce who you were at the time of acceptance. Passing a bond is much easier and less painful. A bond can only be passed if the beings share the same bond structure.

A bond can remain even in death, some claim.

"It doesn't say that people cannot bond with other people." Miranda smoothed her unkempt hair. That and the dark circles beneath her eyes made Ethan believe she'd been here all night.

"What does 'bond structure' mean?" Jayden asked.

"It's the type of animal your group of talents allows you to bond to. Though it seems Feravolk may be able to bond to more than animals. I wondered if it was something similar to a three-oath bond." Miranda tapped her lip as she scanned the open books on the ground.

"What's a three-oath bond?" Jayden asked.

The question seemed to pull Miranda out of her thoughts. She glanced up with a faraway look in her eyes that focused slowly on Jayden's face. "When you make a blood oath with the same individual three times within a certain amount of time, some type of bond takes place."

"A kin bond," Ethan said. His father had spoken of a kin bond before. Something he'd had with his uncle.

"Serena called me a sister-kin."

Miranda's eyes opened wide, then she practically dove toward the books. "That is helpful." She flipped pages in three different books before she paused. "A kin or brother- or sister-kin is someone with whom you share such a special, familial bond that you can experience things through your bonded kin's senses as your own. Tabitha and Lydia call themselves sister-kin. It's because they made a three-oath bond. This could make sense. The Creator could have connected the Deliverers this way." She covered her mouth and stared at the pages, but Ethan guessed she was thinking more than reading. Finally she looked at Jayden. "And you feel this bond?"

"I do. I feel connected to Serena. I feel like we are supposed to be together, like we are sisters."

"And you?" Miranda turned to Ethan. "Do Protectors feel bonded to the Deliverers?"

"I do. That's how we found her."

"And you would protect Serena?"

"I would die for her."

Jayden shot him a wide-eyed look and her mouth opened. How could she be surprised? How many times had he told her he'd die for her?

"Curious." Miranda's voice broke their eye contact.

Now she was just insulting him. "Why?"

"No one protects Healers. We have been human shields for people for centuries. If I stab you in the heart, you'll die. If you stab me in the heart, I'll heal."

"But you *can* be killed."

Miranda paused, her narrowed eyes searching his face. "Yes. The only way to kill a Healer is to cut out her heart or chop off her head."

"I'll protect Serena. You have my word."

"That's what the two of you must tell the Circle. Beware, they might somehow be able to thwart your feelings of this bond and pass it off as something else. Ethan, you were Serena's first heal. That will count for something. Healers usually heal someone they care deeply about first. But you were a stranger to her. She must have felt a strong enough connection to you."

"Like a bond?" Ethan asked.

"Don't be certain it will be enough for them to let their most powerful Healer leave. If she shares our whereabouts with others, it could lead to another Imprisonment, or worse." Miranda's head turned toward the door. "Someone is coming. Quickly, go out the back."

They left Miranda and found the back door. Ethan grabbed Jayden's arm and put his finger up to his lips. Standing there, he opened the door, then let it shut. If Miranda didn't know they were still there, she wouldn't be able to give them away. Jayden stared at him with her eyes wide before a smile slowly formed on her face.

Then she plucked a book off the shelf and handed it to him. "So you can tell anyone who sees you that you were reading," she whispered. Her impish smile was enough to make him want to tug her closer and kiss her.

He backed away and took the book. Opened to the middle and read a line: *Gryphons are impervious to venom.* Then he placed it back on the shelf just as the door opened.

More than one set of footfalls hit the smooth floor. Ethan tilted his head to try to distinguish from where. Stupid ear. Torn between the desire to get closer and the possible danger he'd be placing Jayden in, he stayed put but strained to hear.

"Miranda. Miranda!"

"Rochelle, calm down. What's wrong?"

"Belladonna is here. And she's stolen the Sword of Black Malice."

Sword of Black Malice? What in Soleden was that?

A slow burn spread across Ethan's chest and collected in the middle like a coal on top of his heart. The heat intensified. Ethan gripped his sword hilt.

Now who did his talent urge him to protect? Not Jayden. The flare over his heart didn't quite feel the same, but it was just as strong. Ached just as much. Like his need to protect Ryan or . . .

Serena. Someone wanted Serena.

"Did you see which way Belladonna went?" Miranda asked.

"She's headed toward the crystal lake, and she wants Serena." Rochelle's voice betrayed her fear.

"Go. Warn the Circle."

Ethan faced Jayden. "Run to Serena. Warn her. Stay with her. I'm going after this Belladonna."

"Ethan."

"Please."

Jayden nodded, then she ran.

The urge to protect pulled his heart. No need to ask where the crystal lake was. The threat was getting closer. Ethan raced out of the library. Woods surrounded him. Someone screamed. A surge of heat shot through his chest. He ripped off the white shirt so the whole forest wouldn't see him coming. People who wore shirts like this clearly didn't have to hunt for food.

He stepped farther into the woods, careful where he placed his boots. Too many of those oddly colored silver leaves littered the ground. Crunched beneath his weight.

Voices.

He tipped his head. Turned it slightly, trying to get the best angle to hear. It seemed like the low voices were north. He scanned the gaps between the mossy bark. Found movement. Yes. People congregated there. Maybe four?

His talent urged him closer.

Closer.

The voices grew louder.

The tree he hid behind obstructed his view. He moved left. Carefully. Thick tree bark pressed into his back as he peered around the other side of the tree. There. He could see all of them.

One woman against three. At least that was how it looked. Three women in white—likely Healers—stood with their backs to him. It was the woman in black he had to worry about. When he looked at her, the threat pulsed. That was new. And helpful.

She wore skin-tight clothes—no dress—with leather overlays. Like an assassin. Kara and Thea wore clothes like that.

She faced the three Healers with a huge, two-handed, strange-looking sword. It was black. Thick. Spiraled like a . . . like a unicorn horn. Must be Belladonna. And that had to be the Sword of Black Malice.

"Belladonna, you won't get away with this."

He'd heard that voice before. It belonged to that white-haired lady who wouldn't heal Logan. Tabitha. Perhaps the dark-haired woman with her was Lydia. Ethan's jaw tensed. What was going on here? And what exactly would this Belladonna not get away with?

Belladonna tilted her head and a smile snaked across her lips. "I already have, Tabitha. Now tell me where Serena is."

Ethan's heart pounded.

"Never. Give me the sword and we might spare your life."

"My life? You would kill me? After everything we've been through together, Tabitha? After you practically raised me?"

Spare her life? Didn't Healers take a vow to do no harm? He ran his fingers over the scar on his oath hand. If he broke an oath, it would slowly harm him, perhaps make him sick or go crazy. But if a Healer broke an oath, it killed them. Maybe the history of Healers he'd heard was more myth than truth.

"Your being here is a death sentence. Any Healer who sees you will try to kill you."

"Even with this?" Belladonna held up the weapon.

Whatever was going on, it smelled like a fish left in the sun.

"You won't take all of us, even with the Sword of Black Malice."

A wicked grin spread her dark-red lips. "Give me Serena and I'll spare the rest of you."

That was it. Ethan clutched his weapon in both hands and stepped from around the tree. "The lady told you to hand over the weapon."

All four women looked at him. Tabitha's eyes widened most. "You should not be here, boy. We can take care of ourselves."

Boy? This woman really knew how to burn his straw.

Belladonna's eyes scanned Ethan's body and a smile curved her lips. "Since when have you taken in a man and healed him? The only one I can think brave and stupid enough to bring a man here is Serena. She must be close. I could hurt him. She'd sense it enough to come running, wouldn't she?" Her eyes locked onto Ethan. Bored deep as if trying to extract an answer to her unspoken question.

The flame in his chest flickered.

She'd get nothing from him.

"You wanted my weapon? Come get it. But you should know, I'm not alone."

Five men in chain mail stepped out from behind trees, swords ready. Ethan's stomach twisted. Great. How many more was she hiding back there?

All three of the Healers drew their weapons. Two held long daggers, but the young brown-haired Healer had a short sword. This was going to get ugly.

Ethan gripped his hilt tighter and raced forward.

One of the huge beasts in chain mail raced out to meet him. Steel clashed against steel and the familiar jolt ratcheted up Ethan's arms. Invigorated him. He swung again. The sword met his. Clashed. Screeched. His talents rushed into him. Strength fueled him. Speed electrified him. The man's side was open. Ethan's blade hacked into the man's ribs. Through chain mail, through leather, though flesh, and into bone.

Ethan ripped his sword free as his opponent fell, and stabbed him through the heart.

Then he turned and surveyed the scene. The young Healer was farthest from him, her sword chopping at the man fighting her. He sliced into her arm, but the cut sealed itself shut. Right. Healers. Useful talent in a fight.

Lydia held her own. Tabitha backed away from Belladonna, daggers raised. Ethan raced to help the aging Healer.

"Run, boy. This is not your fight."

The young woman behind him pushed him out of the way. Sword in hand, she ran to her mother.

Two more soldiers raced through the woods the way Ethan had come. Blood already smeared their swords. What had they been doing?

Belladonna chuckled. Ethan pulled out his belt knife and threw it at Belladonna. The blade sank deep into her side. Should have punctured her lung.

"Nice shot, boy." Belladonna pulled out his knife and her wound sealed. She was a Healer, too? Great.

Ethan braced for her onslaught, but Lydia and Tabitha advanced toward her together. Good, let them take her on. He raced to the young Healer instead.

The soldier she fought pushed her, and she slammed into a tree. Fell. The man pulled back his sword to stab her heart. Ethan skidded between the Healer and her attacker. His sword clashed with the enemy's weapon. Both men drew back and faced off.

Ethan clutched his sword hilt. Red trailed down its blade. His talents pulsed through him—his desire to protect Serena throbbed.

His opponent swung. Ethan was faster.

Weapons clashed. Ethan was stronger.

He pushed the man back, kicked. The man stumbled. His sword dropped. Ethan struck.

The blade hitched as he caught bone. The man's arm fell and Ethan finished him off.

"Mother!" the Healer behind him screamed.

Ethan turned. Belladonna thrust her weapon into Lydia's stomach. She fell. Tabitha shrieked.

Belladonna pulled out the weapon.

A quiet overtook the woods. Trees seemed to still and no one breathed.

But Ethan had just witnessed these Healers fighting and healing themselves. Hadn't Miranda just said the only way to kill a Healer was to cut out her heart or chop off her head? Neither of these things had just happened, yet Lydia didn't move. Didn't get up. The gaping, bloody wound in her chest continued to pulse blood.

It had to be the sword.

"Mother!" Mary, the young Healer, raced toward Belladonna, who stood in front of Tabitha, ready to strike.

Ethan's legs burned as he ran faster. He caught Mary's sleeve. Fabric ripped. He gripped her wrist.

Belladonna swung the Sword of Black Malice at Tabitha's head. She ducked and held up her sword, but it fell to the ground. Her hand fell with it, now a useless part of the weapon.

A shudder raced through Ethan's body, and he flung Mary behind him.

Tabitha collapsed, holding what was left of her arm. Ethan's stomach roiled. Belladonna stepped past the broken Healers, eyes on the girl behind him.

Ethan summoned his strength and held his sword up in front of him, staring at Belladonna with the blade in the center of his vision. Deep, body-shaking sobs sounded behind him. Ethan swallowed, not thinking about anything but defending himself. Defending her.

The black blade thrust toward him. He whirled around and toppled into Mary, pushing her out of the way as the weapon cut through the air.

An earthquake seemed to shake the ground and a unicorn reared, kicking at Belladonna with its hooves. She backed away, slashing the sword at the creature. When its hooves hit the ground, the earth shook.

Ethan gripped Mary's elbow and towed her up. "Run." He shoved her away from the battle.

Light flashed. A deafening boom resounded and the earth quaked. Ethan flew off his feet and landed hard on the ground paces away. He got up to his knees, bracing himself on all fours. What was that?

A burn pulsed in his chest.

Serena.

Speed fueled him before he called it.

Serena lay motionless on the ground and Belladonna stood over her.

Ethan skidded in front of Serena. "You'll not claim another Healer today," he said quietly.

Belladonna laughed, dark and screeching.

She was close enough now. Ethan waited. Watched. Called on his strength.

She swung.

The sword met his. A jolt shook his arms. Spread through his whole body. The Sword of Black Malice kept moving despite Ethan's strength. He couldn't hold it. His sword blade bent more than normal. Metal shrieked and his blade tore off from the hilt.

It sailed through the air, wagging like a dying dragon's wing, and hit the ground with a shuddering bounce.

Useless.

Ethan stared at Belladonna over his empty hilt.

Belladonna approached him. "Another round, stupid boy?"

He had nothing to protect Serena except himself. But his talent urged him to keep her safe. It was his job. His desire. His choice.

He could only pray to the Creator that this weapon didn't kill others like it killed Healers. Belladonna didn't hesitate. The blade pierced his chest. Sank deep. Cracked ribs. Shot pain through him like a flash of light. So bright and consuming. It felt warm and cold at the same time. Dust motes glimmered in front of him, untouched by the movement around them, if anything was moving at all—it seemed that everything had stopped to take a breath.

Strange to think of dust motes. Was this what Kinsey had seen when Scarface stabbed her through? Had time stopped for her? Had this light bathed her?

He'd seen this light before. That thought sent a tremor through him. Not again. Who would protect Jayden and Serena now?

Belladonna bent near him. So close he could count her eyelashes, if he remembered how to count. How to breathe.

"Do I know you?" she asked.

Pain shot through him, blinding him to everything else and he sucked in air.

Every breath ached. Something warm, metallic-tasting filled his mouth. Dripped over his lips.

"You know where the Deliverers are, don't you?"

He tried to tell her he wouldn't say anything. But he couldn't say anything. Couldn't see. Couldn't think. Forgot to breathe.

CHAPTER 45

THE SWORD
OF BLACK MALICE

Jayden shook her head, dazed. She'd landed hard, but nothing was broken. What happened? She sat up and tried to clear her head. Dash had raced toward Belladonna. When his horn connected with the strange black sword, sparks zapped in the air. It had almost felt like a storm, but not quite. More like an explosion of light. But when Dash's hooves smashed the ground while his horn was connected to that sword, it was like a lightning tremor through the ground. An earthquake of light. Had everyone felt it? Had it thrown all of them?

Where were they?

Jayden's heartbeat stilled. Stopped. Everything stopped. Her limbs wouldn't support her, and her knees hit the ground as Belladonna removed the sword from Ethan's chest. He dropped to the ground like a sack of apples.

Something inside her shattered.

Not Ethan. Anyone but Ethan.

Jayden found her legs and raced forward.

Dash beat her. His horn met the black weapon and he whirled his head around. The black sword flew from the woman's grasp. It landed near Tabitha. Yes. Tabitha could reach it in time. The old Healer extended her arm, but the vile woman caught the weapon first. Then she threw something on the ground. Purple smoke whirled around her like a funnel cloud, then vanished.

Belladonna, Tabitha, and the black sword—gone.

Jayden reached Serena's side. "Ethan?" she whispered.

"He just jumped in front of you!" Mary was hysterical. "We can't heal him. Doesn't he know that? Why would he do that? No one can heal him."

Jayden pressed her hands to her mouth and muffled words came out. "Is it true?"

"Yes." Serena sniffed. A tear slipped down her cheek. She knelt next to him. Blood covered his chest. She touched the wound. "There's nothing I can do."

A sob choked Jayden.

Ethan's eyelids fluttered. "Serena?"

"Ethan? How—?"

He grabbed her hand and winced as he tried to sit up. "Your hands are cold."

"Cold?" That was all he had to say? She wiped the blood away from his wound and Jayden gaped. No wound. Just a dark, black scar.

"Ethan." Her voice seemed to be so far away.

He turned to her and his eyes softened. "Hey." He pulled her close and pressed his cheek against her head.

She gripped him back so tight. "Are you—"

"I'm fine."

"You're not fine," Serena said.

Jayden pulled back from him, even though she didn't want to, and stared at Serena. She was right. Why would that woman spare him? She reached in to feel Serena's emotions. Confusion topped everything. And longing. A deep longing.

Serena leaned close and inspected the scar. "Belladonna spared you. Why? How?"

"I—I don't know."

Serena hovered her hand over Ethan's wound. "I need to know."

Mary grabbed her hand. "Serena, don't."

"But I—"

"I already felt my mother's wounds. You don't—you don't want to feel that." Tears spilled down Mary's cheeks.

Serena stared at Lydia's bloody stomach. "We have to get you to the Tree of Wisdom."

"No. No Healer can heal me, Serena."

That might be true, but Jayden didn't need Healer powers to care for a wound. "I can try. I trained under wise women at home." Jayden knelt beside Lydia. "Yes. I think I can heal her. I need—"

"Dear Child, there's nothing you can do now." Lydia's wrinkled hand cupped Jayden's. She shifted her eyes to look at Serena. "Belladonna killed Midnight and Diamond. They're gone."

Serena covered her mouth, but Jayden didn't understand.

Lydia shook her head. "I won't last the night. The rip is too deep."

"No." Jayden protested. "I can stitch this up. I—"

Serena laid a hand on Jayden's arm, and compassion flooded through her. "She means the rip from the bond. Midnight and Diamond were Lydia's and Tabitha's unicorns."

Serena's face scrunched up as she hugged Lydia. So much sadness welled up in Jayden's heart, and she turned off her talent.

Ethan touched Serena's shoulder, and she reached up and grasped his hand. "Dash, please tell the Circle to form. This can't wait."

She locked eyes with Ethan. "You should take Jayden and run."

Oh no. This was bigger than the Circle. "We're staying with you," she and Ethan said together.

"Yes. Stay." Lydia's voice was so weak. She motioned to Ethan. "You protected my daughter and Serena."

Serena shook her head, stared at him. "No one protects a Healer. We heal ourselves."

Ethan nodded toward Tabitha's severed arm. "It wasn't working against whatever that weapon was."

"But you protected me against that mortal weapon, too." Mary's voice was quiet. "They're right. You're different."

"Why didn't it kill me?" Ethan pointed to the black scar on his chest.

"Belladonna wanted to keep you alive for some reason." Serena looked at Ethan. "What did she say to you?"

"Just—" Ethan's chest rose and fell. "I don't remember."

"It's okay."

Mary nodded. "I'll tell the Circle what you did for me. For my mother and Tabitha. I think they'll trust you. I know I do."

Serena stood. "Let's get you back to the tree. I don't know what's going to happen next, but—"

"We have to go after this Belladonna. I only came out here because she wanted you. She's a threat to you, Serena."

Serena looked at Jayden. "She's a threat to all of the Deliverers." Serena stared at Ethan. "I want to come with you. I think you need a Healer to fight this war."

Jayden expelled a breath.

Ethan smiled. "I think so, too."

Serena nodded. "I'm going to plead my case to the Circle."

Jayden grabbed Ethan's hand in both of hers. He turned, eyes soft. "You okay?"

This moment, right here—the Healers sobbing, the Sword stolen, Logan still sleeping, streaks of dried tears stretching her cheeks— everything around her was falling apart, but the answer was yes.

Yes, because he was alive.

So right here, this moment was worth holding on to.

"Uh oh," Serena whispered.

Jayden looked up to see a petite, dark-skinned woman lead a group of eleven Healers up the hill toward them. The woman pointed to Ethan. "You, boy."

Ethan's subtle touch on Jayden's arm guided her behind him, but she resisted. "Easy, Ethan. We want them to befriend us so we can take Serena with us."

"What happened here?" the petite Healer asked.

"Hello, Ruth." Serena placed her hand on Ethan's shoulder and whispered, "Ethan, be careful how you answer."

CHAPTER 46

FALSE ACCUSATIONS

I asked the boy a question. Do not interrupt," Ruth snapped. "Where is the sword, boy?"

Ethan stared into this Healer's eyes as the throb of a threat heated his chest. She had it out for him. "I don't know. That woman took it."

"Where?" Ruth closed the distance, her eyes hard. She wasn't about to back down, but neither was he. He'd had enough of this Circle.

Serena stepped in front of him. "Ethan was—"

"Were you in the library, boy?" Ruth's gaze didn't leave his eyes.

"That's not my name."

"Ethan, you don't have to answer her." Serena held her hands out as if she was trying to calm him. Wasn't he already acting calm? He thought he seemed pretty calm.

Ruth dropped a white shirt at his feet. Blood stained it as if someone had cleaned their sword on it.

Wait. That was the shirt Rochelle had given him. Now it was personal.

"Mary gave this shirt to Rochelle to give to you. Were you wearing it at the library just before this?"

"I was." Serena covered her mouth with her hands. Why was she worried? Surely the truth would clear up this whole mess. "I didn't steal any sword."

"Ruth, what is going on here?" Serena asked.

She snapped her fingers and two Healers grabbed Serena. Two others grabbed Jayden.

Dash reared.

Ethan calmed his breathing. So far they meant no harm to anyone but him. If he remained compliant, he could keep the girls safe.

Ruth's glare melted butter. "Miranda is dead in the library. Rochelle said you were there with her."

"What?" Serena gasped.

"I didn't say you killed her." Rochelle's voice came from the cluster of other Healers. They were holding her, too.

Ethan shook his head. "I'm sorry Miranda died, but I didn't—"

"You were alone with her in the library, were you not?"

"I was."

"And you were alone beneath the gray alor tree. With the sword?"

Ethan didn't say anything. If they weren't going to listen to the whole story, he certainly wasn't going to tell them what they wanted to hear.

Ruth tilted her head and cocked an eyebrow. "Shall I take your silence as admission?"

"Once you hear my side, I'm sure there will be no doubt of the fact that I didn't kill Miranda or steal the sword."

"What's that black mark on your chest?" Ruth pointed to new scar.

"Someone named Belladonna stole your sword. I didn't. Her men killed Miranda. And I'm sorry about that, but it wasn't me."

"The mark."

"It's from the sword. She stabbed me."

"And then used the sword's dark magic to heal you?"

"I guess."

Serena squeezed her eyes closed.

Ethan stared at her. Why was she so worried? "Can't you see I'm telling the truth?"

"Anyone with the mark of the sword can lie to a Healer," Ruth said. "Your testimony means nothing. But you already know that, don't you?"

Ethan's heart crumbled.

"What about mine?" Serena strained against those who held her close.

Ruth's lips formed a thin line. "Only Healer blood can open the door. Was it yours?"

Serena opened her mouth, but didn't speak.

"Answer me."

"Yes."

"You helped him. Rochelle told you Belladonna stole the sword, but that could have been what she believed. He covered his tracks well. He knows everything about Healers from Belladonna. He was working with her. Why else would she heal him? Why else would he come here and make threats to Tabitha? I'm sorry, Serena, but he betrayed you. Bind his hands and lock him up."

Ethan stood there while the Healers bound his hands and led him away. As long as he complied, they wouldn't harm Jayden, and that was what mattered.

CHAPTER 47

TEDIOUS ROAD

Leaves flitted off the trees and fell along the path, making no sound as Belladonna's black boots pounded them into the mud below. The potion she'd thrown on the ground should have been enough to take her back to the castle, but apparently Tabitha's extra baggage cut half the traveling time. Now she was in the middle of the woods approaching a city, and she didn't even know which one.

Didn't matter. That unicorn would have killed her. She had to get out of there. And she'd gotten what she went for. The sword, a powerful Healer, and destruction. So what if she hadn't been able to grab that young man who knew the Deliverers? She had ways of getting back to him later.

And true, she'd wanted Serena, but Tabitha would have to do. It's not like Franco asked for specific Healers.

The wind picked up, kicking dried leaves into the air, and they hissed and flitted on the breeze. Wind made inconspicuous travel harder. Sounds distorted, and scent carried.

Tabitha stumbled along after her, mouth covered and hands bound to the rope Belladonna held. Healing the woman's missing limb had taken a lot out of Belladonna. She found she could heal the arm when she held the sword. Now black veins snaked up Tabitha's right arm—well, the stump that remained of it. Hopefully it hadn't distorted her power at all. Surely the death of her unicorn made her weaker.

Those white beasts had been all too easy to slaughter with the help of her black lion and Cain. He'd done as promised, and he was a warrior. Her warrior. She glanced at the sky. He should be returning to her any moment now.

Belladonna tugged harder on the rope. Tabitha squeaked. So cumbersome. Belladonna sighed. But his majesty wanted a pure Healer—one untainted by lies and code-breaking like herself. Obedient servants were a pleasure to their masters. Masters who could be overtaken when the time was right. A purr rose in Belladonna's throat. Her black lion, Mist, echoed. Good, the creature had found her. Hopefully the creature hadn't bitten Cain. Belladonna would not like it if her favorite guard had been killed.

She halted. The familiar tingle on her wrists caught her attention. She might be bonded to a black lion, but she could still sense another Healer. She glanced back at Tabitha. The woman was staring at her wrist. So she felt it too. The presence of another Healer.

Too easy.

She tied Tabitha's rope to a tree. "Wait here. I think I can bring the king two of what he asked for after all." She crept closer to the pull and peered around a tree. A young woman with long brown hair and round, green eyes stood talking to a man with a black beard. Belladonna strained to hear anything important.

"You ready, Miss Madison?"

The young woman nodded. "The faster we get on the move, the better. I have to tell my sister I found the young man with the distorted birthmark."

Belladonna smiled. *Oh, you're not going anywhere, Madison. "Mist, bring me Cain."*

The black lion thumped at her side and Cain slid off the beast's back.

"You asked for me, milady?"

She smirked. "Yes. Do you see that man? It looks like he might be her bodyguard."

"I see him."

Franco would be able to finish his spell with a young, powerful Healer after all. And he'd reward her. He'd better, because once he performed the spell he wished to, she still knew how to kill him. A wicked smile stretched her lips and she looked at Cain. "Kill the guard. Bring me the girl."

CHAPTER 48

STRANGE HEALER CUSTOMS

Jayden glared at Ruth as she stood there, tapping her fingers against her biceps, watching the Healers "guide" her and Serena and Rochelle back to the Tree of Wisdom. Guide. Right. "Force" would be more accurate. But at least she'd be able to keep watch over Logan. Once inside the tree, Serena let Rochelle and Jayden pass, then she stood barring the way.

The Healer who had escorted them cocked an eyebrow at Serena, who merely lifted her chin into the air and crossed her arms. "Are we prisoners?"

"No. Ruth says—"

"Then leave us be." Serena said each word deliberately.

The woman huffed. "The trial will be at sunset. Ruth says you are welcome if you can be compliant to our rules."

"Have I done something wrong, Anita?"

A deep growl resounded outside the door and Anita practically jumped. She moved aside and Westwind, Aurora, and Scout trotted in. Westwind loped up to Jayden and bumped her hand with his cold nose.

"They've accused Ethan of killing a Healer and are taking him to trial."

Westwind's head swung around and he lowered his neck. Bristled.

Scout lunged at the woman in the doorway and she jumped back, but Jayden caught Scout by the neck. "Easy. We're going to get him back."

"Have we done something wrong?" Serena repeated.

Jayden inched closer to get a look at this Anita's face. Then she opened her talent. Frustration was all she could read off the woman. And a bit of haughtiness.

"Not that I am aware of, Serena. But if your friend wishes to remain a guest here, she needs to be compliant as well." Anita's eyes met Jayden's and the haughtiness grew.

Jayden glared and fisted her hands. These Healers didn't have the right to hurt Ethan. Sure, he'd killed—many times—in self-defense. But she trusted him with her life.

"You have her friend," Serena said.

"And evidence, may I remind you, that he murdered Miranda." Anita cocked a challenging eyebrow.

Westwind growled. Scout lunged again, but Aurora blocked him.

Jayden's blood heated. "You don't know him!"

"Oh?" Anita jutted her chin. "And you do? His past? His heart? Are you a Healer, that you can sense his lies and intentions? He is not above blame, and we both know it."

A hollow pull caused the center of Jayden's heart to feel as though it were caving in. That man he'd killed—the prisoner—after Kinsey's murder. He had killed recklessly then. Hadn't he?

Her chest ached. No. Ethan would have a reason. Her eyes burned and her throat tightened. She looked right into Anita's eyes. "I trust him with my life."

"And you would vouch for his character?"

"Yes." Her heart beat faster in her chest. Would they give him a chance?

Anita's eyes narrowed. "I will tell Ruth you wish a seat in the trial to provide character witness for the murderer."

"He's not—"

Serena's hand on Jayden's arm caused her to stop. Then she breathed deep. She was going to say Ethan wasn't a murderer, but her heart betrayed her. She wasn't certain. That one prisoner he'd killed. Jayden blinked back tears. Angry tears. Scout whined and faced her.

Westwind and Aurora stepped in front of her, growling.

Anita backed up a pace. "Be ready for the trial."

"We will be." Serena shut the door in her face.

Then she turned around and pressed her back into it, releasing a sigh. Her eyes met Jayden's and her worry mingled with doubt.

"Now what?" Rochelle asked.

Serena shook her head. "They'll put him on trial. We have to do everything possible to not get caught in their trap, because right now we are Ethan's only hope if they're to see his innocence." She bit her thumbnail. "Jayden, you almost lied. Would you like to tell me about that? Because right now I'm the only coach you have. And we don't have much time."

Jayden's mind reeled. "I know he didn't kill Miranda."

Serena nodded. "We have to prove it."

Westwind nudged Logan's arm and Scout whined.

"They won't be able to wake him before the healing process is finished." Rochelle motioned toward the canines.

Jayden's heart sank. She could really use Logan right now. "How heavily guarded is the prison?"

"Too heavy for you to try breaking in." Serena chewed on her thumbnail as she began pacing the length of the tree.

"But a serving girl could easily sneak in unnoticed." Rochelle bit her lip.

Serena narrowed her eyes. "Don't go off doing something rash. They know you're on Ethan's side. There's no way they'll let you in."

"I know." She frowned. "I just might know who's on duty, and getting past her could prove . . . doable."

"Don't you dare."

As Serena paced the room, Rochelle looked in the cupboard. "You would think they would have at least brought us food."

While Rochelle's back was turned, Serena leaned closer to Jayden and whispered, "She lets her thoughts jumble when she's trying to think of a way out of something." It didn't ease Jayden's mind at all.

Serena guided Jayden to the table while Rochelle checked Logan's temple.

"How is he?" Jayden asked.

Rochelle smiled, small and unconvincing. "Not ready to wake, but he's healing well." She glanced at Serena. "I can't think without food. I'm going to get some fruit." She grabbed a basket and left.

Serena turned to Jayden. "We have to get you ready to speak to twelve Healers—all of whom want Ethan to suffer for murder—and you're going to have to give the most confident speech of your life because they'll be looking for ways to dismiss what you have to say."

"Not too daunting." She laughed weakly, but then smiled because she felt that was something Ryan might say. And she missed Ryan right now because she missed home.

Serena cocked an eyebrow. "That's exactly the kind of talk you'll have to avoid. It feels as though you're trying to deceive us."

"Feels?"

Serena sat in the other chair. "Yes. We feel hearts. Sense intentions to lie or deceive. A lie comes across as a bad taste or smell. A half-truth—those are bit harder to discern. They come across more as a feeling."

"I can understand this. Not the deception part, but I feel things as well."

"Okay." Serena traced her lower lip with her thumb. "The women you are about to convince will be able to feel deception—uncertainty. Even if you can convince one, you still have to convince all. Because if even one senses a lie, her case to getting the others on her side will be very strong. Remember, they want Ethan punished."

Jayden rubbed her hands over her face. "So I've put him in more danger?"

"Potentially." Serena touched her hand. "But if you can find a way to speak from the heart, in truth, then you could help him."

Jayden looked up, pleading. "What should I say?"

Serena smiled and tilted her head. "Do you have a talent you could use? Something that could help you here?"

She shook her head. "No."

"Well then, you must tell them how Ethan is your Protector, and you trust him with your life. You must choose your words carefully and think before you speak. You must believe he's innocent with all of your heart."

"I do."

"Good. Then we have somewhere to start."

"Serena, what will they do to him if they find him guilty?"

The shiver of fear that pulsed into her from Serena's emotions made her clutch a hand over her heart. "They'll give him a Healer's death. The one Belladonna would have gotten if she hadn't escaped."

"A—a Healer's death?"

"If they don't cut off his head, they'll carve out his heart."

Ethan slumped against the moist rock wall of his cell. At least they'd let him grab his own shirt. But they'd taken his weapons. What was left of them. No sword.

He fingered the dark scar on his chest. Numb. But deep inside, it ached. Did the scar really make it possible to lie to them? Maybe he should just try and see what happened. At least he felt no threat for Serena or Jayden. But the moment he did, he'd get out of here if he had to pry those bars apart.

Right. Like that was possible.

No one could say he didn't kill Miranda. Mary's testimony of how he'd saved her was the only way out now. Hopefully she'd pull through and they'd all believe her.

He leaned closer to the cage door. Was someone coming? He strained to hear.

"Psst." Rochelle appeared in front of the door and jingled keys. "Ready to get out?"

He grabbed the bars, cold against his palms. "They believed Mary?"

Rochelle looked over her shoulder, then slipped the key into the lock. "Actually, I'm here to break you out."

"Do you think that's wise?"

"I think the only way you're getting out of here is if you pass the Circle's tests. Lie to me."

"What?"

She opened the door and handed him a torch as he stepped out. "I like the blue shirt. It suits you."

Ethan looked down at his clothes. "Um, thanks. Wait. Why do you want me to lie to you?"

"Just do it." She led him down the tunnel the opposite way he'd come in.

"You're the ugliest woman I've ever seen."

She giggled. "You don't even remotely believe that. I'm flattered."

"You can tell that I'm lying?"

"Of course I can. So can they, if they would just listen. The sword has them so scared."

"Why?"

"It was a weapon forged by the Mistress of Shadows herself. The fact that the wards guarding it were weak enough for Belladonna to take the sword means the Mistress is getting stronger. Readying herself to break free of her prison."

Rochelle turned a corner. "The weapon was built so that whatever wound it creates cannot be healed by any Healer. Even Healers would not be able to heal themselves if the weapon strikes them. They can be killed by the Sword of Black Malice as any man is killed by a sword. The Mistress wielded that weapon in the wars. She killed many Healers with it."

"So why didn't it kill me?"

"The sword is made from a murdered unicorn's horn. Then the Mistress put her venom in it. It's the same venom that black lions—another of her creations—have. When a unicorn stabs you with its horn, it can choose to heal you as it takes its horn out, or it can remove its horn and leave you wounded. I guess the sword has that capability, too."

Ethan touched the scar.

They'd reached a staircase. Rochelle started up. She turned when Ethan didn't follow.

He eyed her, not willing to take another step forward. "How was it so easy for you to rescue me?"

"It wasn't." That voice was recent enough to be recognized. Ruth appeared at the top of the stairs. She descended toward Rochelle, a dagger glinting in the torchlight. Three other Healers backed her.

CHAPTER 49

ON TRIAL

Ethan looked past the dagger and into Ruth's hard eyes. "Tell me you've heard from Mary."

"I have. Her mother and sister were both killed. She really isn't in the best state to give testimony."

"I'm not sure what I've done to make you not trust me."

"Do we have to go over the evidence again?"

That little thing Ruth did with her eyebrows was starting to burn his straw. "Sure. I'll give you the same answers. If you listen, I think you'll see that I'm telling the truth."

"I'll deal with you in a moment. As for you, Rochelle, this little escape attempt has consequences. Punishment is a necessary evil." She held up the dagger. "It's laced with enough bandy weed to stop you from healing for a day. Then you will receive twelve lashes. One from each of us."

Ethan's heart pounded. "Whoa. Wait. She thought she was doing the right thing. Look, I'll just go back to the prison. There's no reason to hurt her." This insanity had to stop.

"You don't make the rules here, boy."

If she called him "boy" one more time, he'd take her dagger and—

Ruth looked him in the eyes. "As it stands, it's time for you to face the Circle."

Yeah. And he'd make sure they really knew how he felt about this system. "Bring it on. You Healers are very violent for a peaceful group."

"We have to be."

"Really? After everything you've told us about the Imprisonment? Armies used you as shields, and you choose to use pain like this on each other? It doesn't make sense."

She stepped awfully close to him. "As long as men live, Healers will be hunted. Desired. Mistreated. It's best that we learn to defend ourselves against the things that could happen."

Ethan shook his head. "Defense, sure, but this is ridiculous. I don't know what kind of men you've been hanging around, but they clearly aren't the right ones. Maybe you've been hiding for too long."

Ruth straightened her spine. "Bind his hands. Cut Rochelle. Lead them both to the stone of trial."

Two Healers marched behind Ethan. He complied, putting his hands behind his back. But a third took the dagger from Ruth and approached Rochelle.

"Wait!" Ethan yelled.

They all paused, Ruth included. She lifted an eyebrow, waiting.

"Listen." He flinched as one of the Healers tightened the rope on his wrists. "This is a huge misunderstanding, but it's somehow my fault. Please, don't hurt her. She heard the truth I'm speaking. I'm sure your Circle will, too. Don't—don't whip her."

"Someone needs to be punished for your escape, boy."

"Punish me then."

Rochelle gasped.

Ruth faced him fully. "You feel much guilt, don't you?"

He looked into her eyes. Begged for her to hear the truth. "I didn't kill Miranda. But I'm not going to let you hurt an innocent girl. Not on my account. Please. Let me take her place."

"Ethan, no," Rochelle whispered. A tear rolled down her cheek.

The women holding his hands loosened their grip.

"Very well," Ruth said quietly. "Let Rochelle go. Bring him before the Circle." She turned slowly, and the confident bounce in her step had disappeared.

Jayden sat beside Serena on a wooden bench. Seven wooden benches in the shape of a crescent surrounded what they called the trial stone. It wasn't just a stone. To one side sat two wooden pillars to secure people who would be whipped. Behind that were twelve wooden chairs—the Circle's thrones, no doubt. And in the center sat a square stone. A dark stone. Stained with blood. Serena had said much blood was shed here over the years. Here, Healers had lost hands. Arms below the elbow. Lives. And angry, brown blood stained the stone's smooth surface.

"Why?" Jayden asked.

Serena looked at her lap. "The Circle's rules are to keep us safe, or so they say. I do not condone the barbarity, but this is the only place I belong."

Jayden turned to her and grabbed her hands. "No, Serena. You belong with us."

Rochelle raced toward them. Sobbing, she fell at Serena's feet, resting her head against Serena's knees. "He's taking the punishment."

"What?"

Jayden's heart thundered. Stilled. A roar split the sky and a bolt of lightning cracked the clouds. "They're not even going to give him a trial?"

"No. No, they're going to—this is all my fault—I wanted to help, but now they're—"

Jayden didn't wait for her to finish.

The crowd started to stand and the Healers brought Ethan up to the stone.

Jayden ignored Serena's cries to come back and wove through everyone. Everything. All she saw was Ethan. He walked, head high, jaw tight, hands tied behind him, toward the stone.

This wasn't right. They'd promised him a trial. They'd said they would listen to him. Hands tried to stop her, but she ducked and dodged their grasp. She was a hidden dagger now, using her speed to get past the enemy. And she ran right over to the Healers who led Ethan out to the stone.

As soon as he saw her, emotion flooded into her from him. Worry, fear, and a trickle of hope. Hope. That was all she needed to know she was in the right place.

"Jayden, what are you—"

"Ethan." She stopped in front of him, not caring how many voices rose up around her. Some in outrage, some in shock. The thunder above rumbled and quieted her heart. She placed her hand on his cheek and looked deep into his eyes. Hoped he could sense how much she cared for him in what she was about to do. "I can't let them do this to you. I hope you understand."

"Jayden, I—"

She stepped around him, faced the Healers, and drew her dagger. Voices of surprise broke up around her. She didn't care. Tears threatened. "You promised him a trial."

"And he will have one." Ruth stepped forward, her gaze landing on Jayden's dagger. "I thought you meant to be a good witness to his character."

"I do. But you had no intention of giving me the chance, did you?"

Ruth narrowed her eyes. "What would give you that impression, Child?"

"Rochelle said you were going to punish him."

"Yes." Ruth nodded. "He convinced us to let him take Rochelle's punishment."

"Rochelle's?"

"She broke him out of his cell."

Her heart dropped into her stomach. Of course he had. That was her Ethan. She closed her eyes as tears crept out. "What's the punishment?"

Rain dotted her clothes. A small sprinkle. Ethan's body brushed against her back as he leaned closer. "Jayden." His breath touched her hair.

She faced him. "Did you kill Miranda?"

His eyebrows pinched together. "No."

She itched to hug him. "Did you harm her?"

"Of course not."

She released a shaky breath and turned back to Ruth and the rest of the Circle. And her emotions started to lose control. Her talent wanted to feel. She had to finish this before she let anger take over. She breathed deep, trying to control her talent, and looked at Ruth. A pang of sorrow hit her heart. Sorrow? From Ruth? Not only sorrow, but guilt and confusion.

Jayden squared her shoulders, sheathed her dagger, and spoke softly. Maybe her talent could help. "If he says he didn't hurt her, he didn't. Serena coached me on some things to say—true things. But what I want to say is that Ethan is my Protector. And I am yours. I'm a Deliverer. Sent to deliver you from an evil that would seek to destroy you. I trust this man with my life. And I think you can see why. I know Rochelle can. I know Mary can." She turned toward him. "Ethan, you would give your life for mine."

A mix of emotions poured out of him, but the strongest was confidence. Confidence in the answer he was about to give. "I will protect you unto death."

She turned back to the Healers, tears wetting her cheeks. "See? What more proof do you need? This Belladonna is a threat to me. He's not working with her."

Ruth breathed deep and stared at Jayden for what seemed like an eternity. But as her heart softened, Jayden's hope rose. And the storm abated.

Finally Ruth nodded. "Unbind his hands. The prisoner has not killed our sister."

Gasps filled the crowd. A Healer cut Ethan's hands free.

Jayden smiled at Ruth. "What changed your mind?"

"Not my mind, Child. My heart." She looked over Jayden's shoulder at Ethan. "She has pulled the blinders from my eyes. Blinders created by the Sword of Black Malice. Its power is stronger than even I thought. But now I see we were about to make a grave mistake. Please accept my apologies. And take my allegiance. Your heart is the purest I've ever seen, Ethan. And Jayden, you have the ferocity and compassion of a true leader. If the two of you ever need the Healers of the Forest of Legends, we will follow you into battle."

Jayden bowed. "Thank you."

Ruth smiled. "The Circle grants your request to take Serena."

"Take?" Ethan crossed his arms and widened his stance. "No. Serena gets to choose."

"Of course." Ruth turned, and Jayden followed her gaze to see Serena standing behind them. "Your choice, Child." Serena nodded.

As the crowd began to disperse, and Ruth with them, Serena's voice stopped her. "The stone of Ishkar. Do you think it's time to show someone where the Whisperer is?"

Ruth stared for so long, Jayden feared they might have another strange custom to have to defeat, but Ruth finally nodded. "We've been guarding the stone for so long, it seems strange that the time has come to use it. Come with me."

She turned, but Serena walked up to Ethan. She kissed his cheek. "Thank you. For letting me choose. You have no idea what that means to me." She squeezed his arm and walked after Ruth.

Jayden tamped down a flicker of jealousy as she headed after the others, shaking her head and telling herself that Serena was doing nothing more than expressing gratitude, but a tug on her sleeve caused her to turn around.

Ethan stood there, eyebrows pulled together. Slowly his crooked smile spread across his face. "That was extremely reckless."

"It's not every day my Protector needs protecting."

His lips parted and his eyes widened. "I'm sorry. I—"

"Don't be." She shook her head. "I needed to do that. I needed them to see what I see in you."

He seemed to gravitate closer. "And what do you see?"

"Your heart."

CHAPTER 50

MOMENT OF TRUTH

Ethan stood, facing Jayden as she watched him with her bright, blue eyes. His heart? Could she truly see it? Because the darkness in there would surely have scared her away.

She blinked and looked at the ground.

He closed the distance between them and smiled the way that always seemed to light up her face. "They're going to show us where the Whisperer is. Logan will wake up soon. Serena is coming. Everything's going right, but you're frowning."

She glanced away, a blush coloring her cheeks, and a smile finally formed on her face. "I know. I'm sorry."

"Hey, it's okay. I've been through more tests here than ever in school, and I have a feeling they're just getting started."

"Any advice?" She looked up at him through her eyelashes, and he realized he was standing much closer than intended.

He swallowed. Took in every inch of her face. Every heartbeat seemed to propel him the tiniest bit closer to her, and with each rest a pang gripped his heart. A pang that reminded him Jayden was Ryan's betrothed.

"Ethan?" Her voice tremored.

"Yeah." He cleared his throat. "Yes. Don't lie to them." He smiled, but it felt different on his face.

"Of course not."

Neither of them moved. He couldn't tear his eyes from her.

"Are you coming?" Rochelle's voice broke the hold, and Ethan remembered to breathe.

He motioned for Jayden to walk ahead of him. She did, but she watched him over her shoulder for a long time. Was she feeling his emotions? He buried them. Became a stone. Her eyes squinted, and she bit her lip.

He'd have to be more careful, apparently.

At last they'd caught up to Ruth and Serena.

Ruth led them down below the tree and into the room beneath the canopy of roots. Ruth didn't produce light in her hand like Serena had. She used a torch.

The deep chill below ground reminded him of the little cell they'd kept him in.

Ruth didn't open any box or produce any key. Instead, she told them to look up. In the center of the tangle of tree roots nestled a sphere. Jayden cocked her head and peered into it. A shimmering light, not unlike the one Serena had created in her palm, shone in the center of the sphere. It widened until it filled the whole stone. As it dimmed, a scene was left in its center. So similar, yet so different from the seeing stone Connor had given him.

The picture was of a young girl chained to a wall of blue rock. A slow burn overtook Ethan's chest that had nothing to do with a threat. Quinn? "Is this the Whisperer?"

"Yes," Ruth said. "She is at Castlerock."

"She's in the same location as the Mistress's prison?" Serena asked, but Ethan barely heard her question. Quinn. This young girl was their Whisperer. The one his talent urged him to protect. Maybe he was supposed to be paying more attention to his talent that he had been.

He clutched his hands into fists. "Who did this to her?"

Jayden touched his shoulder, and some of her calm strength filtered into him. Heavens knew he needed it now.

"I don't know." Ruth's eyes held a trace of compassion. "Whoever took her there most certainly died unless they defeated the beast in the water."

"Beast in the water?" Ethan asked.

Ruth nodded. "No one has touched the water and lived."

Then how were they supposed to rescue Quinn?

Serena followed Jayden and Ethan as they walked back to the Tree of Wisdom.

"We wait for Logan to wake, then we go find our Whisperer," Ethan said. "And we leave as soon as possible. We aren't the only ones looking."

That was apparent. Serena stopped walking. Her feet were like lead, her heart like a hummingbird's wing.

Logan.

They were going to wait for Logan.

So much had happened that she'd forgotten. She'd wanted to go with Jayden and Ethan, but now the fear crept right back into her veins and wrapped tentacles around her heart.

Ethan took two steps back toward her. "You're not coming with us, are you?"

She had to, right? Yet he gave her a choice. Her freedom. "I . . ." She wanted to respond, but she'd lost the words.

Jayden opened the door to the tree and three canines raced out. Westwind whined. He ran a tight circle around Jayden. Scout jumped up and pawed at Ethan's shirt.

Her heart dove off a cliff.

Ethan motioned to Jayden. "Go. Someone should be with him."

Jayden cast one last look at Serena, then ran inside the tree, the canines with her.

Serena wanted to follow. Couldn't.

Ethan held out his hand. "He won't hurt you. If he tries to, I'll put a stop to it."

Truth.

Serena looked from Ethan's hand to his face. "You're either not a very good friend, or you're certain."

He smiled. "I hope it's the latter."

She took a deep breath, let it out slow, and slipped her hand into his.

Together they entered the tree. She peeked from behind Ethan's shoulder, unwilling to let Logan see her yet. Scout and the wolves were all trying to lick his face. He laughed and it sounded warm. Happy. Nothing like any father she'd known.

Jayden raced to Ethan and hugged him so tight. "He's all right!" She looked at Serena and whispered, "Thank you."

Serena's throat constricted. "Did you tell him about me?" Even as a whisper, the words were hard to get out.

"Of course not."

"Ethan." Logan nodded. "Westwind tells me I owe you one."

"Let's not go keeping track or I'll be making too much debt to repay. It's good to see you." Ethan chuckled, yet seemed to hesitate—as if he wanted to hug Logan but wouldn't for Serena's sake. He stayed, blocking her from Logan's view. "You ready?" he whispered.

No. Never. And yes. She nodded.

"Jayden says I'm in a tree." Logan glanced around the room.

"At the camp of the Healers. Serena healed you," Ethan said.

She hid behind him and Jayden, biting her lip.

"The same Serena who healed you?" Logan's voice seemed closer. Was he moving toward her? Her heart pounded like a wild horse fighting a bridle. Jayden touched her shoulder and a sensation of calm blanketed her. Hugged her tight. Serena breathed deep.

"Yes." Ethan stepped aside so she could see Logan and he could see her.

His eyes were blue. Kind. She hadn't expected that. They opened wide, then softened. Glistened. Slowly his arms braced against the bed and he started to stand. She fought hard to remain grounded.

"Serena, you should have told me." Dash's thoughts reached out to her. Gave her courage.

"I think I'm okay."

"This is Serena." Ethan kept his body between them, though not directly. But his soft smile reassured her.

Logan stared at her. "Of course it is." He leaned against the bed.

Serena dipped her head in a greeting. "Do you know who I am?"

"In a sea of faces, I would recognize yours."

Truth. "Ethan says you'll protect me."

"With every breath I have left."

Truth. Her hands shook. She stepped closer. "I've been told you're dangerous."

Logan's face sprouted a half smile, and it made him seem so human. So normal. Could the Healers be wrong about men?

"Some would consider me dangerous." Logan's eyes scanned her face. "But to you, daughter, never."

Truth.

Logan stared into his daughter's eyes. Blue. Like his. She looked so like her mother, but her eyes were his. He wanted this moment to stop and wait for him to catch up. He needed to see her. Every detail about her. He wanted to hug her. The last time he'd held her . . . a burn shot through his nose. He sniffed and wiped his eyes. She didn't seem to want him close to her now. He'd wait. He'd give her all the time she needed. All the time he'd stripped from her when he'd given her to someone else.

He reached out to Westwind. *This is happening.*

"She healed you. All of us. We would be dead if not for her," Westwind said.

Logan smiled. Of course she did. "Westwind says you saved us." Uncertainty tinged her smile. What thoughts raced through her mind? Would she ever forgive him? "How did you get here?"

She blinked rapidly. Then she breathed deep and glided over to him. She placed her fingers on his temples, and he held perfectly still. "That's a long story."

"I have time for anything you want to tell me, daughter."

She stepped back, but this time her smile seemed warm. "You need rest and food. And I think Ethan and Jayden have much to tell you."

A cool breeze entered the room. Ethan turned, hand on his sword. Logan groped for his, but it was nowhere near him.

A young girl, also dressed in white, entered. Her eyes met his and widened. "I thought you might need new candles and more food, but I didn't expect to see Logan awake yet."

"Thank you, Rochelle." Serena took the tray from her and handed it to Logan. He took it.

"I didn't bring enough." Rochelle motioned toward the tray. "I'll have to go get more. Later, so I can be discrete about it. Otherwise the Circle might suspect he's awake." She curtsied. Then she turned to Ethan. "I wanted to thank you for—" she broke off and threw her arms around his neck.

He backed up a step before steadying himself. Slowly he hugged her back. "Hey, thank you for helping us from the beginning when no one else but Serena would."

She sniffed and let him go. "You're welcome." Her eyes were as bright as her smile when she ducked out the door.

Serena turned to Logan. "You can trust Rochelle."

Logan's eyes narrowed. "I thought all Healers were trustworthy."

Serena pursed her lips. "Truthful, yes. Pure in heart, certainly. But they aren't all on your side, Logan."

He glanced at Ethan, who shrugged. "Some of them want to kill you, and the rest want to see you dead. Thankfully, they're letting us leave as soon as you're well enough." He grinned.

"You're serious?"

Westwind growled. *"He is."*

"Then let's go." He put down the tray. "We don't have any time to lose; we've lost so much already."

"Wait." Serena laughed and handed Logan the plate of food.

"It's night. You're tired. Sleep in my home tonight, and we'll leave first thing in the morning?"

"Before sunrise." Logan took a roll and offered the plate to the others.

"All right." Serena pushed it back toward him. "You should know that Rochelle wants to come with us, but I've asked her to stay here for now."

"Good." Logan's mouth was full and his plate half empty. "I've picked up enough strays already, and I don't take anyone unless they can fight."

"Oh, she can fight." Serena gave Logan a leveled look. "Healers can fight."

He'd heard that. "So you're trained?"

She nodded.

"Strays, huh?" Ethan laughed.

Logan chuckled. "Yes. Strays."

Serena went toward the small table near the cupboard and pulled out a charcoal stick and paper. "I'll leave a note I know only Rochelle will find. Having an ally here will be better than not."

"I like the way you think, daughter." The last word made her flinch, and his heart hurt. She didn't forgive him. "Serena, I'm sorry."

She looked up at him, her eyes intense. "For what?"

"I thought putting you in hiding would keep you safe from the queen."

"It did."

"I'm sorry I missed your whole life."

Her mouth opened, but she said nothing. Just stared deep into his eyes. He got up and moved toward her. She backed away one step. He stopped and put his hand up. "I won't press you to do anything you don't want to."

"I see that. You speak truth. That's enough for now."

"Enough for what?"

"I need to show you something." She walked around the table, pulled a yellowed piece of parchment from a creased envelope, and carefully unfolded it. Then she handed it to him. "My mother wrote this."

Logan's eyes scanned the page, and his jaw clenched.

> *Please care for my child. She is one of the Deliverers and needs protection from the queen. Beware, her father Logan Laugnahagn will do everything in his power to take her to the queen. He must never find her.*

His hand shook and he crushed the corner of the paper.

Serena placed her hand on his and lowered it, moving the letter farther from his eyes. "Jayden and Ethan tell me differently. I believe them. But I need to hear it from you."

She waited until he looked at her.

"Your mother wrote this. She took your brother to the queen. I'll get him back, and I'll keep you safe. You have my word." He prayed she heard the truth in his words. The love.

She took the paper from him and crumpled it up. "I'm sorry."

He grabbed her wrists. "You have nothing to be sorry for. None of this is your fault. It's mine. Mine alone. And *I'm* sorry."

"Thank you. I meant I feel sorry for you. You loved her, right? My mother?"

Logan rubbed two fingers across his forehead. She deserved to know. "I did. Another mistake. What's done is done."

"It is." She squeezed his hand and smiled. She looked so much like Rebekah.

He breathed deep, wishing he had something he could give her. Then he remembered. He got up, found the long velvet case Anna had given him, and took out four daggers and their sheaths. "These are for you." He handed her one of the two long daggers. They were almost long enough to be considered short swords. "I can show you how to use them if—"

"I know how." She smiled. "But why would you give me these?"

"These weapons identify the Deliverers."

"They'll bond with you," Jayden said.

Serena picked up the weapon. The milky opal in the hilt blazed with her touch. It looked like a shimmering unicorn under an uninhibited full moon. The white light wrapped around her arm. "Oh."

"There's no doubt now." Logan handed her the other long one and the two small daggers. Each lit up in her hand.

"They're the most beautiful daggers I've ever seen."

"They were made for you, by a Wielder." Logan rolled the remaining swords back into the red velvet and tied the strings carefully around them. He glanced at all three of them. "These are a secret."

Serena smiled and Logan's breathing hitched. *"She's so like her mother."*

Aurora's mood felt content. *"She is."*

Perhaps he could learn to see that as a good thing like she seemed to.

Westwind chuckled. *"That's a lot of human emotion for you to deal with, friend."*

Logan reached down and patted Westwind's head. Teeth touched his hand in response. *"Don't get carried away."* He chuckled at his wolf friend.

"Before you put those weapons away, Logan, Ethan could use a new sword." Jayden shot Ethan a smile.

Logan cocked an eyebrow. "What happened?"

"It's a long story." Ethan shrugged. "And it involves a pretty ugly scar."

"Here. Just until we get you something to replace it." Logan handed Ethan one of the swords from the case.

Ethan pulled it out and ran his fingers over the cross guard. He weighed it. "Feels good. Feels great, actually. This is a far superior weapon."

"Don't get too used to it." Logan chuckled. "We'll head toward—"

"Castlerock," Ethan said. "Our Whisperer is there."

"Sounds like I missed a lot."

Jayden laughed. "You did."

Ethan slumped against the wall. "And be glad you slept through most of it."

CHAPTER 51

EYES LIKE HONEY

Eyes like honey stared at Connor. Fire flickered, danced in the amber irises. A black pupil—blacker than anything he'd ever seen—focused on him. No light reflected off these pupils. Blacker than night. Blacker than the stone. Light didn't exist there.

He shivered. Tried to close his eyes, but the gaze entrapped him.

"Would you like to see?"

See what? Something from those eyes? No way.

His skin crawled, and every hair on his body stood on end.

Then he realized he was a wolf. Always a wolf in his dreams. This had to be a dream.

"Who are you?" he asked.

"Do you have to ask? Don't you know?" The voice sounded like rocks moving, mountains shifting . . . a prison breaking.

No. A shudder shot through Connor so the tip of his tail even shook.

"Yesssss."

Connor tried to flee, but every way he turned, the eyes still stared at him. Bigger. It was almost as if he were caught in the stone. He couldn't be. He'd left it under his pillow.

If his pillow had moved . . . perhaps it had. The eyes were watching him sleep, getting inside his head. He had to learn to fight it.

"What do you want?" His voice echoed in the nothingness around him.

The answering chuckle was deep like an earthquake. An avalanche.

"You're afraid of your powers. You know where they come from."

No.

"Yesssss. They come from her."

Stop. He wanted to cover his ears, but he had only paws.

"The Mistress created your powers. They may have brought balance once, but not anymore. Now they only breed destruction. You would keep yourself away from the others to protect them. But you cannot. Your powers will consume them."

"I'll learn to use them."

"Learn how? From all those books you read?"

How did it know about the books? This had to be a dream, nothing more.

But it was something more. It was true. All of it. All of his fur stood on end. If he couldn't learn to control his powers, how would he survive?

"Your power brings death. You are Death Bringer. Even the creatures of the deep can be destroyed by you, but not unless you learn to use your power. You will be the most powerful of them all."

A shiver raced over Connor's skin. He hunched his back and held his head low. Tail tucked between his legs. "You can't be what I think you are."

"I am Sssssmoke, the mount of the Mistress, and my wings are stretching."

Connor sat up and breathed heavily in the darkness of his room. Little moonlight spilled through the cracks of the windows. The fire still roared but he shivered. Wet from sweat.

The rock beneath his pillow glowed and he picked it up. No sign of the deadly eyes. Eyes the color of his own. It didn't mean they weren't watching. They could be. Could be staring at him right now. But Smoke had seemed to see inside Connor's head. That, as far as he knew, was not possible. It had to be a dream.

If Smoke were truly waking, it meant the Mistress was breaking free of her prison. He had to be sure Ethan rescued Quinn before it happened. If only he had broken free of this trace spell earlier. Thea had been the one to want him to stay. Why had he listened? She'd also said he'd push his mother out a window. He should have known never to trust Thea. She was an assassin.

But Smoke was right. Connor was too afraid of what he'd do to the others. If he hurt them. If he couldn't control his powers. Logan would come looking for him. He wouldn't join them. Maybe he could help from afar.

The rock heated in his hand, and he covered it in the folds of his bedsheet. Then he got dressed. There were a few things he needed to figure out. One of them was how to get out of the palace.

What he needed was some fresh air so he could formulate a plan.

He dressed and headed out of his room, sure to keep the door closed and the fire going in the hearth. He sniffed. Listened. Only the steady creaking of the wind through the drafty corridor. A mouse padded down the hall, tiny paws against the cool floor. He barely heard it with his wolf hearing.

Connor crept toward the west end of the palace, the quickest way to the tunnels. He shed his clothes in the Bard's Way, then morphed into a wolf. The smithy was empty, so he exited with ease. Outside he gazed up at the moon.

All the sounds and smells came to him more clearly. The cool autumn air didn't chill him now. The leaves rustled, dry on their branches. And the wind swept over the field of long, dry grass.

As he paced, he thought.

So far Thea had been right to tell him not to leave yet. Getting the bracer from Balton was worth being here.

Maybe she hadn't led him astray. But she was crazy if she thought he'd push Rebekah out a window. He shook the thought from his head. Rebekah's plan to leave was a good one. But he really wanted to find out what the bracer did before he lost access to the library.

A light flickered in the window. Connor crept closer to the side of the palace wall.

A metallic scent hit his nose and he stopped. Sniffed the wind. Blood. Thick in the air.

His stomach roiled. Who was being killed?

Another scent burned his nose, a scent he'd never smelled before, but his powers gave him immediate recognition. Black lion venom.

Belladonna was there. Franco. A young woman with long, brown hair was there, too. She was bound and scared. The scent of blood choked him. So much blood.

Connor raced back inside. Whatever was happening in the palace, it needed to be taken care of and quickly.

As a wolf he rushed to the spot of light that shone in the white throne room. He'd have to be small to get into that room unnoticed. He remembered his mouse friend. That could work, but how long would he be able to keep to a form that small? He'd never done it. He might only have minutes.

It was worth a try.

The halls of the palace seemed to grow tall and wide as he shrunk into mouse form. The carpet smelled so much more potent from here.

He scurried beneath the door and into the white room.

Light flickered from every torch, every candle. It almost looked like daytime here.

Franco leaned close to Belladonna, and the two men flanking her eyed the king. "You're sure she's powerful enough?" Franco motioned to the poor girl, whose hands were tied in front of her. A gag choked her, and she glared at Franco.

Belladonna nodded. "The most powerful I've ever encountered."

Franco walked up to the young woman and grabbed her chin in his fingers. He held a ring in front of her nose and removed the gag. "I found this in your pocket, Madison. To whom does it belong?"

"I—I don't know. I've never seen it before."

He smiled. "Well, you've seen it now." He clutched it back in his hand and stepped away.

Kara's silhouette filled the doorway. "You found the prisoner?"

"I found her." He motioned to Madison.

Kara charged at her, knife out.

"Wait," Franco said in his most musical voice. "Remember our deal. There is something you must do for me first, then she is all yours."

What was he up to? Connor wanted to change into a wolf and lunge at Franco's neck, but there were too many in here for him to fight.

"I want her now," Kara sneered.

Franco smiled. "Put the knife away. I'll let you take care of her. But first hear and have no doubt."

Kara sheathed her weapon and crossed her arms.

Belladonna chuckled. "Such a good little assassin."

The knife was back in Kara's hand before Franco could even say anything. Kara tossed it right at Belladonna, but before it hit her, one of her new guards dove in front of it. The knife imbedded in his shoulder instead of Belladonna's stomach.

"You idiot!" Belladonna hissed at Kara. Then she knelt next to her man.

"Did—did I save you?" he choked.

"You did well, Cain. Let me help you." She pulled out the weapon, pressed her hands against his wound, and healed him.

He practically groveled at her feet. "Thank you, my lady."

A shiver shot through Connor's fur. His skin seemed tight. This form wouldn't last much longer. Wait. He twitched his nose. The scent of black lion venom was strong here. He inched out from beneath the chair and looked up. There, perched on one of the room's buttresses, lurked a black lion. Its wings spread, and the beast dropped to the floor, pressed against Belladonna, and purred.

Connor swallowed. If that cat smelled him, this wouldn't end well.

Franco turned his attention to Kara. "It seems you just wanted to throw your knife. For the rest of this meeting, no one does anything without my approval. Is that clear?"

She nodded.

"Good." He picked up the knife, cleaned it on the man's shirt, and then handed it back to Kara. He motioned for his guards to hold Madison steady. "This is the woman who killed your sister."

Not true. Connor's heart thumped.

Her eyes widened. "I didn't kill anyone!"

"Lie." Belladonna's tone was bored, and the woman looked at her fingernails. Franco smiled.

"I didn't kill her sister."

"How do you know?" Franco asked.

"I-I—"

"Have you ever seen this ring? We found it in the folds of your robe after the cart crashed."

Madison shook her head. "I've never seen it—"

"Lie." Belladonna yawned.

She looked right at Kara, tears in her eyes. "I'm telling you, this is a set-up. I never killed—"

"I've heard enough." Kara's voice was like venom. She curled her hands around the dagger at her waist. But she looked at Franco.

He nodded once.

She threw the knife.

The knife hurtled toward Madison and sunk deep into her stomach. She shrieked. Crimson spread onto her dress, staining the blue fabric. Clutching the handle, Madison slid down the wall.

Connor squeezed his body against the chair leg. He knew who killed Thea, and it wasn't this poor girl. Whatever Franco's game was, he'd have to get to the bottom of it.

"That was for my sister," Kara said.

Franco smiled. "Belladonna, pull the knife out."

Belladonna gripped the handle. Madison's shriek filled the room, and the bloody weapon clattered to the floor.

"You're still alive." Franco bent over and touched the young Healer's cheek. He grabbed the blood-stained portion of Madison's dress in two hands. The wet material tore easily and revealed her woundless stomach. "You can't just kill her, Kara. But the deal you made with me will make her suffer for the rest of her life. Are you ready?"

Kara glared at the Healer. "I'll do whatever you ask."

"I thought you might." Franco picked the bloodied knife off the floor and headed over to the glass table. He placed the reddened knife blade into a goblet and stirred. "I just need your blood."

No. Not a spell. *Kara, don't fall for it.*

Kara sliced her palm. "Where?"

Franco smiled and tapped the goblet. He let the blood trickle into the glass. Then he poured the black liquid into three different glasses. One he handed to Kara. "Drink."

The next he pressed to Madison's lips. She struggled. He plugged her nose. As soon as her mouth opened, he poured the contents down.

Then he looked at their black-stained mouths and raised the final glass to his lips. "Now." He looked at Kara. "It's your turn." He plunged the knife deep into her gut.

She crumpled to the ground near Connor.

His breathing quickened as he stared into her lifeless eyes. Blood dripped onto the white marble floor. Out of her mouth.

"What did you do to her?" Madison screamed. Blood wet the whole front of her torn dress, but she didn't seem to be in pain.

Franco leaned over the young woman. "Heal her, Healer."

"She's dead."

"That's right, but she's still bound to us by the life-debt. You can bring her back."

The girl's eyes narrowed. "What?"

Connor scanned his memories for the term *life-debt*. He'd read it before. Dark, evil magic. It involved something about black venom and death, but it could give the wielder of the spell near immortality. Of course that was Franco's plan.

Something Thea had said to Connor quickly snapped to his mind: *"When my sister is at her most vulnerable, you will see her. After this, you must tell her what truly happened to me. Not before."*

"That's quite cryptic, Thea."

"I know. But I have to be careful not to change things. You'll know what I mean when you see it."

"And what am I to tell her about you?"

"You'll know that, too, Wolf."

He'd thought her strange then. But now, if Kara truly came back, Connor would tell her that it was Franco who killed her sister.

"Madison," Franco stepped closer. "You will bring her back now, or I'll kill your twin sister."

"You don't have her."

Franco dangled a necklace in front of her. "You haven't seen all of my cells."

"Show her to me."

"If I bring her in here, you will see a corpse."

Madison narrowed her eyes.

Franco snarled. "I will tattoo you, girl, and then you'll have to heal who I say, when I say. You will lose your soul to me."

Madison held her head high and made direct eye contact with Franco. "I don't believe you have my sister. And you can threaten me with the tattoo, but I know the spell for such evil has been lost. I'll heal this girl because you had no right to use her grief to get what you wanted. You are not worthy to be called king."

A guard raised his hand to smack her.

"Wait," Franco said. "Don't hurt her, I need her to perform this ritual. She needs all her strength."

Connor's body started to feel as though it pulled. His skin was getting too tight. He needed to either be in his normal human form or his normal wolf form. And soon. He eyed the exit.

Two eyes, bright like a pale moon, locked onto him. The black lion crouched low and thrashed its tail.

Madison leaned over Kara's body.

If he didn't make it to the door in time, he wouldn't be small enough to get out and his secret would be revealed. He had to go. Now.

Madison cried out. Sweat beaded on her forehead.

The cat purred.

There was an opening.

Color drained from Madison's face. She fell over.

The lion pounced. Huge paws blocked light from view as they cast shadows over him. Connor dodged, but one paw pinched the tip of his tail, causing his paws to slip on the floor. His heart hammered as he tried to gain purchase. A purr rumbled through him from the creature, and he thought his heart would burst. He scrambled against the marble and at last pulled his tail free. His body seemed to stretch. Pulling his skin. Yellow eyes locked on to him. He raced beneath a chair. The lion followed. The door was just in view. He dove, sliding along the marble, and squeezed beneath the frame.

And he heard Kara gasp.

He morphed into a wolf too soon, his tail not even on the other side of the door. That was close. He shook off his fur, turned—and Oswell, the king's personal servant, stared at him with narrowed eyes.

"What are you?"

CHAPTER 52

A SPY

O swell circled Connor, torch in hand.
Connor shook like something inside of him had awakened. His talents. Oswell's display threatened Connor's life—with fire, nonetheless—and his talents emerged from dormancy. He growled. Everything he'd done to keep them contained would be ruined if he used them now. He breathed deep, trying to calm himself.

Oswell slunk closer. "Who are you? What are you?"

Connor backed away a step, heart skittering. Oswell had seen him change as he'd slipped under the door. Oswell knew the color of Connor's eyes. He might be in wolf form now, but Oswell wasn't stupid. He'd figure this out.

If Connor didn't use his talent now . . . maybe there was one more use for the bracer.

He bared his teeth, jumped forward, and pushed Oswell to the ground. Oswell hit with a thud and grabbed Connor's leg. Kept him from escaping. Heat charred his fur and seared his skin. He grabbed Oswell's arm in his mouth. Bit. Crushed.

Oswell swore and dropped Connor's leg.

Connor sprinted away. Every movement pulled at the burn on his side.

"Stop that wolf!"

Guards sprang to attention, but Connor was too fast. He dashed into the kitchen, morphed long enough to open the door, then escaped into the night.

He rounded the palace, headed for the back.

"After it! It's a Feravolk spy!"

A spy, huh? Yes. Oswell was on to something. Connor would have to be very careful not to get caught now. The searing pain in his side told him this would be a difficult wound to hide.

He made it to the back and limped through the long grass behind the smithy. Too many guards had headed that way. Of course his clothes were in the tunnel with no more access to the outside. Now he could either go back inside as a wolf or a naked man. Or wait for the palace guards to give up searching for him so he could slip into the smithy and into the underground tunnels.

He waited in the dark of the night. Waited until the lights dimmed in Oswell's room. And licked his wound.

By the time he deemed it safe to go after his clothes, his side was stiff and the hair matted to the sticky skin pulled with each movement. If he could be a bird right now, he wouldn't even be able to fly. He found the tunnel and his clothes.

His skin hurt worse when he morphed back. His whole side was red and blistered. Pulling on his shirt was torture. So was moving.

When he reached the top of the steps, he pressed his ear to the door. Nothing. At the door to his room, he smelled something. Someone had been by here. He sniffed. Kara. Only she smelled different. What had that spell done to her? To Franco and that poor Madison girl?

Hopefully something in the library had answers.

Connor's stomach twisted, and he wanted to throw up. Maybe he should go patch up his side. He limped toward the infirmary to get some salve, but someone was coming. He sniffed. Lavender. Belladonna. He stepped aside and leaned against one of the recesses in the wall behind a golden statue of a man holding scales.

She marched past without so much as noticing him, but the Healer who followed behind looked right into his eyes. Madison.

A crease formed between her eyebrows and she opened her mouth. He held his finger up to his lips, hoping she'd stay silent.

She turned away from him and he stared at the shackles around her wrists. Poor girl needed to be rescued. Especially if she looked at him like that. But what had Franco done to her? Would it be safe to free her, or would someone notice?

Footsteps shuffled ahead.

"How dare you step in front of me?" Belladonna's voice boomed in the halls.

A fire rose in Connor's throat, and he stepped out of his hiding place. A new serving girl had nearly crashed into Belladonna and spilled soup on the floor.

Connor had met her—her name was Eve.

Belladonna pulled out her whip and Eve dropped to her knees, trembling. She held her hand up, bracing herself for whatever Belladonna was going to do.

Connor rushed between them and placed his hand on Belladonna's wrist. She glared.

"The tea and cakes. You mustn't be late." He nudged Eve to her feet while Belladonna stood there, frozen.

Eve stared at him.

He pulled the napkin off the tray and wiped up the spill, then placed it back. "Hurry." If she didn't see the urgency in his eyes and run, there wasn't going to be much else he could do to help her.

She scurried away, glancing over her shoulder.

He faced Belladonna. "You have authority to whip Franco's servants now?"

"You? Oh, how noble." Belladonna scoffed. "Cleaning up messes for serving girls. Surely Balton will want you as captain in his guard soon. Keep groveling."

He wanted to snarl.

Madison caught his eye, and a smile flashed across her face.

He would do what he could to help her. Trouble was, he didn't know how yet.

Belladonna pushed him out of the way and led Madison down the hall.

Side screaming, he stumbled across the hall and into the infirmary. He just needed some salve. Or something to take away the pain.

"What are you looking for m'dear?" A pretty, young blue-eyed lady smiled at him.

"I, um—"

"Sit." She looked at the blood seeping through his shirt. She lifted the fabric, and he couldn't hold back a sharp cry. Her other hand flew to her mouth. "You should have told me it was a burn. I'm so sorry, dear. Let me get you something."

Burned skin dangled off the fabric, but the tender skin beneath was angry red and oozing.

She returned with some sort of salve, and he could almost feel the relief.

"That's a nasty burn. What hap—?" She froze. She knew.

He started to stand. "I have to go."

She grabbed his arm. "No." Her eyes met his. "I saw what you did for that serving girl. She's my sister. I won't tell a soul that you came here, but Oswell has told the staff here to be on the lookout for the wolf he hurt. He said someone might come here looking for burn supplies to take to an animal. Be careful."

"Thank you . . . ?"

"Molly." Her smile was rueful. "Don't thank me yet. This is going to sting."

As she applied the salve, he bit the collar of his shirt and thought about how he had one choice to get out of this. He'd have to use the bracer on Oswell.

CHAPTER 53

A WINK
AND A SMILE

Jayden followed Logan through Balta's city gates. A gust of wind rode through the town, encompassing her with the scent of approaching rain. Heavy rain that the clouds had become weary of holding. This she understood.

She hadn't seen Westwind and Scout since they'd left the Healers. Logan had said he was sending Aurora to find Gavin and Melanie so they could meet up at Castlerock, but maybe they had all gone. Logan had wanted to keep going, but Jayden's warning of the storm along with Thea's predictions had him conceding to stop early and stay a night at the Winking Fox.

When Ethan heard her proclamation about all of Thea's predictions coming true, he didn't say a word—just stared at her through squinted eyes. Of course, she hadn't shared a thing about her heart's desire . . . or her death.

As that thought touched her mind, the clouds seemed to fall closer to the earth, so heavy with rain.

Logan had tapped his finger against his chin, then shrugged, stating that he had no reason to go against what Jayden thought was right.

That both comforted her and burdened her heart.

Logan led them farther into the city. Serena walked close to Jayden, watching street performers with as much interest as the local blacksmith. Had she ever been in a city?

Jayden glanced behind her, and immediately Ethan smiled. That made her cheeks flush, and she turned back to watch where she was going. Suddenly the clouds didn't feel quite so heavy.

"Would you look at that?" Serena motioned up toward the sky.

"It's still going to rain tonight, Serena." Jayden caught Serena's look of wonder. Clearly cities put her out of her element.

"I just mean that—the ray of light peeking through. Like hope. There's always hope if you look for it."

Jayden's boots paused as if by their own accord, and she watched Serena for a beat.

Ethan touched her shoulder and she nearly jumped. "You okay?"

Maybe Serena was wrong. Maybe hope couldn't penetrate some things. Hope and fear warred within. Rumbles of thunder echoed the ache. She had to stop letting him have a hold on her heart. She moved from Ethan's warmth and faced him. "Just feeling the storm."

He stared back at her, but all his emotions winked out. Probably better that way. He tipped his head the direction Logan and Serena had gone. "Should we catch up, or were you planning to get wet?" His lopsided smile filled his face.

The storm sent a rush of prickles over her skin that excited her. She'd love to be outside when the rain broke free. A drop pelted her. One dotted Ethan's shoulder. But the rain wouldn't come yet. Scout had stayed with the wolves, but typically he never left Ethan's side during a storm. Maybe she could give him comfort in Scout's absence. "I'm sorry you don't like storms."

"Maybe I just focus on the wrong part."

He touched her back and nudged her to follow Logan and Serena. As her leaden feet started moving, he dropped his hand, but she still felt the warmth there. Like a ray of hope.

Hope she didn't want to crush.

In the distance, lightning shot through the sky.

Light shone through the windows at the Winking Fox. A couple exited the inn, giving Jayden a glimpse of the crowd inside. Wooden tables, wooden booths, wooden walls all reflected a warm, yellow glow from the candles. Cool air swirled around her, bearing the clean scent of a storm. Ethan stiffened as they neared the inn. It wasn't just the storm—he felt different. Not terrified, but . . . anxious.

The more she tried to keep from sensing others' emotions, the more they clamored to be felt. She gritted her teeth, but who was she fooling? If she'd felt his emotions sooner during that fight with the black lion—his pure fear, his willingness to sacrifice himself to save her—she would have done as he'd asked. No question. No hesitation.

Her talent would have helped her protect him.

Maybe Thea had been right about that, too.

Maybe the old woman at the library had been warning her to let her emotions in. To trust her talent.

Jayden drew closer to Ethan. "Is something wrong?"

Ethan avoided eye contact. "No."

Serena turned her head sideways. Her amused eyes, visible under the shadow of her hood, held an impish gleam.

Jayden opened her mouth and stared at him. "You're lying to me?"

Ethan looked pointedly at Serena. "I meant, I don't feel any danger."

Her smile didn't fade, though.

Logan's dark chuckle brought all of their attention to him. "You afraid of your past, kid?"

"Franco's got people looking for us. Someone here will recognize me. It might not be safe."

"Next to Nivek, this is the most Feravolk-friendly place I know. If it's not safe here, it's safe nowhere. And we need shelter tonight." He glanced at Jayden.

If Thea had tricked them again, it would be her last. Still, Jayden felt that trusting the assassin on this one was a good idea.

"All right. I'm going in through the kitchens." Logan headed down the hill closer to the inn.

The wooden sign carved with a winking fox fluttered in another gust. Ethan's emotions filtered into her again. She walked closer to him, and he smiled for it.

As promised, Logan led them around back. He lowered his hood before he knocked on the kitchen door. A heavy-set woman with rosy cheeks and friendly eyes opened the door a crack. Warmth from the kitchens spilled out, as did the aromas of lamb stew, fresh bread, and potatoes.

"We are still serving in the lobby until—" She stopped short and drew herself to her full height. "Logan?" She emitted a girlish laugh and pulled the corner of her apron to her blushing face. "Logan Laugnahagn? Is it really you?" She pushed the door open and extended her arms. Logan let the woman hug him. "The Lone Wolf has returned!"

Jayden stopped where she stood, and her mouth dropped open as she watched the woman usher Logan through the door.

"Come in." The woman stepped aside.

"Lone . . ." Jayden looked at Serena, whose eyes were just as wide as she imagined her own to be.

Jayden found her airy voice. "Did you say 'Lone Wolf'? As in the most famous swordsman—"

"Didn't you know?" The woman laughed. "Logan, you didn't tell your traveling companions?"

Jayden finally stepped through the door. "Lone Wolf." Her mouth was dry. If her brothers were with her, they'd be clamoring past her to talk to him. And she'd been traveling with him all this time.

Logan chuckled, hearty and loud. "Jayden, please. It's still me."

"But you are *him*?" The heat of the kitchen must be getting to her. She felt flushed and giddy. How many times had she sparred with him in the last months? She pressed her hands to her mouth. "The Lone Wolf has been teaching me to hone my technique?" Her voice escaped in a squeak.

He hugged her into his side. "And I'm impressed by your ability."

"Now introduce me to your friends." The woman who had invited them in looked at Jayden and then Serena, but when her gaze fell on Ethan, her mouth opened. Jayden and Serena had to move as the woman hurried toward Ethan and wrapped him in a hug. When she stepped back, she kept her hands on his arms. "Let me look at you. I thought for sure they'd—well, I should have known you'd find a way to escape. Bless you, Child. Bless you."

"Hello, Martha."

Her attention was for Logan again, her face ripe in a smile. "You and this boy. I should have known, for all the times I compared him to you."

Jayden caught Ethan's swift glance to Logan.

"How do you know him? Is he—" Martha looked at Ethan and

her eyes grew wide, but she offered no one a chance to interrupt her. "Of course. He's your son. I should have seen it. He's always reminded me of you."

Logan grinned and patted Ethan's shoulder. "I'd be proud if he were."

"I could have put money on that one." Martha shrugged. "Now, who are these lovely young women?"

"This is Serena and Jayden." Logan put a hand on each of their shoulders as he introduced them.

Martha smiled warmly at each of them. "You must be famished. I'll get a table for you. Wait here." She barked some orders to get them hot food and two rooms prepared. Then she scurried into the dining room.

Jayden hoped the clatter in the kitchen hid her stomach's rumble.

The kitchen door opened again after Martha left, and a tall, slender young woman entered. Her long, dark hair was tied behind her back in a loose braid. She set a serving tray on the counter. "Ethan?" She practically jumped into Ethan's arms and hugged him tight.

He squeezed her back, lifting her off the floor. Heat spread across Jayden's chest.

Serena touched her shoulder and whispered, "Careful, Jayden, your jealousy is showing."

Her what? Jealousy? How silly. Why should she be jealous? They were obviously very old, very dear . . . very good friends.

The door opened again, letting some cool air in, and Jayden prayed her face would cool, too. The storm seemed to be picking up speed out there. Rumbling more. Getting angry.

Martha interrupted the hug. Finally. "Tessa, there you are. I went out to find you, but it seems you've found our Ethan."

Our Ethan? Martha's smile was suddenly unappealing, too. Jayden tried to keep from narrowing her eyes while Martha introduced all of them to her daughter.

Finally Martha led them into the tavern area of the inn. The scent of alcohol hit Jayden, as did the warmth of the atmosphere. She couldn't help but look around. The high ceilings provided an echo and carried the music from the fiddle player. A staircase led up to the second floor where a few people leaned over the railing watching the commotion below. Carvings in the wood trim resembling floating leaves bordered the walls in the greater dining area. The candles in the chandeliers gave off the soft, golden glow that filled the whole room. Then there was a magnificent stone fireplace with a carving of a winking fox.

They passed tables of people laughing, eating, drinking, and playing games with cards and dice—there was even a chess set with metal pieces—but none of the cheer seemed to infiltrate Jayden's sour mood. It was strange, really. Even if she didn't open her talent, this much laughter should have at least made her smile or feel warmth inside. She wrapped her arms around her stomach and squeezed. Maybe she'd been trying too long to push emotions away. Apparently now those around her only affected her mood with emotions like fear or anger. Maybe jealousy.

Martha led them to a booth where a hot meal already waited, guarded by a serving boy. He bowed his head and left when they approached. Steam still rose from bowls of stew, and butter left a shiny glow on the rolls. Jayden's mouth watered.

Martha left them, and Jayden slid into the booth and had the spoon in her mouth before Serena had even finished straightening her skirts and untying her cloak.

The warm stew heated her whole stomach but did nothing to unclench the knot that had her all worked up.

Serena cocked an eyebrow and stared at Ethan. "So you fought for sport here? Or just at the Blind Pig?"

Ethan nearly choked on his bread.

Serena looked at Logan and shrugged. "I met him at the Blind Pig." She dipped her chin to her shoulder. "Swallow always fights in a mask."

Logan's turn to choke. "You fought for sport? I am sure the Healer's Circle didn't know of these adventures."

"I needed money to buy books, among other things. And no, of course they didn't. It would have ended my fun." She looked at Ethan again. "I might not have been a legend, but I did go up against Stone Wolf."

Jayden stared, mouth open. "*The* Stone Wolf?" She pressed a hand over her mouth. "You're not serious? He's famous! I would love a chance to fight Stone Wolf. I've heard he's amazing."

Ethan chuckled. "He's not that amazing."

Jayden rolled her eyes, which made Ethan smile. Then she turned her attention back to Serena. "How did the fight go?"

"Well, technically I beat him, but I can't say it was much of a challenge. He hardly fought back."

Ethan grinned. "I told you, I don't fight women—for sport anyway."

Jayden's eyes widened. "Wait. *You?*" He'd practically made her tell him all about her tiny operation with her brothers. And she'd just gushed like a rain-drenched brook. "Why didn't you tell me this before?"

"You never would have believed me."

Jayden stared at him. Memories flooded in of the time on the hill when he'd killed ten men all by himself. Ten. "Yes, I would have," she whispered.

Her words made him wince.

Logan slapped his back. "You're a good swordsman, kid. I had my suspicions."

Ethan pretended to be interested in his soup, but he didn't even touch it. His eyes darted up and met Jayden's stare. So many emotions flooded into her. Regret. Fear. Why? Did he think she thought less of him? Maybe he knew what she'd remembered.

"Stone Wolf?" A new voice interrupted their eye contact. A redheaded woman showing off more than a little cleavage stood by their table.

Ethan set down the rest of his bread. "Francesca."

The woman batted her eyelashes. "You've returned for Harvester's Moon feast. I knew you couldn't stay away from me and my dancing shoes."

"Dancing?" Serena giggled.

Ethan cleared his throat. "Actually, I—"

"Don't you dance, Ethan?" Serena tilted her head.

Francesca's eyes narrowed to slits. Jayden half expected a forked tongue to flicker out of the woman's mouth. The redhead crossed her arms under her ample bosom. "Hasn't he ever danced with you?" The syrup coating her voice was enough to raise Serena's eyebrows and her chin.

Tessa approached. Jayden noticed the cold glance she gave Francesca as she placed more bread on the table. "I have chicken soup, Ethan."

"Please." He returned her warm smile.

She gave him a different bowl of soup. Didn't he like lamb? Apparently he and Tessa knew each other well. Jayden breathed deep and touched her dagger's hilt. Serena was right. Why all the jealousy? Hadn't she decided Ethan wasn't hers?

"Thank you." Ethan's smile seemed to linger and, dagger hilt or not, Jayden's heart beat so fast it skidded.

"Tessa." Serena's voice stopped the other woman's departure. "Ethan was just deciding if he'd dance tonight."

"Ethan never turns down a dance." Francesca sniffed.

"Never?" Serena cocked her eyebrow at Ethan. "You must be a very good dancer. I'd like to see that in action."

Jayden's chest burned. She folded her napkin, pretending this conversation had no effect on her whatsoever.

"I am a good dancer. And anyone who thinks they can keep up with me can have a dance." He winked at Serena, then winked again at Tessa. He looked at Jayden, and the absence of a wink was clear. The playful look in his eyes melted, too. Had she been blind this whole time? Did he really want nothing to do with her? Maybe it was best that she'd decided not to show any feelings toward him.

Who was she kidding? Of course it was best. She rubbed her hands over her very warm face. Letting the emotions back in was turning out to be a mistake.

"I can keep up with you." Francesca breathed in, accentuating her bosom. As if they needed to be reintroduced. Then she walked away, her curly red locks bouncing behind her.

Serena's hips hit Jayden's as she scooted over. Then she patted the bench next to her for Tessa to sit down. Jayden rolled her eyes. Really, Serena? Make friends with the enemy?

"Well, I for one am ready to see my room." Jayden slammed her napkin on the table. It was a lie. She was still hungry, but she couldn't stand all this—this jealousy.

Maybe she should just kiss the man. As if that would help. Ethan's eyes weren't for her.

"Jayden." Serena placed her palm on Jayden's arm. "You haven't finished your stew."

Really? Jayden tried hard not to roll her eyes. Could no one see the jealousy erupting from her like—like lava from a volcano? Apparently not. Moods were her thing.

Oh, for once couldn't someone just read her so she didn't have to explain herself? She huffed and noticed Ethan's brown eyes had locked on her.

He mouthed the words, "Are you okay?"

Her heart stuttered. She took her napkin back. "Sorry, I'm just so tired."

"You won't be dancing tonight then, Jayden?" A familiar voice came from behind them.

She whirled her head to see a truly handsome man with smoky-gray eyes and hair the color of wet sand. It was cut short, but his bangs still hit his eyelashes. He looked different somehow, more confident. And he carried a sword at his hip.

"Ryan." She managed breathlessly.

Ethan was free at the end of his bench and stood to embrace his brother. They fell into fast conversation about fighting and swords while Tessa and Serena scooted out so Jayden could reach him. Serena would hardly get out of the way!

At last Jayden was free of the confines of her bench and table, and she darted past Serena and wrapped her arms around Ryan as if holding him could wash away her jealousy.

He hugged her close. "I'm happy to see you, too, Jayden."

He released her and nodded toward Tessa. "And it's always nice to see you, Tessa."

Of course he knew Tessa. Everyone knew Tessa. Jayden crossed her arms and leaned her hip against the edge of the table while Serena blushed at Ryan and Ethan laughed at something Tessa said.

Tessa glanced at someone behind Jayden and cocked an eyebrow. "Ryan, you didn't tell me you knew the local heroes."

"What local heroes?"

"Lone Wolf."

Ryan's gaze hit Logan and his mouth fell open.

Logan slapped Ryan's shoulder. "It's still me, kid. Don't go getting all tongue tied. Besides, your brother is Stone Wolf."

Ryan turned to Ethan. "This sorry excuse for a ladies' man?"

Ethan smiled. "Do I sense a challenge?"

"You bet."

"So tell me, Ryan, do *you* have time to dance?" Serena asked.

He smiled widely back at her. "I do."

"Then I'll see you later tonight?"

"Most assuredly." Ryan might as well have been drooling, the way he ogled Serena.

Jayden backed out of the tight circle. They were all laughing. She was unable to control her emotions. No one seemed to notice she'd stepped away. Oh. Good. So now she was invisible. Shaking her head, she tore her eyes from Ryan and Serena—conversing as if no one else existed—and tried to calm her nerves. She pressed her hands to her face and turned away from them, willing her emotions to calm. Someone came up behind her. She turned around.

Ethan stood so close she almost whirled into him. "You aren't going to take me up on my offer?" he asked quietly.

He wanted to dance with her now, did he? "Why would I, Stone Wolf?" She raised her chin the way she had seen Serena do it many times before.

He smirked. "Don't you think you can keep up with me?"

"Oh, I can keep up with you all right."

"Good. I'd like to see you try." He smiled before he strode away.

Apparently Tessa was showing them to their rooms after all. And Ryan eyed Serena as she walked away.

"Jayden, you'll be coming back?" Ryan had eyes for her again, did he?

She was too angry to answer so a curt nod had to do, but the man had the audacity to look attacked. She turned on her heel and stormed after the others.

As she reached the stairs, thunder cracked. It was odd for her to feel so flustered during such a lullaby. But now the storm seemed flustered, too. As if storms could feel. These emotions were steadily getting the best of her. She'd have to learn to control her talent, control her emotions, or nothing was going to be okay.

CHAPTER 54

FORBIDDEN METHODS

At the top of the stairs, Jayden followed the others down a hallway to two rooms. Logan and Ethan were already going into theirs, but Serena was still making friends with Tessa.

"Really, you must come and stay with us tonight." Serena was begging her to—what? Stay with them?

Tessa's smile faltered when she glanced at Jayden, then her eyes darted to the floor and she left. Jayden sighed. She wasn't trying to make Tessa feel unwelcome.

Serena practically herded Jayden into their room and closed the door. "You are not making this easy for me."

"This?"

She began to rummage through her belongings. "Tessa has information I need."

"Fine. You befriend her. I don't need to."

Serena's eyes narrowed and she sat on the edge of the bed. "Well, I need some time with her."

"Here?"

"Yes." Her chin jutted out.

"If it's that import—"

"I joined you to keep you and Ethan safe. If that means I need to know more about my powers than Healers will teach me, I have to learn by any means necessary, even unconventional ones."

"You mean forbidden?"

Serena scrunched up her nose. "I am still under Healer code, but no longer under the rules of my camp. The lines of whether or not this is forbidden are a bit blurry."

Jayden frowned. Maybe she shouldn't have been so angry with Serena. Or Tessa. "And Tessa has these answers?"

"I'm not sure what you have against her. Tessa's heart is pure."

Pure. Like that made everything better. Purely in love with Ethan, that's what she was. Jayden paused and shook her head. If that was the root of the problem, she'd have to stop herself right there. Ethan wasn't hers. Couldn't be hers. "I don't have to befriend every pure-hearted person."

"Jayden." Serena sat on the edge of her bed and patted the mattress. "Why are you holding your dagger?"

She was? "It's bonded to me. It helps me control . . . I can feel other people's emotions, and lately I haven't been able to turn my talent off. My own emotions seem to be difficult to tame."

"Because you've been bottling them up?"

Jayden sighed. "That's the thing. Lately I've been trying to use my talent instead of push it away. And the problem seems worse."

Serena tapped her finger against her bottom lip. "It's possible that you're overdue for a bond."

"What?"

"When Feravolk's talents start to become out of control, they need to bond, otherwise the talent could be lost to them forever. It's like a volcano erupting. Everything starts to bubble to the surface. If an animal bonds with you, it can show you how to control your talent. It's something it has lived with naturally its whole life. We have to find your bonded animal."

Serena pried the dagger from Jayden's hand and gave it back to her. "Put this away. Let yourself feel the pull. It will be buried in the turmoil inside you. The animal is usually so full of human desires that it breaks free of its family, and it's so clouded by new thoughts that it gets trapped somehow. Keep your thoughts open so you can find it. Lead us to it. Then you'll know what to do."

Jayden heaved a sigh. "So that's what's wrong with me?"

"Well, it's not what's making your own emotions so volatile." Was that a smirk? "Jayden, why don't you just tell Ethan how you feel?"

Jayden stared at Serena. Was it that obvious? "What if there's nothing to tell?"

Serena cocked an eyebrow.

Jayden's heart sank. It might be good to tell someone. "All the Deliverers in history died saving the Feravolk. It's not fair for me to let my heart belong to someone when I know it won't beat very long." Especially because of Thea's warning.

Serena sighed.

Jayden bit her lip. Now she'd done it. Stolen all of her sister-kin's hope. Only Serena didn't feel hopeless.

Serena grabbed Jayden's hands. "You can't let some account of history that doesn't even recount all the Deliverers dictate your future. That's fear talking. Stop being afraid to let yourself love and be loved. You can't let fear control you like that, sister."

Could Serena be right? Would letting Ethan close be fair? "It's not that easy. Ryan was my betrothed."

"Was?"

"Our parents died. I told him I couldn't have anyone because I'm a Deliverer."

"And what did he say?"

"He seems to agree with you. But we never had the ceremony, so he released me."

Serena touched Jayden's knee. "Then I fail to see the problem."

"Ethan is Ryan's brother."

"Oh."

Oh? So there was no hope. It was as bad as she thought. "If I choose Ethan, do I lose Ryan? I can't lose any more brothers."

"Ryan is like a brother to you?"

Jayden traced the pattern on the bedspread with her fingers.

Serena smiled. "I believe you can control your feelings and overcome your weaknesses, but giving up love isn't the way. Embracing it is. If you want me to get a truthful answer out of Ryan or Ethan for you, I can."

"No." Her face flushed.

Serena just sat there, wearing a soft smile.

"What?" Jayden asked.

"I think you know what. Stop letting fear win."

"How do I do that?"

"For starters, give Ethan a dance tonight."

Jayden sighed. A dance? With Ethan? While Ryan was watching? None of this sounded like a good idea.

Serena giggled and towed Jayden off the bed. "Let's call Tessa up here and see if we can't get you ready for a dance for Harvester's Moon. I think there's one young man whose heart you need to make happy."

CHAPTER 55

MIXED EMOTIONS

Most of Jayden's hair was pulled back from her face. A few wavy tendrils hung loose down her back and laced her chest. The dress Tessa let her borrow brought out the blue in her eyes. Jayden scarcely knew who the woman in the mirror was.

Serena wore a bluish-green dress. Her golden hair was pulled back similarly to Jayden's, but she had done it herself. Tessa's long hair was fastened into a curled ponytail with a few loose strands. She looked beautiful in her soft yellow dress.

Serena beckoned Jayden to follow her. Shyly, she stepped out of her room and down the staircase. Serena glided down in front of her and Tessa behind.

Jayden peered over the rail. Clusters of people dressed in their finest waited around an invisible line on the floor sectioning off the dancing space. The musicians, different from the entertainers who had played while Jayden had been eating, were getting ready to play.

At the bottom of the staircase Serena fixed a strand of Jayden's hair, then pinched her cheeks gently. "You look beautiful."

"She's right." Chloe offered a smile.

"So do you, Chloe." Her emerald green gown complemented her red hair, as did the tall brown-haired young man who swept her onto the dance floor and made her eyes glimmer.

Serena turned around and placed her hand in Ethan's.

He smiled. "Beautiful dress."

She dipped her head. "Thank you."

He led her past Jayden, paused. His eyes met hers for a heartbeat, and he leaned in closer. His breath warmed her ear, her neck. "You look stunning," he whispered.

Warmth exploded over Jayden's skin, and her heart thundered. Music transitioned to a lively tune, and she tore her eyes from Ethan's back. Ryan was waiting for her with his hand extended. She took it and more heat hit her face. Partly because he'd caught her staring at Ethan, and partly because of his roguish smile.

"You look amazing, Jayden." Ryan paid her the compliment she'd already seen in his eyes.

He led her to the dance floor, and she fell into step with his lead. She'd never met someone who twirled her and her clumsy feet so effortlessly. Everything about him was comfortable. Easy. Everything reminded her of home. A fire she could never tame. A brother.

Ryan let her go as they took on temporary partners. Her eyes didn't leave his until another set of strong hands enveloped hers and that familiar electricity shot through her. Surprised, she met Ethan's eyes. Warm, brown, nothing like a storm cloud. But he was like the wind. Soft against her cheek, hard and powerful when needed. He stole her breath.

His eyebrows pulled together. "Something wrong?"

With her hands in his, there was no denying how much she wanted this. She couldn't stop her growing smile. "Everything is perfect."

He smiled softly. "I'm glad."

Before she could respond, he passed her back to Ryan, but Ethan's eyes never left her.

She let out a shuddering breath and faced Ryan. He smiled, charming and perfect.

Dance after dance swirled on. The room was cheerful, the music happy, and the firelight inviting. Jayden hadn't had so much fun in a very long time. She shared a few lively dances with Ryan and some other cocky swordsmen who made her laugh, but her eyes always found Ethan. And they always found him with a different woman on his arm.

When at last she stopped to catch her breath, she took a seat and Serena bounded up to her. Serena's hair was still perfectly placed, and her cheeks were slightly flushed in a way that made her becoming. Her eyes practically sparkled. "Ask him."

"He's been occupied all night."

"If you ask him, he'll dismiss anyone else."

Jayden didn't share her sister-kin's certainty. "I need to talk to Ryan first."

"Good." Serena flicked her gaze to Jayden's right. Ryan was headed right toward her. Oh dear. She should hide. No. She breathed deep and stood. It was time. Serena patted Jayden's knee and walked away.

"Jayden." Ryan smiled. "I have to go. Would you walk me out?"

She straightened her spine. "Of course."

He held out his elbow for her to slip her arm into his. She did, and he watched her with his eyebrow cocked as he led her outside. Cool evening air brushed against her skin. The storm's rage had calmed, leaving a gentle patter of rain. Ryan stopped on the porch under the overhang and faced her. Rain hit the roof above, reminding her of the passage of time as she stood there hesitating.

"Ryan—" It was time to let him down gently and tell him how she felt about his brother. She could only hope for his blessing. "I need to talk to you."

"It's about time."

"What?"

"You don't have to say anything." He stared at her, a smile blossomed on his face. "I know where your heart is, Jayden. You tell Ethan to take care of you."

"Ryan?" How did he feel? He seemed fine. She forced herself to meet his gaze and opened her talent. No sadness. Contentment was strongest. Happiness even throbbed from him. How? Maybe he'd never—

He grabbed her hands and squeezed. "Jayden, I'll always love you, and I know you love me, too, but it's not the same kind of love as you have for Ethan, is it?"

Her heart hammered like a bird watching the door to its cage open. A bird about to be freed. "No."

His lazy smile filled his face. He kissed her forehead. "A guy can never have too many sisters."

"Oh, Ryan. Thank you." She was weightless, like a cloud freed from rain.

He leaned in and wrapped her in a hug. His heart beat in her ear. It didn't sound broken. "You have my permission to move on. Even with Ethan. Especially with Ethan."

She searched his emotions. Happiness under the surface broke free and filled every vein. Then he smiled. "I'll see you soon."

Jayden stood there and watched him leave. Her heart had been freed. And Ryan wasn't hurt that she'd fallen for his brother. She'd gotten everything she wanted. She stared into the darkness that had swallowed Ryan. Serena was right. Letting go of that emotional war made her feel better.

She watched leaves fall as the mild wind pulled them from the branches. They were between storms now, but the rain still fell, light and steady. The scent of wet trees, sodden soil and displaced worms filled the night.

A breeze blew into her, swirled her hair around her, and wrapped her in the sweet touch of the approaching storm. She leaned against the porch railing, closed her eyes, and breathed in. Her heart felt as free as the storm.

The sound of the tavern door closing registered in the back of her mind, and she glanced over her shoulder.

Ethan stood a few paces behind her.

Warmth rushed through her and she froze, facing him. "Hello, stranger."

"Stranger?" His familiar lopsided smile warmed his face.

"You've been avoiding me all night."

"Avoid—no. What makes you say that?"

She leaned back against the railing and smiled. "A different woman for every song. Stone Wolf has certainly made an impression on the young women of Balta. Doesn't he have room for his other friends?"

He laughed uncomfortably and scratched the back of his head. "One Eye has this thing about dancing being like sword fighting." He took a tentative step toward her. Ethan, tentative?

"And is he right?"

That uncomfortable laugh returned, and he seemed to struggle with an answer. Then he looked into her eyes. "I suppose it depends on who you're dancing with."

Silence seemed to stretch the space between them. She should ask him for a dance. Heavens knew she wanted to dance with him. She just wanted to be near him. But he hadn't offered at her subtle prodding. Did that mean he didn't want to?

He joined her at the railing and rested his elbows on it. "Another storm coming?" He smiled. It was such a small smile, but that only made it seem more intimate.

"I thought that was *my* talent."

"I just notice how happy you seem to get right before a storm."

He did? "You still hate them?"

He glanced at his hands and shrugged in response. Then, very quietly, he added, "They're not as bad as they used to be." His eyes met hers and his gaze was intense. Soul-searching.

The soft push and pull of his emotions seemed to bring her closer like a tide. Contentment pulled. Regret pushed. A quiet war inside him.

What did he regret?

She didn't realize she'd gravitated nearer to him until her hand brushed his. He didn't move away. His gaze still held her captive. Her blood ignited. The air turned electric. What if he knew how *she* felt? What if she told him?

"Ethan?"

"Yes?"

Her heart raced. He leaned closer. Warmth encompassed her.

The door opened, bathing them in candlelight. "Is everything all right out here?" A red-headed, full-busted woman poked out of the doorway. Francesca.

Ethan backed away, letting cool air swirl around Jayden, and she groaned. Actually groaned.

He stared at her, a hint of a lopsided smile returning. "Everything's fine. We just needed some fresh air," he said to Francesca while staring at Jayden. "We'll be right in."

"Good. You haven't danced with me in a while." She batted her long eyelashes, then made a show of swinging her hips as she walked back in.

Ethan led Jayden toward the door and opened it for her. "I did agree to dance with whomever could keep up, you know." A mix of emotions pulsed through him like whitecaps hitting stone, and it winked out before she could untangle it. Then he dropped his gaze and turned toward the dance floor.

"Ethan?" Jayden touched his arm.

He turned back to her. "Yes?"

"Save a dance for me?"

"Anything for you. Anything."

He turned to go, but Jayden just stood there. Heat flushed her cheeks. A joy gushed forth from her heart. She couldn't stop the smile that hit her as she watched Francesca practically drag Ethan onto the dance floor.

Love. Of course. That was Ethan's mix of emotions. He loved her.

Her heart beat like a thousand wild horses racing through a thunderstorm.

Ethan looked up and caught her eye. He was about to look away, but she smiled at him. That small smile returned, and he didn't break eye contact even as he twirled the flirting Francesca around as if she were a feather.

Jayden sighed. She wanted to laugh. Ethan loved her.

Eventually the music changed. The evening's festivities would be ending. People were clearing out. Another song over, Serena, Ethan, and Logan made their way to where she was standing. Ethan and Serena walked together, laughing. Serena wore the dreamy look of one who had danced a magical night away, and her emotions were oozing with contentment and complete bliss, but Jayden's face didn't flush with jealousy.

Serena glanced at Jayden, the smile still on her face. "I think it's time for me to get some rest. But I'll wait for you, Jayden, if you're going for another round."

"Just one." Jayden turned toward Ethan and held out her hand. His eyes opened wide. Had he doubted her desire to dance with him? "You promised."

Ethan's return stare was soulful.

"All right." Serena rose. "Bring her back safe."

He didn't take his eyes off of Jayden. "Always."

"I'll retire, too." Logan nodded toward his daughter.

Serena eyed her father. "I can take care of myself, you know."

"You don't have to remind me, Miss Swallow. But that won't keep me from being one room away." They walked upstairs together.

Jayden took Ethan's hand in hers and towed him toward the remaining dancers. The night was ending, so the musicians started to play a less lively tune, "The Princess and the Pauper." A sad song, mostly in minor chords, about a princess who couldn't marry the man she loved because he wasn't royalty.

She reached the floor, faced Ethan, and dipped into a curtsy. He bowed but didn't take his eyes off of her. They circled one another, hands suspended in the air, palm facing palm, not quite touching. It symbolized how the Princess and the Pauper were just out of reach of one another.

Ethan cast a fleeting look into Jayden's eyes. Just before he looked away, she smiled, hoping to trap his gaze. It worked, but he didn't smile back. The intensity in his stare heightened. Captivated her.

She studied his face, the deep swirls of dark brown in his chestnut eyes, the two moles on his right cheek, little details that she typically admired from afar. Or with secret glances. This time, nothing inhibited her. She wanted him to see how she felt. If he had her talent, she'd make sure her emotions were open to him.

He grabbed her hand now. Strong and gentle at the same time.

And she slipped her other hand on his shoulder. Pulled him closer. He didn't resist.

Neither of them said a word. But his gaze remained on her. As if he were reading her soul.

She listened to the beat of his emotions, the perfect mix of so many feelings blended together. She'd never felt anyone have this kind of love toward her. It was . . . beautiful.

She didn't even think about the dance steps anymore, just let him lead her across the floor, and it was effortless.

The last strum ended the song and Ethan dropped her hand.

Jayden laced her fingers behind his back, keeping him close. "Thank you, Ethan."

He smiled, even if it was only half of a smile, and his eyes narrowed. "Something changed tonight?"

Jayden smiled. "Yes."

"Didn't things go well with Ryan?"

"Better than hoped."

Ethan nodded curtly and backed out of her arms. He glanced at the floor. "Must be hard for you to leave him again."

"I'll see him soon." She reached for his hand again, but he scratched the back of his head. "Ryan wanted me to tell you to take care of me."

"I'm sure he did."

"Ethan." This time she caught his hand. He managed to look like a wounded animal in a trap. "Ryan knows—"

"He does? Jayden, if you want me to leave—"

"Leave?" She drew nearer. "Ryan knows my heart isn't his."

"It—it's not?" He was trembling. Or was it her?

"He says you won't be betraying him." Her hands slid up his arms, over his shoulders, rested in the dip of his collarbone, drawing him closer.

A moth couldn't have flown between them.

His palms pressed against her waist, her hips. Warm. Strong. She touched the back of his neck and didn't have to coax him any more than that. Ethan leaned in and Jayden closed her eyes as his lips touched hers. He cupped her neck in his hand. Both hands. His thumbs brushed her cheeks and her heart thundered, melted, ached. She leaned into him, closer and not close enough. Tugged his shirt collar, and his arms wrapped around her back. Pulled her against him. Heavens, he was strong.

Her fingers slid up his neck, into his hair. The din of the tavern quieted. Low burning candles snuffed out. There was no sound except the approaching thunder and rain pelting the ceiling like Ethan's emotions on her heart.

And she opened her talent.

Desire, longing, hunger, she felt it all, like she felt every brush against her skin, every new touch against her lips. And she wanted more.

CHAPTER 56

A FUEL
FOR VENGEANCE

Connor headed to the palace library first. He needed a way to save Madison. Now. Chances were, he'd have to leave after using the bracer, because when questions started arising, fingers would point back to him. The sooner he left, the better.

He'd have to be very careful which books he was seen looking at, but it was one he'd read before. Problem was, he'd read hundreds.

Once in the library, he headed toward a specific shelf. Hopefully he wouldn't need to use the ladder. He didn't think he could climb one right now. The burn on his side made every movement agony. What about this one? He touched the spine of a leather cover. Embossed letters read *Dark Spells.* He pulled it off the shelf and headed to a table.

"I knew I'd find you here."

Kara. Of course she'd be here to taunt him. Well, better get it over with.

She sat next to him. "What are you reading today?"

"You don't have to share books with me."

"But you're always reading the book I want."

"So we have one common interest."

She leaned over and slid the book from his grasp. "This one looks good." Her fisted hand shot toward his injured side. He spun in his seat and caught her wrist in both of his hands, but the movement tore at his burned skin and he couldn't hide his grimace.

She stared at her trapped arm. "So it *was* you."

"What are you talking about?" He released her and took the book back.

"Maybe you should see Madison about that burn."

"Who's Madison?" He thumbed a few more pages.

"Don't play dumb. I know it was you waiting outside the door, little spy. You can't even sit up straight."

He closed the book over his arm and glared at her. "I don't know what you're talking about."

"Did you know Madison killed my sister?" Her return glare was harsh.

"No, she didn't."

Kara leaned back one vertebra at a time. Like a strike of lightning, she shifted toward him, grabbed his shirt collar, and the sharp prick of a knife pressed into his injured side. "Talk."

He pulled away, but her grip on his collar tightened. "You don't need to do that. I'm going to tell you."

Slowly she released him.

He eased back in the chair and pivoted to face her in case she tried anything again. "Your sister came to me and asked me to tell you something. Her message was so cryptic until now. She pulled out her seeing stone the day she was killed. I saw it happen. Madison wasn't even there."

"You're just telling me this now?"

"She told me to wait."

She pointed the knife at him again. "My sister told *you* she was going to die?"

This time he grabbed her wrist and growled. If she wanted to see what he'd be like as a wolf, she'd see it. "Will you let me tell you the whole story, please?"

She must have sensed the change in his behavior because a hint of her smirk returned. As if she dared him to take her on.

He released her. "When your sister was killed, I watched it happen in the stone. Before she left for Meese, she told me that I'd need to tell you what happened to her, but I had to wait until after I saw you at your most vulnerable. I figured seeing you dead on the floor counted as 'most.' She said everything would make sense to me, and it does. She must have had the gift of foresight."

Still didn't mean he'd toss his mother out a window.

Kara leaned back in her chair. "She told me her talent was to know certain things about people, like what they were meant to become. I wanted to think that was true. The gift of foresight killed my father. Those with the gift generally don't live long. Especially if they share their secret." Her eyes turned hard. "Who killed her?"

"Franco."

Heat flooded her eyes. She sheathed her weapon and got up.

He stood with her, in case she meant to strike him again, but the movement sent pain through his side and he leaned on the table for support. "Where are you going?"

"My sister left me a note. I'm going to make sure I complete it. And get my vengeance."

"How will you do that?"

She cracked a smile as she turned to go. "Good little wolf, just keep playing your part, and I'll play mine." Then she stopped. All trace of her haughtiness faded. "I'm sorry I hurt you." She darted out the door before he could respond.

He shook his head. She certainly was strange. He gingerly sat back down and flipped through the pages of the book. His burn throbbed with every heartbeat.

Here. Life-debt.

This is a powerful kind of tainted magic created after the fall of the Mistress. With this potion, one can bond oneself to Healers. All the person needs is a willing sacrifice—someone to die for them—but it must be someone they've betrayed. The person who becomes a life-debt forever links the person they die for to the Healer who brings him or her back to life. If that person should become injured, the Healers bound to them will heal those wounds—no matter where they are. Any Healer who heals one with a life-debt will become a slave to the bonded person. The Healer's powers will be siphoned from them, sucking life from their years to give to the bonded individual. The only way to truly kill this individual would be to cut off his or her head.

No ordinary weapon can do this, though. It has to be a weapon forged by a Wielder. And the head must then be burned.

Connor closed the book. So Madison was bound to Franco through Kara. Every time Madison healed the king, it would take away from her powers. Suck life from her bones.

That settled it. Maybe he would get his mother out of here and stay at the palace.

As soon as Connor placed the bracer on his wrist, a heavy feeling of dread shrouded him like a layer of grime. He crept down the hall toward Franco's quarters, every movement agony. Oswell hadn't been in his own room. Perhaps he'd been summoned by the king? Before he entered, a sound caught his ear. Someone crying? He approached the entrance to Franco's room and glanced in.

The king wasn't here. Neither was Oswell. There, on the floor, huddled in a heap on her knees, was the same young Healer. She gasped and sat up. Her eyes were wet and red-rimmed. She sniffed and wiped her nose on her tattered sleeve. Her other hand was chained to Franco's bed.

Connor's heart thudded. What was the king planning to do to her? Had he already done it?

Madison shrank away from Connor, her eyes huge.

He held out his hand. "I won't hurt you."

She just stared at him as if he were a walking ghost.

"Did—" Connor motioned to the bed. "Did he hurt—"

New tears sprang into her eyes and she turned away, restricted from moving farther because of her chained arm.

"Let me help you." He reached to take the chain off her. "Oh, I need a key." He always knew how to get keys, but getting one in time could be tricky.

Her hand touched his, firm but gentle. "You can't. He'll find out. I can't lie."

Connor sighed. "Don't worry about me."

"He hasn't . . ." She looked at the bed. "Not yet. But he plans to."

Connor noticed the flash of the bracer on his arm. "Not if I can help it."

"I don't think you can, unless you have a key like the one he holds around his neck."

The bed's post was made of solid redwood. Thick and strong. No getting through that. He smiled. "Don't lose faith."

"Are you all right?" She reached toward his injured side and he recoiled. "It's okay," she murmured. "Let me help you."

Her eyes met his and he nodded. Gently, she touched his side. His skin grew hotter. He gritted his teeth. Then it cooled. The ice that rushed through his side sent relief, and the wound was gone.

She looked up at him and smiled. "I haven't lost all faith."

"Thank you."

A creak sounded. Franco had returned. Madison's wide eyes did, too. "Please, get out of here."

He stood and faced the door as Franco entered.

Franco's eyes narrowed, and he nearly dropped the goblet he held. A clear liquid, like white wine, sloshed over the rim. "What are you doing in here, brother?"

Connor stepped closer to the king. A sense of unease swept through him, nauseated him. Well, at least the bracer was working. "I knocked. You invited me in."

Franco blinked. "Of course. What were you here about, brother?"

"I went hunting today. Missed you out there. You've been quite busy since your mother's passing. I'm sorry I haven't been more help to you. Is there anything you need me to do?"

Franco set his goblet on the table. "Aren't you going to lecture me about keeping a girl tied to my bed? You've never liked my wanton ways, brother."

Connor's hackles wanted to raise. "Pleasantries first, lecture second. I see no reason to enrage the beast since I'm going to ask you a favor. What are you drinking?" Connor motioned to the chalice. He'd seen it in the room on many occasions when a lady visited Franco. Never had he suspected the use of spells.

Pain vibrated behind Connor's eyes like his head might explode. He staggered forward and leaned on the table.

"Are you all right?" Franco leaned to catch him.

Connor waved him away. "A little too much wine, I think."

Franco laughed. "Doubtful."

Connor faked a laugh with him. It echoed in his ears. He was about to pass out. If he was going to complete this task, it had to be now. He looked right into Franco's eyes. "You will pour this drink out the window, untouched by her lips." The pounding hit harder. His voice echoed in his head like a shout. "You will unchain her. There is no reason to keep her locked up. And defiling your own personal Healer is a very bad idea."

Something warm trickled out of his ear. Then his nose. He wiped it away, unwilling to look for fear that he'd break eye contact and this wouldn't work.

He braced his hand against the chair. "You will leave . . . her . . . unsoiled." His head hit the floor, and he watched Franco pick up the goblet and head toward Madison.

CHAPTER 57

FOREST OF WOES

Logan readjusted his pack and checked his sword again. Morning orange hung low in the sky, chasing pale yellow upward. He could see his breath, and they were headed north to Castlerock. That meant colder nights loomed in their future.

He could only hope they'd reach it before Franco.

"*Westwind?*"

"*I'm here.*"

"*How far did you make it?*"

"*I sent your message. Hopefully it will reach Beck and Reuben's ears soon. Aurora is far from earshot, but I feel her. She's moving fast. She should reach Melanie and Gavin soon, if she hasn't already.*"

"*Good. We head toward Atta and then the Forest of Woes.*"

"*Not a journey I'm looking forward to. The wolves around here say that place isn't fit for animals. Scout and I are close to Atta. We'll wait for you. It's all open out here, Logan. Food is scarce.*"

"*Martha was quite generous. Still, we'll have to find our own food when we can, friend.*"

"*Yes. Hurry. I hope that man you were talking to was trustworthy.*"

"*Don't worry. Serena heard every important word. She said he wasn't lying.*"

Speaking of Serena, she certainly was having a long goodbye with Tessa. Logan peered closely. Serena glanced to her left and then right. Interesting. Whatever she was about to say was a secret. Only she didn't say anything. She just handed Tessa a folded piece of paper. What was going on there?

Perhaps Jayden knew. The girl's cheeks were redder than the sunset, and she stared at Ethan.

Logan glanced at Ethan and cleared his throat.

That got the kid's attention.

Logan nodded in Serena's direction. She was finally headed toward them, and he led them out the city gate.

"What's turned your mood sour?" Westwind's smirk was palpable over the bond.

"I think Ethan and Jayden may have finally admitted their feelings to one another."

Now Westwind laughed outright. *"It was only a matter of time. Stop being such a wolverine about it."*

Now it was Logan's turn to chuckle. It wouldn't be so bad. He just worried that one of them would end up getting hurt. This journey was going to claim lives. It already had. He'd try his best to make sure it wasn't one of them.

"Where is Castlerock?" Ethan asked.

Logan glanced over his shoulder. "Last night I managed to talk to a few of the locals as well as a man who lived north of here. No one goes into the Forest of Woes, but that's where we're headed. Castlerock is in the center. No one has seen it in hundreds of years."

"A hidden city?" Jayden asked. "Like a Feravolk camp?"

Logan nodded. "If the Whisperer is there, she will draw us in. That's what Anna did to me. The problem is, that poor girl is chained to the prison. She won't be able to come to us. But if she can use the trees to pass along her messages, we'll hear her. For now, we need to get there as fast as possible. Westwind and Scout will meet us once we get outside the city. Aurora should be close to finding Melanie and Gavin, and Westwind has already passed along a message to Reuben and Beck. I figure we'll need all the help we can get."

They kept up with Logan's quick pace. Urgency spurred them forward. Lush green hills filled the expanse between Balta and the northern city of Atta. By midday the second day after leaving Balta, they had reached the outskirts of Atta. Logan took them around the city, unwilling to risk being seen in a place that palace soldiers may have frequented. Chances were high that Franco had sent men this way, looking for Castlerock.

They would definitely need all the help they could get. They were setting up like a game of chess, and they needed to make sure no one knew what their next move would be.

As the day grew older, their destination drew closer.

Up ahead lay the Forest of Woes. A wall of trees spread out before them. Their dark trunks contrasted with the sunny green hills and the white fog that flooded between them. This place reminded him of the strange foggy area they'd walked through before meeting his friends from Moon Over Water a few months ago. Only this place was much larger.

Westwind loped along the edge of the wood. *"You're not really going in there?"*

"We have to."

Westwind's golden eyes met Logan's with a flash of uncertainty. Logan felt it, too. They were going in. Would they come out?

Logan squeezed his hand into a fist, clutching his oath scar. *"You are not bound to this quest, my friend."*

Westwind chuckled. *"I am. I'm bound to you. Love and loyalty and all that human stuff."* He looked up at Logan. *"And I mean to see this through."*

Beside him, Scout sat. *"I'm not afraid. Of love and loyalty, that is."* He looked back at Logan, his long tongue lolling out of the side of his mouth in a goofy grin.

Logan patted the dog. *"You warm my heart, friends."*

"All right. Let's go find this Whisperer and save the Feravolk." Scout stood.

Logan glanced at his traveling companions. "It's clear why no one goes in there. I thought the Forest of Legends was intimidating."

Westwind chuffed. *"Scout and I are going back into the hills to hunt. I don't smell any animals in that forest save . . . well, I'm going to guess that's what a dragon smells like."*

Logan shared this with the others.

"Dragons?" Serena's eyes widened. She covered a small smile. Dash whickered and his nostrils flared.

"It will storm tonight, Logan." Jayden's voice was almost a whisper as she stared at the wood in front of her. Seemed she didn't want to take shelter beneath these trees either.

"We'll camp near the border of the woods tonight. Tomorrow we'll venture farther in. Hopefully we find Castlerock soon." Logan led them into the wood.

The thick mist seemed to dissipate as they walked through it. The towering trees weren't the same as the Forest of Legends. Blue-green moss had covered healthy trunks, but the trees here were tall, spindly, and gray. Almost like they were in mourning. Where the ground in the Forest of Legends was dark, moist soil filled with lush life, in this place the ground was hard, packed dirt, void of nutrients and covered in rocks.

Ethan scanned the wood as he stepped inside. Without a word, he strung his bow. The place smelled like hot ash. If dragons lived here, an arrow wasn't going to do any good. Thankfully they all carried Wielder-crafted weapons. Those would pierce dragon armor.

"Logan. I have a message from Aurora. Melanie and Gavin are headed this way. They made alliance with the Feravolk from Island in the Swamp. It looks like we have more friends than we thought."

"How far away is she?"

"Too far for me to hear. This message came from a prairie wolf."

At least there was some good news. Depending on who or what lay in these woods, they might need reinforcements.

Logan stopped not too far in. He could still see the green grass of the foothills outside. "We'll sleep here tonight. Ethan?"

The kid nodded once. "I'll take first watch."

○

Jayden neared the fire Logan had made near the border of the woods. She couldn't get warm. Not that she expected the fire to warm her. She wasn't cold on the outside. This chill came from within. Possibly from fear. Possibly worry. Mostly she felt the way she thought these trees looked.

Even the approaching storm felt different here. Like the ground groaned and thirsted for water, never to be quenched. And the vines, old with cracked, woody bark, seemed to hang from every tree like bindings they'd stopped trying to escape from long ago.

"You okay?" Ethan joined her by the fire, skinning a rabbit. His gaze met hers, and that new, miniscule smile tugged his lips.

"I'm just on edge."

"I think everyone is." Serena sat on Ethan's other side.

Dash was the only one who seemed at ease here. *The forest is full of magic. That's what you feel,* he said.

"What do you mean?" Jayden leaned toward the unicorn.

He stood still and breathed in. *The magic in the Forest of Legends is full and rich, life giving. Here the magic is repressed. Wounded. Something terrible happened here.*

"You can talk to him?" Ethan eyed Jayden.

"Yes. I can't read his thoughts like Serena can, but if he speaks for anyone who understands to hear, I can. He says something terrible happened here. Do you think it's the prison? We're so close to the Mistress."

The ground seemed to tremor.

"Shh." Logan pressed a finger to his lips. "I might not speak her name here."

"Yeah." Jayden picked up one of the rabbits and the soft fur seemed to comfort her . . . until she remembered it was dead. She dropped it. "That's a good idea."

Logan sat up straight. "Westwind found them."

"Found who?"

His eyes weren't focused on her. He had to be listening to Westwind. "There's a camp. Franco's men are here. They're not a bowshot from Castlerock. Westwind says it's hidden. They might not know it's there." He stopped talking and held up his finger. Everyone waited, staring at him. "Franco's men are here. General Balton is here." His voice was a near growl. "There are too many for us to take on ourselves. He says Aurora is less than three days out with Melanie and Gavin. It'll be too dark soon to move. As soon as it's light, we'll head back into the foothills and wait for Melanie. She's bringing reinforcements from Island in the Swamp. Then we go after the king's men."

Jayden breathed deep. This was it. They'd get their Whisperer. Franco wouldn't be able to complete his ritual to set the Mistress free. Or they would fail and the Mistress would escape and hunt the Deliverers until she got what she wanted—the Creator's power.

Jayden glanced at Ethan. If they won, she could be with him.

Unless Thea was right.

She had to tell him. It was only fair that she told him. Her heart sank.

CHAPTER 58

HOLD ON

Jayden joined Ethan at the base of a tree. Scout lay pressed up against Ethan's legs. The wind howled and grabbed at her hair like a frightened child looking for something to cling to. Clouds swirled overhead. Tonight's storm would start loud as they crashed together in resistance. Ethan's scent mingled with the scent of approaching rain. When a spray of lightning spread above them, she found herself staring into the dark pools of his eyes. She grabbed his hand and slipped her fingers between his. He squeezed. She cuddled closer to him, rested her head on his chest, and listened to his heart whispering in her ear.

"Will you sleep at all tonight?" she asked.

His heart beat a bit faster. "Are you staying here all night?"

"If I do?"

"Then yes."

"Then I will." She sat with him in silence for a time. But the question that plagued her had to be answered. "Do you think it will be harder for you, now that there are two of us to protect?"

Fear sparked through him like a flash of lightning. There one moment, then gone. He seemed to be getting better at controlling his emotions around her. "It's always harder with more than one, but I won't be alone. Logan is here. Dash, Westwind, Scout. We'll protect you."

"That's not what I'm worried about."

His heartbeat sped. "No?"

She sat up and looked into his eyes. "I'm worried about you. After Kinsey died, you blamed yourself."

He stared at her, silent for so long she wondered if she'd upset him, but a wall seemed to prevent her from reaching his emotions. She pushed. Nothing rushed out at her, but there was some give, as if a door opened. She pushed further, and just on the outskirts there seemed to be a pull. Mentally she reached. Like strings on a lute, she strummed, and his emotions leaked into her. Of course he felt guilt. Pain. Anger.

"I didn't mean to upset you."

"I know." He cupped his hands together and rested his elbows on his bent knees. "Kinsey's death was my fault." He spoke slowly. "There was so much going on. I wasn't sure which direction to shoot first. I hesitated."

"You're too hard on yourself sometimes." She swallowed, her mouth suddenly dry. "I can't let you blame yourself when I die." There, she'd said it. Her breathing shook.

He turned toward her. In the dark, it was so hard to read his face, but he placed his hands on her arms. "*When?*" Sadness poured out of him. "Jayden, you can't think like that. Being ready to die and believing you're going to are two very different things. You can be ready. But please, don't give up hope. Never give up hope."

A tear spilled down her cheek. "Thea can see the future. She told me I was going to die."

His grip on her arms tightened. Then he let go. Touched her chin so gently. "Did she say when?"

"Not exactly."

"Did she say how?"

Jayden closed her eyes and shook her head.

He touched her hand, sending a tingle through her skin, and she looked at him. "Can you feel my emotions?"

"Yes." Her voice sounded breathless.

"And what do you feel?"

Hope. Love. Desire. All of them so contagious they beat into her. "I feel your hope."

His thumb brushed along her jaw, and he leaned close. Kissed her gently. Warmth coursed through her whole being. "Good. Hold on to that."

Wind picked up, rustling leaves against one another in a dry, whispering sound. They swirled past her and sent a mild breeze over her skin. Tonight's storm seemed to be changing the way it felt, as if it were connected to her emotions.

Her foremost feeling was worry, but his hope comforted her like a blanket. "How did you know I could hold on to your emotions?"

He smiled. "I didn't. But it makes sense. You calm me down all the time. It's a useful talent. If you use it while you're fighting, to calm your enemies or push an emotion into them, you could really throw someone off."

Her talent was useful? "It's not as useful as detecting threats, but I'll remember that."

"Good. Now, let me protect you. Please? It'll make my job much easier."

"Okay, but your oath isn't forever."

"No, but I have a talent that makes me sense threats for people I love, so I'll always know when you're in danger, oath or not."

"People you . . ." *Love?* "You mean your very good friends?"

He chuckled. "Yes."

"Like Ryan and Serena?"

"Yes." He grabbed her hands. "And you."

"Then trust it." She laid a hand on his chest. "If your talent stems from love, perhaps it's not a weakness. Perhaps you just need to trust it more. Listen to your heart, not your fears."

He placed his hand over hers and his thumb rubbed against it. "I'll try to remember that."

So would she. It was time to face fears with the hope that she could overcome them. And it started with her facing the one person she never wanted to lay eyes on again. Franco.

CHAPTER 59

A BRIDGE TO CROSS

Ryan concentrated on the position of his opponent's feet, the angle of his sword, the placement of his arms, and the sweat rolling down his own back. Still, he brought his sword up to defend against a blow nearly too late. Focus.

He chopped his sword at his opponent, a tall, muscular man with a perpetual smug grin. The man swung again, and Ryan could see that he had nearly missed that advance because he lost sight of the other's footing. Too many things to remember.

A shift in his opponent's step caught Ryan's attention. He braced himself for the strike. Catching it, he staggered backward. Perpetual Grin was stronger, but Ryan was faster—thanks to his talent.

One Eye and his crazed theories about dancing and sword fighting. Sure, they worked . . . if he could focus his attention on everything at once.

In the heat of a fight? Not so much.

Perpetual Grin twisted and spun.

Spinning. Dancing.

Whoa, whoa, whoa. Could it be that simple? Yes and no. When Ryan was dancing, he could twirl a girl, catch her in a dip, and take the next partner without losing a step. What if he danced with Perpetual Grin? Not a structured dance, but a dance nonetheless. After all, it took a lot of talent not to let a girl who was resisting his lead step on his toes. And he was a master at that.

He studied the man in front of him as if he were a pretty girl come to dance. Okay, an ugly girl. Just as well, because the object of the dance was to not let her touch him. Perpetual Grin spun. Ryan blocked the blow as easily as if he would have grabbed her hand. He pushed, moved back, and spun. Music seemed to strike up in his head.

As he saw the movements, his body reacted—and all those drills One Eye had made him do for the past months finally counted for something. His muscles remembered what to do. How to block, dodge, strike.

The veil had been lifted. All he had to do was dance.

He struck with his sword, causing Perpetual Grin to back up. Ryan dislodged his opponent's sword and placed his blade on the man's neck. Perpetual Grin lost his signature smile and kicked at the ground as everyone began cheering for the Knight.

Ryan shook his head. He'd done it again. But this time, not by the skin of his teeth. Sweat rolled down his back. His arms ached. But he'd done it.

"Nice crowd today." Tessa slapped his back. Her nose wrinkled, and she wiped her hand on his sleeve. "Looks like you attracted an old friend."

Serena? No, she wouldn't—

A slender woman dressed in deep blue stood staring at him with pretty green eyes. Madison. Pleasant surprise.

What had she been up to? He was about to head over to her when a burly man with a patch over his eye appeared from the crowd and patted Ryan's back.

"One Eye?"

"I see you finally got the lesson." The other's gruff voice resounded over the clapping. "Tomorrow I won't hold back." He winked.

Ryan shuddered. It just wasn't natural for a one-eyed man to wink.

As quickly as the man had appeared, he ghosted back into the mingling crowd. Ryan stood staring. In the dissipating crowd he'd lost sight of Madison, but he figured she'd gone inside. He wiped the sweat from his face before he decided to go in himself and get a drink.

Heat met him at the door. Martha had the kitchens fired up today.

"Excuse me?" A small but distinctly feminine voice caught his attention.

He turned toward Madison and smiled. "You look lovely this evening. Would you care for a dance with the Knight?"

She stepped back, eyebrows scrunching together. "Cocky thing, aren't you?"

"I've been called that before. You should come up with something more original."

She scoffed. Then she leaned close, and her eyes swept the room. "Can I talk to you?"

Well, she was acting strange. "Of course, but we'd better do it while dancing." He smiled his best and extended his hand. "The Knight has many suitors, and after tonight's performance—you were watching, weren't you?"

"That's not why I'm here."

"Clearly." He shot her his most charming grin and offered his hand again.

She simply looked at it. "Dancing? You're serious?"

A flock of other girls started to approach. He'd be busy tonight. He nodded in their direction, and Madison glanced that way.

Ryan took her hand. "I'd rather dance with you. After all, you've always been honest with me."

"We hardly know each other."

"All the more reason." My, she was playing hard to get tonight. "Has something changed?"

"No. I still need to have that discussion." Madison sighed, grabbed his arm, and led *him* out to the dance floor. "Dancing it is."

When the music started, she didn't rely on his leading. In fact, he wasn't leading at all. She was. Ryan narrowed his eyes and searched her face. Something was different about her. "You seem to have had some lessons."

She tilted her chin up. "Of course."

"Are you going to let me lead?" He raised an eyebrow, wondering what game she was playing.

Her eyes softened and she smiled. "I'm sorry, yes."

Well, now she looked more herself. "Are you in some kind of trouble, Madison?"

The hope that sprung into her eyes made his stomach squeeze. "Yes. I need your help. And I'm not Madison."

"A secret name?" He glanced around the room. The man who had escorted her last time was nowhere in sight.

Her smile turned coy. "I've never met you before. Madison is my twin sister."

"Well, that explains things. You must think me awfully forward, then." Ryan spun her.

She faced him again and grabbed his hands. "I do, but I like you anyway."

"All right. I'll take that. So tell me, Not Madison, what is your name?"

"Morgan."

"Ah."

"You don't believe me?"

He laughed. "No."

"Well, it's true." She rolled up her sleeve and showed him the blood moon birthmark.

He covered it with his hand and scanned the room. "You can't just show that off. Even here."

"Your concern is heartwarming." She pulled her sleeve back down and smiled. "But I had to make sure you're taking me seriously. I speak the truth, and I need your help."

She was more confident on her feet that her sister had been, and much less cozy. Ryan had no trouble believing she was Madison's twin. What puzzled him was who these girls really were. And what kind of help this one expected.

When the dance was over, Morgan dragged him to a table and sat. He thought about protesting, but his curiosity had the stronger pull.

Morgan's eyes grew pleading. "My sister's in danger."

"What happened?"

"She was on her way to the Forest of Legends when she came through here, but she's been captured by the king."

Ryan lowered his voice. "And what do you expect me to do about that? I'm no friend of the king."

"I know. You're one of the Feravolk, aren't you?"

It was true, if not recently. "Yes. I'll be heading back to my Feravolk camp soon. I could get some of the others to—"

"There's no time. It has to be you. You save her. I've seen it."

That didn't sound good. "Seen?" He recalled Chloe's comment the first time he'd seen Madison. "You're the sister who can tell the future, aren't you?"

"Not exactly. I have . . . a gift. I can see things. Future things. Not the whole future. But I saw you. You and a pretty blonde-haired girl saved my sister."

Ryan slowly leaned away. What was it with clairvoyants confiding in him? "Listen, I wish I could go storm the castle and rescue your sister, but it just isn't practical." And what pretty blonde? Could she mean Serena?

"You were there already, close to the king and some strange dark-haired woman."

So she wasn't going to give this up. A chill crawled up Ryan's spine, and not because the room was cold. "Close to the king? I think you've got the wrong guy."

"I don't. I saw *you*."

"Listen I'll—" Oh no, not tears. Heavens, not tears. It was like he could feel his heart softening. He reached for a handkerchief and handed it to her. "I'll do whatever I can."

A smiled blossomed on her face, but the tears continued to drip down her cheeks. "Thank you. I knew you would."

The way she looked up at him reminded him of the times his sisters changed his good intentions into blood oaths. A sinking feeling settled in his stomach. He'd just made a promise as far as she was concerned, not only to do what he could but to rescue her sister. What was he, some hero meant to go storming castles and winning pretty girls? No.

She wiped her cheeks with his handkerchief. "I just get pieces of visions. I can't make them come. They just do."

He sighed. "You might as well tell me what happens."

Her eyes practically glimmered. "I see you in the palace with my sister. She gets onto a horse, a brown stallion. A man is there with her. Then you get on a white horse, behind the woman I mentioned. You kiss her, so she must be someone you know. Or—well, I suppose that's beside the point. *You* save my sister."

So there was storming and castles and kissing. The kissing might be okay—she did think he was a hero. Snare heroes.

She winced. "It's not very helpful, is it?"

"What about me being close to the king? And can you tell me more about this dark-haired woman?"

"Yes. Go to the palace. You belong in the king's inner circle."

If he didn't know better, he'd have thought a thousand tiny spiders were marching over his skin.

Morgan continued, "You wore the apparel of one of the palace guards, and you carried the king's key."

"Key?"

"He always carries that key around his neck. I don't know what it's for, but no one carries something around their neck unless it's valuable to them."

Perfect. Now he had to rescue a girl, wear the uniform of the king's men, *and* take the man's key? Snare the key, snare heroes, snare all of it. Except the kissing.

"Morgan, I just don't see how any of that is possible."

"It always is."

"Like when you saved my sister and brother from the king's men."

She tilted her head to the side and narrowed her eyes.

He tipped his chin toward Chloe on the dance floor.

"Oh."

"You remember her?"

She nodded slowly, seeming to focus on some internal thought. "And Ethan. He's your brother?" Her words came out quiet. Soft. Like someone trying to spare him bad news.

Ryan's heart forgot to beat for a moment. "What are you not telling me?"

"You go after my sister. I'll help your brother. I've—I've seen him recently."

"In your visions?"

"Yes. And the people he travels with."

"They're my friends."

Her green eyes met his, full of determination and purpose. "I can help them. Will you help Madison?"

Snare me. "Morgan, I'll do whatever I can."

She rose.

He stood with her.

"They call you the Knight."

Ryan rubbed his hand over his face, but had no time to protest before the warmth of her palm touched his chest. He looked at her and those big, hopeful eyes.

"Thank you, Knight Ryan. I'll never forget you." She stood on her tiptoes and kissed his cheek. Then she darted out of the tavern.

I'll never forget you? What was that supposed to mean? Would he survive this rescue? Ryan stood there rubbing his cheek. Francesca's grip on his arm brought him back to reality. For once he was glad to see the redhead.

CHAPTER 60

TIME OF DEATH

Connor opened his eyes to darkness. He sucked in a breath and sat up. The light glow of a candle across the room revealed his mother curled up in a chair. His chair. His room. How did he get here? The last thing he remembered was being in Franco's quarters with Madison.

The chair skidded against the floor as she flew out of it. "Connor?"

"I-I'm okay." He cupped his head in his hands. The bracer was gone. Probably just as well. Whatever it had done to him, he had no desire to relive. Unless it was necessary. "What happened? How did I get here?"

"Balton carried you. Franco alerted me that you'd collapsed, and I persuaded the general to carry you." Rebekah's eyes creased in the corners.

Connor cocked an eyebrow. "I don't see how that's funny."

She poured him a glass of water. "He's been quite compliant, actually."

She handed him the drink and the bracer peeked out from under her sleeve.

"Mother."

"It doesn't affect me the way it did you." Her hand smoothed his hair like he was little boy in her lap.

"You shouldn't use it. Not until I can figure out more about it." And why it pulsed with evil.

"I only used it to get you back here safe and sound." Her brown eyes softened.

"Thank you."

She took his empty glass to the table and refilled it. "How's your head?"

Aside from throbbing like he'd played with a mountain goat? "Fine."

Rebekah rolled her eyes.

"Why ask then?" He smiled, a little.

Her forehead creased and she ran her light fingers over his hair again—it did feel nice. "Get some sleep."

He swallowed the water and his head hit the pillow. "How long have I been sleeping?"

Silence.

Connor shot up, then grabbed his head. With one eye open, he stared at his mother's back, willing the pain to go away. "Mother?"

"Two days."

Two . . .? "I need to get to the library."

She faced him, chewing her lip. "You need to sleep. Tell me what to bring you."

"The truth is, I don't know."

"If you wait until morning—"

He threw his sheets to the side. "I think the sooner we get out of here, the better."

"At least eat something." The tray she held up for him did remind him of the ache in his stomach.

He grabbed a roll and held it with his teeth as he laced up his boots. Then he took another, and an apple. Picking up a lit candle, he headed out the door.

Each step brought a new pounding to his head. Maybe he did need more sleep. No, he had to find out what that bracer had done to him, especially if his mother was walking around using it.

He stepped into the library and the scent of musty books surrounded him. His shoes landed softly on the smooth wood floor. He scanned the walls of books, then walked to the section on the west wall where he'd first stumbled upon a copy of the *Old Custom*. Maybe something about the Creator's split with the Mistress of Shadows would be there.

He moved his fingers across the spine of a burgundy cover that seemed familiar. A stab of pain shot through his head, and he bent over, clutching his knees. Black spots smothered his vision. Hot wax hardened on his knuckles and the candle clattered to the floor.

Breathing deep, he leaned against the bookshelf as the intensity of the headache passed. That could not keep happening. Now he'd have to get another light. He slid down to the floor.

"Connor?"

He froze.

"Connor?"

He didn't recognize the soft whisper just outside the library. His heart beat faster. Slowly he rose to his feet and crept closer to the doorway.

"Connor, please answer me. I know you're close."

He stood, back pressed against the wall, ready to spring into the doorway if needed.

The footsteps stopped just outside of the library's entrance. Light spilled into the room. He stayed just clear of its rays. Someone stepped closer.

"Connor? Please answer me." She moved far enough into the room that he could see her.

"Madison?"

"Yes. Where are you—oh!" She turned just as he resolved to show himself, and they nearly collided.

"Sorry," Connor said.

She smiled. "You startled me."

He stared at her, waiting for her to speak, but she didn't say anything, just searched his face with her big, green eyes. "Thank you. For rescuing me."

"He hadn't touched you?"

She shook her head and tears coated her eyes. "And I'm no longer chained, though I can't leave the palace or he'll know."

That sounded familiar. He took a step back from her. He didn't really want Franco to come looking for her here and find him. "Can I help you?"

"No." She walked past him and set her candle on the table. "But I can help you."

He leaned against a bookcase and crossed his arms, ignoring the ache behind his eyes that magnified with his every movement.

Madison's eyes seemed to grow larger, if that were possible. "You don't want my help?"

"Are you reading my mind or something?"

Her smile sprouted. "Of course not."

"How did you know where to find me?"

"I'm a Healer, Connor."

"I know what you are."

"Well, that headache you're walking around with is interrupting my sleep."

He pushed off from the bookcase. "Pardon?"

"I need to help you."

"So you can sleep?" And risk Franco knowing what she'd healed him from? "No, thanks."

He walked by her and stooped to pick up his candle. Might as well light it before his unexpected company left. When he stood, another stab of pain shot through him. He clutched the edge of a shelf until it passed.

When he straightened, Madison was right behind him. "It's getting worse, isn't it?"

"Not really."

Her eyes didn't leave the firelight as he touched the wicks together. "Connor, you need my help."

"It's a headache. I think I'll live."

"You won't."

His eyes met hers. She could be putting herself in danger. Or both of them. Or she could be exaggerating. Maybe she had a message from Thea. It was possible.

He studied her face. "Why are you really here?" The candlelight revealed a shiny coating glazing Madison's eyes. Why was she crying?

Connor's heart thrummed. Heat flushed through every vein. "Do you think—am I really dying?"

A tear dripped down her cheek. "Yes."

He set the candles on the table, his mind reeling. "How—how long do I have?"

"I can heal you." She reached for his head.

He stepped back from her and grabbed her wrist. "No."

Her mouth dropped open. "Why not?"

"Franco. You're bound to him. Won't he feel it? Last time, he came right after you healed me."

"You saved me from his wrath once." She touched his arm.

"I won't be able to do it again."

"It's a chance I'll take. You have days maybe."

Days? His heart sank. That wasn't enough time. "How sure are you?"

Another pulse of pain exploded in his head. He buckled over.

A soft touch rubbed his back. "You believe me now?" Chair legs scraped against the floor. "Sit."

Not heeding her advice, Connor stood. He needed more than a few days.

"Madison, I need to ask you a favor."

She pressed her palm against his forehead and cupped her other hand around the back of his head. Heat coursed through him, consuming the ache. Then it cooled, leaving him headache free. Madison's hands slipped from his head and she fell against him. Catching her, he guided her to the ground as dizziness begged him to.

She gripped his hand. "I had to use a lot of energy from both of us."

He leaned against the table leg. "Since when does a headache cause this much trouble?"

She laughed. "I don't know."

"So you don't know what was wrong with me?"

She shook her head. "Just that I needed to help you."

"Why risk Franco's wrath? We don't even know each other."

"It's hard to know who to trust here." Madison pulled a piece of paper from her pocket and handed it to him. "But my sister warned me that I'd meet a young man with golden eyes and that I should not anger him." She smiled. "And that I'd know something was wrong with him and if I didn't help him, he'd die. Then she told me that you couldn't die. Something about the fate of the world or something."

Connor unrolled the parchment. "You have a picture of me."

"I just saved your life, you know."

He shot her a grin. "Thank you."

Now he needed to find out why the bracer had nearly killed him, and if it was doing the same thing to his mother.

CHAPTER 61

STORM WITHIN
A STORM

Jayden opened her eyes as the thunder pealed. The storm traveled closer. Her heart beat to it.

The yellow-green glow of Westwind's eyes stared back at her. Her head still lay comfortably on Ethan's chest, but he slept, Scout curled up beside him.

"It's my watch?"

Westwind nodded.

Rain fell steadily and thunder erupted, preceded by lightning. Ethan looked peaceful, though. Perhaps she'd been able to ward off his bad dreams for a change.

The electricity in the air shifted, almost as if the storm warred within itself. Some of it wanted to form into a wild, raging monster with whirling clouds and impetuous lightning, and the other half wanted to bask in a moment of contentment with a drenching rain.

Jayden sat up. The wild part of the storm pulled at her until the skin behind her ears tingled. An overwhelming need to follow the source of the static in the air flooded her. She stood and crept out from beneath the tall pine.

Westwind rose with her, emitting a soft rumble from his throat.

"I feel something . . . pulling me."

He followed her as she walked into the dripping rain. The pull led her to a place overgrown with vines. She moved a vine and crept past it.

Westwind hunched forward, tail tucked beneath him. A whine escaped his throat. A deep, thunderous growl responded. Westwind bristled.

"What is it?" Jayden's breath caught.

Westwind jumped in front of her and stood growling. A deafening roar, like thunder, returned from the other creature's throat. Jayden's feet became like iron. She shivered. She tried to leave, but she couldn't. The beautiful horse had captivated her.

Not again. Her heart melted.

The horse tried to move toward her, but it shook its head wildly and reared back as if dragged. Its reckless movements matched the part of the coming storm that wanted to break free. But this creature emanated fear. Whinnying loudly, the horse reared up, and from its sides unfolded two enormous wings.

This was no kelpie.

Wait. Stars. There were stars on the token. It wasn't a picture of a horse. Not a kelpie. It was a pegasus.

She reached for the horse's nose. Her fur was like satin. Smooth and soft. The animal's fear pulsed into her, and Jayden pushed her calm confidence back. "You're caught in a vine. Can you understand me?"

"Yes." The pegasus's voice rang clearly in her head, and the animal breathed a sigh.

"I'm going to help you."

The animal stilled. Jayden crawled under the pegasus and took out her dagger. A thick tangle of vines wrapped around the creature's back legs. "Stay calm. I won't hurt you."

The pegasus remained perfectly still as Jayden hacked at the woody vine. The storm seemed to calm with her. Now uniform, no longer battling wild against control. Could this be her bonded animal? Jayden's insides buzzed with that hope Serena always urged her to cling to.

At last the vine loosened, and green serpentine plants dropped to the forest floor. A blast of wind eddied the air around Jayden. She looked up as the pegasus lifted skyward. Gone.

Jayden's shoulders drooped as she glanced at Westwind.

The wolf still bristled.

Jayden rose and wiped the grime off of her clothes. "There's nothing to be worried about. It's gone."

She turned to see the pegasus standing behind her.

Thunder pealed and Ethan woke with a start. His heart raced as he remembered the picture in his mind of his parents dead on the ground. Blood pooled around their bodies. Flowed from their necks. And the rain. It didn't wash away a thing. Just splashed into the blood, making streams out of red puddles.

Rivers that drowned him in his dreams.

He'd felt the threat. The danger had pulsed hot across his chest for the first time in his life. A warning he didn't understand but that told him to move. Told him to take the reins his father had left unattended and urge the cart horses forward. But he hadn't. Not at first.

They'd died because he hadn't tried to save them.

In his nightmares, the blood always drowned him. Splashed red against his hands. His face. And the thunder laughed. The lightning revealed his mistake in stark detail.

A cool nose pressed into his hand.

"Hey, buddy." He patted Scout's furry head.

Scout whined.

"I'm okay."

Scout pawed at his arm, pulling it closer. As soon as Ethan cracked a smile, Scout practically crawled into his lap and licked his face.

"All right, all right." He pushed his dog down and Scout rolled over to have his belly scratched. A thanks he deserved for banishing those vivid pictures away.

Ethan sat up straighter. Where was Jayden? He didn't feel a threat. "Did Westwind go with Jayden?"

Scout nodded and grabbed Ethan's hand in his teeth to get him to resume belly-scratching. He complied.

Everyone else was asleep. The unicorn nestled next to Serena with his eyes closed.

"Help me. Help me. Help me."

A breeze filtered around Ethan, carrying a soft, small voice. The Whisperer.

The stone. He could talk to her in the stone, but the last time he'd looked in it, Scarface had seen him and come after Kinsey.

Ethan's heart seemed louder than the rumble of thunder. He stuck his hand in his pocket. Curled his fingers around the stone. Should he look?

It was night. No one else would be watching. Right?

His fingers dove through the light folds of the material and touched the smooth surface of the stone.

The girl's voice seemed to echo in his mind. *"Help me."*

He had to.

Red, like burning embers, spread over the black surface and revealed the girl still huddled close to a rock wall, shivering.

"You're sure they'll come?" the voice in the stone asked. It was dark where they were, too. Only a light flickered in the background. A fire. The flames seemed to dance in front of a rock formation. Could that be Castlerock?

Then he saw Quinn. Bound. Gagged. Tear streaks on her young face. Her eyes pierced him. How did she always sense his presence? His talent warned him, and ice chilled his stomach, just like his mother telling him not to come out of the wagon. Not to come save her.

This time he would save her. Save where he'd failed Kinny, his parents.

Someone stepped into the line of sight. Blocked his view. A fire in Ethan's chest raged when he recognized Scarface. So the man had survived.

Revenge pushed at his talent, the fire in his chest boiling.

Scarface bent over the girl, and she trembled. *"You be good while I'm gone, because if you try to escape, we'll run you down."* He laughed. *"Don't worry, I won't be that long. Just until mid-morning."*

Shaking, Ethan curled his fingers around the stone and put it back in his pocket. She'd be alone? It was dawn now.

How was Scarface getting across the water? There would have to be a boat there, waiting for him. If Quinn was on the island, chances were that the beast had already been killed. Or died on its own two thousand years ago.

Ethan glanced at Scout. His paws twitched in a dream.

He smiled. It looked like a good one. "Stay here, buddy." He gently stroked Scout's head, then he stood, keeping his hand on his borrowed sword so it wouldn't hit the tree.

He had to save Quinn. It was time to follow his talent.

Alone.

This way, he wouldn't be stretched too thin.

○

The pegasus's dark mane shimmered from the rain. Marbled gray swirled through the feathers on her wings and fur on her coat. Jayden had never seen a horse with such an arrangement of colors. The pegasus stepped closer, her hooves quiet like Dash's.

"My name is Jayden." She didn't know what else to say to the elegant creature.

The pegasus lowered her head and Jayden saw, in her mind's eye, one billowing, deep gray cloud crashing into another, and wave of lightning fanning out between them.

"That's your name?"

"*Yes.*"

Jayden stared in awe. "It's like a storm cloud."

"*Stormcloud.*" She reared up onto her hind legs, letting her magnificent wings spread out beside her. Her coat changed to black as night, then faded into a purple, then midnight blue. A streak of what looked like lightning flashed out across her wings before she settled to the ground. "*My name is Stormcloud.*"

"How are you doing that?"

"*Doing what?*"

"Changing colors."

Stormcloud folded her wings against her sides and became the color of an evening blue sky with her mane and wings a shade darker. "*This is normal for a pegasus.*"

Pictures of other pegasi flying in the air, changing colors from orange to magenta to deep purple as they danced around through the clouds at sunset, infiltrated Jayden's thoughts. "It's like camouflage."

Stormcloud dipped her head down and tossed it up a few times excitedly.

Westwind whined and Jayden turned to the wolf. The sky was lightening. "I should be getting back to camp."

"You travel with the wolf, too?"

"Yes."

"You can speak to them?"

"Just this one. Westwind is my friend."

"Westwind." Stormcloud closed her eyes and Jayden could sense a gentle breeze, warm to the touch. It carried a sweet scent like early blooming flowers and thawing snow and season-worn grass.

Jayden blinked. "That's the west wind?"

Stormcloud flicked her head again. Her excitement flooded into Jayden like a spring downpour.

Jayden looked at the ruddy wolf. "What's Aurora?"

Joy burst through Stormcloud and pushed into Jayden like a gust of wind inside her soul. Her thoughts spilled again into Jayden's mind, showing her a dark sky lit up with dancing colors, like perpetual lightning strikes never disintegrating into the night. Blue, green, and purple. Stormcloud reared up and her expressive coat captured the scene as well.

"It's beautiful," Jayden mused and she looked at Westwind. She turned her gaze back to Stormcloud. "I feel your emotions as if they're my own."

"I feel your wonder. You are like a changing wind right now. Not sure which way to blow."

"We're bonded, aren't we?" Jayden stroked Stormcloud's nose. It was the most natural yet amazing conclusion she could come to.

"Bonded. That sounds right," the pegasus mused.

"A pegasus. I can't believe it. You're more amazing than anything I ever expected." She smiled and Stormcloud dipped her head low. Jayden stroked the mare's incredibly soft nose. "You're beautiful."

"Thank you."

Westwind chuckled as he loped back the way they came, looking over his shoulder to make sure they followed. Stormcloud stayed near Jayden. After they had almost reached camp, Stormcloud's head pulled from Jayden's hands and her ears swiveled forward. Jayden glanced over her shoulder. Ethan was walking away from camp. Alone.

She glanced at Westwind. "Does Logan know?"

Westwind shook his head slowly.

"He's going to save the Whisperer. We can't let him go alone."

"The Whisperer?"

"She's a prisoner of someone who plans to release the Mistress of Shadows."

Stormcloud reared and lightning flashed across her wings. *"That can't happen. Tell me what I need to do."*

CHAPTER 62

UNEXPECTED CONCLUSION

Connor sat on top of the hill in silence. Moonlight spilled across his paws. His tail swished back and forth as he stared at the palace. Something in its belly beckoned him to stay.

Today he was to leave with his mother. Today they were to break out. It was perfect because most of the soldiers had headed out—less reinforcements to go after them—and Franco himself had left ahead of this group.

But today Connor felt the urge to stay. To protect. There was a strange pull tugging his heart. Luring him to remain as if he were needed here. He stood and loped back toward the massive gray structure. Perhaps this was what Ethan felt when he needed to protect the other Deliverers.

If that were the case, maybe the Deliverers were headed here. Maybe he needed to stay because they were coming to rescue *him* now.

Heeding his gut had never been a problem. Getting Rebekah to understand this decision might be, though.

Creeping in through the assassin's gate, he padded through the dank halls in his wolf skin, sending the rats skittering. He took the back stairs and slipped into the hallway, then down toward his room.

Footsteps echoed down the corridor. Connor morphed back into his human form and hurried into his room. He pulled on his breeches as the sound drew closer. The footsteps stopped outside his door. With no time to put his nightshirt on, he tossed it on the ground, flipped his blankets to the side, and climbed into his bed. Then he waited.

A gentle creaking betrayed the opening door. A hooded figure slipped into his room. He sniffed. The familiar scent of roses wafted toward him. His mother? She was early. Hours early. She looked his way and he nodded once. Then she glided toward his dressing room. He lay back down, but his ears remained alert.

She wore her travel clothes, including her gray hooded cloak and boots. It was time, then. The guards outside her room would be disposed of. The warmth of a body neared his bed. For a human, Rebekah was soft-footed. She'd always been.

"Are you ready?" Her eyes met his.

He wouldn't go with her now, though. "Mother, I can't—"

She handed him a vial. "Drink this."

Sitting up, Connor took the potion. Whether or not he was staying, he'd need to break the trace. He drank. It slid down his throat like honey seasoned with bitter herbs. He shuddered.

Why had he done that? It would bring more danger for him now, knowing he was going to stay. And yet, he'd done as she asked without thinking.

She took the glass from him and he noticed the bit of gold peeking out from her sleeve. "I imagine Franco will want to make sure you are still here when he sees I have gone missing. He must see you sleeping. Then we can leave together."

"I am not—"

"Connor."

"Mother, don't use that bracer to make me do as you wish."

She placed her hand over her mouth and her eyes grew wide. Then she removed the bracer and held it out for him. "I didn't intend to use it on you. It was an accident. I never want that to happen again."

Did she mean it? He stared at the evil thing. New footsteps in the hall broke him of his trance, and he wrapped his hand in his blankets to avoid touching the weapon as he slid it under his pillow. As the footsteps drew nearer, Rebekah withdrew into his dressing room again.

Connor concentrated on calming his breathing. Heels clicked harshly against the marble floor in the corridor. At least four sets of footsteps stopped outside his door. One of them light with a cocky bounce. Oswell. Accompanied by . . . soldiers?

Connor's throat tightened. If they'd trailed Rebekah here—

The door handle turned. Rusted hinges creaked. Connor tried not to smirk. His mother had been quieter. Torchlight preceded the intruder.

Connor gripped the knife under his pillow. The door burst open. Connor sat up, knife in hand. "What is going on here?"

Oswell tilted his chin. "You dare raise a weapon against the king's second?"

"You busted into my room, scaring the pants off of me when I would be sleeping is all." He put the knife on his pillow and raised his hands. "I meant no disrespect."

The three soldiers Connor had expected filtered into his room.

He tipped his chin toward them. "What did I do to earn the greeting party?"

Oswell being in charge during Franco's absence could prove terrible, especially if the man suspected Connor was guilty of more than sneaking food from the kitchens. Oswell had always had it out for Connor, ever since Franco first called Connor "brother." And now Franco wasn't here to step into the middle of a disagreement.

Oswell crept farther into his room. "Your mother is missing."

"Missing?" Connor jumped out of bed and grabbed his sword and shirt.

"You didn't know?" Oswell stared at him, and a wicked smile slid across his lips. "Be careful. I'm borrowing Belladonna's power."

Connor swallowed. A spell made her power viable for a few hours. He'd have to take care with his words tonight, or it could be his mother's last.

"That she was missing? How could I?" Connor pulled his shirt over his head. Then he flew to his window and opened it. The cool night breeze billowed in like a welcome friend. A hint of gray rose up from the horizon. The gray of morning.

"See anything?" Oswell came up behind him.

Connor looked down the four-story drop to the ground from his tower. The wind shifted, sprayed him in the face. "No." He turned away from the window and headed toward the door. Soldiers impeded his exit.

He whirled around. "Are we going to look for her?"

"We have scoured the whole castle and she is gone."

"Gone? What do you mean, gone?"

Oswell narrowed his eyes and searched Connor's face. "Since the king has always felt the two of you were brothers, I doubt he would have told you, but I'll not spare you the gory details about your mother."

He locked eyes with the king's second. "What details?"

Another gust of wind fluttered against the edge of the valance.

Oswell leaned on the fireplace mantle. "She killed innocent soldiers tonight. Two men in training who stood watch in the east wing. Boys, only fifteen."

"Killed? What proof do you have?"

Oswell smiled. "If dead soldiers aren't enough, once we find her, we will have the proof we need. Now have you seen her?"

"Seen her? I was in my bed before you barged in." That was close. Oswell didn't seem to notice a lie. "If you think I'll believe she killed innocent boys—"

"If I can prove it?" Oswell asked.

Connor shook his head. The bracer. She'd been wearing the bracer. She'd made him drink the potion. Was it possible that she'd killed the guards? Or made them kill one another so she could lie? "Then—then she has gone against everything she ever taught me."

"I am glad to hear you say that." Oswell straightened. "I was beginning to think you might have changed."

The soldiers started nosing around the room. The sun sent a soft glow through the window as its early morning rays touched the skyline. They would find her.

Panic clawed at his gut. He stood. "What are you doing?"

"She may have snuck in here. You are the only person she trusts." The way Oswell stared into Connor's eyes unnerved him. "Do you want to tell me if she is here and get on my good side?"

"I told you—"

"Leave him alone." Rebekah came out of his dressing room and threw her daggers down.

"Mother."

A burly man grabbed Rebekah, but she didn't struggle. "Let my son go."

"I thought we could be reasonable." Oswell rubbed his hands together.

Connor walked over to his mother. "Is it true? Did you kill innocent men—boys?"

Rebekah stared at him open-mouthed. Tears filled her eyes. "Tonight was the only chance I had."

Oswell waved his hand. "Take her down to the dungeons. She will be beheaded today."

"Wait." Connor looked over his shoulder at Oswell. "Please. I need answers first. You know King Franco would give them to me."

Oswell's eyes narrowed. "Very well."

Connor drew his sword and pointed it at his mother. Oswell didn't intervene. Instead, the guard released Rebekah. Connor's sword tip motioned toward the window, and Rebekah moved there, away from everyone else. Thea had told him this moment would come. How had she known?

Truthfully, when she'd said Oswell would make him see that Rebekah had betrayed him, Connor didn't believe it for a moment. But now . . . now that she stood before him, after all she'd done to get him to leave with her tonight—against his will—he understood just how powerful Thea was. And he prayed that she was right.

If she wasn't, he was about to make the worst mistake of his entire life.

He moved so her back was to the open window. "You taught me to be kind, mother. Was it all a lie?"

"No. Of course not."

"You killed harmless boys?"

A tear slid down his mother's cheek. "The queen poisons her soldiers. Then she makes General Balton give them a tonic to stop the poison from killing them. But it's too late; it's already infected them. They are no longer the same. They become monsters with black hearts."

"That makes it okay to kill them?" He advanced, pushing her closer to the window. "To make people do things they don't wish to?"

Her eyes widened. "I'm not the only one guilty of that."

So she had made him drink on purpose. The wind howled. Everything was set up just right. Just like Thea had told him. How could he have doubted her? She knew it all. Knew he would have to do this to his own mother. His heart ached. Rebekah would choose her own fate now.

"Connor." Oswell placed a hand on his shoulder. "We can take care of Rebekah."

He snarled. "She betrayed *me*, didn't she? Everything she taught me? Everything I lived for?" He turned toward his mother. Made his voice soft. "Answer my question. Does that make it okay to kill them?"

"Sometimes we have to do things against our values in order to save the ones we love."

Connor lowered the tip of his sword and walked toward her. "I trusted you."

Her golden hair fluttered around her angelic face as she stared back at him with tears in her eyes. "Connor, I love you. I had no choice."

"There is always a choice. You taught me that." He reached up and cupped her cheek in his hand.

She kissed his palm. "Yes. There's always a choice."

The wind hit his face. Warm. His heart trembled. What could he say to her now?

"I choose to trust that you know what you're doing."

A voice filled his mind. *"Now."*

He dropped his sword. "I do. And I choose justice." He placed his hands on her shoulders and pushed. How easily she fell out the window.

Gasps staggered behind him.

Connor lurched toward the window, clutched the cold sill in his hands, and watched his mother fall. His heart throbbed with every beat.

Warm air rushed up to greet his face as Cliffdiver swooped beneath her. She grabbed hold of the gryphon and he carried her to the ground. She lay down, twisting her form as if dead. Cliffdiver looked up at him, and another gust of the mild wind hit Connor's face before the gryphon ghosted into the shadows.

Oswell pushed him out of the way. "He did it." A smile snaked across his face. "I didn't think you had that kind of darkness in you." He looked as though he'd tasted something sour. "The king will be pleased."

Connor closed his eyes. Rebekah was free. Almost. "She got what she deserved." He sighed and turned toward Oswell. "Let me take care of her body."

"Of course. Make a pyre."

Connor squeezed his eyes shut and nodded. He walked away from the sound of Oswell's chuckle. Once out of his room, he descended the stairs without torchlight. His wolf eyes didn't need it. When he reached the ground, he scooped Rebekah into his arms. She stayed limp, her head lolling with each step as he walked out of the palace court, across the drawbridge, and out toward the cemetery.

He would build his funeral pyre. No one would think to bother him.

As soon as they were out of eyesight, he spoke to his mother. "I'm so sorry. I—"

She raised her head and gripped him around the neck. "I trusted you. You did well in there."

Connor smiled ruefully. "Nearly killing you?"

"I never doubted."

He set her down and began collecting wood from the woodpile. "What are you doing?"

"Oswell wants me to burn your body, but you can go."

"Go? I'll wait for you."

He tore his gaze away from her. "I'm not coming, Mother."

"Connor?"

"I have to follow my Destiny Path."

"You can't stay. Franco will return, and he'll know the trace spell was broken."

"The king believes he has my loyalty. This will get back to him and make him more sure of it."

"But Belladonna."

"I'll guard my tongue. That is an art you taught me well." He grabbed her hands and watched the tears fill her eyes. "Did you really kill the soldiers?"

"No." She shook her head and managed a tearful laugh. "I used the tangle flower as planned. They will wake in the morning." She hung her head. "But I imagine Franco will order Oswell to kill them now, to keep your loyalty."

"Maybe not. Maybe I can get them to safety."

"So you are really going back?" She smoothed his hair.

"Mother, something—someone—needs me to stay."

A faint rustle in the trees announced the white-headed gryphon. Connor nodded toward the animal. "Thank you for saving her."

Cliffdiver cocked his head and eyed Connor. *"You look different, but smell the same. And I can feel your power."*

Connor smiled.

"You smile the same, too."

"Who is this?" Rebekah eyed the creature.

"Cliffdiver."

"You're bonded to him?"

Connor nodded.

Rebekah held out her hand to the gryphon. "Thank you." She looked at Connor. "He does not seem to recognize you. Has he ever seen you as a man?"

"No."

Rebekah turned to the gryphon. "You will take care of my son?"

Connor shook his head. "Don't worry about me, Mother. I'll join you as soon as I can."

"How will you find me?"

"Moon Over Water? I could find it in my sleep by pull alone."

"They need you."

"Since when have I been one to neglect my duties?"

She pulled him in for a hug. "Never." When she released him, all evidence of tears had been erased, but she sniffed. "I won't be able to protect you now."

"You need to go to the others. They pull you?"

She nodded. Then she turned, leaving him to finish the pyre.

At least his mother had made it away. And the plan had been flaw-less. Well, not entirely. He swallowed. He'd need to free himself from Franco's clutches before Franco found out what he and his mother had so desperately tried to hide from him. And now that the trace spell was broken, he'd have to remain more visible.

Neither of those things would be easy, especially since Thea had no more guidance to offer from the grave.

CHAPTER 63

MYSTERIOUS WOMEN

Ryan lowered the bucket into the well. Cool autumn air rippled his shirt. He couldn't get his thoughts off Madison and Morgan. He was beginning to wish he'd never met either of those two mysterious women. Still, he wanted to help Madison. But he wouldn't do it alone. No matter what Morgan saw, going to the palace alone was suicide.

He was no hero. Hadn't even completed his training. And here she was, trying to send him off on some rescue. Now Logan—*there* was a hero. The Lone Wolf, for heaven's sake.

And Ethan was Stone Wolf. That didn't surprise him. For some reason, he'd always suspected his brother to be that swordsman. If Morgan wanted to help them, why didn't she just ask them to save Madison? Who was Ryan Granden anyway?

No one they needed.

I can use you if your friends won't. I will prize your talents where they ignore you.

"How long does it take you to get a bucket of water?" Chloe interrupted his thoughts and stood there with her hands on her hips.

"It's coming." His calloused hands pulled the rope.

"You've gotten dangerously good with that thing." Chloe motioned to his sword.

"You have, too." He nodded to her daggers.

"Thanks. But not as fast as you."

"Well, I did like to pretend I knew what I was doing with one before we even left home."

"And you think I never played with daggers?"

He hefted out the bucket and handed it to Chloe, then took her empty one. "Well, if you hadn't spent so much of your extra time doing penance—"

Chloe splashed water all over him. "You were saying?"

Ryan tried to squeeze the excess water from his well-worn clothes and scowled. "You're getting dangerously good with *that* thing."

She giggled. "And now you have to bring up more water. You'd best hurry. You don't want Estelle and One Eye to come home from the market to no supper." Her grin turned impish. "Might as well bring both buckets. I'll be cutting up carrots."

Ryan rolled his eyes as he lowered the bucket back into the well.

Stag followed Chloe to the house, the bounce in his tail matching the bounce in her step. Ryan laughed to himself.

When he had two full buckets, he lifted both and headed toward the house. The cool breeze chilled him to the bone as it filtered through his wet clothes. A few stray leaves rustled past. He looked up at the clouds racing across the gray sky. The sunlight barely broke through.

A shrill scream carried through the wind.

Chloe.

Ryan's heart tripped on a beat.

He dropped his burden and dashed toward the cabin.

The scream still echoed in his ears, but another came. Chloe raced out the back door, looking behind her. Ryan caught his sister. She was trembling and covered in blood. The kitchen knife in her hands dripped red.

"Chloe?"

"They killed Stag."

The back door opened and spewed out a woman dressed in tight clothes with black leather overlays. The queen's emblem decorated her uniform, and she had long, dark hair. He remembered her. The lie detector from the palace. He'd bested her with his wit once before. A sword was a different matter entirely.

Ryan placed himself between the woman and his sister and drew his sword. "Who are you and what do you want?"

"You." The woman stepped forward. Her hair swung in a ponytail behind her.

Three men came out of the house. One was covered in blood.

The woman in black narrowed her eyes. "Your dog killed one of my men. I like to return favors."

"I guess you've made an enemy." Ryan tightened his grip on his sword. Dance. He just had to dance.

The woman smiled a perfectly wicked smile. "And any friend of Logan's is an enemy of mine. Especially you."

Ryan pushed his sister farther back with his right hand and clutched his sword in his left. "Run, Chloe."

"No."

"Run, Chloe!"

"No!"

The three men raced toward them. Ryan concentrated on the dance and the steps of the fight began to map out for him. Every muscle showed the direction the soldier would move. Ryan gritted his teeth, clutched his sword, and let his instinct take over.

With the first clash, the man's strength pushed against him. The man lunged again and pain shot through Ryan's shoulder. This guy was good. Trained. Ryan didn't stand a chance. That meant Chloe didn't, either.

A new fervor pulsed through Ryan's veins. He had to make sure his sister lived to see another day. He lunged forward, blocked, pushed, and hacked down at the man's right arm. How easily his blade passed through bracer, flesh, and bone.

"Good."

Bile crept up Ryan's throat as reality rushed back to him.

"Now the other."

This was different than the huge giant he'd fought with Jayden. Giants were monsters, not men. This was a man. He pushed his sword through the man's middle, evidence of a scream burning his throat. The man fell.

One Eye's voice pulsed in Ryan's ears: *Someday you will look a man in the eyes and you'll kill him. You'll see the light fade. His screams will ring in your ears long after they're silenced. The world will want to stop around you, but boy, if you're in the middle of a fight and you stop, that will be your last kill.*

That was a voice Ryan welcomed. He willed himself to keep dancing. His arms ached, but he raised his bloodied sword and turned toward his sister's attacker. Chloe staggered back and thudded to the ground. Her daggers, wet with blood, went up to defend her, but they wouldn't stop a sword.

Blood covered her weapons.

And his sword.

Blood.

Death.

He was a killer.

Chloe screamed.

A strange roar resounded in his head, and a white lion leaped toward Chloe. Where had it come from? He hadn't seen one with Belladonna before. Ryan gripped his sword in both hands and sliced through the air at the lion's white head. It dissolved like smoke in the wind, but his blade penetrated flesh and bone. A man. He'd struck one of the soldiers and sent the man's head tumbling to the ground. Ryan's stomach clenched. His shoulders screamed for him to stop.

"You are easily provoked to aggression."

He squeezed his eyes shut, but the lion was there, too. And only her head was white. Everything else was red.

"I saved your sister. You owe me."

I owe you nothing. An arrow zipped past. Wide-eyed, Ryan looked for the source. A man on horseback was charging up the hill. More men crested the hill behind him. "Chloe, run!"

"No." Her voice trembled.

He looked into her scared eyes. "Please, Chloe. One of us has to. I'm the right age; they'll follow me. Run!"

She scrambled to her feet. "No."

Tears blurred his vision. He pushed her. Pushed his own sister.

She stumbled away from him and ran right back to his side, eyes wet. "Ryan?"

He touched her cheek. "Please, run?"

"Snare you, Ryan. Snare you!" Tears streamed down her cheeks, but she turned and ran.

Thank the Creator, she ran. *I love you, too, Chloe.*

Ryan turned back to the men advancing up the hill. He dropped his sword and spoke to the lion in his head. *If you want me to kill, I won't do it.*

"Fool."

No. You don't control me.

"We'll see."

The woman in black held up her hand and the five on horseback, now congregating at the top of the hill, stilled their arrows.

"What are you doing, boy?" She stepped closer to him.

"I'm surrendering. *If* you'll let my sister go."

The sound from her throat sounded like a purr. "She is of no use to us anyway, not if we have you." She stopped in front of him and pulled a knife from her belt. "What's your name?"

There was no use lying. "Ryan."

Her dark eyes were wild, crazy almost. "I'm Belladonna."

A cool blade pressed against his neck, but he wouldn't move. Wouldn't give her the satisfaction of seeing his fear.

"The king wants you alive, lucky for you. But even so, you are quite handsome. And strong. And I do need more men since you've robbed me of three perfectly good ones." She stroked his bloodied arm. "Cain was my favorite, but I think I can train another."

Ryan clenched his jaw.

Crazy Belladonna stood on her tiptoes and her cheek brushed against Ryan's neck. "I will keep you for my own, if he'll let me. Would you like that?"

"I'm nobody's pet."

"Honest, too." The flat of her knife blade slid against his neck, but the edge sliced him anyway.

He flinched as sweat seeped into the open wound.

"Oh, how clumsy." She traced her fingers along the cut. It grew hotter.

Then cooled. No more sting. Then she touched the wound in his shoulder.

Heat burned through him like the fire from the black lion. Just before panic set in, it cooled. No more gash. No more pain.

Ryan flashed his eyes to meet Belladonna's dark ones.

She smiled. "That's right. I healed you. Now if you continue to be this compliant, you'll find yourself a knight of the king in no time."

The king? Ryan's stomach squeezed. What exactly had Morgan seen?

"Raph, Travis," Belladonna shouted, and two men moved their horses forward. One was smaller, weasel-looking, and the other was a burly man with an eye patch and a wooden leg. "Follow the girl, but don't hurt her. I want to know where she's going. Don't get caught."

The two men spurred their horses down the hill.

Ryan closed his eyes as his stomach squeezed. *What have I done?*

CHAPTER 64

INK-BLACK WATER

Dawn's rays pierced through the trees and lit the rocky shore bordering the moat. The flare of protection in Ethan's chest burned stronger with each step toward the ruins. Danger for Quinn. For himself. Maybe the beast wasn't as dead as he'd hoped. Great. Hopefully he'd be able to help her before the others found him missing and tried to follow.

Ethan pulled the stone out of his pocket. Just one more glance to make sure nothing else had changed. A flash of red, like the glow of fire in a fanned coal, spread over the black surface and she appeared. Alone.

He breathed deep and replaced the stone. Then he stepped into the clearing and looked across the water to the island's south side. Listening. Feeling. Trusting his talent. That last one was hardest.

Water, black as pitch, surrounded the ruins. A strange rock formation jutted up from the center of it that looked like a dwelling built on a mountainside. Only it was no mountain. By the black rock-rubble at the bottom of the formation and the lush, living vegetation surrounding it, this was most certainly a volcano.

The water around the island resembled a moat. Manmade, but archaic. The rock formation could have been an ancient castle tarnished with lava and centuries past its once-formidable prime. This was the place.

Ethan scanned the base of the volcano for the girl. Scanned the shore for a boat. There. Farther up the shoreline, where it curved around the massive volcano. The scent of ash was faint in the wind. He moved closer, his boots crunching on the rocky soil.

"Ethan."

He stopped. Heart sinking deep. Why did they have to follow him? He was the Protector. Couldn't they see that he was trying to keep them safe?

He turned to face Logan, but Serena and Jayden followed him right through the clearing. Scout bounded up to him. Westwind stood beside Logan, Dash stood behind Serena, and a black horse—no, a pegasus—stood beside Jayden. Ethan stared.

"Her name is Stormcloud. I'm sorry I left you alone—"

"You bonded?"

She beamed.

He sighed. "Quinn is only alone for a few more hours. I didn't want the rest of you to get hurt."

Logan walked up to him and squeezed his shoulder. "Kid, this isn't your burden to bear alone. I thought you'd get that by now."

"I'm supposed to protect them, not drag them into danger. Besides, I couldn't wait for Melanie and Gavin. I had to make a move now."

"Yes, but not alone. And how were you planning to get across the moat?"

Ethan glanced at the pegasus. He had to admit, the timing was good.

Logan's eyes crinkled in the corners. "Sometimes letting your friends—no, *family*—help you is better than going alone."

Sometimes.

The heat of a threat pulsed in Ethan's heart for Jayden and Serena. He fisted his hands. Why couldn't Logan ever listen? "Sometimes going alone is best. Get them out of here, please. I don't know what the danger is, but I have a bad feeling, and—" A low moan seemed to shake the ground. "And it just got worse."

"What was that?" Logan's eyes were wide.

"The beast." Serena's soft whisper hung in the air like thick mist.

A girl stepped into view on the island. She strained to reach the end of her chains so she could see them.

Ethan let out a trapped breath. She was alive. He cupped his hands to his mouth. "We're going to get you out of there."

"No! Run before it kills you. It will kill you!"

The ground quaked. A thunderous bubble rose from the dark liquid. Ethan pulled out his sword and stepped back. He glanced at Jayden, pleading. "Will you run now?"

Jayden stood next to him with her daggers out. "Not a chance."

"Actually, it might be a good idea." Logan grabbed Jayden's wrist. "Let's go."

Water shot up from the moat like a spire. It towered above them so high, Ethan couldn't see the top. Then, like a firework, it burst apart in five directions. Ethan pushed Jayden into a run. They all headed toward the trees.

A snakelike neck, bigger around than an old oak tree and covered with green and yellow scales, slammed onto the ground ahead of them, knocking Ethan off his feet. He pushed off the ground, but the earth shook as four more necks crashed to the ground, separating him from the others. The creature could have separated all of them, for all he knew.

One thing was certain, his chest was practically on fire. Not like he needed the warning.

The single black eye on a scaled, cyclopean head focused on him. Smoke leaked from its nostrils. White fangs lined its massive jaw. It opened its mouth and an orange ball of flames festered in the back of its throat. Ethan rolled and scrambled to his feet. "Now what?"

"We hope our swords cut through it." Logan's voice came from behind one of the necks.

He raised his weapon as a stream of fire spewed toward him. Fighting this was not like fighting a man—its heart was still safely in the water. Great.

The pegasus soared into the air and one of the heads tracked it. Jayden was atop Stormcloud.

The best way to save her was to kill the thing. He focused on the head tracking him and raced toward the water's edge. Two heads swiveled in his direction. One head lunged at him, opening its mouth. Two rows of serrated teeth dripped with saliva. The orange glow was a good tip-off, at least.

Ethan dove to the ground. Rough pebbles grated against his body as he skidded away from the flame. The second head snaked closer. He scrambled to his feet and hacked at the beast. He hit it. A shock of resistance shot through his arms, leaving his muscles quivering. Its scales were like a rock, but the sword had cut through. The red on his blade proved that.

An ear-splitting screech emitted from the creature's five throats. The heads targeting Ethan recoiled as if in pain. He spun to see what had happened. A head lay on the ground under Logan's dripping sword. Blood cascaded from the twitching neck as fire spewed from the remaining heads. At least Logan's sword got through.

Fire flared around Ethan. Scout valiantly jumped at the snakelike creature, but it knocked him away easily. Then the beast lunged at Scout's fallen form. Ethan's heart sped as he looked at his helpless dog. He raced forward, calling his speed. It coursed through him. Fueled every muscle.

He brought down his sword right at the base of the creature's skull before it could claim Scout's life. He swung. The head dangled, still attached on one side. Sparks spouted uncontrollably from the mouth.

Then heat washed over his chest. This time the threat was for him.

"Ethan, look out!" Jayden's voice rang out above him.

Another head raced toward him.

Flames spouted and Ethan jumped. For a heartbeat, he was suspended in the air. Acrid heat shot past him, singeing his sleeve.

The half-severed head sailed toward him. Unable to change direction, he braced for the hit. It bashed into his arm, sending his sword flying across the ground.

Ethan slammed into the unforgiving earth and slid across the wet sand. Gasping for air, he tried to push himself up. The world spun. How far was he from everyone else? Panic shot through him. His hands were empty.

"Scout, I don't know if it's safe."

His ears dipped down. *"Then let me be the one to test it. If I make it across, you'll know it's safe."*

Logan stared at the dog. Was he willing to let Scout make that kind of sacrifice?

"It's my choice, Logan. You know I'd die for my human."

Logan crouched down and Scout pressed his soft fur against Logan. Licked his hands. *"You can't stop me."*

Logan nodded. "All right."

Scout bounded to the moat and jumped into the dark waters with a splash. They consumed him, lapped over his golden fur. Tainted it. But the dog surfaced. Then he swam.

"You made the dog go?" Serena grabbed his sleeve.

He stood. "No. It was his choice."

She released him. "I hope he makes it."

"Logan." Westwind's voice was wild. *"Do you smell that?"*

Logan stopped and sniffed the wind. He didn't smell anything out of the ordi—wait. Faint traces of sword oil. Leather. Chainmail.

"I hope the dog makes it, too." That voice sent a flash of heat and ice through Logan's blood. "It'll mean the way is clear for my men and me to get across."

With a growl in his chest, Logan faced the man with his sword ready. He stepped in front of his daughter and looked into the eyes of his enemy. The old scar on his chest that General Balton had carved into his skin pulsed, and he touched it.

The man stepped out from the trees onto the shoreline, a cluster of men and horses following.

It was too late to get Serena out, but hopefully he could keep Jayden and Ethan from coming this way.

"Scout. There's a trap over here. Don't let Ethan come back this way."

A shudder surged over the bond. *"I'll get them to safety."*

Logan prayed he could. He glared at the man before him and growled. "Balton. I see you're using your left hand."

General Balton chuckled. "Hello, Lone Wolf. It seems all you could take from me last time was my thumb. I'd like to collect my payment for that. Oh, and don't worry about your friends on the island. They've walked into a trap. I can take you to them."

"I'd rather die."

"I was hoping you'd say that."

○

Stormcloud sailed over the waters, surprisingly clear from above.

Ethan hugged Jayden tight. "I don't think it's wise for you to come with me."

Her hand touched his. "I know. But I don't think it's wise for you to go alone. She can't talk to you. It's safer if I'm here."

Not for him.

They landed and slid off Stormcloud. She whickered. "Shh." Jayden stroked her nose. "She says it's quiet, and she smells something dangerous."

Great. "We'll get Quinn, and you two can go."

Stormcloud whinnied, but it sounded more like a scream.

A huge animal with a head, chest, and legs like an eagle's and curved talons to match flew toward them. Golden-brown feathers fluttered in the wind, and massive wings beat against its sides. As it moved, Ethan saw that the back half of the animal wasn't feathered at all, but covered in short, tawny fur. Like a lion's body. A gryphon. A chain encircled its brown, feathered neck. Its long, muscular body shifted as Stormcloud took flight, and it caught her. It growled like a lion, and Stormcloud's answering rumble was thunder. It slammed her into the ground and pinned her there.

Its tufted tail swished like a whip warding off predators. Its feathered ears lowered like an angry horse's, and it locked eyes with Ethan. *"Leave. Run."*

The words seemed . . . desperate. Ethan caught a glimpse of its eyes. Huge, round pools. Terrified. Of what?

"I'm sorry. I have to obey."

It wrapped its talons into Stormcloud's flank. The pegasus shrieked.

"Leave her alone." Jayden charged the animal, dagger aimed at the gryphon's face. It turned away, eyes closed. The look made Ethan grab Jayden to stop her.

"What's wrong with you, Ethan?" she shouted.

"I knew you'd come."

They froze, but heat flared in Ethan's chest at the sound of that voice. Scarface. He turned. The man stepped into view and smiled, puckering the scar on his cheek. "You just couldn't resist setting her free." He held the other end of the chain that controlled the gryphon. Must be a magical chain if the beast didn't just drag him away.

That had to be it. He'd trapped the gryphon. Leashed him.

Ethan's talent warned him. Urged him. Whispered to his heart for him to free the gryphon and leave with Jayden.

That didn't make sense. Why would he free the enemy? Why would he leave Quinn? He had one chance right now to make Scarface feel the pain of a broken heart—even if only for a moment.

Ethan gripped his sword tighter. The familiar fire of revenge fueled him, filled the void his talents wouldn't touch. "You'll die for what you did."

He could kill the man, then save Quinn and Jayden.

Scarface grabbed Quinn by her tangled mass of hair. She shrieked, trying to claw at him with fettered hands.

"Let her go."

"Or what?" Scarface smirked.

Ten men with swords came out from behind the volcano, cutting them off from Stormcloud. From their escape.

Scarface pressed the knife to Quinn's neck, and she whimpered. "This looks familiar, doesn't it? You hand over the Deliverer or your little friend dies. I think you know by now that I mean what I say."

CHAPTER 66

EASILY UNDERESTIMATED

Jayden watched the tip of Ethan's sword tremor. This was exactly what she'd feared. He'd have to make a choice to protect her or someone else. Just like with Kinsey. Her heart clutched with double the strength. Ethan's fear was running through her, too. He didn't know what to do, whom to protect. She had to do something. Save him before he sacrificed himself again.

The man with the scar jammed the blade against Quinn's throat, and she choked on a scream. Jayden's blood heated. Quinn was just a child.

Jayden dropped her daggers. "I'll go with you."

"No." Ethan looked at her with wide, wild eyes.

He reached for her. That look in his eye and tug in his heart meant one thing—he was going to protect her by any means necessary. But who would die in her stead? Last time Kinsey died. This time Scarface would claim no one.

She shook her head and backed away from him. Closer to the scarred man. "He won't kill me, Ethan. Franco needs me."

His eyes flicked between her and Quinn. The panic on his face matched that in her own heart. It ached. "Jayden, if you go, everything we've been fighting for—"

"You'll still be fighting for it. Only this time you won't lose anyone."

"How could you say that?"

"Give it up, dog." The scarred man's deep voice boomed behind her as if it vibrated through her being. Shook her to the core.

"What are you doing?" Stormcloud's voice was strained. Maybe the gryphon would let the poor pegasus go.

"I'm saving everyone. Just like I'm supposed to."

"Are you sure you're not just giving up?"

"I never give up." She looked right into Ethan's eyes, willing him to hear those words she'd thought. Hoping they rang true through her eyes. She wasn't giving up. She was saving him.

The ache in his chest sprang into her like a geyser rushing forward from the earth. "You said you'd let me protect you."

"Apparently, she lied." The scarred man threw Quinn toward Ethan and grabbed Jayden's arm. "Revenge taints your soul. You can't control it, can you? The way it eats at your flesh? When the time comes for the Deliverers to die, I'll slit Jayden's throat myself. How does it feel to know you willingly endangered her?"

"You die today, Scarface." Ethan lunged forward.

The grip on Jayden's arm tightened and cut off circulation. She couldn't slip out of his fingers. He was too strong. Was everyone from the palace this strong? Franco had been this strong.

Ethan's sword headed her way, straight at the scarred man. She tried to anchor her heels into the rocky ground. The scarred man pulled her closer to himself despite her furious fight against his grip. As if it didn't matter that every muscle in her body strained to get away from him. He still yanked her closer until she was in front of him.

A shield.

Sunlight glinted off Ethan's blade as he raced forward. He seemed to move slowly as she fought the scarred man's grip. Ethan raised his sword above his head, and it came crashing down.

Down.

At her.

The sword's shadow covered her vision as the blade descended.

"Ethan!" Her voice got lost in the slow motion of the moment. She willed time to speed so Ethan could hear her. Everything in her shrieked for her to close her eyes, but she looked into Ethan's instead.

They weren't soft. They were hard and full of fire. And they looked right through her.

Her blood boiled from his hatred. A tear dripped down her cheek. *Please, see me.*

Ethan jolted as if he'd run into a wall. The clouds seemed to clear from his vision, and he shook his head. He stood there, chest heaving, and the scarred man's chuckle vibrated against Jayden's back.

She squirmed, trying to break his hold, and he pulled her closer still. His peppermint breath hit her face, and she craned her neck to look at him. Pain shot through her arm and a sick feeling spouted in her stomach. She wanted to vomit. It couldn't be.

"You aren't Scarface." Ethan's voice was a whisper.

A shudder rushed through Jayden's body.

"Ah. You won't fall for the same trick twice?" The man chuckled. "Just think, even if you had killed me, it wouldn't have quelled your hunger." A strange haze overtook the scarred man's face as if he weren't really himself. More of a reflection in a pond. The scar faded, his eyes changed color, and then the man's face sharpened into focus, but it wasn't the scarred face she'd been looking at. It was a face she knew well. It haunted her dreams enough.

Franco.

He pulled out a vial of dark, purple liquid. "Thanks, dog."

"No!" Jayden pushed against his grip with everything she had left, but it wasn't enough.

"What's happening?" Stormcloud's panicked cry echoed through her.

Franco tossed a vial on the ground and purple smoke exploded. Snaked up around Jayden. It misted against her skin. Made her feel light. Everything swirled and Stormcloud's voice winked out.

Hard, dirt-packed ground became solid beneath her feet, but she lost her balance and rolled.

She was free.

She stood, ready to make a dash for her daggers as soon as the haze cleared.

It did.

But there were no daggers.

No Ethan.

No Stormcloud.

She stood on black, scorched earth. A circle of dead, leafless trees surrounded her, black lines shooting up the dead bark. White fog misted in, blinding her to everything outside the circle. What was this place?

"You're mine now." Franco's voice made her turn. He was right behind her.

She kicked at his thigh, her shin making hard contact. He fell to the earth, and she raced for the white mist.

Two black eyes the size of dinner plates met her, pushed her back into the circle. The creature's head followed. It resembled a goat with massive, curled horns, but its fur looked like flames. Danced like fire. It tipped its head and thrust it upward. A long neck grew up toward the sky, and Jayden fell to the ground as it encroached her space and opened huge, leathery wings.

Franco chuckled. He straddled her and pressed against her biceps, pinning her arms in place. "All I need is to release the Mistress, then use her power to get you to kneel willingly to me."

She spit in his face. "It'll never happen."

"Oh." His thick finger trailed against her cheek. "I think it will."

That was a mistake. She pushed against his chest. He bobbled and her other arm was free. She pulled the knife from its sheath beneath her sleeve and slit his throat. Blood gushed out onto the blade. Dripped onto her face. Her hands. She'd done it. And it was so easy.

Franco put his hand on her wrist and pushed her arm back. He wiped the blood off his neck. No cut. No scar. How?

He smirked. "Did you think I'd come to this fight unprepared? I know what you're capable of, my love."

She shivered at his use of that word. "You know nothing of love."

He squeezed tighter, grinding her wrist bones together. "We'll see." He yanked her to standing and finally let go. She rubbed her sore wrist, then pulled out her dagger and clutched the hilt tight.

A deep chuckle struck up behind her. Smoke poured across the ground. She backed away from the sound. The earth shook. A huge, scaled nose, with nostrils big enough to swallow her whole, crept through the trees, cracked and snapped them in half. A black, horned head followed, and the two amber eyes—eyes of the biggest creature she'd ever seen—focused on her.

A dragon.

CHAPTER 67

THE DOG BITES

Ethan shook his head. Gone. Jayden was gone. He'd seen that before. Always the vial. He focused and felt the pulse of her pull. She wasn't too far from here. Good. Also bad. That meant Franco wasn't far, either.

He stared at the ten men and their arrows. "He left you here."

One of them laughed. "He has a very special plan for you. We're supposed to make sure you don't leave."

"Free me, and I'll help you."

Ethan ignored the gryphon. But his talent burned in his chest. Throbbed. Pushed against the fire of revenge. He shook his head. Why had he let revenge take a hold of him again?

He glanced at Quinn. "Don't worry. I'll get you safe."

She rubbed her raw wrists and looked up at him. "How?"

"She's not what you think she is. Free me. Please?" The gryphon's eyes pleaded. His claws receded. Slowly he released Stormcloud. She reared, hooves flailing, but the gryphon shrank away.

"Stupid beast."

Ethan turned at the sound of the voice. It was the girl? She was controlling the gryphon? The dark chuckle in her throat didn't seem to be anything a little girl could make. It was a chuckle he'd heard before.

"Fool, dog. I told Franco his plan would work better if he looked like me. I knew you'd come for me. You should have seen your face as he held the knife to my throat. It was just like I remembered." Quinn's face morphed, melted into Scarface. He shucked the cuffs on his wrists and pulled a sword from behind a boulder. "Surprised to see me?"

"Surprised you're alive."

Scarface laughed, dark and evil. "I know a Healer." He twirled his sword. "That revenge you wanted? Come and get it."

Ethan backed up a step. "You killed my sister."

"You let me."

His chest throbbed.

Heat spread across it. He'd recognize that pull anywhere. Jayden. Franco was going to hurt Jayden, and he'd brought her into this whole mess.

All because he'd chosen revenge. He didn't deserve to be a Protector. Not anymore.

"This is all because you wanted to kill me, isn't that right, dog?"

Those words he'd heard over and over. *Dog*. As if a creature who loved so fully was something to be ashamed of. He'd never forced Scout to stay with him, never once forced him to endure pain because of a leash, and his dog had stayed. Would have sacrificed himself. That word would no longer get to him. If this was how Scarface treated dogs, he was about to be bitten.

Something whispered in the back of his mind, a feeling more than words, but he knew exactly what it prompted him to do: *Use the sword. Free the gryphon.*

His talent had clearly told him what to do. Had been trying to tell him all along, and he'd failed. Ethan's sword came down hard on the gryphon's chains.

The animal screeched like an eagle and dove at the men with arrows. His body and massive wingspan shielded Ethan from the enemy. Freed him to face Scarface.

He clutched his sword hilt. "It's you and me now."

Scarface lifted his hand and tossed something. A vial. He'd get away. Ethan charged forward. Purple smoke burst up from the ground. Not this time.

He thrust his sword into the violet haze and hit something. He twisted. Laughter punctured the air. Then died.

Purple dissipated.

Nothing but blood on his blade.

Ethan sank to his knees, his talent urging him to stand. To fight. But he had nothing left. He'd failed Jayden. He'd failed Kinsey. And he'd let revenge flood into him with such vengeance that he hadn't listened when his talent had warned him to free the gryphon and go.

It was all his fault after all.

"Look out!"

The gryphon's voice warned him with the same intensity as the flare in his chest, but Ethan didn't want to listen.

Let it kill him. He wasn't worthy to protect Jayden anymore—Logan was right about that. He couldn't even trust himself. It wasn't his talent that had wronged him. It was his own weakness.

A growl joined the sounds of men screaming and the gryphon screeching. Ethan stood, sword in hand, and turned, puzzled. The gryphon was faltering in flight, arrows sticking from its body in all directions. But the growl he'd heard was from Scout.

Scout! Black water dripped off his fur. He'd swum over? Why?

The answer thudded into Ethan. To protect him. To make sure he wasn't alone.

Ethan picked up his sword and joined his dog and the gryphon. He breathed deep. Called on his talents, which rushed into him like a dam had broken. He had people to protect, and it started with getting off this island alive.

Man after man fell to his sword. To Scout's teeth. To the gryphon's claws. When at last the rocky ground was covered with bodies and blood, Ethan wiped his blade on the dead men's cloaks.

The gryphon slumped to the ground, and Ethan raced over to the creature. "Hang in there, buddy."

A burn flashed across his chest.

He turned.

One man reached up and pointed three arrows at Ethan's chest. There was no way he'd catch three arrows. Perhaps his fight was over.

The gryphon tried to get up, but its wing hung limp and it stumbled.

Scout jumped up. His lithe body sailed toward the archer. He grabbed the man's arm in his teeth. Pushed the enemy to the ground and bit the man's neck.

A burn spread across Ethan's chest. For Scout?

No!

He raced toward his dog, but the man shoved an arrow into Scout's stomach.

Scout's yelp silenced everything.

Ethan's heartbeat stalled, then he ran forward and stabbed the man through. He pulled Scout's body off the ground and into his lap. "Scout?"

His voice cracked. Scout's pink tongue flicked across Ethan's hand, then stilled. His head went limp.

"No!" He clutched his dog to his chest. His dog. His friend. His family when he'd had no one.

He held his dog amidst the bodies of scattered men. Scout had saved him when he wasn't willing to save himself.

The gryphon crawled next to him. Ethan was going to push the animal away, but it nudged Scout's head with its beak, then closed its eyes. Ethan patted the gryphon's head. "Thank you."

Blood seemed to pulse in his oath hand and he looked at the scar. Three distinct lines merging into one. His promise. Tears dripped down his cheeks, and he dug his fingers through Scout's fur. He kissed the top of his dog's head. "You're a good boy, Scout. I almost forgot how important this promise was to me, but you reminded me. I'm not alone. I love you, buddy. Thank you."

CHAPTER 68

TURN IT OFF

They're Feravolk! Take down the animals, too!" The man called Balton yelled, and Serena's heart clutched.

Dash's nostrils flared. He whirled, kicked a man, and stabbed his horn through another. When he pulled the horn out, he'd left a hole in the man's chest. A hole. Serena gaped as pain flooded her. The pain of others. Pain that lead to death. Five men fell to Dash before she unsheathed her daggers. Logan's sword was already bloody and Westwind lunged at a man, knocking him to the ground. She looked away as his teeth clamped down.

Serena breathed deep. Focused. Clutched her new daggers tighter. A man advanced toward her. She spun. Her heel met his stomach, then she slashed his arm. Blood.

A wound she wouldn't have to heal, but she still felt the stab of pain.

She was a Healer, not a killer.

"*Serena, this is a fight. Your desire to heal cannot be your immediate response. You have to fight.*" Dash's words resounded in her mind.

She breathed deep again. And something in the daggers seemed to flood her.

"*Dash, can you turn it off? The need to heal?*" Her thoughts made her voice sound small.

"*I can, young one. When I use my horn to harm, I turn it off.*"

She slashed a man's thigh and jumped back. She stared at him. At the blood on her blade. The daggers seemed to knock on her soul. She opened the door to them and something hollow seemed to fill her. Like an expanse of nothing. Her desire to heal turning off. That's what it felt like? This was what true fighting did to Healers? This was not what she wanted.

The man lunged toward her again. He held his sword high over his head. She should toss her dagger into his heart, but she didn't want to. Now he was so close.

Logan's sword stabbed the man in the chest. Then he spun toward her. His sword clashed against a man behind her. A man who'd almost struck her down.

"Serena, don't stop fighting." Dash's thoughts spurred her forward. Blood stained his white fur, but his wounds kept healing.

Her daggers clashed against another man's sword. She kicked his leg. His knee buckled. She stabbed his arm and moved to another attacker. Cracking in the brush sounded between the clash of steel. A swarm of men infiltrated the threes. Hundreds of men.

"Get on Dash and get out of here." Logan shouted over his shoulder. Where would she go?

Logan cried out as three men took him on at once. Westwind jumped up and grabbed one of them by the throat. Logan's pain filled her first. She whirled to face him again, still battling men, stopping as many of them from getting past him as he could.

She couldn't leave and let him fight alone.

"No!" She charged at them. Her dagger bit into one of the men, but someone struck her from behind. She whirled around. Clashed her dagger against another blade.

Another soldier sliced her arm. The cut was deep. She turned and hacked into his arm. But there were too many.

"Serena, look out."

She turned in time to see a blade coming toward her head. Logan's sword met it. Stopped the fatal blow. Another sword cut deep into his side.

He fell.

"Stop." The voice of the man Logan had called Balton rose above all the rest. "We have them now. Don't kill the girl or the unicorn."

She fell against Logan's side. Westwind stood beside her, facing the encroaching men, head low and fur bristling. His ears flattened and his blood lips peeled back to reveal reddened teeth.

Dash stayed on her other side, bloody horn pointed at the soldiers. Blood stained his hooves. His fur. The ground. And Logan's clothes. And they were completely surrounded. Beaten.

She turned on her talent. It was as she feared. If she didn't heal Logan, he'd die. She pressed her hands against his wound.

"No, Serena. They can't know what you are."

Her breathing stilled. He was right, but her wounds had already healed. "They already do." She took his pain inside her. It filled her middle, burned like a fire. And his wound closed.

"Take them!"

Dash's wild whinnies would not be tamed. Westwind's growls resounded and men screamed. She couldn't focus; she had to heal Logan. He had saved her. He was her father. Imprisonment or not, she would not let him die.

They wrenched her arms behind her. "Stupid girl. We're just going to kill him anyway."

Balton poised his sword above Logan and plunged it into his gut.

CHAPTER 69

BLACK BLOOD ARMY

Ethan pulled Scout tight to his chest. There was no way he'd leave his friend's body on this island. Not if it was the Mistress's prison.

His chest burned with warning of a threat. It was so hard to explain, but since he let his talent back in, it had become stronger. Easier to understand. He could tell which place in his chest was the warning for Serena, which pulled for Jayden, without thinking. And the one for Jayden was most urgent. Serena had Logan with her. Jayden was alone with Franco.

How would he get to her? He stopped and set Scout down.

The gryphon turned to him. *"What are you doing?"*

Ethan touched the animal's silky feathered chest. "Wishing I could give my dog a hero's funeral. Trying to figure out how to get off this island." Ethan smiled ruefully at the creature. "Thank you for saving me. I don't even know your name."

A sensation like a warm wind hit Ethan's face. It smelled so familiar, like harvest wheat in the fields, sweat grass, and flowers in bloom. The west wind. Warm. "That's your name?"

The gryphon seemed to smile. *"How do you say it in your tongue?"*

"It's the warm wind, like a zephyr."

"Zephyr. Yes, that is my name."

"Well, thank you, Zephyr. I don't know how to repay you."

"You freed me first. When you broke the spell and cut the leash."

That made sense. And now the animal felt indebted to him. Having a gryphon around could be a good thing—especially since it could fly—but this one was injured. "I can't leave you here, either. You saved my life."

"You're in danger if you stay here. Let me carry you both off this island," the gryphon said. *"We can give your friend a funeral."*

"You're hurt."

"I'll be able to get you off the island."

He clutched his dog to his chest and stood.

Zephyr's legs wobbled. Ethan planed his hand on the creature's feathered chest. "You're not okay."

"If I have to protect you, I won't feel it. Hurry, we won't be alone here soon."

He wouldn't feel it? That was the same as Ethan's talent. *"We're bonded, aren't we?"*

"Yes. Like the dog, I'll protect you unto death."

That word send a pang through Ethan's chest.

"Family protects family. You don't have to go alone."

Like Logan had said. Maybe he really did need to start leaning on others. Ethan opened his mouth to speak, but those expressive eyes cut into his soul. Big and brown, like Scout's. Family didn't have to be something you were born into. It was those whom you loved enough to die for. He reached out and touched the gryphon's feathered head. "Thank you, friend."

Zephyr curled his talons gently around Scout's body and Ethan climbed onto his back. In the air, wind pushed against him, rippled through everything, making him feel exposed and alive, weightless and grounded, all at once.

And his purpose shone clear. He would make sure Jayden could save them from the Mistress.

Zephyr took them to the shore across from the island's east side, but that was the wrong way.

"My friends aren't over here. They're south."

"You mean to go after the girl?"

"Yes."

"The other way puts you in danger."

Zephyr landed and let go of Ethan. This side of the island was so different. Ruins, as if another massive castle sat here, towered up to the heavens. Rock, fire-stained black on one side, towered as high as the volcano. Beyond the ruins was a lake, bluer than the sky on a summer day—except for the mouth of a tiny stream that emptied from the black water of the moat into the lake. "Where are we?"

"The Forest of Woes used to be called the Forest of Prosperity."

Ethan spun around at the sound of that voice and pulled out his sword. He scanned the place for anyone. *"Zephyr?"*

"I smell them." He stood next to Ethan.

Hundreds of rocks seemed to move all around him. Not rocks. People—wearing Feravolk cloaks. One person, a young woman, lowered her hood. She looked familiar with her piercing green eyes and long, brown hair. She smiled, revealing a dimple.

Ethan approached her. "Morgan."

She shrugged. "I have a talent for being in the right place at the right time, remember?"

Did he ever.

Her dimple reappeared with her sweet smile. "You saved my friends, the Dissenters, once. They seem to think we should return the favor."

"How did you—"

"Your brother sent me for you this time."

"Ryan?"

She nodded. "I was coming this way regardless. Franco is bringing his black blood army here. We've been following them. That's always been our purpose. That and rescuing Children from becoming part of the army. The closer I came to this place, the more often your familiar face frequented my visions." She shook her head. "I see you still have the same propensity for getting into trouble?" She turned to a younger girl who looked very similar to her. "Lana, will you heal them?"

An innocent-faced young woman stepped forward, and Morgan wrapped her arm around the girl's shoulders. "This is my little sister. She's a Healer, like my mother. Will your gryphon friend allow her to heal him?"

As if in response, Zephyr lay down.

As Lana healed him, Morgan picked up a stick and began drawing in the sandy soil. "There are two armies on the mainland. One on the west shore and one on the south shore—"

"I left friends there."

"One of them has a unicorn?"

"Yes."

"They're in danger. We will go fight with them." She paused.

"I'm not going with you. Is that what you see?"

She nodded and chewed her lip.

Ethan's talent pulled him elsewhere, even though his heart burned with the knowledge that Serena was in trouble. He needed to listen. "It's all right. I have someone else to protect."

"Go quickly." She touched his shoulder. "After we leave here, the place will be surrounded. Franco is returning to complete the ritual. I'm sorry, I don't know more than that. This is the hard part about seeing the future. This scenario has so many possible endings. I don't know what happens from here."

"The future changes?"

Morgan nodded. Then she touched his hand and placed something in his palm. Flint and steel and a char cloth. "As for your dog, I'm so sorry. We came across the lake, same as Franco's men. But they didn't go around the crescent. They stopped on the north side." She motioned to the lake that the moat's waters trickled into. "Use the small boat. Give him a hero's farewell."

Ethan sucked in a shuddering breath. "Thank you." He grabbed her arm as she started to turn away. "You say Franco is coming back here to perform the ritual?"

"Yes."

Then he'd be bringing Jayden.

"What about the man with the scar on his face?" Ethan drew his finger over his cheek to show her. "Have you seen him?"

"Yes. He will meet Franco here to perform the ritual."

"Can I stop him?"

She touched his shoulder. "I hope so."

She smiled softly, then led her Feravolk army toward the shore across from the south side of the island.

Ethan turned to his dog and picked him up. He'd have a hero's funeral after all. He laid Scout into the small, empty boat and set it ablaze. *Thank you again, my friend.*

As the fiery craft floated away from the island, Ethan wiped his eyes and breathed deep. *Okay, talent, where to?* The burn in his chest surged. He had to go now, and he knew exactly where.

"Someone you love is in danger." Zephyr lowered his head and Ethan mounted the creature.

"I know this plan is going to sound crazy, but I need to know if you trust me."

"Of course."

"Remember the man with the scarred face?"

Zephyr growled.

"Show me where his camp is."

"Why?"

"I need to get to Jayden."

"You think she's there?"

"I think Franco and Scarface are together."

○

Logan stared into Balton's eyes as the general pulled out the sword.

Pain crushed his insides like an avalanche.

Westwind howled. *"Aurora, where are you?"*

A dozen arrows spattered Balton's chest.

He looked down at the shafts sticking out of his chainmail. Blood dripped over his bottom lip.

"Take them out. Rescue the Feravolk."

Feravolk? The voice was fuzzy, like a dream he was waking from. And he was so warm. Hot. Someone leaned over him. Rebekah?

"Please don't die. Please don't." Her voice chanted. Not Rebekah. It was Serena's beautiful face. So like her mother's. She looked at him, smiled. "Father?"

That had to be the most beautiful thing he'd ever heard. *Father.* In the rest of his days, may he never forget how wonderful that name sounded. Strength filled his limbs as her healing power coursed through him. Again.

He grabbed her hand. "Thank you."

"I wasn't going to let you die. Not if I could help it."

"It's about time you woke up." Westwind's voice was shaky.

Logan's attention snapped to the reality around him. Hundreds of men and women in Feravolk garb fought the king's men. *"How?"*

"The Dissenters sent help. Seems they thought we might need it."

"The Creator bless them." Logan stood, sword in hand.

Dash ripped his horn through a soldier. The Dissenters shot arrows into the line of men. A young woman approached them, a bloody cut on her cheek. She looked familiar. "I'm Morgan. Ethan sent me to you. He went after Jayden. We have to get away from here. More soldiers will be on their way. Franco plans to use the island to complete his ritual."

"How do you know this?" Serena asked.

"Sometimes I see the future. Franco plans to surround the island so no one can get to him while he performs the ritual."

"He can't get to the island without boats."

"I'll show you where they're keeping them. The mainland's west shore."

Logan scanned the fighting men. Feravolk fought against the Royal Army just like during the Blood Moon wars. "If Franco wants his men to protect him, how many more does he have coming?"

Her green eyes grew round and she seemed to look past him. She pressed her hand against his arm to steady herself.

"Morgan?"

She didn't answer. Finally she shook her head and looked into his eyes, horror plain on her face. "Franco knows we're here," she whispered.

Logan gripped her arms. "He's sending more men?"

"His black blood army is bigger than I saw. I don't know how he kept that from me. He—" She shook her head wildly. "My talent failed you. Failed all of us."

Black blood? Logan recalled the man who had thrust himself onto the sword blade. His blood had flowed black. It had to be some sort of spell. He looked out at the battle. That meant these soldiers were under a spell. His heart ached. "Morgan, call a retreat. We fight where we can hide best. In the woods. Call the Dissenters back. Do you understand?"

She nodded, regaining her composure. "Fall back!"

"Logan!" Westwind's voice cut into his thoughts. *"Watch your back!"*

Logan looked at the tree line he planned to escape into. Men marched out of the trees. Men bearing shields with the mark of a muzzled dragon—the crest of the queen. Only this crest had been changed—likely Franco's own design.

This muzzled dragon wasn't red. This one was black.

The black blood army.

And they were sorely outnumbered.

○

Zephyr flew low and Ethan saw the tents among the trees. Yes, here. His talent urged him to be here. "Okay, buddy." He patted Zephyr's head. "I'm going to go alone here."

"What? No, I can—"

"I'll need you to help me get out. I have to get close to Jayden. But I don't want them to know about you. You're my way out."

"You think she's at this camp?"

"I do. But if she's not, I have another idea. Though it involves going back to the island as Scarface's prisoner."

Something filled Ethan as if a string tied to his soul. It made his stomach squeeze, but it wasn't his emotion. It was Zephyr's. From the bond? Was this what Jayden felt? Zephyr landed and Ethan slid off his back. He looked into the gryphon's huge eyes. *"I'm not sure I like either of these plans."*

Ethan sighed. He didn't really have much time to think of anything else. "I didn't say it was ideal. If I can sneak in here, can you get Jayden and me out?"

"I'll try."

"I think a surprise is our best bet. We're too outnumbered otherwise."

"That's the only thing that makes sense about this plan of yours."

He patted the gryphon. *"I'll be fine. One of my many talents is the ability to become very still—like stone—so that no one notices me."*

"I share this talent. It's not as foolproof as you suggest with your cocky attitude."

Ethan smiled at his new friend. Then a pang hit his heart. How many times had Scout thought the same things of him? He'd never know. *"All right. Then you stay hidden, too. I'll sneak in and find Jayden."*

"Can you feel her presence here?"

"No. But my talent pulled me here so I can protect her. That must mean something, right?"

Zephyr's eyes squinted. He cocked his head and peered down at Ethan. *"Do what you must to protect her. I will do what I must to protect you."*

That was all he could ask for. Zephyr melted into the woods, and Ethan sneaked near the camp. Heat pulsed across his chest.

An arrow pointed right at him.

Zephyr screeched and charged toward Ethan.

"Shoot it. I want the boy alive."

Ethan's heart skipped a beat. He knew that voice. Scarface wouldn't make it out alive this time.

Zephyr landed in front of Ethan as arrows rained down around him.

No! Ethan darted in front of his friend to deter another volley—the soldiers had been ordered to take him alive. Too late. The arrows were already unleashed. Behind him, Zephyr's wings beat. Wind swirled around him and shot the arrows away from Ethan, sending them into the ground, the trees, the enemy.

Neat trick.

Men leaked out from the cover of trees.

"Stand down!" Scarface barked.

One arrow loosed and sailed toward him. Zephyr covered Ethan with his wing.

"You fool." Scarface raised his bow. "The arrows are coated in black lion venom. I need the boy unspoiled." He shot an arrow at the offender and that man tumbled down, an arrow in his heart.

"Venom?" Zephyr fell.

"Zeph?" Ethan leaned over his friend. Not venom. Not that stupid black lion venom. Again.

"Bring the boy to me. I'll bring his heart to Franco personally."

Ethan braced himself, listened to his talent as the men approached. His sword met the first attacker. He sliced through that man's arm then stabbed him through. He grabbed that man's sword. With two blades he faced the men circled around him. Ethan called on his speed. Called on his strength.

Three more men fell to his sword.

Then his talent spoke to him softly. *Surrender.*

What?

"*Surrender.*" It was Zephyr's voice this time. "*I'm okay.*"

"What?"

"*You said if this didn't work, you needed to go as a prisoner. It's better if they think I'm dead.*"

"But, Zephyr, the venom—"

"*Won't hurt me. Gryphons are impervious to venom. Now do you trust me to rescue you?*"

"Yes."

"*Then I'm going to play dead now.*" Zephyr closed his eyes and lay motionless.

Ethan dropped his sword and fell to his knees.

Scarface stepped through the men surrounding Ethan and smiled. "A dog always returns to its master."

"You aren't my master."

"Tie him up." Scarface chuckled. Then he picked up Ethan's borrowed sword and hit him in the back of the head. He fell to the ground, trying to hang onto consciousness. His arms no longer obeyed him. Everything grew hazy, but he heard Scarface's dark chuckle again. "Thanks for the untraceable seeing stone. Franco has everything he needs now. Thanks to you."

CHAPTER 70

ALL THE INGREDIENTS

S ay hello to Smoke." Franco stepped away from Jayden's weapon and laughed.

Jadyen shuddered as she stared at the massive beast. Its amber eyes seemed to look into her, probe the depths of her mind. Its massive, curled horns ended in spikes large enough to pierce a hole through a bison. And the teeth. They dripped with hunger for death. The emotions spilling from that creature turned to pleasure as it watched her squirm beneath its gaze.

"He's not mine." Franco stroked the dragon's nose. "My mother was holding on to him for someone else. The Mistress has picked out someone special to bond to him."

She recoiled.

"Smoke can't fly yet, but he'll have his strength back soon enough." Franco pointed to the fiery animal with the goat face. Its long body slithered forward, and Jayden saw that it was long and slender, like a weasel. "The firegoat is mine."

Claws extended from lion-like paws, and it raised its neck so that it towered over Jayden. Its head crashed down. The curled horn bashed into the ground. Jayden fell, teeth chattering in her skull.

Heat warmed her skin. She scrambled to her feet.

Lava oozed from the charred and broken ground where the coiled horn had struck. Blood from the earth. She backed away, only to bump into Franco's chest. He held her steady while the beast sniffed her arm.

A forked tongue slid out of its mouth and touched her. A flame on her skin.

She jerked back.

"Now that you're acquainted, let's ride. Oh—wait. How rude of me. I should tell you about your friends. Yes, I know they were on the shore near Castlerock Island. And they are sorely outnumbered. Your revenge-seeking friend played everyone right into my snare. They brought reinforcements, but I sent more men. They're outnumbered again. And surrounded."

A boulder sank in the pit of her stomach. How would she save them now? How could this happen again? For all her trying to protect them, her family kept getting caught by the enemy.

Franco mounted the firegoat, and she noticed the saddle for two on the creature's back. Franco patted the seat behind him. "Join me."

"Never."

Smoke's black talons curled around her stomach and she fought the iron grip. Useless.

The dragon set her on the firegoat's back and its fur scorched her legs.

Franco pulled her onto the saddle. "Careful, she'll burn you." His smile was wicked. "Now, all I need is your blood, a Whisperer's tear, and an untraceable seeing stone. I have you, and thanks to what Belladonna saw in the stone of Ishkar, I have your Whisperer. Well, I didn't have her until you and your friends killed the last guardian. Then my men sailed across the moat and set up the rest of my trap. Oh, and Captain Jonis informs me that he just secured my stone. Looks like I have everything to set the Mistress free, and I have you to thank, Deliverer."

As they flew over land and water to get to Castlerock, Jayden scanned the ground. Blood. Everywhere blood. And this time it wasn't her imagination. It was real. Men and women in cloaks fought the soldiers in black. Cloaks? Feravolk? Her heart lightened. Had Aurora already returned with Melanie and Gavin? She searched each person, scanned for any sign of Serena, Logan, or Ethan, but she couldn't pick them out at this height.

She wanted desperately to hang on to any form of hope, but it seemed so futile now. Between Franco and his beast, how would she defeat him? How would she stop him from breaking the prison open? She couldn't.

Despair washed over her.

Snuffed any rising hope.

He would take her blood. Even if she were dead, he would be able to take her blood. She buried her face in her hands. *Oh, Creator, why did you choose me?*

Her stomach plummeted, and she gripped Franco tight for fear that she'd fall. The firegoat dove to the island, and Jayden rolled free as soon as they landed. There, on the ground, were her daggers. If she could just get to them, she might be able to strike Franco down.

The firegoat snaked in front of her, its leathery wings extended, and hissed. She backed up, and Franco's tight grip forced her into the rocky exterior of the volcano.

A group of men surrounded them. "We are ready, your majesty. And we have the Feravolk prisoner you asked for."

One man kicked and pushed a bound prisoner to the ground. Ethan. A leash roped his neck, and the scarred man held the other end. Hadn't Ethan told her he never wanted to be leashed again? Her heart broke.

Ethan struggled to stand up. His eye was bruised, and blood stained his face and hands. He looked at her, and the guilt that pulsed into her made her knees weaken. Ethan's guilt. He made soulful eye contact with her and mouthed the words, "I'm sorry."

Franco and Scarface slammed Jayden's back into the wall of the volcano and tied her bound hands to a metal ring buried into the mountainside. They placed Ethan on her left and a small girl crouched next to her on the right. Quinn. For real this time.

Her clothes were nothing but rags, as dirty as the ground. Her arms were scarred as if they'd been burned. When she looked at the firegoat, she shook.

Jayden's heart hurt. Wasn't there something she could say to comfort this poor girl? She glanced at Ethan. He said nothing, just stared at her and let the regret lap against her like a riptide.

Because he'd wanted revenge. Again. Only . . . she'd searched his heart and didn't feel him giving in to revenge. He'd been trying to protect her.

Quinn clutched her knees with her arms and buried her face between them.

"Are you Quinn?"

Her brown eyes met Jayden's and she trembled.

"You don't have to be afraid, Quinn." Ethan's voice was soft and calm. "We're going to do all we can to rescue you. Won't we, Jayden?"

Quinn focused on Ethan. "I saw you in the stone. I hoped you'd come for me. But they got you first. And look, they're bringing more men over."

Jayden glanced to the shore where Quinn's eyes stared. Three more boats headed over the black waters. Franco's soldiers lined the opposite shore where a battle continued behind them. How many soldiers did he have at his disposal? How many more were coming?

"Hey, chin up," Ethan said. "We killed that five-headed beast, didn't we?"

Quinn's whole body shook. "It killed the others. The ones who put me on this island. It ate them."

Ethan smiled. "It's gone now."

She nodded toward the firegoat, and a tear dripped over her cheek. "That is a terrible creature. The only creature in the underworld that fire does not consume. You can't beat it."

"Now don't lose hope." Ethan stared at her as though he meant it. Then he looked at Jayden. There was hope in him. It poured into her. She drank it in. It was just strong enough to refuel her desire to succeed, to make it, to persevere. Maybe her talent was a gift after all. She just had to find the right emotion to latch onto. She mouthed words back to him, "Thank you."

"Anything for you. Anything."

Another emotion washed over her. Relief. Not hers. Not Ethan's.

Jayden, I knew I'd find you. Stormcloud. She was close. Warmth bubbled up in Jayden like a hot spring and tears coated her eyes. *"I can draw the firegoat away from you."*

Not that it would do any good. Unless she could get free. She wriggled her hands, trying to loosen the ropes. Overhead, Stormcloud coasted over the island.

The firegoat lifted its head and a menacing rumble escaped its throat. It tore into the sky after the pegasus.

Jayden scraped her bindings against the rock's hard surface. She looked at Quinn. "If fire doesn't hurt it, what does?"

Quinn blinked. "I don't know. Water, maybe? It's always in a thunderstorm in the stories where it's frightened."

Thunderstorm? They wouldn't have one of those today. Only a drenching, heavy rain that covered them and grayed the skies. The hope slipped. She looked into Ethan's eyes.

"Jayden, I—"

"Quiet." Scarface kicked Ethan's chest and he groaned as his body slammed into the craggy rock. His head drooped forward and his chest heaved.

Hope shattered.

Quinn started sobbing.

Franco approached her. Grabbed her hair and wrenched her head back. He held a shiny, black stone up to her cheek, and her tear dripped onto the surface. It sizzled. Franco grinned. The smile made his eyes look as though they were on fire. "Ingredient one."

The air left Jayden's lungs. Her blood boiled. She twisted her wrists. She would get out of these bindings and Scarface would pay, he would . . . the fire that bubbled up inside her dimmed to a simmer. Chest heaving, she glanced at Ethan and he shook his head.

No revenge.

She'd fight for her people.

Franco laughed. "Now all I need is the Deliverer blood and the heart of a Feravolk." He motioned to Ethan. "Cut out his heart."

"No!" Jayden screamed so loud her voice scraped against her throat. If she could just find a sharper bit of rock to scrape these ropes against.

Scarface approached Ethan with his dagger—no, *her* dagger. Ethan stared at his enemy with a tight jaw. His shoulders squared. Jayden scraped her bindings harder. Scarface would not kill Ethan with her weapon.

A shard of lighting cracked across the sky, and the clouds billowed black and ominous.

Something had turned the sky angry.

Stormcloud flew out of the dark clouds. *"This is just what we need."*

The firegoat spread its wings and chased her.

Jayden pulled at her wrists.

What sounded like an eagle's shriek filled the air.

Jayden's heart hammered in her chest as she watched a gryphon race toward them with the speed of an arrow. The same gryphon that had hurt Stormcloud. *Could nothing go right?*

Her wrists screamed as the rock cut into her skin, but she kept scraping the rope against the mountainside.

The gryphon hurtled into Scarface, knocking him flat. Stunned, Jayden stared as the gryphon ripped the ropes off of Ethan's hands and tore the leash from his neck.

"Kill the gryphon! I need the girls alive!" Franco's voice rang out.

Hope leaped inside her as Ethan cut Jayden's ropes with her dagger and the gryphon kept Franco's men at bay for precious seconds.

"I'm so sorry, Jayden. Please forgive me." He touched her cheek. "Get Quinn. We're getting out of here. Alive." He handed her the daggers. "Don't hurt Zephyr."

She looked at the creature who dove toward Franco's men. "I won't."

"You can't get me out of here." Quinn held up her hands. "These won't open without the key."

Ethan looked at her. "Where's the key?"

"There." She pointed up the face of the volcano to a rocky outcropping far too high to reach. "On that ledge."

Ethan pulled out his sword. "Call Stormcloud. Get the key. I'll help Zephyr hold these guys off." He faced the enemy with a clash of steel.

"Stormcloud?"

"The firegoat loves pegasi. If I come, he'll follow."

"We'll be ready."

She stood guard in front of Quinn.

Stormcloud dipped down. *"Look out!"*

Jayden turned too late.

Franco pushed Jayden to the ground and pinned her arms and legs down. "I'm not done with you." He laughed as he dragged a knife across her cheek. A drop of blood dripped off the blade and hit the stone with a sizzle. "Ingredient two."

His fingers curled around her throat. "Now call off your dog." He forced her head to look at Ethan. Men surrounded him, but he held a sword in each hand and slashed with more speed than she'd ever seen.

"No." She choked out.

"Then die."

She looked right into his wild, greedy eyes. "You still need me to get the Creator's power."

His eyes narrowed. "Then suffer."

Ethan stopped. He turned toward her.

And one of the men stabbed him in the back.

Franco's fist met her face and everything went black.

CHAPTER 71

FUELED BY FIRE

Ethan slashed open his attacker's neck and the man fell. He ran another soldier through. Strength fueled him. He didn't even have to call on his speed. It was a part of him.

Warmth exploded across his chest.

Jayden. Ethan turned. Franco had her and he meant to hurt her. What would he do now? Who should he protect first?

"Trust your talent." Zephyr's voice was calm.

He breathed deep and focused. The heat pulsing over his heart was made of a thousand tiny dots pointing out where each threat lay in relation to him. The hottest was the one he'd need to deal with first.

Not the threat behind him.

The threat in front of him.

A sword bit into his skin, but Ethan was already racing toward Jayden. A sword cut into his back, but not as deep as it would have if he hadn't moved toward the threat his talent pulled him toward. Zephyr killed the attacker behind Ethan. That spot of heat winked out. More took its place, but Ethan knew how to listen now.

He approached Franco. Whatever his talent told him to do, he would do. This time he would obey.

On the east shore, a boat pulled up into the rocky sand. Five more men rushed toward him. They cut him off from reaching Jayden.

Ethan swung his sword. Clashed with the enemy's blade. Another sword sliced his side. He barely felt it. His protective instinct kept the pain at bay. Instead he turned. Thrust his sword through that man.

Chopped at the next. Sweat trickled over his skin. Three more men fell to his blade.

Now he stood in the alcove facing Franco, who shook his head. "Not bad. You would make an awesome warrior if I could turn your blood black."

What did that mean?

"But I already have the Deliverer's blood. Now I need a Feravolk heart."

"You won't get mine."

Franco shrugged. "I no longer need it." He motioned to a body on the ground beside Jayden's still form. Lana? The young Healer girl. Morgan's sister? Blood soaked her clothes. "You weren't the only one who had more soldiers waiting. Your little army is no match for mine. Look. More join us on the island every moment. I have men to spare. Your friends on the mainland are being killed as prisoners as we speak."

A flame in his chest seemed to take over for his talent. Revenge.

No. Ethan clutched his borrowed sword tight, as if clutching it would help him hold on to his talent instead. It seemed to work.

"My men brought me one of the Feravolk." He held up a heart, placed the stone inside.

Ethan raised his weapon and blood dripped down the blade. The storm rolled. This time he welcomed it.

He raced forward, swung. The sword slashed from Franco's shoulder to his hip. The wound healed.

What magic was this?

Franco laughed. "You can't kill me." His smile beamed. "You can't stop me, either."

Warm wind blasted Ethan's side. It was like standing too close to a fire. He shielded his face as it grew hotter, then he dove over top of Jayden as a beast with fur like flames swooped toward him.

Eyes dark as a pit focused on Ethan. Its face was like a goat with huge, curled horns, and its neck was like a dragon's. Ethan covered Jayden and looked away from the bottomless eyes.

The creature bashed a curled horn into the side of the volcano. The earth shook. Red oozed from the crack. Lava. And the creature took flight.

Ethan crouched over Jayden and patted her cheek. "Jayden."

Her eyes fluttered open and she clutched his arms. "Ethan."

Quinn tugged his shirt with her bound hands. "The evil man is going to drop the stone into the volcano and start a fire. It will set the Mistress free."

Jayden's eyes rounded and she stood. "I know how to stop him. I need Stormcloud."

Ethan grabbed her arm. She shouldn't go alone.

"Ethan." She placed her hand on his. "This is what you've been protecting me for. I can do this. Let me go."

For once, his talent didn't beg him to protect her. She was right. And it was killing him.

"Get the key. Save Quinn. I'll see you on the other side." Her smile was beautiful. All he needed to keep going. She mounted Stormcloud, and the pegasus carried her toward Franco.

Ethan clutched his sword in one hand and turned to Quinn. His talent still burned for him to protect her. "Let's get you out of here." He scanned the island. Zephyr had taken down the remaining men, but a new boat was fast approaching. *Zephyr? I need that key.*

The gryphon soared above him and dropped the tiny metal object onto the rocky ground. Ethan grabbed it. *Please tell me that was the last of them.*

The boat is making another trip. Let's get out of here before fresh soldiers land.

Sounds great.

Look out!

The pulse in his chest burned.

Quinn screamed.

Ethan whirled as Zephyr flew to meet the new soldiers on the shore.

Ethan pulled out his sword and faced the incoming soldiers, but a new threat burned stronger. A threat from behind. He turned.

Scarface stood with his axe held up to Quinn's neck. "This game gets better every time."

Not this time.

Ethan breathed deep. Revenge clawed at his heart. He wanted to give in. Let it banish the fear and fuel him with strength. Jayden's words echoed in his head: *If your talent stems from love, perhaps it's not a weakness. Perhaps you just need to trust it more.*

More than revenge.

Scout. Kinny. No more loss.

Listen to your heart, not your fears. Jayden had said to him. She was right. No more revenge. This was for love. He called on his speed. Zephyr was faster than Ethan. If he could get speed like that. . .

It fueled him.

Scarface brought the axe back to swing forward at Quinn.

Strength coursed through Ethan.

In one heartbeat he was at Scarface's side. He pushed against the man's arm and braced himself with all his strength. Scarface's arm remained stationary, unable to swing. Ethan plunged his sword into Scarface's side. Clean through his lung.

The man's breathing hitched. He gasped. Fell backward. Blood. Black blood oozed out of him.

Ethan looked at his sword. At Scarface. The man's eyes changed. His blood ran red.

"I'm sorry . . . about . . . the girl. Idla spelled us . . . turn the blood . . . red."

Scarface slumped against the rock, his eyes open. No rise and fall of his chest. Ethan closed the man's eyes. What in Soleden had he meant?

No time to wonder. He unlocked Quinn's chains and scooped her into his arms. She was like a newborn lamb. "I'm going to get you out of here, okay?"

Her head nodded against his chest.

"Zephyr?"

Ethan's hair seemed to stand on end. The air tasted off. Electric.

Zephyr swooped in. His wings beat with a fury over them. *"Hold on to her."* He picked Ethan up.

Lightning cracked. Hit the ground. Even the sky seemed to jolt.

Zephyr slammed into the earth. Everything shook. Ethan lost his balance and curled his body around Quinn and rolled as they fell. Jagged stone bit into him. Fire sparked, crackled on a dead tree. It fell toward them. Ethan scrambled to his feet, picked up Quinn, and dove out of the way. Rock tore into his skin, but the tree missed him.

He opened his arms and looked at Quinn. "Are you okay?"

She tugged his shirt tight and curled into a ball in his arms. "F-fire."

He tried to scan her body. "Where? You're hurt?"

"No. I—I'm—" Tears streamed down her face.

He saw the burn scars on her arms. "Oh. You're scared."

She clutched his shirt tighter.

"It's okay. I've got you. I'll get you out of here."

The ground ruptured, sending him sprawling. The volcano cracked. A sound like thunder vibrated up the gullet of the rock. Tremors plagued the earth. He tightened his grip on Quinn and ran. Rocks slid down the face of the volcano—racing past them, threatening to make them stumble—and another roar belched from the mouth of the volcano. Grit sprayed from the heavens, raining down in chunks and blinding him.

The ground shook.

He fell. His elbows hit the ground, and Quinn tumbled from his grip. Tiny rocks pelted him, each hit stinging his skin, too thick to see through. Ethan shielded his face.

On shaking legs, he stood. Black coated the air. "Quinn?"

"I'm here."

He cocked his head, trying to tell where she was with his good ear. "Where?"

"I'm scared."

Ash stung his lungs. Fire, like a pillar, streamed from the top of the volcano. Smoke billowed toward the sky. Lightning stretched out from the darkness above them. In the flash he caught sight of the girl's small form. She lay on the ground covering her head.

"I see you. I'm coming."

Chunks of burning rock rained down around them. The earth groaned. Everything trembled.

The ground split.

Lava sputtered up from the crack. Smoke descended. Ethan lost sight of everything but the red glow. His talent told him exactly where Quinn was, and he dove over her shaking body. *Zephyr, can you fly in this mess?*

"I can if I have to protect you."
Heat flashed across Ethan's chest. *"Jayden's in trouble."*
Quinn screamed.
A torrent of flame cascaded toward them.

CHAPTER 72

ISLAND IN THE SWAMP

Logan sank his blade into another man. His arms burned with fatigue. His lungs ached. And lacerations covered every limb. Serena and Morgan fought near him, valiantly, but they were clearly tired, too.

Those in the black blood army seemed unable to tire. Perhaps the unnatural substance that pulsed through their blood kept them from weariness.

"Logan, I think it's time to surrender." Westwind's thoughts even sounded breathless.

Logan looked at his blood-covered friend.

Dash even bore more black on the front of him than white. Black from unnatural blood.

"Westwind, we can't—"

"Logan! We're coming. Hang on!" Aurora's voice broke through distant and quiet, but no less urgent. *"Gavin says Glider can see you. You're losing."*

"Aurora, the few of you who would come could not dent this army."

"Logan, I bring Beck and Reuben with the fighters from Moon Over Water. Melanie and Gavin found Island in the Swamp—the Feravolk camp in Meese. We come thousands strong to fight with you. Humans and animals."

A strange feeling lifted his heart. Hope. For so long he had refused to acknowledge its tiny rays of light, but now her words shone like the sun in this dark moment. A surrender would buy them time.

"Morgan. Call a surrender."

Her glance was incredulous.

"Trust me."

"Surrender! We surrender!"

One by one, the Dissenters dropped to their knees as the army accepted their surrender. Logan knelt beside Morgan. He placed his hands behind his head. A young man—a Child by the look of him—walked to the center of the group of soldiers where Logan knelt on the blackened, sandy soil.

"You surrender?"

Logan nodded. "Take us to Franco."

"We will take the Deliverer."

"I go with her. I pledged my life unto death. I will go with her." He reached out to Aurora. *"Where are you, friend?"*

"Right here."

A volley of arrows rained out from the tree line. Hundreds of black blood soldiers fell.

"Retreat!" Logan called to the bruised and wounded fighters. He looked at Serena. "We'll need you to tend to the wounded."

"I have strength."

Morgan gripped Serena's arm. "We have a few Healers, too. You won't be alone."

Dissenters raced for the trees. The Royal Army began to fall on the shore. Logan made sure Serena and Morgan made it into the safety of the trees. Westwind limped next to him. *"We might defeat them now."*

Logan glanced at the island. *"If Jayden and Ethan can stop the ritual. We have to figure out how to get over there and help them."*

The ground shook. Lightning cracked across the sky. And the volcano rumbled.

CHAPTER 73

BURNING HEART

The firegoat streaked up into the dark clouds like a backward lightning strike. Jayden kept the beast in her sights. Though the thought of going after this beast terrified her, this was what she had been born for—keeping the Mistress imprisoned—and Jayden wasn't about to let Franco set that monster free.

Stormcloud sped toward the firegoat. *"The goats hate water. If only this storm would cry. We need rain. Can you make it rain?"*

"No. I only know when it will."

"Are you sure? The sky shares your emotions, does it not?"

"Sometimes it seems that way." Wind whipped Jayden's hair as Stormcloud flew higher. Her wings, midnight blue and black rolling together in an angry gust, beat hard and fast. Had the storm changed? Could she connect to it?

Whether or not she could, storms were her heart. They beat and pulsed through her. She wasn't afraid to get wet. Thunder pealed. Jayden patted Stormcloud's neck. *"Are you sure you're ready for this?"*

"We are bonded. If it is your purpose, it is also mine."

"He's headed for the volcano. We have to cut him off."

Stormcloud chased the streak of orange light in the sky. *"It craves the taste of pegasus. I might be able to lure it after me again, but we have to get there in time."*

Stormcloud climbed higher, and two black-hole eyes locked onto her. The firegoat veered off course. *"It's working."*

Franco's shouts were audible now. Jayden felt a surge of pleasure.

Lightning pulsed through the sky as if she'd called it. Then Stormcloud dove around the other side of the volcano. *"Okay. It wants me. Now what's the plan?"*

"To keep Franco from getting that stone into the volcano."

"Good. We have to stop him from lighting the volcano on fire and waking it. Rain would be nice about now." Stormcloud zoomed higher into the clouds.

Weakness. What was the firegoat's—an image of Idla lighting up from the inside out filled Jayden's mind, and she shuddered. *"We have to strike the firegoat with lightning. That will render its wings useless. It will turn it to glass like a lightning strike on a beach."*

"That is a good plan." Stormcloud seemed to smile. *"Do you feel that?"*

A tingle shot over Jayden's skin, and her heart nearly leapt. "Lightning."

It cracked and hit the island. A tree burst into flame too close to the volcano. Ethan was down there. If the volcano woke—she'd have to make sure it didn't.

Jayden looked at her daggers. *"Stormcloud, if you get me close enough to the lightning, I can absorb it and—and I can throw it."*

"So can I." Stormcloud tossed her head. *"I know where it will strike. Hold on."*

Where was the goat? She'd lost it. Her heart stilled like a frightened rabbit.

A streak of fire punctured a dark cloud and headed toward them. "Look out!"

The goat passed close to them. Franco's fiery eyes met hers and he held a knife. Jayden covered her head. Soft feathers encompassed her. The firegoat slammed its horn into Stormcloud.

Stormcloud's fear shot through Jayden's heart. *"My wing."*

Jayden's stomach started to plummet as Stormcloud fell. Fast.

The firegoat flew right toward them. *"Stormcloud, can you get me closer?"*

"Jayden, if—"

"If you're not carrying me, can you fly?"

"Yes, but not for long."

The firegoat made another pass. Jayden could make it if she jumped. It was now or never. Her legs pushed her forward and she grabbed burning fur. Hung on. Dug her dagger into the beast and pulled herself up. It screeched. Fur singed her arms, licked against her clothes, but she climbed higher. Closer to the double saddle.

Free of Jayden's weight, Stormcloud used her wings to carry herself up, but she was faltering.

Franco sneered. "You are not immune to the burning fur. It's going to be so easy to torture you."

She pulled herself onto the saddle and stood.

Franco dipped the heart onto the monster's fur and flames spouted from it. Below, the volcano had awakened. If he dropped the heart in, it would be consumed and crack open the Mistress's prison. No way she'd let that happen.

She thrust her dagger into Franco's side.

He cried out. But the shriek morphed into a laugh. He pushed her with one wickedly strong hand. She lunged and struggled to grasp the heart in his other, outstretched hand. She could almost reach it. He pushed harder and she lost her footing.

Her stomach lurched as she fell. She gripped the saddle in one hand and punctured it with her weapon. Franco kicked her arm. She swung her legs up and kneed his calf.

He fell on his knees, his face right next to hers. He sneered. "You lost."

The heart still burned. Didn't the fire hurt him? Perhaps not since he was bonded to a firegoat. Her fingers slipped, but her legs were on the saddle now. One hand gripped the saddle and she pulled herself up. Ripped her dagger free of the leather. Stabbed Franco in the neck.

Blood ran down her fingers. Ran everywhere.

He grabbed her wrist and pulled the blade out. Then he slammed her back against the saddle and turned her wrist toward her, trying to stab her with her own weapon. The closer he leaned, the closer he brought the burning heart.

She pulled her blood-slicked arm free and stabbed again.

Laughing, he gripped her neck. Squeezed.

She kicked and the fiery heart bobbled. She tried to breathe. Clawed at his face. His crazed eyes terrified her. She couldn't . . . breathe.

"You lost, princess."

The heart was closer. All she had to do was hold on to her dagger, but her fingers were opening.

Something Ethan said rushed into her mind. Could she calm Franco? As terror throbbed through her, she calmed herself, willed the calming waves to lap over Franco.

His laughter stilled and he stared at her with his eyebrows pinched together.

Calm down.

Air trickled into her lungs. His crushing hold was lessening. She breathed. Gripped her dagger tight and pulled it free of Franco's flesh.

"Stormcloud?"

"Yes?"

"Can you lure us closer to the lightning?"

"I won't be able to catch you."

"I know. It's okay."

She'd felt emotion travel over a bond before, she realized, as Stormcloud's sadness flooded her. What she felt from Ethan was truly a bond. Somehow she was bonded to him. It was different, as Miranda had said, but a bond nonetheless. And he might not be able to hear her, but right now, right before her only chance to stop Franco, she thought about Ethan. Thought him a final farewell. Because when Stormcloud tossed her the lightning, Jayden would use it to destroy the goat. And she would die, too.

I love you, Ethan. I always will.

The heavens opened and rain poured out.

The firegoat shrieked as the water sizzled on its fur. With unsteady wings, it drew nearer to the volcano mouth. The heart stopped burning. Franco lost his smirk. He put the heart inside his shirt and choked her with two hands, still pinning her arms down with his legs.

How was he so heavy?

A tingle washed over Jayden's skin. Stormcloud rose from the other side of the volcano just as the firegoat crested the top.

The sky crackled.

Franco released her and grabbed the heart from inside the fold of his shirt. Dipped it in the weak flame of the firegoat.

She sucked in life-giving air.

Stormcloud flicked her tail as light darted across the sky, and it changed its course. Raced straight for Jayden. She just needed this one moment.

She caught the lightning with the tip of her dagger and looked into Franco's wide eyes. "This is how I killed your mother."

She slammed her dagger into the goat. It screeched as a bolt of lightning pulsed through it. Pulsed through Franco. Through her.

The heart fell from his hand. It smacked against the volcano's rocky edge and bounced off the side.

"You failed." She fell from the firegoat, but Stormcloud would not catch her. The pegasus was falling, too.

Franco and the goat fell down, down, down.

She'd done it. Completed her mission. The lightning may have spared her, but the fall wouldn't. Looked like Deliverers didn't survive after all. Thea was right. But Jayden didn't regret it. Not one moment.

Her body fell onto something, and she didn't even feel that much pain. It was soft. Like feathers and fur. Like . . .

A gryphon?

Jayden sat up. Zephyr looked over at her, but the fear in his eyes was wild.

The goat landed like a meteor falling from the heavens and shattered on contact.

"Stormcloud?"

"I'm here." The pegasus' voice was weak. *"It's your friend. He's trapped on the burning island with the girl. I—I can't get to him."*

Ethan.

"Zephyr, can you get me down there?"

CHAPTER 74

A NEW FAMILY

The ground rumbled again. There was no way this island was going to make it. And Ethan couldn't get to the water. Lava bubbled up everywhere. *"Where are you, Zephyr?"*

"Jump . . . now!"

Ethan clutched Quinn tight to his chest and jumped into the thick, dark smoke. Claws grabbed his arms and he hung on to Quinn. Wing beats started to overpower the sound of sizzles and exploding rock, and he opened his eyes.

Finally out of the smoke, Ethan breathed easier. Cold wind hit his face.

"Fly lower, Zephyr. The lightning is striking northwest." That was Jayden's voice. Her beautiful voice.

Zephyr dipped, doing as told.

"There. Stormcloud says that's the Feravolk camp."

Serena leaned over another man and healed his wounds so that they were no longer fatal. That was all she could do.

"You need to rest." Dash nuzzled her shoulder with his nose. Some of his strength warmed her.

"What are you doing?" she asked.

"I don't want you to faint."

Logan found her. Blood stained his clothes, a few cuts marred his face, but she'd healed his deep wounds despite his denial that he needed it. "How are you?"

"Weak." She couldn't lie.

He touched her arm and she let him. "Rest, then. Those who are deeply wounded have been cared for, thanks to you. The rest are on the pyre."

"Logan." A man, Logan's age perhaps, came up behind them. He had hair the color of wet sand and gray eyes, very much like someone she'd met before, and he stared at her.

"What's wrong, Gavin?" A woman stepped around him. Her gaze caught Serena and she stopped, too.

Serena stood slowly.

"Serena," Logan said.

Her heart stuttered. "Is this . . . my mother?"

Logan looked away and closed his eyes.

"Your mother is my sister. I'm your aunt Melanie." Her eyes shimmered with tears.

Serena pressed her hand to her chest. "My aunt?"

Melanie nodded, spreading her arms. "You're beautiful. Look at you."

Serena hugged her. The embrace was so warm, so . . . was this what it was like to have a family? Tears burned in her eyes and she blinked them away.

"What news, Gavin?" Logan asked.

"We've moved camp away from here in case Franco had called for more men. There are a few prisoners. I want to start taking them back to Moon Over Water. Most of us can travel, thanks to Serena. I actually came to thank her myself."

"Good. Start moving some groups out. I have to go for Jayden."

Another young woman appeared in the clearing. She had such a familiar face, but Serena was certain she'd never met her.

Logan's strong arm pushed Serena behind him and he drew his sword. "Kara." He basically growled her name.

She crossed her arms. "Hello, Logan."

"You know each other?" Melanie's eyes grew wide.

"She's the one who led us straight into Idla's waiting arms."

"And I led you straight out again. I'm the reason Soldier is still alive."

Truth. Whoever this Soldier person was. Serena touched Logan's arm. "Look." Something shot through the air. "It's that gryphon and Stormcloud. They're alive. The gryphon is carrying—"

Logan clutched Serena's shoulder. "Have you saved your strength?"

"Yes."

The prickle of pain from her friends grew stronger—she could almost tell exactly what kinds of injuries they'd sustained. How much strength she needed to conserve to heal them. Was it wrong to want to heal her friends completely when so many other wounded had only received what they needed to be mobile and out of mortal danger?

She'd never felt this way before. She'd only ever wanted to heal people. But these people, this family she'd created—she wanted to make sure they were free of all suffering.

Finally they were close enough for her assess their wounds. Relief flooded her. They were all hurt, but not too bad. She had the strength to heal them.

The gryphon landed and Serena rushed to her friends.

"Hey, it's good to see you." Ethan set down the girl. She was so thin. And curled into a little ball. "Quinn, this is Serena. She can heal you." He looked at Serena with pleading eyes and she took the girl's hand.

Then he turned and helped Jayden off the gryphon. "You okay?"

She nodded. "Franco's dead."

Serena placed her palms on Quinn. "Let me heal you, sweetie." There was nothing she could do for her old injuries. The sight of them lit a torch in Serena's gut. Quinn had not had the fortune of being able to self-heal, like she had, when others hurt her.

Quinn shivered as Serena reached for her.

Serena looked into the poor girl's eyes. "Please, it'll only be warm for a moment. Nothing like fire."

Finally Quinn nodded.

When she was done, Quinn hugged her, tight. She hugged the girl back and whispered, "It's okay. No one will hurt you anymore, if we can help it."

Drained, she turned her attention to Jayden. "You certainly took a beating." Jayden breathed in through her teeth as Serena touched her wounds and mostly healed her. "It's good to see you."

Jayden clasped Serena's hands. "You, too, sister."

Sister. She looked into Jayden's eyes and smiled. A sister. Jayden had no idea how much this meant to her.

She sniffed and turned her attention to Ethan, taking away most of his pain. "How you walk around this injured, still saving people, I'll never know."

His smile was rueful. "It's my talent."

She swayed and he helped keep her steady. "You okay?"

"I will be." She hugged him tight and whispered, "Next time, you two don't go without me."

He chuckled, and the sound was glorious. "I hope there's no next time for this."

"Serena, do you have strength for one more?" Melanie's eyes looked concerned, but Serena nodded. She always had strength for one more. Right?

Be careful. Dash touched her with his nose and tried to filter a bit more strength into her. But he had little to give.

CHAPTER 75

CRAZY EYES

The insides of Ryan's cheeks dug into his teeth as Belladonna forced him to open his mouth for another drink of water.

"You have to drink, pet." Her voice used the same purr as the white lion's.

He spit the water back in her face.

She slapped his cheek, and his head knocked into the tree she'd tied him to. Eye-to-eye, she glared at him. Growled. If he didn't know any better, he'd have pictured a thrashing tail. "It's unwise to upset me, pet."

"I'm not your pet." His voice scratched against his dry throat.

"You are." She stood up, her hand caressing the whip on her belt.

Ice stabbed Ryan's heart. Bits of bone and sharp-looking rock stuck out in jagged edges from the tails. He'd never been whipped, but he'd seen a whipping. No one knew the man whose back had been ripped open by it. The man who'd been left in the middle of the town square, tied to a wooden pole, drying in the sun, begging for water, then begging for death.

A shudder chilled Ryan's skin. The Royal Army had tied that man up to show what happened if the queen didn't receive money and allegiance.

Incentive enough.

Surely this crazy woman didn't mean to use her whip on him? Incentive or not, Ryan Granden was no one's pet.

"Don't be so sure."

Ryan groaned. The voice was getting too comfortable in his head. His hands, tied behind him, made the twig Thea had given him unreachable in his pocket. "Where are you taking me?"

The back of Belladonna's hand stung his face again. His head throbbed. Nettles of fire stung his cheek.

"Quiet, pet."

"What's your name again?"

One of the two men who traveled with them leaned over the cook fire and chuckled as Ryan toyed with Belladonna's patience again.

The woman huffed. "Belladonna. I told you to *remember.*"

"Sorry." He shrugged, sending a pulse of pain through his aching shoulders. "I think all this slapping keeps jostling my memory, Bell . . . Bell. Oh, Bell something. It's got a pretty ring to it."

Both men snickered.

Ryan smiled.

Belladonna scowled. "You little—" Her hand rose to slap him again and he played a card—he shrank away, wincing, and closed his eyes.

Nothing.

He cracked one eye open, chest heaving. Truly, it wasn't a hard act to pull off. The woman made him tremble already. Crazy shone in her eyes like a comet lit up the night.

"Be careful who you call crazy," the voice in his head purred.

Belladonna leaned closer, eyes slits. "You killed Cain."

"Sorry?"

She nodded. At least something seemed to appease her. "He loved me."

As Ryan remembered, her henchmen had been trying to kill him and Chloe. Oh, Chloe. He hoped she made it to Logan or someone who could help.

Belladonna thrust out a hip and tapped her fingers against it. "You'll make a fine replacement."

Ryan stared. That did not sound good.

Her hand flashed near his face, and he flinched without meaning to, but she rested her palm on his throbbing head. The pain started to recede and he sighed audibly.

That made a wicked-looking smile stretch her red lips as she moved her hands over his body. She didn't touch him, but pressed the air around him so that it rubbed against him. Abrasive. Dangerous. Her brown eyes latched onto him. "Yes, you will make a wonderful replacement for Cain."

Ryan almost told her he'd never fall for her the way Cain—whoever he was—had, but he'd just gotten rid of the headache. It was really tempting to keep the pain at bay for a little longer.

The voice in his head purred.

Maybe he should say something then. "I don't know how you got Cain to fall for you, but I'm pretty sure—"

"You *are* pretty." She licked her lips, and Ryan's stomach squeezed. "Cain loved me because I healed him."

Ryan swallowed. The voice in his head laughed.

Belladonna lifted the water to his lips again. "Drink, pet. We'll be at the palace soon. Then I'll show you how you're going to fall for me."

This time Ryan drank. His father had always told him no one could break a Granden. They were too strong, too stoic. Chloe seemed to think they were also too stubborn, which was likely more accurate, but Father wasn't wrong. Grandens were strong. And they were stoic. Belladonna could try all she wanted, but she wouldn't break him.

Not Ryan Granden.

Belladonna crouched in front of him, holding a piece of cooked venison. "Eat, pet."

He stared at her. If he was going to survive this, he'd have to play her game and get into the palace. From there he could figure out how to save Madison, find the bloody key Morgan had mentioned, and kiss the pretty blonde she'd talked about. To do that, he'd still have to be himself, or Belladonna would notice a change and think he was up to something. But now he had an agenda, which being called "pet" was not a part of.

She backed up a little. "What's with that look?"

"He's more dangerous than you think," one of the men said. The broad-shouldered one. Not to be confused with the other one, who had legs like tree trunks.

"Oh." Belladonna's smile made Ryan's skin crawl. "I know he's dangerous. That's why I like him. He's like a dragon in its lair, protecting his mountain of secrets. That's why the Mistress likes him. But I'll get his devotion. She will not."

The voice in Ryan's head hissed, but he recalled something his mother had said: *A dragon in its lair lures you close so it can eat you.* How true that was.

"Eat, pet." Her words were harsher this time. He opened his mouth, but didn't change his glare. She smiled. He smirked. She glared. He stared.

She raised her hand to smack him.

He held her gaze. No flinching.

Her hand connected with his cheek.

He spat blood on the ground by her feet. Ryan would be a dragon.

The voice in his head seemed appeased.

And he would be her dragon, too.

CHAPTER 76

LOVE AND PROTECT

Jayden sighed and her breath shook. It was done. Franco was dead.

"We're moving everyone out, right? I don't like the looks of that." Logan looked over his shoulder at the red lighting up the sky. "That volcano isn't stable."

Gavin nodded. "Most of the group has moved. We're the last ones."

"Good. Get moving." Logan paused and faced Ethan. "Kid . . ." He rubbed the back of his neck. He remained quiet for so long, Jayden opened her talent. Regret pumped with his every heartbeat. His arms fell to his sides. "Earlier, when I told you—"

Ethan clasped Logan's shoulder. "Don't worry, I won't stop protecting them, oath or not."

Logan nodded, then he held out his hand for Quinn. "All right. Let's get out of here."

Quinn ducked behind Ethan.

He knelt near her and smiled. "You can trust Logan. But if you want to walk with me, you can."

"I do."

Logan chuckled. "I don't blame you, Quinn. That kid has saved all of us at some point."

Quinn's eyebrows pulled together, and Jayden sensed the confusion pouring off of her, but it changed. Warmed. Grew into understanding. "You're all so different from everyone else I've met. You all . . . love each other."

"Hey." Ethan touched Quinn's shoulder. "That's what family does. Loves and protects."

He was right.

Quinn hugged Ethan tight. "Thank you."

Logan smiled at the two of them, then followed Melanie and Serena. That was everyone. They were finally heading away from this awful place.

Jayden turned to go with them. A soft touch brushed the hair away from her neck and she faced Ethan.

He wrapped his arms around her waist, nudged her closer to him. "You had me worried."

A lump formed in her throat. "So did you. They leashed you."

"It was a price I was willing to pay to get to you."

"Willing?" Her arms circled his neck and she stared into his eyes. Dark. Deep. Every emotion in him exploded. "You had that whole thing planned with Zephyr, didn't you?"

The small smile she was starting to love appeared. "It didn't all go as planned, but I had to get on that island."

She smiled back. "You had to protect me, huh?"

"Anything for you." His fingers brushed against her jaw. "I think I learned to trust my talent. It was the hardest thing to let you go after Franco, but you were right. It's what you were born for. And you did it." He smiled softly. "You're amazing. *You* protected all of us today. Thank you."

"Anything for you." As soon as she said it, a knife slayed her heart, then warmth like a summer rain melted it. Those words. Every time he'd said them, it had been an admission of love.

His lips touched hers softly, slowly at first, matching how vulnerable she felt. Then stronger, showing her his desire. His love, fierce and protective and unbreakable. His emotions swirled into her. Her knees melted. Her being tingled. She pulled him closer, held him tighter, as if nothing could tear him from her arms. As though he was the only thing keeping her standing. Wind whirled around them, tugging her hair, pressing their bodies together. His passion joined hers. She didn't need to open her talent. He was giving her everything. No walls. No barriers. And her heart overflowed.

His forehead touched hers, as if he was unwilling to let go yet. She smiled as his fingers brushed her face again. This man would have died for her, would have let her follow her heart if it didn't include him, would give her anything she asked for. All she wanted to do was tell him that she felt the same way. "Ethan, I—"

The ground rumbled and a shattering screech split the quiet. Ethan gripped her arms and pushed her behind him. Quinn grabbed her hand. Fire spread across the land as if a hard wind blew it toward them. Flames slammed into the volcano.

She trembled. "What is that?"

"She's coming." Quinn whimpered.

Jayden knelt close. "Who?"

"The Mistress."

CHAPTER 77

BLACK CHASMS

Connor jolted from sleep. A muffled scream resounded through the corridors. Black bathed the night sky. True black. Not a single star shone. Something blocked their light.

Black night—he was supposed to know what that meant. He'd read about it often enough. He climbed out of bed and pulled on his trousers. *When the night turns black . . . when the night turns black . . .* What was the rest?

A scream punctured his thoughts. His ears perked. That came from somewhere in the palace. He headed toward his door.

When the night turns black, the dragon has returned.

He paused, hand almost on the door handle. No. It couldn't happen. Not now. He hadn't found a way to stop it.

The sky seemed to laugh like the dark chuckle of someone choking on smoke.

Goosebumps spread across his skin, and his body wanted to morph into wolf form. Someone called for him. He stilled himself from changing.

The scream resounded again. This time, his wolf hearing picked up his name. Someone here in the palace was calling his name, and she sounded like she was in pain.

"Connor!"

Someone banged on his door, frantic and wild. He didn't have time to pull on a shirt as the door burst open. Molly, the girl from the infirmary, stood there holding a torch. Its light reflected in her wide eyes.

"She—she keeps calling for you. She's writhing and screaming. There's nothing wrong with her. I—I don't—"

His heart stalled. She couldn't already be here. "Who?"

"Madison."

Oh. The Healer? Connor grabbed his shirt. "Take me to her."

"Follow me."

He didn't need to. The screams led him down the spiraled stairs. Madison was in the stairwell, curled into a ball, screaming.

"Madison?" He moved her hair so he could see her face. She was slick with sweat, and in the dark she looked so pale. "Madison," he whispered.

She clutched his shirtsleeves. "H-he—" her words broke off into a shriek, and she pressed her hands into her middle.

"What's wrong? Where are you hurt?"

"Not me." Her wet eyes met his. Her breaths turned shallow. "Franco. He's clawing his way back from the grave."

Franco. His bond to her made her heal him no matter where he was in relation to her. And she was feeling every part of it. "Hold on." He scooped her into his arms and carried her back toward his room.

"What do you need?" Molly asked.

"I need some rosemary, chamomile, ginger, and willow bark. Please."

She patted his arm and hurried off. Connor carried the screaming Madison up the stairs. She shook in his arms and rested her head on his shoulder. Heavens, she had no strength left. "He's drained you."

"I'll be fine." Her voice was so weak.

"Can you still heal if you're knocked out with tangle flower?"

"It doesn't work on me."

Of course not. "Bandy root?"

"No! No. I'll just have to heal him later then. Just—will you stay with me?"

He clutched her close and opened his bedroom door. "Of course." He laid her on the bed and smoothed her sweat-soaked hair away from her face. "You'll be safe there."

And then he held her all night while she screamed.

The herbs Molly had brought seemed to help a little, and hours later, when morning came—dark and red, trying to break through the black—Madison finally stopped screaming.

She thanked him several times, even though he'd done nothing to deserve it. Then she fell into a deep sleep.

Connor sank to the floor, resting his back against the bed. So they'd almost killed Franco. He hadn't found a way to break Franco's bond to Madison in time. Some help he was. He needed to figure out how to undo what Franco had done before—

The ground quaked and knocked Connor over. As he righted himself, he realized nothing in the room had moved. Only him. Madison still slept.

He swallowed. Something terrible and familiar surged through him.

A feeling, thick and long, that made his hair stand on end. A deep, frightful laugh followed, then broke into thunder as if it were thunder all along. That laugh had haunted his dreams enough. He knew what—or rather who—it was.

Smoke.

And if that grounded dragon was flying, it meant one thing—the Mistress had broken free. They'd failed to keep her contained.

They had no choice but to open the door of death.

They had to banish her away for all eternity.

Somehow, his heart wasn't surprised by this. He'd known all along, deep in his soul, that she'd break free. That he'd be forced to use his powers to help the others.

He looked at his hands.

Calloused by weapons.

He'd been running so long, learning to use the sword, the quarterstaff, any weapon he could get his hands on. He'd become a fighter so he could help without using his powers. Now there was no more running.

As all trace of tiredness slid off of him, he stood. Why hadn't he left with Rebekah? Why hadn't he tried to escape with Ethan? If he'd been there when they fought Franco, would the Mistress still be imprisoned? Heat pulsed through his core and ebbed out to his skin. He'd worked so hard to not lose sight of his purpose. Nothing would make him use his powers. Nothing. None of the others had powers as terrible as his. He'd fulfill his destiny without them.

And he'd stay as far away from the others as he could. He'd always known he'd have to help from a distance. But now he felt more alone than ever.

WHISPERS IN SMOKE

The ground rumbled and Quinn looked toward the volcano. Angry black and red rose from the top of the place that had been her prison.

A massive, snakelike form cut through the clouds, and her heart clutched.

"A dragon!" Ethan shouted. "Take cover!"

She knew that beast. His face had appeared in the stone enough times. Terrible. Evil. Dangerous. Every time its amber eyes appeared, Quinn wished she could crawl behind the rock and hide. But the chains weren't long enough. She'd had to stay there, under that gaze, exposed.

It had introduced itself to her. Smoke. The way the dragon had said it sounded like the hiss of fire. Fire against her skin.

Quinn rubbed her scarred arms.

The fire burned.

Hot tears dripped down her cheeks.

Cracked rock slid off the face of the mountain and into the moat. Water splashed onto the shore with a hiss. The ground started to crumble. The volcano split in two.

The things Enya, her bird, had warned her about were coming to pass.

It was time for her to fly. To protect the humans.

Quinn glanced to her right.

Jayden steadied herself against a tree. "What's happening?"

Quinn stepped away from them, arms spread out.

"What are you doing?" Ethan reached for her, but she moved from his grasp. Her slow steps taking her closer to the danger.

"It's time." She spoke to the trees, and at once thousands of whispers filled her mind. Crept into her thoughts like a welcome wind.

A strong wind.

Many voices.

They wanted to know why she'd woken them. She uttered her request. *"Please, help us! Hide us. The false dragon is searching."*

The trees swayed. Moved. Some fell into the cracks created by the split. Others formed a wall between the volcano and the Feravolk. Quinn's lips moved, though all her words rang in her mind. Her hair blew in the wind. Her eyes closed as the trees showed her what they saw. She trusted their vision. They were closer. Their roots dug deep into the dark, decaying ground around the prison.

There, like an open wound, a red gash in the ground lined the prison wall. Large enough for Smoke to get inside.

She waved her arms and the trees swayed with her. Filled the spaces with their protective branches. A tear slid down her cheek. So many of them would die because of the poison. They'd perish so life could continue.

Quinn's eyes popped open. The dragon rose from behind the volcano, black as night. Smoke poured from its nose. It sniffed. Forked tongue flicking out of its mouth. Quinn shivered as those amber eyes locked onto her. Eyes so different from the kind wolf who'd watched her in the stone. The one who had sent the gryphons to protect her. Sent Ethan to save her. These amber eyes were the enemy of the other amber eyes.

"Quinn," Jayden reached for her.

"It won't see us." Quinn stood her ground.

The dragon nosed almost to the tree line. Then it huffed, turned its long neck, and dove into the chasm. Forever the scaled hide seemed to descend, until at last its spiked tail tip slithered over the edge.

Then silence.

But the ground rumbled again.

Smoke's head burst forth, creating another rift in the ground. Up, up, it rose. Forever higher, cradling the limp form of a woman in its claws.

As the ground settled, Quinn turned to Jayden and Ethan. They started at her with their mouths open. She felt taller. Older. Her hair now flowed past her shoulders.

"Who was that?" Jayden asked.

Quinn looked right at her. "Smoke. He's freed the Mistress from her prison."

S.D. Grimm's first love in writing is young adult fantasy and science fiction. That's to be expected from someone who looks up to heroes like Captain America and Wonder Woman, has been sorted into Gryffindor, and isn't much taller than a hobbit. Her patronus is a Red Voltron Lion, her spirit animal is Toothless, and her lightsaber is blue. She has been known to write anywhere she can curl up with her laptop and at least one large dog. She has been caught brandishing a wooden spoon in the kitchen while simultaneously cooking dinner and "head-writing" a fight scene.

She believes that with a little faith, a lot of love, and an untamed imagination, every adventure is possible. That's why she writes. Her debut novel was *Scarlet Moon*, the first book in the Children of the Blood Moon series. Learn more about her books at *www.sdgrimm.com*.

Facebook: *www.facebook.com/SDGrimm*
Twitter: *www.twitter.com/SDGrimmAuthor*
Instagram: *www.instagram.com/s.d.grimm*
Pinterest: *www.pinterest.com/SDGrimmAuthor*

The final chapter in the
CHILDREN OF THE BLOOD MOON saga

BLACK BLOOD

Visit us online for the latest updates:
www.sdgrimm.com
www.enclavepublishing.com

an imprint of
GILEAD PUBLISHING

Jayden's journey concludes in January 2019.